The Necklace

Pamela Smith Allen

ALL THINGS
THAT MATTER
PRESS

To Larry

Acknowledgments

First of all, much gratitude goes to Deb and Phil Harris, from All Things That Matter Press, for agreeing to publish my debut novel, The Necklace. I am especially grateful to Deb Harris for her editing efforts and to Phil Harris for his valuable marketing advice. I am also grateful to my friend, Paulette Millander, for putting me in touch with one of the authors from All Things That Matter Press, Marina Neary, who encouraged me to submit my manuscript for consideration.

Next, I would like to acknowledge Catharine Clarke, my creative coach, for helping me with countless revisions of *The Necklace* in order to make it presentable for submission to potential agents and publishers. Thanks also to my friend, Maura Richman, for referring me to Catharine.

Finally, I would like to acknowledge Larry for listening to excerpts from *The Necklace* over and over without complaint, always offering valuable suggestions and encouragement, and to Dianne, Kerry, and Hal for their willingness to read the manuscript and to give me their valuable input.

Thanks also to family and friends who encouraged me to keep going until *The Necklace* was finally completed and ready for publication.

Prologue

Dublin, Ireland
1895

Anne-Elizabeth Benet sat alone in her room gazing at the picture in her hands—her parents' wedding photograph—tears flowing down her cheeks. An only child, born at her mother's death fifteen years before, her dear father now also taken from her.

"What would Jeshua say?" she cried out, still in disbelief weeks after her father's death. Yet, in His name, she must forgive those men who had shot him. But how *could* she?

She warmed inside as she studied the photograph: her mother, Anne-Catherine's beauty, her long dark hair piled on top of her head, her eyes serious, her new husband Gaston, standing tall beside her. Gaston wore the gold pendant that now hung around Anne-Elizabeth's neck. Designed with a circle in the center, covered with mother-of-pearl; around its perimeter, seven colorful gems had been set, and, engraved in the middle, a gold fleur-de-lis, its outer petals filled with pink rose quartz and blue sapphire, its central petal, golden topaz.

Trusted family friends had brought Anne-Elizabeth from France to eastern Ireland, where she'd been taken in by a family who needed a nanny. Although she might not be allowed to practice her faith openly in this new country, her angels would still hear her prayers. Of this, she felt sure.

She closed her eyes while touching the pink and blue petals of the fleur-de-lis on her necklace, repeating the phrase she'd been taught as a young child: "I am grateful to Mother-Father God for my life." Touching the golden topaz in the middle, she continued, "May the center flame of their union burn forever brightly in my heart."

As she touched each of the bright gemstones surrounding the centerpiece of her necklace, a peaceful sensation washed over her, and her father's last words echoed in her mind. "No one need know what is soldered inside your locket. Let that be our family secret. Wear it over your heart and know that you are never, ever truly alone in the world."

Her eyes smiled through her tears, as she thanked God for her faith and for her parents' love, which she would always carry in her heart.

PART ONE

Jessica

Paris, France
1968

Relieved to feel the crisp morning air after the night's cold rain, Jessica relished the sensation of early morning sunshine on her cheeks as she approached Saint-Germain-des-Pres, one of her favorite neighborhoods in Paris. She nearly skipped with delight as she searched for the art museum listed in her guidebook. An integral part of her course work at Paris University-Sorbonne, such museum visits invigorated her with the anticipation of being surrounded by what she loved most in the world: art. Now that the faculty at University College in London had approved her application to study in Paris for another semester, her sophomore year, she could stay through the summer and maybe extend her studies into the fall. What better place to study art history? The Louvre alone was like a university itself.

She breathed in the intoxicating fragrance of baguettes and croissants that filled outdoor stands and smiled at patrons in outdoor cafés, sipping cappuccino as if they had all the time in the world. A market just ahead, with its colorful fruits and vegetables neatly displayed, looked just like a postcard. Passing a *patisserie*, she inhaled the aroma of chocolate and warm sweet rolls, following their scent inside the door. She allowed herself to indulge in her favorite French pastry: a chocolate éclair. After savoring every crumb of her treat, she continued on her way, open to the vibrant sensuality of her beloved Paris and its array of tastes, sights, sounds, and aromas.

Lost for a moment in reverie, Jessica stopped suddenly. "Here's the address," she said to herself, looking more closely at the guidebook. "*Un trois deux* Saint Germain." But no sign to identify it. Drawn to the design of a tree, carved on the door, she marveled at the way its roots and branches swirled upward and downward. Puzzled, she opened the door and peered inside where a construction crew was working. Across the room, a strikingly handsome young man with dark hair stood next to a matronly-looking woman. Captivated by his appearance, she found herself staring at him, unable to speak.

"*Bonjour,*" the woman called while walking toward her. "*Je peux vous aider?*"

"*Bonjour,*" she replied, catching her breath and turning her attention to the woman. "*Je m'appelle Jessica Taylor. Je suis de London.*"

"You're English," the young man said, walking over to join them.

"Yes, I'm an exchange student from London, here in Paris to study art history." She pointed to the small book in her hand and brushed a strand of hair out of her face. "I thought this was a museum."

"It used to be," he replied in a deep, warm voice, "but it's being converted into a Catholic convent."

"Really?" she said, sensing her cheeks warming. "That's not mentioned here," she continued, flustered.

"You must have an old issue. All the art from this building has been transferred to Montmartre."

"Monsieur Murphy," the other woman interjected, "may I take a break, since you're conversing in English?"

"Of course, Monique," he answered without looking directly at her.

The woman turned a bit abruptly, Jessica thought, and hurried away.

"I'm sorry to have bothered you," she said, her heart racing, her eyes meeting his gaze.

"No bother," he assured her, reaching out to shake her hand, his deep brown eyes engaged and curious. "I'm Joseph Murphy."

"So very nice … to meet you," she stammered, shaking his hand as firmly as she could. His grasp, warm and energetic, steadied her.

"I'm an architect from Boston, consulting on this project," he said, breaking into a grin. "Since you're here, would you like to look around?"

"I'd love to," she said, excited that he'd asked. "By the way, the design on the front door is exquisite."

"I agree. I found it by chance in an antique store and its compelling design caught me immediately. I *had* to buy it."

"I know what you mean. It has a serene quality that seems appropriate for an entrance to a convent."

With a sweep of his hand, he led her to the end of the hall and opened the door. "Eventually," he explained, pointing to the building next door, "that church will be incorporated into this building and will serve as a vital part of the convent."

He closed the door and opened another that led into an open courtyard. She followed him outside to a grassy area surrounded on all four sides by the two-story building.

"We'll be landscaping this to create a beautiful prayer garden for the nuns," he shared, his eyes sparkling with enthusiasm as he spoke. "The kitchen, dining hall, library, and Mother Superior's cell and office are under construction on the ground floor."

"You really love what you're doing, don't you?"

"I guess my excitement shows." He smiled, motioning for her to follow him upstairs. "Along the hall on the street side there won't be any windows. Instead we'll hang iconic religious paintings. On the inside, we'll create the nuns' cells, each with a small window, overlooking the courtyard."

"It's a wonderful project," she said, catching some of his enthusiasm. "How long will it take to complete the conversion?"

"Hopefully, we'll be finished by the end of the year. That is, if everything goes according to plans. The only problem is, I'm losing my interpreter next week. I must find a replacement as soon as possible."

"You know," she said, an idea popping into her head, "I'm looking for a job to help me with expenses. I'm planning to stay through the summer and maybe into the fall. I speak fluent French." She pressed her hand to her face, trying to hide her blushing cheeks. Perhaps she'd been too impulsive.

"How's your shorthand and typing?"

"Pretty good," she said with renewed confidence.

"You're hired."

"You're kidding."

"No, I'm not. Can you start next Monday?"

"Well, I think so," she said, her mind in a whirl. "But I'll need a few hours each week to complete my art critiques."

"I mainly need you in the mornings when I'm coordinating tasks with the chief architect. His English is better than my French, but things definitely move along more smoothly when we have an interpreter. You'll be free most afternoons unless I need to dictate a report."

"It's a deal," she said, her heart fluttering with anticipation.

They shook hands again, lingering an extra moment as if both realized this was no ordinary meeting.

***

On the following Monday, Jessica arrived at the exquisite tree door and crossed its threshold into another world, eager to plunge herself into a new adventure. Thrilled to have a job where she could practice her French, she also looked forward to working with such a vibrant and exciting man.

At noon, Joseph offered to share his lunch with her. His charm had a childlike innocence, although she imagined him to be a few years older than she—probably in his mid-twenties.

Despite an overcast sky and cool breeze that promised afternoon showers, they walked toward the River Seine and found an empty bench to share. Joseph took two cheese croissants from a plain white bag and casually handed her one in its pastry wrapper.

She asked, "So why this project? Was it Paris?"

"My firm's been working for quite a while with the Catholic Church," he explained, "and, since I'm Catholic, they thought I'd be a good person to send. Plus, I'd also worked on a similar project in the States."

"I recently converted to Catholicism—from the Anglican Church."

"Really? That's unusual."

"My parents were horrified when I told them."

"What made you convert?"

"My boyfriend at university was Irish Catholic and took me to Mass. I especially loved the rituals, you know, the candles, symbols, everything. After we broke up, I kept going to the same church and soon I started taking classes. It just felt right to me. Can you believe that I even considered becoming a nun?" *Why did I tell him that? Not even my parents know I considered that.*

"Very interesting," he said, with a surprised look. "What made you change your mind?"

"The priest helped me see that I was trying to escape from the pain *in* my life rather than accepting a call *to* my life."

"Sounds like a wise priest," he responded, nodding his head in agreement. Then, looking directly into her eyes, he continued, "And have you dealt with the pain?"

"She looked down at her lap, realizing she'd barely tasted her lunch. "I think about it, try to understand it," she stammered, "but it's hard to stay with what hurts."

"I'm willing to listen if you want to talk about it."

"Thank you." She smiled. "Maybe another time."

"I didn't mean to pry," he said softly, touching her arm.

"It's all right."

As she gazed into his inviting eyes, a feeling of déjà vu swept over her. *I feel as if I've known this gentle man for a very long time.*

They sat together in silence, until drops of rain began to fall. Joseph stood first. "I guess we'd better get back."

"Yes, looks like it." She shivered.

"Perhaps we can continue our conversation tomorrow." He smiled.

"I'd like that," she said, her heart warming. "My turn to bring lunch."

"It's a deal," Joseph agreed with a wink. "I'm off to meet the Mother Superior who'll be heading up the convent." As they approached the street outside their building, he added, "Are you doing art critiques this afternoon?"

"I'm on my way to the Louvre to focus on the Italian painters," she shared breezily, glancing up to see the sun breaking through the clouds.

"Maybe you'll take me with you sometime. I have lots to learn about fine art."

"I'd like that. But I have much to learn myself." Sensing his eyes still upon her as she walked away, she turned and they both waved goodbye.

Joseph

After work, Joseph heated some chicken soup and made a salad. As he sat down in his small dining room to eat, an image of Jessica, her long blond hair catching the breeze, crossed his mind. *I love her accent and the way she waves her delicate hands to express herself. And the way she talks — blending English with French. It's almost musical. I've been too busy to see much of Paris. Maybe she'll agree to explore with me. Our interests are so related: her art, my architecture —*

The phone's ringing startled him out of his reverie.

"Hi, Joseph," his dad said in a cheerful voice. "How's it going?"

"Great, Dad. The project's moving along really well."

"Did you get a new interpreter?"

"Yes, I did," he said, suddenly feeling awkward. He tried to sound nonchalant. "An art student just happened by, wanting to see the museum. When I told her what we were doing, she showed much interest in the project. We got to talking and I found out she was fluent in French. Long story short, I hired her."

"That's great. By the way, your mother and I saw Father Anthony the other night. He sends his best. He's hoping you'll enter the seminary when you get back."

"Well, Dad, you know I'm considering that, but I still haven't made up my mind."

"I'm sure you'll make the right choice," his father said in what Joseph heard as a presumptuous tone.

After the call, the message behind his father's words gnawed at him. *I should never have told Dad or Father Anthony about my interest in the priesthood.*

***

The next morning at the work site, the hours flew by as Joseph worked side by side with Jessica. When it was time for lunch, he led her to the same spot where they'd eaten the day before. She broke open a baguette and handed him half.

"Joseph," she began, "I realized something after our lunch yesterday. You're a wonderful listener. I really mean that. It's a wonder I didn't tell you my whole life story."

"Hey, I'll take that as a compliment," he said, smiling. "If we keep having lunch together like this, perhaps you will."

Suddenly, a pigeon landed near her to beg for a crumb; she threw it a piece of her baguette.

"You'd better watch out or you'll lose your entire lunch," he said, laughing as he watched the bird swoop in to grab some of the bread right out of her hand.

"I see what you mean," she said, shooing the hungry bird away and turning back to him, noticing the necklace partially covered by his outer shirt.

He followed her glance and fumbled to take out the Celtic cross to show her.

"It's beautiful. I've never seen anything quite like it."

Unlike typical Celtic crosses, where the inner circle creates an outlined edge, mother of pearl filled the center of this one and a gold fleur-de-lis had been engraved within it. There were three colorful stones set in its petals. Seven more stones surrounded the circle's perimeter.

"There's a story behind it," he explained. "My Irish grandmother, my dad's mother, inherited it from her mother, who I believe was French. The story goes that *she*'d inherited it from an ancestor who'd been a priest. Anyhow, my father ended up with it. As he prayed over it one day, he had a vision of me, dressed in a priest's collar. He decided this was a sure sign that it was my destiny to enter the clergy." *Now that I've opened up the subject, I hope it won't scare her away.*

"That's quite a story," Jessica exclaimed. "What do you make of it?"

"Well, I've been in a bit of a quandary … trying to decide what to do with the rest of my life. It's not that I don't love architecture. I truly do. There's this gnawing feeling inside of me that won't let me go. A *calling*, maybe, toward the priesthood."

"Really?" she said, her eyebrows lifting in surprise.

"Really. It shocked me when Dad told me he'd even considered becoming a priest himself … before meeting Mom, of course."

"That's interesting. Have you talked with your mom about it?"

"I have, and she's not keen on the idea at all. She feels strongly that I'd regret not having a family. I tried to explain that I'd be part of a spiritual family, but she encouraged me to go to college before making up my mind."

"Joseph, I appreciate your sharing this with me. It's probably not easy to talk about."

"Actually," he said, noting the kindness in her eyes, "it's amazing how comfortable I feel with you, even though we've only known each other for a few days."

"I feel the same way," she admitted after a noticeable pause.

They sat for a few minutes in silence. Reaching for his cross, he took a deep breath and said, "When I'm alone and in prayer, the priesthood seems like the most natural path in the world for me. But when I'm with my brother and his family, I can't imagine going through life without a wife and children. I'm really crazy about my nephews."

"How old are they?"

"Charlie's two and Sean's almost a year."

"I think you'd make a great father," Jessica said. "Have you ever been in love?"

Taken aback by her question, he paused before answering. "I thought I was in love … once … with a woman I met at Boston University. We'd gotten pretty involved and she wanted to get married, but I couldn't make a commitment. Finally, she left me for another guy." He looked at Jessica, a bit embarrassed. "I don't know why I'm telling you this."

"I asked and you told me, that's all," she said, a charming pink glow coloring her cheeks, mesmerizing him. "But maybe I'm asking too many questions."

"On the contrary," he said. "I appreciate your interest. Real connection with people helps us make sense of it all. Don't you think?"

"Yes, I do."

***

One afternoon at work while dictating a report to Jessica, Joseph found himself studying her face—lovely, young, but also a look of wisdom in her soft green eyes. A wave of warmth washed over him and he began to stumble over his words.

"What is it?" she asked, looking up from her notes, "Your voice is trailing off and I can't follow what you're saying."

"Let's stop for now," he suggested, trying to compose himself. "We'll start fresh again tomorrow."

A bit awkwardly, Jessica stood to leave. Mother Superior entered the room, taking them by surprise.

"Hello, Joseph," the nun greeted him.

"Hello, Mother Marian," he replied, jumping up. "This is my interpreter, Jessica Taylor."

"I'm glad to meet you, dear," the older woman said.

"Likewise, Reverend Mother," Jessica responded. "Joseph has told me all about you. And, by the way, your English is excellent."

"Thank you."

"Well, I'd better run along." Jessica said. "I hope to see you again."

"She's quite a lovely young lady," Mother Marian said as she watched Jessica leave the room. She turned to face Joseph, her clear blue eyes cutting through his outward attempt to appear nonchalant.

"Yes, she is," he stammered.

"*Bonjour*," a cheery voice interrupted.

Marc DeLeon, the French architect, breezed in and Joseph audibly sighed, grateful for the distraction.

"*Bonjour*, Marc," Mother Marian greeted him.

"What do you think of your new convent so far?" Marc asked.

"I think you've done an excellent job," she replied.

"Joseph worked on a similar project in Boston," Marc explained, "and he's been invaluable to us."

"Marc tells me you're interested in becoming a priest," Mother Marian said, looking directly into Joseph's eyes.

Her comment took him by surprise. "Well … I'm … I'm giving it some thought." Obviously, sharing that with Marc hadn't been a wise decision. "Sorry, I must run now, but Marc will show you your new office."

"Thank you, Joseph," she said kindly. "*Au revoir*."

"*Au revoir*," he echoed, leaving the room as quickly as he could and made his way to the church next door. Once inside its sacred space, he sat down in a pew, bowing his head. *Father, I'm so very confused*, he prayed silently, fingering the gems on his cross, a gesture that usually centered him. *I only want to do your will but I think I'm falling in love. What should I do?*

Jessica

Several weeks later, while sitting at the typewriter in the library of the partially completed convent, Jessica finished putting the final touches on a report Joseph had dictated to her earlier in the day.

"Care for afternoon tea?" Joseph asked, joining her in the room with a teapot and two cups in his hands.

"That would be super," she replied.

He looked almost impish as he prepared a place for them to sit at one of the library tables. A sense of well-being and warmth suddenly flooded her heart. She'd grown quite fond of him over the last few weeks. In addition to the magnetic chemistry between them, he was fast becoming what she might consider *her best friend*.

"Do you agree," he asked while pouring the tea, "that I've shared a lot about myself since we met?"

Caught off guard, she looked at him with interest. "Well ... yes," she answered, accepting a warm cup from him. "And where is this conversation going?"

"I'm just interested in knowing more about *you*," he replied, gently reaching for her hand. "We're friends, right?"

"Of course. What would you like to know?"

"Well, you talk about your mother often, but I never hear you speak of your dad."

"My dad?" she asked as if to keep his question at bay. "I'm afraid it's not easy to talk about him."

"I'm a good listener," Joseph reminded her, squeezing her hand.

"Maybe, I'll try," she hesitated, looking down at her tea. "It goes way back." She paused again, gathering her thoughts. "He cheated on Mum—more than once—and finally left her for a woman half his age."

"Wow, that must have been very hurtful. Do you ever see him?"

"Sometimes, but it's rare. He plays violin in an orchestra and ... his girlfriend plays oboe." An old, familiar discomfort crept into her heart, but she forced herself to go on. "They're off on tour much of the time."

"And your mother? It sounds like you've remained close to her."

"Oh, yes. I'm very close to her. Having been an only child, I'm her sounding board—for better or worse—more like her mother sometimes than her daughter." She paused, hoping she hadn't revealed too much.

"Go on, I'm listening," Joseph urged.

"Well, when Dad left, Mum brought home lots of books from the library where she works. All she did was read. I tried to get her out of the house, to consider divorce, but she wouldn't hear of it. I think she still hopes he'll come back."

"That's sad," he said. "She's lucky to have you."

"I love my mother, you know, want her to be happy."

"Of course, you do. And what about you? How did you cope with your own pain?"

Lowering her eyes, she said, "I relied on my priest. He helped a lot, you know, really listened, as if I mattered. He was kind of like … *you*." Shuddering at what she'd just said, she pulled her hand from his grasp.

"Oh, Jess."

"Don't worry. Really, I'm nearly used to it by now," she explained, attempting a smile. "It's just that I don't usually talk so openly with a man. I mean, most of the men I've known have betrayed my trust in some way." She looked down to hide the flush flooding her cheeks.

Joseph sat still, looking at her, then took her hand again.

After taking a few sips of tea, she decided to say more. "Do you remember the Irish Catholic man I told you about, the one I dated at university?"

"Sure," he said, his head cocking to one side.

"Brian was my first serious relationship. I hadn't yet come to terms with sex before marriage and he convinced me that he respected my values. So, you can imagine my shock when he came back after summer vacation married to his childhood sweetheart. I found out later she was pregnant."

"You must have felt horrible."

"It's true, it hurt," she acknowledged. "Since then, I've had a few relationships, but they were always short-lived for one reason or another. I guess I've been a bit shell-shocked."

"I can see why."

"It does help to talk about it," she said. "Thank you so much."

"I'm honored that you feel comfortable enough to share with me."

She looked at him deeply, as if she couldn't believe he was real. "It's easy to be with you," she finally said. "And I appreciate this so much, just talking this way, just being together."

Their eyes locked for what seemed like a long time until Joseph finally spoke, "I feel the same way, as if we've known each other for—"

Before Joseph could finish his sentence, loud voices rang out from the street. They ran to look out the window. People were milling around, some with signs and others with torches. A young man climbed on a platform and began to speak in French to the crowd.

"I've seen that man before," Jessica exclaimed. "He's from Paris University-Nanterre. He spoke on our campus last week about how unfair the bureaucracy is that controls the school's funding."

"I've been part of similar events back in the States," Joseph said. "Sometimes they can get nasty."

"The elitists in our government," the speaker shouted, "continue to discriminate against those of us who live and study in the poorer areas of the city and we're not going to take it anymore." He held up a newspaper and torched it. "It's time for action."

The crowd cheered as the speaker threw the burning paper into a large trash can. Another student climbed up on the platform, torched another paper and threw it into the fire. Others followed suit; soon the flames rose high above the trash can, lighting up the now darkening sky. Before long, embers escaped, igniting debris on the street. Several students tried to stomp out the fire, but it was too late. A couple of bushes in front of the old building had begun to burn, along with the wood trim outside the window where Jessica and Joseph stood in disbelief.

"Our building's on fire," Jessica yelled, running to the telephone to dial the emergency number. Speaking in French, she reported the fire and pleaded for help.

"They said they'd send someone right away, but apparently there are other uprisings going on in the city."

Suddenly, they heard an explosion as a small motor bike burst into flames. Joseph ran to close the front windows, but fire shot through one of them, traveling up the old, dry paneled walls and crackling into the ceiling of the century-old building.

"Oh, my God," Jessica screamed, gathering up the typewriter and papers. "I'll take these out the side door."

"I'll get the fire extinguisher," he shouted back, running to the newly finished kitchen.

She ran down the hall, but there was no escape from the smoke. She could barely see, and, even worse, she could hardly breathe. Everything went black.

***

"Thank God," Joseph said as Jessica opened her eyes. They were on the ground in the open courtyard, her head cradled in his arms.

"Joseph, is that you?" Her voice was hoarse, her throat so sore she could hardly speak.

"I'm right here," he said. "The fire's out now, but you collapsed — probably from the smoke. I carried you out here to get some air."

Before she knew what was happening, his warm lips were kissing hers. Relishing the tender moment, Jessica allowed her eyes to close again and she and Joseph melted together.

"Are you two okay?" a firefighter shouted, rushing into the courtyard.

Startled, they sat up. "Yes, we're fine," Joseph replied. The man hurried back into the building.

"Can you stand?" Joseph asked, offering his hand.

"I think so," she said, "but I'm a little dizzy."

Once on her feet, she stumbled into his open arms. As he drew her closer to him, safe and secure, she absorbed the joy of his embrace. They walked into the building, relieved to find the smoke had almost cleared. Three firefighters were packing up their gear. "Thanks for your call," one of them said. "The fire's out now."

"Thank you," Jessica said as she and Joseph walked out the front door.

"Oh, look," Joseph said with distress. "Our tree carving has been damaged." His hands outlined the charred wood where the burn had deepened a sculpted limb.

"It hurts me to look at it. We'll have to find a woodcarver who can repair it."

"It looks like a war zone out here," Joseph said, looking around. "I'd better take you home."

Jessica nodded. "You know, I'm not really surprised by this. I've sensed a growing urgency among the students to stand up to the government's conservative attitudes."

"If those protesters were as angry as they sounded, I have a feeling this is only the beginning."

As they walked to the Metro, she felt his arm reaching around her shoulders as if to protect her. Later, by the door of her flat, he bent down again to kiss her softly.

With no words, no question, she led him inside.

Joseph

In a dreamlike state, Joseph caressed Jessica's body in the darkness of her living room, her soft, smooth skin upon his own wrapping him in a warm cocoon. Soon most of their clothes lay in a heap on the floor. They somehow managed to climb into bed together.

"Is this a dream?" Jessica whispered.

"If so, let it last forever," he whispered back, holding her close.

"I don't usually do this, you know."

He kissed her gently parted lips, his hands caressing her small breasts. His mouth found her nipples and the hidden places on her body that brought moans of delight.

"My darling," she whispered, drawing him deep inside her.

Their lovemaking continued as their bodies rose and fell in perfect rhythm. Their breathing intensified as though they were one being. Passion, held in abeyance for weeks, finally exploded, leaving them both breathless and satiated as they drifted to sleep in each other's arms.

The next morning at dawn, Joseph sat up with a start, remembering that Mother Marian was coming to the work site that day. Gazing down at the sleeping woman beside him, he felt again as if he'd entered into a beautiful dream. He reached down and kissed her on the forehead. "Jess," he spoke in almost a whisper, "I need to go home now."

"Oh, please stay," she said, kissing his arm.

Their lips met again and it was all he could do to tear away from her. "We should go into work separately, so we don't cause any unnecessary talk."

"You're not sorry we did this, are you?" she asked with a puzzled expression.

"Of course not. Never. I'll see you later," he assured her, caressing her cheek.

Closing the door behind him, his inner monologue began. *How can I tell her how confused I am? I love being with her, and yet ... what about the priesthood? Is this really fair to her? Or to me?*

***

"It's a good thing you two were here last night," Marc commented later that morning as Joseph walked across the threshold of the smoke-damaged door into the front room of the work-site. "A firefighter came by to check on things and told us you'd done a lot to put out the fire even before they got here."

"Well, we did put out the flames," Joseph said, "but there's a lot of rubble to clean up. Even our beautiful door carving needs repair." *And what about the fire that started between Jess and me? Given my conflicted feelings about the priesthood, will our relationship also end in rubble?*

***

During the next week, Jessica worked beside him, smiling mischievously when no one was looking. His body and emotions responded noticeably to her sensuality. *She's charmed me completely and there's nothing I can do about it.* When she invited him over for dinner that weekend, he eagerly accepted, throwing all caution to the wind.

***

"Would you like a glass of wine?" Jessica asked as he entered her apartment.

"I'd love one," he replied, following her into the kitchen. "It smells great in here. What are you cooking?"

"It's lasagna. I'm afraid I don't know any French recipes."

"I love lasagna."

After a sumptuous meal and a few glasses of wine, he reached for her hand.

Pulling her into his arms, he put his face in her hair, its fragrance filling his nostrils with orange blossoms. An urgency grew inside him and his lips sought hers. Pushing all of his conflicted feelings aside, he lost himself in the ecstasy of the moment.

The lights had been off the last time they made love. Now a small nightlight and the golden glow of candlelight made everything they did seem more honest, more real.

"You're so beautiful, Jess," he murmured while undressing her.

She helped him remove his shirt and trousers, caressing his shoulders and chest. Her touch was irresistible, sending shivers up his spine. When their nearly nude bodies came into contact, the passion inside him grew stronger. He scooped her up and carried her to the bedroom.

Their lovemaking was slow and sensual and he relished every moment. When they finally collapsed on the bed, he drew her into his arms and the rest of the world disappeared.

The next morning when he awoke, Jessica was already up. Following his nose into the good-smelling kitchen, he found her there, preparing eggs, bacon, and croissants.

"Good morning," he said, placing his arms around her from behind.

"Good morning," she said, putting down the croissants and turning to embrace him.

He melted for a moment in the warmth of her body. "This feels so good," he murmured, stroking her back.

"Last night was wonderful."

"It gets better and better," he agreed.

After they had enjoyed breakfast together and cleaned up the kitchen, Joseph noticed a newspaper on the counter and scanned an article.

"Jessica, did you know that the students at Nanterre took over the administration building?"

"Oh, my God. They did?"

"Apparently, a number of poets and musicians joined their protest as well as students from the Sorbonne. But then the administration brought in the police and they were all ordered out."

"What happened next?"

"Apparently they surrendered peacefully, but vowed to continue pressuring the administration for change."

"I'm glad they're doing this," Jessica said. "From what I've heard, the entire university system needs changing. There's a big difference between the Sorbonne and Nanterre in terms of available funds. And there are many parts of the city with no access to university at all."

"I agree that something must be done," he said, noting her enthusiastic response to the article, "but I hope it can be done without violence."

"That may not be possible. Some of the students, even at the Sorbonne, are pretty radical."

"Why don't we forget about this for the time being and go visit someplace that's peaceful and quiet."

"Joseph, you *are* a pacifist, aren't you?"

"Indeed I am. If I'd been drafted to go to Vietnam, I don't know what I would've done."

"I think we've had enough talk about war for one day," she said, wrapping her arms around him. "Let's go see Luxembourg Gardens."

"Great idea. I hear it's an amazing place."

***

They walked through a portion of the serene Luxembourg castle and gardens but, noting the sunshine outside, retreated to the gardens to enjoy the dazzling light. Magnificent sculptures stood throughout the grounds, including even the original Statue of Liberty.

"I've never been to the U.S.," Jessica said, "but, one day, I hope to get there."

"I would love to show you my hometown, Boston," Joseph replied, "but it's the art in New York that would inspire you."

"It must've been truly monumental for those migrating to America to be greeted by Lady Liberty as they sailed into New York Harbor."

"I'm sure it was," he agreed.

During a leisurely lunch in a small outdoor garden café, they took in a free musical performance in the gazebo. *Just sitting here with her*, he mused, *is as natural as the air I'm breathing*.

After the performance, they continued strolling through the gardens, admiring its many sculptures and fountains.

"Art is alive in this place," Jessica exclaimed. "It's a feast for my eyes." But they clouded over as she continued, "Paris is such a beautiful city. I hope it survives all the turmoil it's going through."

"I hope so, too," he said. "It reminds me of the anti-Vietnam War rallies we've been going through in the U.S. and also of the Civil Rights movement. Sadly, we lost JFK just as he was beginning to change things for the better."

"I know," she said. "That was so unbelievably sad."

"I guess we have to focus on what we have right here, right now," he said, reaching out to hold her hand, "because our future is so uncertain."

"Joseph," she said, her eyes watering, "when you talk like that, it reminds me that I could lose you at any time—to the Catholic priesthood." Loosening her hand from his grasp, she reached up to touch his necklace. "I try not to think about it, but it's always in the back of my mind."

"Sometimes I wish my father had never given me this necklace. It constantly reminds me of his vision of me as a priest. But the truth is, I'm totally ambivalent about what to do. On one hand, I'm so happy when we're together. Then, on the other hand, I wonder if my faith is being tested."

"A test of your faith?" she said incredulously, her voice hardening. "If that's all I am to you, then I've been a complete fool."

The shrill quality of her tone and the stark validity of her words hit him like a sledgehammer. "I'm sorry, Jess. I know my ambivalence isn't fair to you." He reached for her hand but she pulled it away.

"I need to go home now," she declared.

He could think of nothing else to say that could possibly make things better. They rode the Metro in silence and then went their separate ways.

Jessica

Jessica spent Sunday afternoon in the Louvre studying some of its famous sculptures. The Winged Victory of Samothrace evoked a sense of exhilaration inside her. Venus de Milo stirred her, too, her cheeks blushing hot as she glanced around hoping no one had noticed. Startled by the aliveness of Cupid and Psyche, something resonated deep within her soul, bringing tears to her eyes. She vaguely remembered the myth of the famous pair and the forbidden nature of their relationship, Cupid, a god, and Psyche, a mere mortal. *I'm beginning to wonder if my relationship with Joseph is forbidden, too. If he feels God may be calling him to the priesthood, how can I stand in his way?*

She stopped in the museum gift shop to buy a few postcards of the sculptures that had moved her and to ask whether they had or could recommend a book on the myth of Cupid and Psyche. The clerk had nothing on hand but recommended Shakespeare & Company on the Left Bank, a notable English bookstore.

***

Jessica realized that she knew the neighborhood not too far from Notre Dame and had even been inside the bookstore before. Once inside she approached the front desk and asked the clerk where she might find books on the Cupid and Psyche myth. The clerk pointed her to the Mythology section.

Bulfinch's *Age of Fable or Stories of Gods and Heroes* referenced the Cupid and Psyche myth and appeared to be a classic. Next she found a much more recent psychological study called *Amor and Psyche: The Development of the Feminine.* "A commentary on the tale by Apuleius," Jessica read out loud from the cover, thinking Amor a better name for the God of Love. Cupid brought little cherubs to mind. *Not very sexy.*

Jessica had hoped to find something by a female author since the myth seemed to follow the emergence of feminine power, a woman's journey, but she found none. She bought both books anyway, leaving the store in anticipation of what she would find between their covers.

***

That evening Jessica began to thumb through Bulfinch's book, noting that he had used an ancient source to gain insights into the myth of Cupid and Psyche: a novel entitled *The Golden Ass,* written in the 2nd century AD by Lucius Apuleius. *Can a myth as old as this speak to me, a troubled, love-smitten woman of the twentieth century?*

After only a few pages, she started feeling sleepy. Several hours later, she awoke, bewildered that the light was still on, struggling to recall her dream. She revisited it in her mind and wrote what she could remember in her journal from her dreamer's point of view:

There's a man over there, sitting among many beautiful women, all of whom are gazing adoringly at him. Another woman sits nearby on a couch, crying and holding her head in her hands. Suddenly, the woman looks up at the man and the other women and I recognize her as my mother. Although I don't see the man's face, I feel he must be my father.

Putting down her pen, a particularly painful memory flashed through her mind: that awful day she'd first seen her dad with his mistress. She and a friend from high school had been having lunch in a local café when they saw him at the counter, with a young woman companion. After paying the bill, he'd placed his arm around the woman, his hand gliding down her hip, as they walked outside. Jessica and her friend had sat in shock as the couple kissed goodbye before parting.

She'd confronted her father that evening. He had made light of it but Jessica didn't believe him. Soon after, he'd told her mother he wanted a trial separation.

Something inside her heart wilted that day, like a houseplant left without water to die long before its time. How could her father have done such a thing to her mum and to her?

Returning her attention to the dream, she wondered if it somehow had something to do with her relationship with Joseph.

Her intuition told her that, although she didn't like to admit it, she was a lot like her mother. *She gave her heart to Dad. He played with her, toyed with her, made her think he loved her when, all the while, he was seeing another woman. Now I'm hopelessly in love with Joseph and have no way of knowing if he loves me enough to stay with me or if he's going to take off ... just like Dad.*

The next morning part of her felt she should get away from Joseph as fast as she could. But a serenity in her heart told her she was fortunate to have him in her life—even if the relationship didn't last forever. Besides, there was no way she could just walk away from the man she loved. Not now, not this way. She got dressed and left for work.

***

"I wasn't sure if you'd come in today," Joseph whispered in Jessica's ear after she'd entered the worksite that morning. "Above all else, I don't want to hurt you."

"You know I care," she whispered back, looking deeply into his eyes, "but this is too hard for me. It sounds crazy after all we've been through, but could we just be … friends?"

Drawing back from her as if slapped, his eyes darkened. Her heart pounded and her eyes welled with tears, betraying her attempts to remain composed. "Please don't look at me like that," she managed to say, turning her head from his haunting gaze. *How ridiculous of me to think either of us can settle for friendship. But I can't think of any other way to handle this.*

"I don't know what to say," he stammered, reaching for her arm.

"Don't say anything," she replied, pulling away, unwanted tears falling down her face. *I feel like such a fool and I certainly don't want his pity.* Softening her voice, she added, "Maybe we should just get to work."

"Okay," he whispered, his eyes downcast, his body slack.

***

For the rest of that day and over the next two weeks, Jessica continued to interpret for Joseph and type his reports, but there were many awkward moments in between tasks. Still, she was determined to keep their relationship only professional.

At night, she pored over the myth of Cupid and Psyche. Neumann had substituted the name Amor, for Cupid in his interpretation, but Jessica preferred to think of the God of Love as Eros. After all, in the myth, he crept into Psyche's bedroom at night and made passionate love to her under the cover of darkness, eventually impregnating her with his child. *You can't get more erotic than that.*

The love affair between Eros and Psyche had begun when Eros's mother, Aphrodite, the Goddess of Love, noticed that the mortals who had always lavished love and praise on her were now lavishing it on Psyche, a mere mortal, instead.

Psyche was, indeed, uncommonly beautiful. Furiously jealous, Aphrodite sent her son, Eros, to kill the young maiden. Instead of killing Psyche, however, Eros accidentally pricked himself with his own arrow and instantly fell madly in love with her. After that, he made sure that Psyche lived in a palace and that her every need was met by *unseen hands.* But, in order to hide his identity, he insisted that she not see him in the light.

Why should Psyche let him make all the rules? She was incensed. *Because she's just a mortal and he's a god, that's why.*

Jessica suddenly identified with Psyche's vulnerability. *He holds all the cards. Just like Joseph. I've put him on a pedestal, like a god. All I can do is wait—wait, hope, and pray he'll choose me over the priesthood. I'm lost, just like poor Psyche.* With that awareness, she closed the book and cried herself to sleep.

In the middle of the night, a disturbing dream awakened her. Accustomed to writing down her dreams, she turned on the lamp and wrote in her journal:

Thieves break into my apartment, wake me up at gunpoint, and demand that I give them my wallet, which contains a good sum of money and all the forms of identification that I keep in it. They also take my passport. I cannot prove my identity to anyone else and eventually forget who I really am.

Why have I dreamed such a dream? And who am I, really, when I dissolve all the roles that I play: daughter, art history student, interpreter, lover—that is, former lover?

***

The unrest in Paris and her own inner turmoil left Jessica uneasy, ambivalent, unsure of her place in it all. When she heard the news that Martin Luther King, Jr. had been assassinated on April 4, 1968, she felt the world's despair as her own.

The conflicts between students and administrators at Nanterre also continued. By early May, the administration had shut down the university.

"We have to take a stand and convince them that this is wrong," Jessica said to herself at a hastily called meeting at the Sorbonne. Inspired to do her part, it took her mind off Joseph. "I'll make posters," she shouted, her hand shooting up to commit her time.

Despite a strong student protest at the Sorbonne a few days later, the police brutally took over the school, spraying many of the protesters with tear gas in the process. To get away from the mêlée, Jessica moved around the outside of the crowd. Suddenly, a shove from behind left her lying on the ground amidst other fleeing students.

"I'm so sorry," a young man apologized, helping her up. "You should get out of here."

"That's what I'm trying to do," she said, exasperated. She began to run, not knowing where to go. All she could think of was Joseph.

The next thing she knew, she was standing on his doorstep like a lost waif, her arm dripping with blood.

"What happened?" Joseph cried when he opened the door of his apartment.

"I was in the middle of a riot," she explained, trying to catch her breath. "Someone shoved me and the next thing I knew I was on the ground."

Reaching out to her, he guided her gently down the hall to the bathroom and tenderly washed the blood from her elbow.

"My knee hurts, too," she sighed, pulling up her pants leg to reveal another bad scrape.

"Oh, dear, it's beginning to swell." He handed her a cloth. "Try to wash it off while I get some ice."

"Thank you," she said shyly through her tears.

"Oh, sweetheart," he comforted her, holding her in his arms and stroking her hair. "I'm so glad you came to me."

They walked together back to the living area where the television was on. Jessica curled under Joseph's arm as they sat down to watch some footage of the riot at the Sorbonne. The phone rang.

"Oh, hi, Marc," she heard Joseph say. "I don't think so. I can't leave Jessica alone. She got hurt in the riot tonight at the Sorbonne and came to me for help." After a pause, "Just some minor injuries, but I don't think I should leave her alone. She's pretty shaken up. And I certainly can't take her with me. We'll watch it from here. I'm sure it'll be televised. And, Marc? Be careful."

"There's another protest planned for tomorrow at the Arc de Triomphe," Joseph explained after hanging up the phone.

"We can go, Joseph. I'll be all right."

"Jess, I really think you need to take it easy. Can't you let me take care of you?"

Her heart melted. Before she could think about it, Joseph was beside her, his lips covering her with tender kisses. Without resistance, she allowed him to lead her into the bedroom where she surrendered to her true feelings, far away from the turmoil in the city.

Joseph

Joseph smiled tenderly at Jessica curled in his lap on the couch, bandaged and dressed in one of his flannel shirts. She looked like a child, her eyes wide with interest as the televised protests at the Arc de Triomphe unfolded before them.

"De Gaulle's traditional ways of doing things aren't working anymore," the newscaster announced. "There's a movement evolving where the people have a voice. Not just students but also teachers and many of the city workers."

More protests continued in the coming days, with riot police brought out to confront the growing crowds, their brutal tactics injuring many. Some of the more radical protestors threw Molotov cocktails into parked cars on the street. By mid-May workers in the city called for a general strike.

"We may as well close down our operations at work," Joseph told Marc by phone on the day before the strike. "Nobody's coming to work tomorrow."

Millions of strikers took to the streets the next day and Paris was in an uproar. Many top musicians joined the movement, staging concerts in Paris and elsewhere to support the cause.

***

Even after De Gaulle's re-election as president, some changes eventually took hold in France. The Sorbonne campus reopened and the students set up committees to negotiate for changes in the system. Many workers followed suit, occupying factories and demanding better wages and conditions.

As tumultuous as the rioting in Paris had become, nothing could overshadow Robert Kennedy's shocking assassination in Los Angeles a few weeks later, gunned down while campaigning for the Democratic nomination for President.

"First Jack and now Bobby." Joseph shook his head despairingly as they watched in horror on television. He took Jessica's hand, his heart aching. "When will the violence end?"

"It's as if everyone on the planet has gone crazy," Jessica said, tears flowing down her cheeks as she jumped up to turn off the television. "I can't stand another minute of it."

Later that day, the phone rang as they sat again mesmerized by the newscast. Joseph answered only to hear his brother's trembling voice on the other end of the line.

"I hate to tell you this, Joe, but Dad's had a heart attack. He's in the hospital and they're planning to do open heart surgery in a few hours."

"Oh, my God. When? Where? Is he conscious?"

"What's wrong?" Jessica whispered, then mouthed, "Who is it?"

"It's my brother," he said, covering the mouthpiece. "Dad's had a heart attack." The words stuck in his throat.

"Oh, no," Jessica said, reaching out to touch his arm.

Gripping the phone cord, Joseph paced across the floor, his thoughts racing as he spoke with Tom. "How's Mom?"

"She's scared, I think. Stunned."

"Tell her I'll be there on the next flight I can get out to Boston."

"Okay. And Bobby Kennedy, I can't believe it."

"I know. I know."

"I'll feel better when you get here, Joe."

"As soon as I can. Hang in there, little brother." Joseph fumbled the phone into its cradle.

"Oh, sweetheart," Jessica said, standing near him but with her hands at her sides, waiting. "I'm so sorry."

He stood stunned, looking at her. "They're doing open heart surgery this afternoon," he blurted, his eyes filling with tears, his heart racing. "I've got to make a plane reservation, get to Boston, call Marc, pack."

"Maybe you should sit down for just a minute," Jessica urged. "You know, find your center."

"I don't even know where to begin," he said, slumping into the couch, shaking his head in disbelief.

"Would you like me to call the airlines for you?"

"That'd be great. I need to get to Boston right away."

She hurried to his desk in the corner of the living room to grab the phone book, then sat down on the couch to place the call.

He watched her movements for a moment and then closed his eyes. *Oh, God*, he prayed, *let Dad make it through this. Let him live. I can't imagine life without him.*

"They've got a flight for you," Jessica announced, "but it leaves in only three hours. Do you think you can make it?

"I'll have to," he said, looking at his watch. "I'd better throw some things together." He jumped up and went to the coat closet by the front door and pulled out a suitcase, knocking over some shoe boxes in the process.

Jessica followed him into the bedroom where he hurled the suitcase onto the bed before pulling random shirts and trousers out of the closet and placing them haphazardly into the bag.

"Here, let me help," Jessica offered, folding his clothes for him. "You'll need your passport and your shaving gear."

"Passport. Of course. But where did I put it?" He hurried to the living room to rustle through his desk drawers where he found his passport under some blueprints.

"I've got it," he announced, returning to the bedroom, throwing on a sports jacket and placing the document in his coat pocket.

"What about your shaving gear?"

"Right," he said, darting into the little bathroom off the bedroom. Grabbing his razor, shaving cream, and a comb, he stuffed them into a small travel case.

"I put some socks and underwear in for you," Jessica said.

"What would I do without you?"

Joseph put his trembling arms around her and lingered there as the fragrance of jasmine filled his senses. *I feel so connected to her. I want to be both here and there. I wish she could go with me.* With that thought, an inner voice told him, *"Give her the necklace."*

While fingering the stones on the cross that hung around his neck, another part of his mind countered with: *How can I possibly give away the necklace my father entrusted to me?*

Jessica is the other half of your heart. The necklace belongs with her.

But—

Before he could complete his contrary thought, warmth flooded his body. *Of course. Giving the necklace to Jessica will build a bridge from my heart to hers. It's the right thing to do.* A deep sense of peace permeated his being. With fingers that no longer trembled, he unclasped the necklace and handed it to Jessica. "Here. I want you to have this."

"But it's far too valuable and means too much to you, especially now," she insisted, trying to hand it back to him.

"No, I want *you* to have it," he said, refusing to take it. "I'm so sorry that my confusion has hurt you, hurt us. I want the necklace to remind you that my love is with you always, no matter where our futures lead."

A shudder ran up his spine. *Why did I say that as if our future is so uncertain?*

She looked at him tenderly.

"Here, let me put it on you," he said, reaching for the necklace. As he placed it around her neck and connected the clasp, the warmth in his heart reaffirmed his decision.

"I don't know what to say," Jessica whispered, tears filling her eyes.

"Just kiss me goodbye," he said, taking her into his arms and kissing her warm, willing lips. It was all he could do to break away from her to call a car.

"Oh, I've forgotten to call Marc," he exclaimed after hanging up the phone. "Will you please let him know what happened? And, please, stay here as long as you like. In fact, it'll be dark soon. Promise me you'll wait until daylight to leave, okay?"

She nodded. "My heart goes with you, you know." Crying openly, she caressed the stones of the necklace as she looked up at him, "Are you sure you want me to have this?"

He inhaled deeply. The gems on the necklace shone brightly in the glow of late afternoon sunlight streaming through the window. "I've never been so sure of anything in my life."

At that moment, the horn sounded from the taxi out front. He gave her another kiss on the forehead and was gone.

***

After arriving in Boston, Joseph took a taxi from the airport to Boston Memorial Hospital. In the waiting room, he spotted his mother, brother, and the family priest, Father Anthony.

"Oh, Joseph, son, I'm so glad you're here," his mother cried, moving toward him on unsure feet.

After giving her a reassuring hug, he embraced his brother Tom as well.

"Thanks for being here," Joseph said, turning to Father Anthony who took his hand in both of his.

"Your father's had a massive heart attack," the priest explained. "The surgery seemed to go well but we haven't heard much from the doctor yet. I've been here waiting with your family."

"He's so young," Joseph said, dazed.

"That's why this is so startling. And with no warning," his mother added. "I still can't believe it happened."

"He's been asking for you, Joe," Tom interrupted.

"Do you think I could see him?" Joseph asked his mother.

"He's probably unconscious, but I bet he'll know you're there," she said, pointing to a nearby hallway. There through the doors, in Critical Care."

He walked slowly down the hall and through the heavy swinging doors, where a nurse accosted him.

"I'm sorry, sir, there's no admittance in this unit except for immediate family."

"I'm here to see my father. I'm Joseph Murphy. I've just flown in from Paris."

"Of course, follow me."

His heart ached as he entered the curtained space where his father lay, tubes and monitors attached everywhere.

"Dad, it's Joseph," he whispered in his father's ear.

Nothing, only the click of the heart monitor.

"Dad, it's Joseph. I'm here from Paris. I love you, Dad. Can you hear me? Please try, Dad."

"Joseph?" His father stirred a little and opened his eyes, his voice very faint. "Is that really you?"

"Yes, Dad, it's me."

"I'm not so good, son," his dad replied in a labored voice, almost a whisper.

"You're going to be fine. The docs are taking good care of you."

Tears shone in the older man's eyes as he squeezed Joseph's hand and took a deep breath in through his mouth, then shut his eyes tight, grimacing.

"I'll get help. You look like you're in pain."

Unable to keep back his tears, Joseph hurried to get the nurse.

"Help, my father seems to be in pain," he called to the first nurse he saw.

"Someone will be right there," she assured him.

"Thank you, please hurry."

Two nurses followed Joseph behind the curtains where his father lay.

"Joseph," his father whispered in a barely audible voice while one of the nurses adjusted his tubes and another noted something in his chart before both left the two alone.

His father's face eased almost instantly. Joseph suspected morphine.

"Yes, Dad?" He leaned in close, gently placing his ear near his father's lips to decipher the words.

"Speak to ... Father ... Anthony." Each labored word was punctuated with coughing.

"You'd like to speak with Father Anthony?"

His father shook his head, his lips forming the word "no" and then whispered something Joseph could barely hear but understood nonetheless. "Priest ... you ... son."

Oh, how he wanted to explain he'd been struggling with his decision for quite some time, but the intense look in his father's eyes and the tightening grip of his hand melted his heart.

"You would like me to talk with Father Anthony about the priesthood. Is that what you're trying to say?"

His father closed his eyes and nodded slightly.

"Okay, Dad, I'll talk with him."

"Promise?" his father said, opening his eyes again.

"Promise."

Instantly after his father heard Joseph's words, his eyes softened and

Joseph felt his grip go slack.

He called for the nurse who was just outside the door.

"I'm sorry, but perhaps you should call in your family and the priest," she said quietly.

Joseph's heart jumped to his throat as he backed up slowly and turned to do as she'd suggested.

***

Seeing the look on Joseph's face as he approached her, his mother simply said, "No," as Tom held her steady.

Father Anthony led the way, a sense of urgency preceding them.

"I think we're losing him," the doctor said in a strained voice.

Joseph watched the team trying to revive his father. Then, all was quiet and the doctor solemnly came over to them.

"I'm afraid he's gone. We did everything we could to save him."

A chill went through Joseph's body.

"No," his mother cried, "It can't be true." She rushed over to her husband and sat on the bed next to him, sobbing.

Joseph and his brother, eyes brimming with tears, looked down on the still body of the man they'd known as their father.

The priest came over to comfort them. "He was at peace with God. We can be grateful for that."

Joseph's thoughts rambled between memories of his father and images of a future without him. He also thought of the promise he'd made. How could he be sure that what his father wanted for him was also his true calling? He longed for Jessica. *If only she was here.*

Oh, God, he prayed silently, *I only want to do your will. If you want me to be a priest, please give me some sort of sign.*

He turned and joined his family as Father Anthony led them in prayer.

***

Thoughts raced through Joseph's mind as he struggled to fall asleep that evening. Finally, checking his watch, he realized Jessica would be awake and placed a call to Paris.

"Hi, Jess, the news is bad." His words stuck in his throat. "It's my father. He … died today."

"Oh, Joseph, I'm so sorry. If only I could be with you."

"I still can't believe he's gone," he said. "He was only forty-six."

"Are you okay?"

"Not really." He paused for a moment and then said impulsively,

"There's something else I should tell you."

"What?"

"I spoke to my Dad at the very end. Almost the last thing he said, his last request, was that I speak with Father Anthony about the priesthood." He took a deep breath before going on. "I felt really torn, but I just couldn't let him down, not then, so I promised him I would."

Jessica did not respond.

"This doesn't mean I've made a decision, but eventually I'll need to talk with Father Anthony about it."

"Joseph," Jessica said in a quiet voice, "I appreciate your telling me, but right now, just be with your family, and take care of yourself."

"Oh, Jess, I hope I haven't upset you. I just couldn't hold it back. It's all too heavy."

"I know, I know. I want to be here for you but, truth be told, it is hard to hear."

"I understand," he said, sensing her pain.

"I'm sorry, Joseph. What am I to say? Or do?"

"Will you please tell Marc what happened?"

"Of course. When do you think you'll be back?"

"I'll need at least a couple of weeks."

"Joseph, I miss you so much."

"And, I miss you, too, sweetheart. More than you know."

The words *I love you* formed in his mind but he couldn't bring himself to say them out loud. "We'll be together before you know it," he finally said. *I know I can't have it both ways and only God can truly help me.*

Dropping the phone in its cradle, Joseph sat on his childhood bed for what seemed like hours. *How can I honor my father without hurting Jess? Soon I will have to make a decision. God help me.*

Now there were even more pressing issues: the funeral, the estate, being there for Mom, Tom. It was more than he could bear. Finally, sleep came, but only to usher in disturbing dream images of doctors in white coats trying to revive his father while he stood by helpless and unable to move.

Jessica

Paris

After hanging up the phone with Joseph, Jessica sat brooding over a cup of tea in her tiny apartment as rain pelted against the windowpane. *Am I on the verge of losing Joseph?* Clasping the necklace he had given her, she squeezed her eyes shut. Tears ran down her cheeks, mirroring the unrelenting rain beating against the window.

Startled by the phone ringing again, Jessica answered quickly, thinking it might be Joseph. Instead it was a flustered Aunt Jane, reporting that Adelaide, Jessica's mother, had been rushed to the hospital.

"Why?" Jessica asked, her nerves jangled.

"Your dad called and asked her for a divorce so he could marry his girlfriend," her aunt declared in an abrupt manner. "Luckily I was here because she went into hysterics. She went on and on about not wanting to live anymore."

"Oh, my God. It was that bad, then?"

"Pretty bad. I couldn't calm her down so I called an ambulance. They gave her a sedative at the hospital."

"How's she doing now?"

"Better, but she's been asking for you."

Jessica got all the information she needed and hung up. *I've been afraid this would happen. I don't know why Mum was so blind. Now she's got to face reality and that's certainly not her strength. I'd better leave right away.*

She held on to her necklace, took a deep breath, and picked up the phone to arrange a flight to London. Then she packed some clothes and scanned the apartment to see if there was anything else she needed. Her eyes fell on the two mythological books about Eros and Psyche on the kitchen counter and she decided to bring them along.

***

Later that day, a nurse directed Jessica to her mother's room.

"You're here," Adelaide Taylor exclaimed. "I knew you'd come."

"Mum, you know how much I love you. Of course I'm here."

"You're a good daughter, dear. I don't know what came over me. When your dad told me he wanted a divorce, I was crushed. I guess I always thought he'd come back home."

Her mother's words cut Jessica to the quick. *Why do women give such power to the men they love?*

"Maybe it's for the best," she said, holding her mother's hand. "At least now you know and can get on with your life."

But even as she said it, her own fear of losing the man she loved hovered about her like a storm cloud gathering overhead.

"I know you're right," her mother whispered. "When did you become so wise?"

"Hardly that, Mum. Now tell me, what can I do to help you?"

"Just finish up your studies and have a good life. That's what I want for you. Your Aunt Jane invited me to come live in the guesthouse on their farm. I've decided it would be a good change for me. She knows the librarian and feels sure he will give me a part-time job."

"Are you sure you're ready for such a huge change just now? What about the house in London?" She couldn't imagine her mother moving out of the family home.

"Maybe I'll rent it to start. Or perhaps it's time to sell."

"Well, being out of the house you shared with Dad should help immensely."

"Yes, it's high time to move on."

Jessica felt her mother echoing her inner state somehow and felt closer to her.

***

The next day, Jessica took her mother home and set about calling realtors. Adelaide had turned a corner and, though she remained weak, her spirits had lifted. With viewings set for only a few weeks away, Jessica began to clean out her old bedroom, finding some solace in sorting through memories of her childhood and clearing the space.

"Thank you for helping me with this," her mother said, appearing at the door, wiping the tears from her eyes with a tissue. "It must bring back some painful memories."

"It does, but I'm glad to let them go," Jessica said, fingering the gems in the necklace Joseph had given to her.

"That's a beautiful necklace. Where did you get it?"

"A friend gave it to me."

"Is this someone I should know about?" her mother asked with a suggestive smile.

"Just a friend." *Is that all he is?* An ominous feeling crept into her heart.

***

Later that evening, Jessica sat in bed, reading the myth of Eros and Psyche.

Despite Eros's insistence that Psyche not see him in the light, the gullible girl had followed her jealous sisters' advice anyway, lighting a lamp one night while her lover lay asleep. She'd had to know if he was a monster instead of a man.

To her delight, Eros was the most amazing and beautiful being she'd ever seen. But, in her nervousness, she spilled some wax from her lantern, accidentally burning his shoulder and waking him. He yelled out in pain, admonished her, and jumped up to leave. Psyche held onto him as long as she could, but, after breaking her pledge, she had to let him go.

Tears rolled down Jessica's cheeks. *My pledge was to myself, to not get hurt. Like Psyche, must I sacrifice my love for Joseph?*

***

The next morning, while sitting on the toilet, Jessica checked her panties closely. It had been ten days since she was due to start her period. How could she have been so careless as to miss taking her pills even once, much less three or four times? Maintaining an air of calm on the outside, but panicking on the inside, she called her family doctor to make an appointment for a physical exam. *I can't discuss this with Mum. On top of everything else, it would send her over the edge.*

***

"You'd better take a pregnancy test," Dr. Thomas said a few days later when Jessica told him her symptoms.

With a deep sigh, she agreed.

"I'll call you when the results come in," he said, patting her on the shoulder.

She continued helping her mother with the cleaning and painting, trying to stay calm, but, on the inside, she was falling apart. *When will the doctor call? What will I do if I'm pregnant? What will Joseph say?*

Finally, the call came, confirming her worst fears. "You're definitely pregnant, my dear."

"Are you sure?"

"Usually these tests are very reliable."

Numbed, she slowly placed the phone onto its cradle. *How could I have allowed this to happen? I feel so alone. Dad isn't around and Mum's so fragile. I'll just have to tell Joseph and let the cards fall as they may.* But a conflicting voice shouted out inside her: *He'll probably think you meant to get pregnant just to trap him into marriage.* Her tears came again in earnest.

That evening, unable to sleep, she remembered how, at twelve years old, she'd figured out that only seven months passed between the date of her parents' wedding and the day she'd been born. *Did Mum trap Dad into marriage and—even worse—have I unconsciously attempted the same thing?*

An emptiness gnawed at her as she realized she'd never been able to please her father. *I tried to play piano and then guitar, but I just wasn't musically talented, except in writing little songs and poems. Then I tried to draw and paint, but that wasn't good enough for him, either.* She could still hear him saying in a condescending voice, "Don't try to be an artist unless you can be the best." *What did he expect of me at such a young age?*

Her hand again on Joseph's necklace, she cried out inside, *Oh, God, please don't take him away. Our baby needs him and so do I.* She thought of poor Psyche, carrying Eros's child, and searching everywhere for him in vain. The striking parallels between Psyche's story and her own overwhelmed her. She cried for her unborn child and for all the women and children who found themselves stuck in such a position.

Joseph

Boston

With the ordeal of the wake and funeral finally behind them, the brothers had been hanging out together for a couple of hours at O'Mally's Irish Pub, when Tom raised his beer for a toast.

"Here's to Dad," Tom said, his glass held high. "Wish he was here with us."

Their glasses clinked.

"So do I," Joseph agreed. "So do I. I'll never forget when he gave us our first beers. You'd just scored the winning touchdown in the homecoming game. Remember?"

"Yep. How could I forget that?"

"You were such a jock. I think you were his favorite."

"But you're the one who was always so *good*."

"Hey, easy. I couldn't possibly live up to the rigid standards Dad placed on me and you know it."

"I know it and you know it but Dad didn't know it," Tom slurred, his voice growing louder. "I can just hear him now: 'Try to act like your brother, Tommy!'"

"Better keep your voice down," Joseph urged, looking around. "The bartender's giving us a nasty look. Besides, I think we've both had too much to drink."

"No way," Tom snapped. "The night is young."

"Look, I promised Susan I'd bring you back with your wits still about you."

"So you were talking to my wife behind my back, eh?"

"You know Susan worries about your drinking. It's no secret."

"Well, I can hold my liquor a lot better than either one of you gives me credit for," Tom balked, his voice getting louder. "And I don't appreciate the two of you talking about me when I'm not around."

"We weren't talking behind your back. It's just that she confides in me sometimes because she knows I'll listen to her. And, according to her, you don't always listen to how she feels."

"Always playing the big brother, huh, Joe?"

"I *am* the big brother."

"Well, Susan is *my* wife, not yours."

"I know that, Tom, and I didn't mean to intrude."

"Time to pay up," the bartender announced, suddenly appearing before them and handing Joseph the bill. "You'd best be moving along now."

"I guess we were getting a little loud. Sorry about that," Joseph apologized, paying the tab. Turning to his brother, he motioned toward the door. Reluctantly, Tom followed him outside.

Once outside the pub, Tom said, "I'm not gonna take any more shit from you. Are you man enough to settle this once and for all? Go ahead, take the first punch. I dare you."

"Let's just go home, Tom."

"You wouldn't dare fight with me, would you? You're not any different from those hippies. Always complaining about the Vietnam War. Make love, not war. What a crock."

Something in Joseph snapped. Without warning, his fist shot out and hit Tom in the nose, sending him tumbling to the ground.

"Holy shit," Tom exclaimed, wiping blood from his nose and stumbling up to his feet.

Barely upright, Tom's fist hit Joseph's right eye, sending *him* to the ground.

While Joseph lay stunned, Tom burst into a belly laugh. "We haven't done this since we were kids!"

Dizzy, but also oddly tickled, Joseph managed to get up, with Tom's help. "We'd better go home before we draw a crowd," he said, breaking into a full laugh himself.

***

The next day, Joseph woke up in his childhood bedroom, recalling the scene from the night before. Although it had ended on a comical note, some truth had broken through the dynamic between him and his brother. Thoughts raced through his mind, worsening his hangover.

Tom and I are so different. He was all set to go to Nam if they'd drafted him, but I would've done anything to avoid it—even going to Canada. He sure was touchy about my talk with Susan, but she needed someone to listen to her. Who do I think I am? I can't even be straight with Jessica. She deserves someone who'll be there for her. Why do I want to be a priest anyway? Is it for my father or is it truly my path? If only I knew.

Climbing out of bed, his head as big as a pumpkin, he stumbled into the kitchen, where his mother greeted him warmly.

"Look who's finally up. Whatever happened to your eye?"

"Tom and I got pretty potted last night. We ended up fighting outside the pub until we realized how ridiculous we were."

"I think you need a cup of coffee. And a bag of frozen peas to put over that eye."

"Thanks," he said, accepting the warm brew from her and sitting down at the breakfast bar.

She brought over the peas and her own cup of coffee, taking a seat beside him.

They sat together for a few moments in silence, Joseph leaning on the bar with the bag over his eye.

"How are *you* doing, Mom?"

"I've never felt so lost in my life," she said, shaking her head, tears threatening to spill, as she stood up to get a tissue from a box on the counter.

"It's okay to cry," he said, standing and wrapping his arms around her, his own tears mixing with hers. She offered him a tissue. They blew their noses and smiled at each other.

"Your dad would want us to be strong," she said.

"What was it he used to say? God doesn't send us more than we can handle?"

"Maybe you *are* meant to become a priest." His mother smiled and looked into his eyes.

"Let's not talk about that, okay?"

"Joseph, whatever you decide to do will be fine with me. I only want you to be happy."

"I know, Mom, and I appreciate that more than you know. Speaking of, I promised Dad I'd talk with Father Anthony. I have an appointment with him tomorrow."

***

Joseph sat down with Father Anthony in the familiar office where they'd shared so many rich conversations.

"Dad's last wish was that I confer with you about entering the seminary," he began.

"I think you'd make a great priest, Joseph." The older man paused before asking, "But are you ready to make such a momentous decision?"

"I'm not sure. I've been dating a woman in Paris and my feelings for her have confused me."

"Are you in love with her?"

"Maybe I am, but I want to do God's will more than anything else in the world. If He wants me to be a priest, how can I walk away from that call?"

"Only you can answer that, Joe, with God's help. The life of a priest isn't easy. You must be willing to give up worldly attachments."

"I know."

"It sounds like you've got some soul searching to do."

"Yes, I do."

"I wish you luck, Joe," the priest said. "Go back to Paris and keep your heart open. God will answer you."

"I hope so," Joseph said, shaking his head, as he stood to leave, reaching out his hand.

Father Anthony took his hand in both of his, saying, "Bless you, my boy. Bless you."

"Thank you, Father," Joseph said quietly, his head hanging as he left the office, feeling Father Anthony's gaze as he made his slow walk down the long hall.

***

That night, Joseph had a vivid dream. He was standing in front of a parish, wearing the robes of a priest, saying Mass. "That can't be me," he heard himself say, not sure whether the dreamer spoke or he had spoken to the dream. He woke up with a start. *That felt so real.* But he still had doubts.

***

On Saturday morning, Joseph suggested to Tom that they get together. Their mother and Susan had gone shopping and the kids were out with their friends. They met for lunch at their favorite deli.

"I was surprised at the strength of your punch the other night," Tom teased. "I'm lucky my nose wasn't broken."

"I guess we did do some damage to each other." Joseph smiled as he removed his sunshades to reveal his black eye.

They laughed.

"Even though it's been a rough time for all of us," Joseph said, "it seems to have brought us closer."

"I feel the same way. Maybe our fisticuffs opened up something for us. You see, fighting isn't always a bad thing."

"You've got a point there. Do you remember the look on the bartender's face?" Joseph chuckled. "I don't know if we'll be welcome back in that pub again."

"Look, Joe, I've been thinking about what you said the other night. Maybe I haven't been listening enough to Susan. You'll be happy to know we actually had a good talk yesterday about my drinking and I promised her I'd cut back. And I really do intend to do that."

"Hey, man, that's great. You've got way too much going for you to let alcohol spoil your life."

"You're right, *as usual.*"

"I'm not always right, that's for sure. Sometimes I don't have a clue about what's right for my life."

"I thought you'd be going to seminary after you finish up in Paris."

"That's what I'm so *conflicted* about. I also realized something because of our ridiculous fight. I'm actually a bit jealous of you and Susan. I look at the life you live and wonder if I'd be sorry if I gave up my own chance to have a family."

"Wow, I didn't know you felt that way. But, hey, maybe you will get married someday. Have you dated anyone in Paris?"

"I've been seeing someone. She's my interpreter, an English girl who speaks French like she's known it all her life."

"How do you feel about her?"

"I think I'm in love with her. That's what makes this so complicated. If I'm destined for the priesthood, I'll have to let her go. I had this dream the other night that I'd actually gone through with it. I was in the church saying Mass. I could even smell the incense. Man, it was so real. But I don't know if I really have what it takes to take on such a huge responsibility."

"Dad always said it was your destiny."

"I know how *he* felt but I've yet to figure out how *I* feel."

"Hey, you'll work it out," Tom said, bumping up against him with affection.

"Thanks for listening." Joseph was relieved, that despite their differences, he and Tom could talk honestly with each other.

***

That night, Joseph had another dream. This time he was making love to Jessica, savoring each caress, when sirens rang out from the street. A loud knock at the door startled them. Grabbing a robe and throwing it around himself, he opened the door to find his dad standing on the threshold with two policemen. "Arrest this man," his dad demanded. "He's deserted God."

Startled, Joseph awoke, sitting straight up in bed. "Dad," he said out loud, "you're even after me in my dreams." *Or is it God, speaking through you in order to get my attention?*

***

The next morning during Mass, Joseph studied Father Anthony serving the Holy Eucharist, mesmerized by the priest's actions. Something also struck him from the sermon: "Listen to your heart for guidance when you're confused about what to do." *He seems to be looking directly at me when he says those words.*

***

On the day before he was due to return to Paris, Joseph took some time alone down by the Charles River. *It reminds me of the Seine, where I spent so much time with Jessica.* Sitting on a bench, he bowed his head and closed his eyes. *Speak to me, God. What would you have me do?*

Something in his heart jumped. "You know the answer already," a voice in his head clearly said. "You've always known." He knew it was God this time, reminding him of what he'd known since childhood. *If I shirk my duty to God to marry Jessica, I'll be haunted forever by whether I've made the wrong decision. It will be excruciating to say goodbye to her. But the sooner I do, the better it will be for both of us.*

***

A few days later, back in Paris, Joseph called Marc to let him know he was back.

"So sorry about your father," Marc said.

"Thanks. I appreciate that."

"Looking forward to seeing you when you feel like coming back in. We're nearly finished, you know."

"I know. I'll be in sometime tomorrow."

"By the way, Jessica called from London. She's there with her mother. I told her you'd be back today. She'll probably give you a call."

***

The following evening, Jessica called.

"It's good to hear your voice," she greeted him warmly. "How are you coping? I know you've been through an awful time."

"I'm doing fairly well, under the circumstances. And you?"

"Well, I've been better. Dad finally asked Mum for a divorce and she flipped out."

"Oh, no. I'm so sorry, Jess. How is she now?"

"Better. She's decided to sell the house in London and move up to the Lake District to live with my aunt and uncle."

"And how are you? Really."

"Exhausted. I've missed you."

"I've missed you, too." After an awkward silence, he continued, "We'll catch up when you get back. How about a dinner out on the town? I'll treat you to some bouillabaisse."

"Sounds wonderful. I'll give you a call when I get back to Paris in a couple of days."

"Okay. Take care of yourself, Jess."

After hanging up, he held his head in his hands. *Oh, Father, help me with this.*

***

Two days later, Joseph sat across from Jessica in one of their favorite cafés. After they enjoyed their soup, he began the dreaded conversation he'd practiced over and over again in his mind.

"I talked with Father Anthony about our relationship," he began.

"You told him about us?"

"I had to. Don't you know how special you are to me?"

They lingered in silence, as if weaving the bond between them more tightly.

"And you to me."

"But I can't go on like this," he continued, reaching for her hand.

"What do you mean?"

"I care for you with all my heart, but ...."

"But?"

"But after a lot of prayer and the conversation with Father Anthony, I've had two dreams that lead me—I mean, they suggest that my father may have been right about my destiny. For example, in the first dream—"

"I don't want to hear your dreams," Jessica cried, raking her chair across the floor as she pushed away from the table and rushed for the door.

Unable to stop her, Joseph threw some cash on the table and ran after her. But when he got outside, she had already turned the corner a block away. His heart raced. *This isn't how I'd imagined the night to be. I'd wanted to share with her—with certainty this time—that I've come to the realization that God has been calling me ever since I was a child to serve Him as a priest. If only she could have listened and understood.*

Instead, I've hurt her, just like her father, just like she's feared. How can I let her go and live with what I've done to her? Oh, God, why, why, why is this so hard?

Jessica

After her devastating experience with Joseph, Jessica caught a cab to the nearly finished convent in order to pick up her things. She had to leave Paris and get away from him as soon as possible. Her worst nightmare had come true, making her sick to her stomach. She reached for the cross around her neck. Fingering its precious stones usually comforted her, but this time, the gesture made her gasp. *I should have given the necklace back to him.*

"Are you all right, Mademoiselle?" the driver asked.

"Yes," she responded with quiet hesitation.

Tucking the necklace under her blouse, as if to hide it from herself and anyone else who might see it, she closed her eyes to think. *I should give the necklace back to him, but I can't bear to see him again.* And then Joseph's words replayed themselves. "I want you to have it," he'd said, "to remind you that my love is with you always, no matter where our futures lead."

No matter where our futures lead. He must've known we wouldn't stay together. Tears stung as the hole in her heart grew.

"Please pull over here and wait for me on the curb," she said to the driver, pointing to the convent on the near corner. "I'll only be a few minutes."

She used the key Joseph had given her long ago to open the front door. *How sad. The beautiful tree carving is still damaged. Just like me.*

Inside, Mother Marian came into the front room to greet her.

"Reverend Mother, I didn't know you'd be here."

"I moved in permanently a few days ago," the nun explained. "May I help you with something, dear?"

"Well, I just came to get my things," she replied, trying not to cry.

"You're upset, Jessica. Come, sit with me in my office and tell me what's wrong."

Jessica needed to talk with someone, and the warmth in the older woman's voice comforted her, so she followed her inside.

"Now tell me what's happened," Mother Marian said.

Jessica broke down.

"Dear child, what's wrong?"

"I'm pregnant," she blurted out, not able to keep the truth to herself any longer.

"Oh, you poor child."

Jessica's tears grew deeper, turning to sobs as the nun took her by the shoulders and pulled her to her breast, sitting them down on the nearby couch together.

When she was able to speak, Jessica said, "I can't believe it. What have I done? How could I be so foolish?"

"Pregnancy before marriage is such a heartbreak. I am so sorry you must endure it."

"Yes, it is the worst thing that could possibly happen."

"Well, child, yes, it is very sad, but a new life will come of it, a part of you and someone you've loved." There was a pause before Mother Marian continued, her voice softening, "Have you told the baby's father?"

"No. I can't. If you only knew—" Jessica's voice broke.

"You must calm yourself. Trust, trust that some good will come of it all."

"I don't see how."

"Can you share your news with your mother? Could she help you?"

"No, no, she has troubles of her own."

"I see. Yes, I understand. Perhaps I can help you, dear, if you'd like."

Jessica lifted her head and looked into Mother Marian's eyes as if she were her only hope. "Yes, but how?"

"First, let us pray together."

As the silence surrounded them like an invisible cloak, the Reverend Mother's love was palpable and the room became calm and peaceful.

"The nuns at my former convent in Provence will surely take you in. You can also receive the medical help you will need there."

"Thank you, Reverend Mother. Oh, thank you."

Taking Jessica's hands and crossing herself, the nun shared, "You will also, of course, need to decide how you will raise your child. You *are* Catholic, aren't you, dear?"

"Well, I was, but now I'm not so sure." She thought of how Catholicism had taken Joseph away from her.

"Jessica, you must think of what's best for the baby. If you should need it, there's an excellent Catholic adoption center in Provence."

"I won't give up my child," she exclaimed, horrified by the nun's words.

"I know how you must feel, dear, but there will likely come a time when you realize you cannot provide the kind of home an intact Catholic family can offer. Keep it in mind as an option, an option close to your heart."

Mother Marian wrote down a telephone number and an address, folded it, pressed the paper to her lips, and handed it to Jessica.

"If you decide to do as I've suggested, you may call this number. I will contact the new Mother Superior and tell her that she may hear from you."

Jessica searched the Reverend Mother's pale blue eyes in disbelief, taking the number as if willed to from beyond herself.

"Please don't tell anyone I've told you this."

"Of course not, dear. You have my word."

***

Provence
Seven Months Later

Jessica screamed as another labor pain pulsed through her body, causing Sister Madeline to hurry to her side.

"I think the baby's coming," Jessica shouted.

"The doctor's been called away on another case," Sister Madeline said, a look of panic in her eyes.

"I don't think the baby's going to wait much longer. Please … help me," Jessica cried in pain as her body convulsed yet again.

"I'll get Mother Catherine. She'll know what to do."

***

Three hours later, the Mother Superior, sweating profusely, but smiling from ear to ear, handed Jessica her tiny baby boy, still streaked with blood as he wriggled in the nun's arms.

With a full heart, Jessica accepted the precious bundle of life into her arms. "He's perfect," she exclaimed. "Thank you, God, for giving me this beautiful child."

"Amen," Sister Madeline chimed in.

"We've assisted in lots of births," Mother Catherine said, "but this was the first time we've delivered a baby without the help of a doctor."

"I'm actually glad the doctor didn't come," Jessica announced. "What could possibly be more sacred than two nuns and a brand new mother bringing the gift of life itself into the world?"

"I'm just relieved that your son is alive and well," Mother Catherine said. "I guess we'd best clean him up now."

"Wait. I want to hold him a little longer."

"Of course. We'll leave you alone with your little one."

After the nuns left the room, her heart fluttered as she gazed at the tiny bundle in her lap. *This is the proudest moment in my life. What a miracle.* When her baby's eyes opened and his gaze met hers, she felt a love like no other.

"Well, hello there, little … André. How about a French name for a little French baby?"

André closed his eyes again at her pronouncement and fell asleep.

***

For the next three months, Jessica lived in the convent, nursing her baby, changing his diapers, and thoroughly enjoying early motherhood, a role she'd never expected to play at such a young age.

This is all so surreal. Just last year, I was a young and carefree student. Can I actually be here in southern France nursing my own baby? The nuns and I are the only ones who know I'm a mother. My parents don't even know. Joseph doesn't know. Maybe this is all my imagination. She kissed André on the forehead. *No, this is a real baby all right.*

That night she woke up with a start from a disturbing dream and recorded it in her journal:

I'm wandering around aimlessly with André in my arms. We must be homeless because we don't seem to belong anywhere. I'm looking into his eyes and telling him I'm sorry. I just don't know where to go or what to do. He's crying and I feel so guilty for not being able to provide a home for him.

In the glow of a nightlight, she could see her baby's face as he slept peacefully in the little cradle by her bed. Closing her eyes, she prayed. *God, what should I do? Mother Catherine thinks I should allow André to be adopted by a Catholic couple here in Provence. But how can I let him go?*

Doubts about her future cast a dark shadow on her initial joy. How could she take care of André and also finish school? What kind of job could she get without a college education? Her father was busy with his own family and her mother was trying to put her fragile life back together. The Reverend Mother had suggested she place André up for adoption. But how could she?

Touching the stones in Joseph's necklace almost always around her neck, Jessica closed her eyes and listened with her open heart. Suddenly, a image of golden sunlight and a field of huge sunflowers filled her inner vision: the Provence she'd seen and fallen in love with the previous summer when she'd first arrived. Since then the shadows of winter had eclipsed the beautiful light that gleamed again in the vision before her.

She marveled at the beauty of the scene. *It looks just like a Van Gogh painting.* A small boy ran up to the largest sunflower in her vision and kissed it as if it were a face. An older man and woman ambled into the scene wearing huge smiles. The man swooped up the little boy, holding him high above his head, while the little boy giggled and beamed into the man's face. The vision gradually faded.

Maybe Mother Catherine is right. She turned to gaze into her child's tiny face. In spite of her sadness, a smile crept across her lips. *I love you more than anything in the world, my darling André, and I only want what's best for you.* Now she knew in her heart of hearts what she must do. And she would leave Joseph's necklace with him as a way to build a bridge from her heart to Andre's.

***

"You've made the right decision," Mother Catherine said the following day, touching her arm gently with comfort.

"But how do you know that?"

"Because I've known these people for a number of years. André will be loved and cared for by both a father and a mother, something that you cannot provide for him."

***

Jessica stayed on in Provence in the town of Arles for another month, not far from the convent, living on the money that had been earmarked for school. Vincent Van Gogh had lived and painted in Arles and Jessica felt the troubled painter's presence as she wandered about the city. *Perhaps he felt lost, too, like me.*

Thoughts of her baby—now living with the Catholic couple who had adopted him—haunted her. She tried to find out who they were, but the nuns would give her no information.

How could I have given up my own child? Was it the right thing to do? Dark waves of despair washed over her, threatening to consume her with guilt. She had to get away, center herself, make some decisions—get back on track with her life. But where could she go? Not London. Not yet. And certainly not Paris.

I'll go to the seashore. If I can just be near the sounds and smells of the sea, I know I'll be all right. I've never been to the French Riviera. Maybe this is the time. She rented a car and drove toward Marseilles.

***

Prior to arriving in the coastal city, Jessica found herself in the village of Saint Maximen. The streets were filled with people and she was forced to park the car.

"What's going on?" she asked a nearby young woman.

"Why, it's the Festival of Saint Mary Magdalene," the woman responded as if surprised someone did not know. "On July 22—today—

we carry her skull through the streets."

"Her skull?" Jessica exclaimed in disbelief.

"Well, it may or may not be her actual skull. That's not important. But here in southern France, we celebrate Mary Magdalene with all our heart and soul."

Jessica had heard of the strange cult of Mary Magdalene followers but had never actually encountered such devotees. She wanted to ask more questions, but the woman had hurried down the street, following the procession.

Without knowing why, Jessica followed the crowd, trying to get a glimpse of the skull, but she could not see over the shoulders of the throngs of people. She made her way across the street, rushing to the front of the procession before it turned the next corner ahead. *Is this a dream? Can I really be so captivated by something as strange as a skull, belonging supposedly to an ancient biblical woman? Where am I really? This can't be real.*

Her thoughts subsided as she rounded the corner and gazed back at the procession. There, held high in a golden carriage filled with white lilies and raised up by four angels, perched the head and shoulders of a woman, her face covered with a golden face mask. A kind of golden helmet rested on her head, surrounded by long golden tresses that flowed around her face. *Is this supposed to be a skull? If so, it's completely covered.*

She followed the procession to a convent, where white clothed nuns led the carriage into an open courtyard. They then proceeded to pull off the face mask. As strange as it was, the sight of the little black skull, with its jagged teeth and hollow eye sockets, touched Jessica's heart and brought tears to her eyes. *Is this really the skull of Mary Magdalene? Could it be? Why is it black?*

She gazed around at the adoring worshippers around her. *Who are they? And what is it about this experience that affects me this way?* Tears flowed, and she found herself sobbing. *What's happening to me?* She turned and hurried out of the courtyard, looking for something — anything — that resembled reality.

Glancing at her watch, she decided it was too late to drive to Marseilles. Fortunately, there was a small hotel across the street.

***

"Do you have a room available for tonight?" Jessica asked the clerk, a rather short, elfish woman with bouncing silver curls and bright amber eyes.

"You're in luck," the woman said. "We've been booked up for

weeks with people coming here for the festival, but I've just had a cancellation for tonight. How long will you be staying?"

"Oh, just one night," Jessica replied. "I was on my way to Marseilles but the festival captivated me."

"People come from miles around to be here on this date," the woman said.

"I'm curious as to why, in southern France rather than Jerusalem or some other place in the Middle East, people would be so devoted to Mary Magdalene?"

"Are you Catholic?"

"I used to be. I guess I'm kind of searching for something to believe in again."

"Why don't we have a cup of tea in the parlor and I'll explain the meaning behind all this celebration. By the way, my name is Theresa."

"And I'm Jessica," she said, taking the woman's outstretched hand.

She followed the little woman into the adjoining room where a welcoming pot of tea and several china teacups sat on a small antique buffet. Several chairs, covered in pink silk, with lace doilies draped over their backs, sat around the room in pairs, with small tables in between. *It's like an English tea parlor.* The room was oddly comforting. Noting a vase of colorful roses on the table before her, she inhaled their scent, and was instantly transported back to her mother's garden in London where she had grown up. Her eyes suddenly brimmed with tears. *I miss my mother and our old home.*

"Are you all right?" Theresa asked gently.

"Yes, I'm just feeling sentimental, I guess."

"Have a seat, dear, and I'll pour us a cup of tea."

"Thank you, Theresa. You're very kind."

They both settled onto their comfortable chairs. Theresa's eyes took on a faraway look as she began to unravel a story, one that left Jessica spellbound.

***

That night, in the privacy of her bedroom, Jessica lay awake, trying to process everything Theresa had told her. Her mind spinning, she pictured Saint Maximen bringing Mary Magdalene and her brother and sister, Lazarus and Martha, to southern France after the crucifixion and resurrection of Jesus.

Was Mary Magdalene really married to Jesus, or Jeshua, as he was called in those days, and *did they really have a daughter named Sarah?*

Theresa had said that Mary Magdalene brought what many considered to be Jeshua's true teachings to France. She'd also added that the Magdalene's descendants were the Cathars, who'd continued to follow the teachings for many years until the Pope and the King of France had them massacred for heresy because their beliefs conflicted with the so-called authorized teachings of Christianity.

Thank goodness some of them survived and continued the teachings in secret. And here in Saint Maximen, they still do. She closed her eyes, picturing the black skull, supposedly of the Magdalene, being paraded through the streets from her crypt in the Basilica of Saint Mary Magdalene to the Dominican Convent, where the nuns greeted her. Theresa had explained that some of the Magdalene's flesh had decayed on the skull, causing it to turn so dark. *I agree with Theresa that this is somehow appropriate because of the way the Catholic Church blackened her name, referring to her as a prostitute until they finally admitted she wasn't.*

She reviewed in her mind the true teachings of Jeshua that Theresa had shared with her. "Love, in all its various forms, is the answer to all of life's problems. First and foremost, we are to love God with all our heart and soul, and then to love our neighbors as ourselves. The basic teachings also stress the sacred nature of love between a husband and wife as well as the love of family, friends, and even those who we may deem our enemies."

Of course, Jesus would choose to embody, as example, the essence of all forms of love practiced on earth, wouldn't he? And wouldn't he have wanted his priests to do so also? Her eyes filled with tears, thinking of her love affair with Joseph and how sacred it really had been.

***

The next day, she awoke from a very special dream, one both erotic and sacred. She wrote what came to her as a poem.

Inner Wedding

In a marvelous mountain cavern
his sweet golden body
caressed me from head to toe.
I trembled as he kissed me
in that dark sweet place
where love rumbles and moves
and seeks release.
Like part of the earth
our bodies joined
the heartbeat of the mountain,
that shook with our ardor,

smiled at our union—
there in its hidden chamber
in the center of the earth.

If only it could be true ....

Joseph

Joseph relaxed with a glass of iced tea as he sat on the couch in the front room of Saint Mary's rectory where he lived with two other priests. Father Douglas, the head priest, had gone to visit one of their parishioners in the hospital and Father Andrew had taken his turn hearing confessions. Joseph had spent the afternoon playing basketball with the boys at the church's youth center. He smiled, recalling the wondrous expression on little Danny's face when he'd shot his first basket.

In these moments of solitude, he reflected on the past year since he'd completed seminary. *I love ministering to the parishioners, but I don't always know how to advise them — like that man who told me in confession that he and his wife had resorted to artificial birth control because they couldn't afford another child. With four already, I could understand their dilemma.*

Although he'd stayed within Catholic guidelines by advising the man to try harder to make the rhythm method work, Joseph found himself questioning not only the Church's stand on the issue, but his own actions in upholding it.

Why shouldn't a couple make love just for love's sake? If artificial means of birth control frees them to do so, what's really wrong with that?

Father Andrew came bursting through the door, interrupting his reverie. Joseph smiled at his fellow priest, a jovial, kind-hearted man, somewhat older than he, and was about to bring up the birth control issue when the phone rang.

"Come for dinner Saturday night," Tom insisted. "Susan's cooking a pot roast and Mom's coming with her new friend — one of the teachers at work. She calls him a friend, but I think he might be more than that."

"That sounds great. I'd love to come. I should be free by six."

"Then come at six. The kids have been asking where you've been."

"It'll be great to see you all ... and meet Mom's new friend." Hanging up, Joseph thought of his nephews: Charlie, at seven, quiet and studious like him; Sean, six, athletic and outgoing like Tom. Suddenly, Jessica's comments in Paris years before echoed in his mind: "I think you'd make a good father."

What would my life be like if I'd married her and had a family? Standing up, he paced the floor, willing himself to stop thinking of her, for doing so aroused something in him not at all priest-like. *I can still sense her fragrance as if I were holding her in my arms. But that was in the past. I made my decision and things are different now. So why does she still haunt me so?*

Regaining his composure, he returned to the living room, noting that Father Douglas had come back from the hospital. Just then, the cook rang the dinner bell; together they filed into the dining room for their evening meal.

***

On Saturday evening, Joseph completed his parish duties and took the commuter rail to his brother's house. Tom and Susan lived in Roslindale, a Boston suburb. He marveled at the historical significance of his hometown as he walked through Beacon Hill to catch the T to his rail connection. After only a short walk to their house, Joseph arrived. Sean greeted him at the door.

"Uncle Joe's here," Sean called to the rest of the family.

"You're getting tall, buddy," he said, admiring his nephew's physique.

"I'm taller than Charlie," Sean announced, standing up as straight as he could, his blond hair tousled and his blue eyes sparkling with mischief.

"Stop bragging," Charlie said, coming to join them. His dark wavy hair hung long around his neck and he wore a pair of round, gold-rimmed glasses just like the ones John Lennon wore.

"Good to see you, Charlie," Joseph said. "I like your new glasses."

"I just got them," Charlie said as they went inside.

Everyone else had gathered in the living room. They all stood up when Joseph entered with the boys. After he'd hugged his mother, sister-in-law, and brother, his mother introduced him to her guest, a tall husky man with thinning gray hair and friendly brown eyes.

"How do you do, Mr. Parker," he said, shaking the older man's hand.

"Nice to meet you, Father. Please call me John."

"John, it is. And you might as well call me Joe or Joseph like the rest of the family does."

As the family prepared to enjoy drinks before dinner, Joseph settled onto a chair on the edge of the circle. Tom handed him a cold beer. It had been a while since they'd all been together. The conversation centered on the boys and on the addition to the house that Susan and Tom were considering, but Joseph noticed that his mother sat very close to John, whose eyes twinkled as he looked at her and patted her hand.

"Dinner's ready," Susan said, brushing a shiny brown curl out of her eyes.

Grounded and practical, she balanced out Tom's flighty personality. *My brother is a very lucky man.* "It smells great," he said as Susan ushered them into the small dining room that would soon be enlarged, its adjacent porch enclosed to make a sunroom.

"Will you offer the blessing, Joseph?" Susan asked when they were seated.

"Of course."

They all bowed their heads.

"Our Father, we are grateful for this wonderful food and for everyone gathered here, for the gift of family and new friends. May this food nourish our bodies as your love blesses our lives. We pray in the name of the Father, the Son, and the Holy Ghost. Amen."

"Great pot roast, Susan," Joseph remarked when they'd almost finished eating.

"I know how much you guys love it. That's why I made it."

"Everything was good," his mother commented. "I'd love your recipe for the broccoli casserole."

"I'll write it down for you after dinner," Susan said, beaming.

"How about that Red Sox victory over the Yankees?" Tom asked.

"Did you catch the last inning?" Sean interjected. "A homer to break the tie and win the game."

"Sure did," Joseph said. "I think we have a chance to win the pennant."

"John and I are taking ballroom dance lessons," his mother announced, abruptly changing the topic of conversation.

"That sounds like fun." Joseph smiled, noticing that she'd colored her graying hair brown and had it cut in a short, trendy style instead of pulling it back in a bun at her neck. *It makes her look much younger. Nice that she's found someone like John. They both look so happy.*

"Maybe you'll tango around the room for us some day," Tom said, giving his mother a wink.

***

Deciding to take a cab back to Cambridge later that evening, Joseph fondly remembered his family's faces. He sighed, gazing out the window at the Charles River on his way back to the rectory. *For some reason, the Charles reminds me of the Seine. Jessica and I used to walk across the Pont Neuf Bridge, the river beside us as we shared our hopes and dreams. There she is again, filling my head with memories. Why is she always in my mind?*

"Because you love her," a voice from deep within his heart replied.

Was it his imagination or had he actually heard a voice? "But I'm a priest now. I'm not supposed to feel that way about a woman," he replied silently.

"Love is everlasting," the voice said. "It stays with you even when circumstances change."

A loving presence filled the cab like a warm blanket, enveloping him with a sense of wellbeing and comfort, as if God had spoken to him inside his heart.

Thank you, Father. He was grateful for the power and presence of love in his life. *Obviously, that includes Jessica.* He smiled. *It's okay to love her and still be committed to the priesthood.*

Jessica

Jessica gazed around the tiny hotel room, the very same one where she'd stayed after leaving Provence and her baby boy four years before. The dainty, antique dresser she remembered had been replaced by a long, modern one. *Seems out of place in this room.*

I'm stronger now. She caught her reflection in the mirror. *After all, now I'm a scholar of European Impressionists, with a Master's thesis to prove it.* Sighing, she turned away from her reflection. *Who am I kidding? Nobody truly recognizes my talent—that is, if I even have talent. I wanted so much to be working in a museum after graduating, but, no, I'll be an insignificant art consultant in an insignificant gallery. Well, at least it'll pay the rent.*

Looking around the room, she frowned again at the attempts that had been made to modernize it, and decided she liked its original quaint look better. Modern Venetian blinds covered the small window where pale, blue-flowered curtains had hung before. She remembered a matching bedspread that had once covered the bed—now replaced by a tan, fitted coverlet.

Neutral, everything is neutral—like my life has been ever since I left France. In London, all I've done is study. Will life be neutral in Paris, too?

She walked into the loo and unpacked her toiletries. Opening the medicine cabinet, she suddenly swooned, as if still the desperate girl from four years ago. Memories of that night came flooding in.

***

The summer of 1969 Jessica had returned to Paris after her experience in Provence of blindly following the supposed black skull of Mary Magdalene through the streets of Saint Maximen. The idea that Mary Magdalene could have been the wife of Jesus, perhaps even the mother of his child, a notion refuting all principles of her Christian upbringing, haunted her with a truth she could not name.

Mary Magdalene wouldn't have given up her child like I did, she thought, pangs of guilt emerging like the dark clouds outside her window. Neither the cheerful blue flowers on the curtains nor the warm coziness of her room could mask the gloominess of the scene outside or her dark mood and its incessant self-accusations.

What if those people harm my baby? It'll be my fault for giving him up.

What would Joseph think? And what does God think?

Pacing the floor, she found herself in the loo, staring inside the medicine cabinet at the small bottle of sleeping pills that the village doctor had prescribed for her just before she'd left the convent. She'd only taken them once, that first night without her baby. She opened the bottle and poured its contents into her hand, seeing her anguished face in the mirror looking back at her.

Stricken, she saw, too, her mother's face when Jessica was a child: so sad, so lonely, so pathetic.

"I will never be like she was then," she said out loud. "I am not a victim."

She returned the pills to their bottle, tears rolling down her face, as she saw her true self reflected in the mirror, sad, but determined, and never pathetic, never a victim.

Jessica turned away from the mirror and returned to the window where heavy raindrops pelted against the pane, muffling the faint sound of chimes in the distance, as a familiar melody came to her: "Let it be, let it be, let it be." A maternal warmth enveloped her.

Through the raindrops, the chimes growing louder, she saw a familiar vision: a small boy skipping through a field of sunflowers. She smiled as, again, the maternal comfort came, knowing in its embrace that she had made the right decision for her André.

***

Four years later, no longer the desperate girl, Jessica nonetheless continued to periodically suffer over her decision to give up her baby. Part of her remained uncertain, unsure of herself and her place in the world, in spite of her accomplishments. The recurring nightmare had come again the night before: she'd heard a baby's cry in the distance but could not find her way to it. She woke in a sweat, unable to go back to sleep.

Another disturbing dream, vivid and real, had brought her back to Paris, back to this very hotel. Opening her travel bag, she retrieved the journal where she'd recorded the dream and read it again to herself:

I'm being rocked like a child in the arms of a very large woman with dark skin. The two of us are sitting under a tree on a patch of soft grass, its branches hanging low around us. The woman looks down at me with deep kindness in her tender, brown eyes. She hums a melody to me that is vaguely familiar and says: "I am waiting for you in Chartres. Come...sit with me...in the darkness."

Jessica unpacked an art history textbook she'd brought with her and looked in the index for the Cathédrale Notre-Dame de Chartres. The building towered at the center of a small village. Encased in ancient stone, world-renowned stained glass windows lit the inside of the cathedral with a blue glow. Intricate sculptures told stories around its outside perimeter. But the two Black Madonnas housed there interested Jessica the most: one in the main part of the sanctuary and another, deep beneath the original foundation, in the crypt.

Turning to the page that pictured the Black Madonna of the crypt, her heart fluttered. The calm face on the Madonna resembled that of the black woman in her dream. She heard her call within her: *Come ... sit with me ... in the darkness*.

She read further that the crypt also housed the Sancta Camisa, believed to be the tunic worn by the Blessed Virgin Mary at the time of Christ's birth.

Theresa, the woman she'd met in Saint Maximen shortly after André's birth, had suggested she visit Chartres Cathedral, especially on the Summer Solstice, tomorrow, June 21, to walk the labyrinth as a way of connecting to the deepest core of her being. She sensed a calling, something she must follow at this transitional time in her life.

The next day, after an early morning train ride from Gare du Nord station in Paris, Jessica walked up the hill to the Cathédrale de Chartres. The majestic sight towering above her took her breath away, its medieval architecture, crowned with two uneven spires, as if it had always stood there. *Reaching for the heavens*, she thought.

At the arched entrance stood carved figures of people and angels, beckoning her to enter. She sidled up alongside a tour group in progress, listening carefully to the melodic French cadence of the tour guide's words as he referred to a huge labyrinth, forty feet in diameter, under their feet, crafted in dark blue-grey and white marble.

"... created in 1205, shortly after the completion of the fourth rendition of the cathedral that had been ruined three times before by fire. We are not sure, but we believe the labyrinth has always been intended for walking meditation. Some say to walk the labyrinth is to walk the path of life. We walk to the center of ourselves, receive the gift of who we are, and we return to the world to give that gift. Its circumference matches the exact size of the western Rose Window, its diameter the same as the window's height. In the unlikely event that the western wall fell inwards, the rose would land directly in the center of the labyrinth, probably the plan of those who implemented the cathedral's sacred geometry."

Jessica gazed up at the Rose window to the west, its blue radiance sparking awe in her heart. Her research suggested that the rose represented Mother Mary, the womb, the center of creation.

The group walked slowly to the back left gallery of the cathedral.

Pointing upward, the guide continued with his talk, "This is Our Lady of the Pillar, The Black Virgin." Adorned in gold and white vestments, the Black Madonna sat upon a tall pillar, holding her child, dressed in gold. Both wore crowns upon their heads. The guide handed Jessica and the others in her group photographs of the statue without its vestments.

"As you can see," the guide continued, "this is a black wooden statue, modeled after the White Madonna on the main altar of the cathedral.

"Why is she black in color?" asked an elderly man in the group.

"Because she represents the mysterious element of the Feminine."

"I would like very much to visit the crypt," Jessica said when the guide paused for a bit. "Will you be taking us there?"

"The Sexton gives tours of the crypt through another entrance to the cathedral," he said, glancing at his watch. "The only tour this morning is at eleven a.m. After we view Our Lady of the Beautiful Window, you must hurry if you want to join the crypt tour."

After taking in the beauty of the stained glass depiction of Mary, the Queen of Heaven, Jessica thanked the tour guide and asked quietly how to reach the entrance for the crypt tour.

"You go out the front door," he instructed. "Turn left and circle back to the southeast corner of the building. You can buy a ticket in the gift shop there and the clerk will show you the entrance."

"Thank you so much," Jessica said. "I have one other question as well. Could you recommend a place where I might stay overnight?"

"If you want to stay on the grounds here," he whispered, "I recommend Hôtellerie Saint Yves, built on the site of an ancient monastery, only fifty meters or so from the cathedral and very reasonable."

"Southeast corner of the building," Jessica whispered to herself as she made her way out through the front doors of the cathedral and turned left, rounding the corner as directed. There, indeed, was a little church store. Next to it, on the right, was what looked like a monastery. Drawing closer, she saw a guesthouse sign, as the guide had mentioned.

No time to make reservations now. They're already lining up for the crypt tour.

She hurried into the gift shop and purchased a ticket, the last one available, according to the clerk. *I guess I'm meant to be here,* she thought, rushing to join the others.

"We will be viewing the only part of the cathedral that was originally built in the fourth century," the Sexton was saying in French. "The rest of the building was destroyed by fire and rebuilt four or five times. The last reconstruction began in 1180 and took about eighty years to complete." He opened the door and waited for everyone in the small group to enter. "We will now walk down these stairs to the crypt, which is actually under the main cathedral and serves as its foundation."

The dark stairway led downward to a series of small, open rooms, like scalloped edges or petals of a flower, that surrounded the chapel. Jessica thought of the rose and wondered if this symbol, too, enveloped the sacred crypt.

The guide pointed out how the Gothic pillars upon the main floor above were built on top of the crypt's original pillars below. They passed a well covered by a grate. "Legend has it that the Druids worshipped here," he said, "long before the first rendition of the cathedral, but there is no clear evidence of this. Jessica stopped at the well and felt the depth of its energy. *Something took place here, something intense and deep.*

"Follow me, please, in silence, as we enter the chapel where The Lady of the Under Ground is located. As you enter, look back over your shoulder and you will see her, sitting on her throne, with the babe on her lap. The statue serves as a focal point for those who come to services still held here. Please remain silent while visiting this very sacred space."

Candles lit the altar where the Black Madonna sat surrounded by a mosaic blue flame reminiscent of the evocative blue of the western Rose Window. Jessica waited until all had risen from their prayers and appeared prepared to exit before she whispered to the Sexton, "I would like to stay behind and pray if that is acceptable to you."

"You may, but will have only one half hour before the crypt closes for two hours for lunch. Be careful to watch the time."

"*Merci.*" Jessica nodded, crossing her heart and entering the silence of the inner chamber.

The Black Madonna, although only a couple of feet tall, seemed larger than life, regal. She sat on a shelf, surrounded by her blue background—blue with streaks of lavender, violet, yellow—resembling the heavens, stars intermingled with other forms of light.

As the Sexton had indicated, Mary—*or perhaps a Druid Goddess or maybe both in one*—sat on a throne with the babe on her lap, her statue carved out of dark wood. Below the Madonna was a small wooden altar and further in front of it, a sort of podium or pulpit. *Probably where the priest stands when doing services.*

Looking around the room, Jessica studied the chapel's other artifacts, including a faded fresco on one of the walls. Beside it, the relic of Mary's tunic was displayed within an ornate gold-encased box behind what appeared to be a tempered glass. Lit only by candles, the ancient sacred place was dark, its stone arches framing the scene.

Jessica entered timeless time.

As the tall shadows of the other individuals on the tour faded one by one from the candle-lit wall, Jessica knelt down on the soft burgundy cushion in front of the closest chair, looking up first toward the dark Mary, the Black Madonna, closing her eyes in silent prayer.

Beloved Mary, please forgive me for giving up my precious baby. Guard and protect him in his new home. And please heal my broken heart that hurts so and my womb where I once carried my baby. Help me to forgive Joseph for leaving me and myself for leaving André.

As she continued to sit silently, she released a long-held sadness that felt to have originated before her present lifetime, arising out of some deep, dark history of the planet itself. *Is this the pain of all women from years of suppression and open denigration in some parts of the world? It seems the feminine in this world is not honored and appreciated as it should be. The world looks down upon even those men who courageously reveal their vulnerability — their grief and sadness — for being weak, less, somehow, than so-called real men.*

She gazed at the Black Madonna before her, a response to her prayer emanating from the tiny form. *There is a hidden side of womanhood — a dark side — for we are part of the earth itself, the very matter from which creation springs. We must acknowledge this truth within us, reveal our wisdom, that it may be lived and known.*

Jessica's heart ached. "I recognize and appreciate the dark feminine," she said softly to the Black Madonna. *My wisdom lives in you now,* she heard with her ears and in her heart.

Glancing up, Jessica caught a glimpse of the Sexton outside the gate, pointing to his watch, alerting her that her time was up. Slowly, she stood and left the silence of the room, exiting through a stairway leading back up into the cathedral.

As she emerged from the darkness into the blue light and spaciousness of the main floor of the cathedral, she noticed another group gathered before one of the stained-glass windows. The sun shone through a small hole in the window, expanding onto the floor. She joined the others and together they witnessed the sun's rays beaming onto a spike nailed into a flagstone that had been laid at a different angle than the others around it. She heard the group's guide say, "At noon on the Summer Solstice the sunlight falls upon this spot, located directly above the well over which the cathedral is built."

She remembered what Theresa had advised about visiting Chartres during the Summer Solstice. *The significance of the well is even greater than I thought. Does it point to our sacred center, our very soul?*

Jessica felt a resonance with the cathedral that she had never felt before. She returned to the western doors under its Rose Window, seeing that the chairs had been removed from the labyrinth as others were gathering. She pulled the flyer from her purse that shared information about the labyrinth's history and modern meaning to pilgrims, including a drawing of its pathways. It contained four sections and eleven circuits. Its center formed the shape of a rose with six petals. One opening from the outside led to the center and back out again. She recalled her discussion with Theresa four years ago.

The labyrinth represents my life's journey, inviting me to walk to the center of myself again, just as I did when I sat with the Black Madonna underground, to find and deepen my connection to the feminine divinity within me. Could this help free my life of pain, guilt, and fear, or guide me to accept what I cannot change?

Jessica joined the others preparing to enter the labyrinth. She removed her shoes and set her intention to remain open and present as she walked, preparing to cross the threshold, noticing that the woman just ahead of her had waited until the person in front of her had made his first turn. She inhaled deeply and took her first step, the marble floor cool on the soles of her feet. Jessica walked in silence, but not alone, sensing a strong presence with her as she took each step.

With each turn on the path, she felt a slight shift inside, as if each step, each movement, aligned her more fully with herself. She began to witness herself on this path as it revealed to her how she walked in life: slowly, cautiously, then erratically.

Jessica wanted to let go, wanted to let the path take her where she needed to go. Soon her self-awareness turned to sheer presence and she proceeded without effort. Images of her childhood came to her. She felt the sting of her father's rejection of her artistic talents. As she glided around the next turn on her path, she also remembered the gifts her father had given to her: appreciation for music and the importance of following one's passions.

Gazing ahead, Jessica felt a slight dizziness that took her step onto the path's edge, and for a moment she felt disoriented as her hand touched another person's arm. She excused herself and regained her balance, thinking she'd lost her way, but recovering it. Suddenly she recalled her mother's passivity, how her father diminished and silenced his wife. She recoiled inside, almost halting, but, with the next turn, compassion washed over her. Rather than fixating on her disgust for her mother's behavior, her heart opened. *I'm sorry your life with Dad was so unhappy, Mum.* Jessica smiled with genuine happiness that her mother had fallen in love again and married Donald, the librarian with whom she worked.

She continued walking, noticing others walking beside her, each at their own pace, some passing by her when she became still.

Thoughts of the men she'd dated entered her mind. *I forgive you all for leaving me—especially you, Joseph. I realize you're off serving God, and who am I to say you made the wrong choice?*

And she saw her precious baby, once swaddled and adored, now playing hide and seek in the sunflower grove. *I love you, little André. I bless you and release you to the Great Mystery, who will guide your way. You will always be my son. Be happy, my darling one, and stay healthy.*

Soon Jessica reached the center of the labyrinth. From where she stood inside the rose, enveloped by its six petals, she looked up at the Rose Window, its radiant blue light emanating in all directions. "Like you," she whispered to Mother Mary, "I brought a son into the world. And, like you, I've suffered the pain of saying goodbye to him. Now it's time to move on with my life, begin my career—maybe even find love again."

She walked into the first petal of the rose, etched onto the floor below her, and the fragrance of a rose came to her, like the ones in Provence, as the entire experience of her awakening in Saint Maximen came alive in her again.

Moving to the second petal, she closed her eyes and sensed the fragrance of lilies. She stood, once again imagining the procession of Mary Magdalene's skull through the streets of Saint Maximen, lilies surrounding its carriage. *And now the Black Madonna is beneath my feet on her throne in the crypt. She guards the unknown, the dark places within, not yet conscious. These, too, are sacred. Perhaps she represents the Magdalene.*

Moving to the third petal, she became aware of the image of the Black Madonna of the Pillar, draped in gold. "*Guarding the present world,*" a voice inside her said softly. Recalling that the skull of Mary Magdalene in Provence had also been draped in gold, she wondered. *Just what is the connection between the two Marys? Maybe mother and daughter-in-law? Could they represent two aspects of the Feminine principle still present in the world, one known, one unknown?*

Moving to the fourth petal, she closed her eyes again as a delicate breeze passed through her. It's as if an *angel caressed my tired soul, lifting my spirit upward.*

Realizing that others would soon be waiting for her to complete her meditation, she prayed that she might make haste slowly as she moved to the fifth petal, sensing a strong white light shining down upon her from above, quickening within her. *Thank you, Father God,* she prayed spontaneously, *for shining your light upon me, for guiding me to trust myself as I am.*

As Jessica entered the sixth petal, an image of stained glass appeared within her inner vision, the window of Mary, Queen of Heaven, draped in her blue cobalt mantle. *Guiding us toward heaven.*

Stepping into the center of the circle, she looked up, once again, at the Rose Window, high above her. *Yes, I am held and supported.* She *savored* the moment. *I am not alone. Both Madonnas, the light and dark, meet inside me. I am earth and I am spirit. My earth, my body, my soul matters. It mothers me. I am a vessel for light, for spirit. I am whole.*

As Jessica returned to the labyrinth path to retrace her steps back to where she'd begun, she realized that she could now walk into the world with her center strong and intact. Where Notre Dame stood tall and erect in Paris, a place of order and masculine sovereignty, Chartres felt like a womb, a place of gestation, devoted to the feminine, personally and in principle: more symbols, sculptures, stained glass windows, and paintings dedicated to the Virgin and, of course, the Black Madonna. As Theresa had suggested to her four years ago in Saint Maximen, Chartres could be considered the Seat of the Feminine.

Each step brought Jessica to new insights. *Not only are there two aspects of the feminine, the pure and the primal, nurturing mother and erotic lover, heaven and earth, but God, too, is both masculine and feminine, light and dark, assertive and receptive.* Her masculine assertion could take her into the world again, and her feminine receptivity, her openness to new ideas and practices, could take her deeper into her own knowing. She knew now that the unfolding of her life remained a mystery, one she could stop trying to figure out, one that she could trust wholeheartedly, no matter what the future held for her.

As Jessica made her final turn toward the opening, a new energy filled her with resolve and hope, as she pledged to honor her inner guidance, her innate wisdom, her own sovereignty, always.

Thank you, Father and Mother God. Thank you for my newfound awareness and for this day, this threshold into a life worth living.

Jessica slowly walked toward the front door of the cathedral, turning once again to savor the radiance of blue light and such inexplicable beauty and comfort. *I'll never forget this experience.* She bowed her head as she passed through the final arch into the afternoon light.

She inquired straightaway at the monastery guesthouse adjoining the cathedral about a room for the night, not yet ready to leave the beautiful village or the surrounding grounds of the sacred place, needing time to absorb what had happened here.

***

That night she had a vivid dream, similar to the one from her time in Provence, in which she'd made love with a golden man in the center of the earth within a great mountain. But this time, she observed the couple rather than participated. Suddenly, the mountain erupted, sending the man upward toward the heavens. Much later, it seemed, the woman, too, hurled upward where the two met in mid-air. She recorded the dream in her journal the next morning in the form of a poem:

Volcano

Earth—woman unleashes her power
sending her man raging outward in flames.
His awesome essence
towers above the mountain,
flowing outward in molten streams
across the land,
fertilizing the earth with her own energy
while she remains hidden
until the day appointed
for her to be free.
Power out of control
until she—no longer to be contained—
Rises from the earth mountain
to meet her true mate,
who descends upon her
in a radiant light.
Towering above the mountain,
Sun and Earth,
Spirit and Matter,
unite as one in mid air,
creating an offspring
magnificent to behold.
In the light of this holy union
fury transforms into beauty,
rage into trust,
darkness into light.
Mysteries long hidden are revealed
and heart flames alight
across the land.

Joseph

Boston, Massachusetts
Three years later

Joseph and the other priests from Saint Mary's planned to take turns getting away to enjoy the Saint Patrick's Day parade, a favorite activity of Joseph's family when he was young. His father had especially enjoyed Saint Patrick's Day. *He would be happy to see me now,* Joseph thought. He could almost hear his father's voice, introducing him: "This is my son, the priest. We're very proud of him."

Later, at the party, he sang along happily with "When Irish Eyes Are Smiling," but when a group gathered at the piano for "Oh Danny Boy," he couldn't sing the last verse, thinking of his father again. *He would be proud of me, but am I proud of myself?*

***

Spring turned into summer and Joseph sat in the darkness of the confessional at Saint Mary's, listening to one of his parishioners tell of her husband's abuse. She had one broken arm. Recognizing Natalie Shannon's voice, he was shocked that her husband, Ronald, would do such a thing.

Ronald Shannon's parents were strong financial supporters of the Church. Joseph suspected Father Douglas would be appalled by Natalie's story, but in order to follow up on her request for annulment, he had no choice but to go through the head priest.

***

"That's preposterous," Father Douglas reacted after Joseph told him Natalie Shannon's story. "Her husband's one of the most respected members of our parish." He took off his thick glasses and looked down his round, puffy nose at Joseph.

"Yes, I realize that, but clearly we don't know what he's like in the privacy of his own home."

"How do you know she's telling the truth?"

"She told me in confession. She wouldn't lie to a priest about such things. I could tell by the fear in her voice she's truly scared of him." *How can I convince this man that some people aren't what they seem to be on the outside?*

"Look, Joseph," Father Douglas said in a rather condescending voice, "I think I'd better take over at this point. I'll call Ronald in and have a talk with him."

"I must remind you," Joseph said sternly, "I'll first have to get Natalie's permission."

***

When Natalie arrived later that afternoon, Joseph ushered her into a small conference room. Her arm was still in a cast, and she looked frail and vulnerable. Anger rushed into his heart when he pictured Ronald using brute strength against her in such a violent manner. *What makes men like that think they have the right to abuse their wives?*

He shared how Father Douglas had responded. Natalie broke down again.

"I was afraid he'd do that. Ron puts up such a good front. He'll make it sound like I'm the one who's in the wrong, not him."

"I know how frightened you are, but please try to hold on to your faith. We do have to confront him, hear his side of the story if we're to continue with a possible annulment."

His words sounded hollow even to his own ears. Though it made him sick to think of it, Natalie was probably right. Ron would blame her—and Father Douglas would allow it.

PART TWO

Jessica

London

Jessica sat down to rest from the busyness of the day. Evening shadows darkened the living room, so she switched on the lamp on the table beside her. Her eyes scanned the small flat that had served as her home while she completed her education and launched her career as an art consultant in a small gallery. After seven years of living on her own in London, she felt it was time for a change.

Picking up the letter on the table beside her from her old friend Stephanie Lawrence in the States, she re-read it carefully.

"Please come to America," Stephanie had written, "and be my roommate here in Greenwich Village. It's the happening place to be in New York, full of art, music, and interesting single men, hint, hint."

There's nothing to keep me in London. I haven't dated anyone who sparks even a hint of soul connection like I shared with Joseph. Mum seems happy in her marriage, and things haven't changed much with Dad. He still basically ignores me now that he's busy raising his son. Tyler would now be almost as old as André. I mustn't think about André or Joseph now. I should go. I could start a brand new life.

Later, she lay in bed wondering if she'd lost her mind even considering such a radical decision. *But how spontaneous is it, really? I've thought of nothing else for weeks.* About to turn out the light she noticed her copy of *Amor and Psyche* on the coffee table. She'd become extremely interested in the mythic story since her experiences in Chartres cathedral three years before. The cathedral stood over an ancient Druid well where the Mother Goddess had been worshipped in ancient times. When Jessica had knelt in the darkness of the crypt before the Black Madonna, she'd begun to embrace the sacred energy of her own womanhood.

Psyche also learned to embrace her womanhood, she mused, picking up the book. According to Neumann, the young maiden had awakened to her sacred femininity when, instead of allowing Amor to keep her in the dark—a mere object for his own pleasure—she'd made the decision to see for herself who he really was.

Yet the journey to womanhood had not come easy for Psyche. After Amor, also known as Eros, vanished, her first inclination had been to find him and bring him back into her life. After all, she was carrying his baby and he had professed his love for her.

Should I have done that, too? Sought out Joseph, the father of my baby, and done everything I could do to bring him back into our lives? Oh, but that's too painful to even think about now. I had to release Joseph to follow his calling and I wanted André to have a better life than I could give him when I was so very young.

Glancing back at the book, she scanned its pages until coming to the part where Psyche begged Aphrodite to send Eros back to her.

Eros was the personification of Love itself for poor Psyche. Like Psyche, I long for that kind of Love in my life. With tears in her eyes, she closed the book. *For now I must find my way in the world without it. Psyche followed Aphrodite's instructions and I too must follow the Sacred Feminine. Maybe in America everything will make sense again.*

***

Two weeks later, after an exhausting flight, Jessica got in the taxi line at Kennedy Airport, her shoulders tense as she pulled her two ample suitcases behind her along with her carry-on bag and purse. Much as in London, the people waiting alongside her appeared to come from all over the world as their various accents filled the air. *Am I really in New York City?* The warm July breeze played with her hair, waking her up and stimulating her senses, but she hurt all over after the long day of travel and looked forward to getting where she was going. Finally, she was the next in line.

The Indian driver jumped from the driver's side and gestured that her bags should go in the trunk. He threw them in and she opened the door to the back and sat down. *London taxi drivers are much more hospitable, and their cars much cleaner.* The driver pulled down the meter's lever and said, "Where to?" as he sped away.

"Greenwich Village, please," she said, handing him the address.

"Do you want to take the tunnel or the bridge?" the man asked without turning around, a small plastic window between them.

"I have no idea. You know better than me."

He grunted. Jessica would have sworn he was not altogether awake. She held on to the strap above the window while he sped along, merging onto a crowded highway at near standstill.

"Goodness, is it always like this?" she gasped.

"It's rush hour, lady," he said curtly.

Jessica stared out the taxi window, noticing that the grounds around the roads were littered with debris. The sides of low buildings, in varying states of disrepair, were covered in graffiti. She locked her door, leaning over to lock the other as well. After an exit to one of the bridges, the city skyline began to emerge from the haze of the white sky.

Marveling at the sheer magnitude of the silhouette of tall skyscrapers, she gripped the strap tighter as the vehicle bounced up and down over potholes and in and out of lanes. Music pounded from some of the cars and horns blew percussively around them. *I could never drive here.*

As they crossed a bridge, she wondered about the body of water and started to ask the driver but decided against it. He was listening to his Walkman. The water looked dingy, like the Thames, but it sparkled nonetheless. Soon they darted across city streets and through yellow lights. People rushed to and fro and buses rolled along amidst swerving cabs and pedestrians walking against the lights. Captivated by the vibrant energy all around her, she could hardly wait to have her feet on the ground and be part of it all—*if I make it out of this car alive!*

Turning left onto Fifth Avenue, she assumed they were driving along Central Park. When she saw a horse and carriage she knew she was right. Passing fancy department store windows and then Tiffany's, she realized she was in the famous midtown shopping area.

The taxi raced down the avenue, chasing the green lights that seemed to change on command as he entered each intersection. Slowly, the tall buildings became more ordinary, and at 14th Street she suspected they had come to the Village, as people were dressed much more casually and many of the buildings looked residential.

Finally, the taxi slowed to a stop in front of a brownstone building with a red door.

This must be it. Jessica heard the trunk pop and she gathered her things. The driver hurriedly placed her two bags at the curb.

"How much do I owe you?" she asked politely.

"Lady, didn't you read the meter? Thirty-five dollars and seventy-five cents, plus tip."

"Oh, well, will you take a traveler's cheque?"

"You've got to be kidding. No way. Give me forty bucks and I'll be on my way."

Annoyed, Jessica reached in the back pocket of her bag where she'd secured her passport and took out two of the five twenty dollar bills that the teller had suggested she convert for emergency money.

"Thank you," she said, handing them to the driver. Without another word, he was gone.

She had to make two trips up the stoop to get her bags to the landing, and, once inside the vestibule, realized that she had three flights of stairs to climb to Stephanie's apartment, 3C. She pushed the button beside her friend's name and heard a loud buzzer. She got the first bag through the door but not the second, and had to buzz again.

Stephanie sashayed into the front hall. When Jessica saw her she nearly dissolved into tears with relief.

Both out of breath upon reaching the third floor, Jessica heard the familiar lilting sounds of The Beatles coming from behind the door to the right of the landing.

"You got it. That's *our* place."

"I'm so excited," Jessica said.

"You're going to love it here."

Jessica pulled the heavy bag across the threshold, Stephanie just behind her holding open the door, and stepped into a small room that was filled with potted plants. It looked almost like a nursery. She felt at home immediately.

"This is fantastic," she exclaimed.

"I knew you'd love it. My folks helped me get it. You wouldn't believe how expensive it is here. But, with their help, we'll be just fine." She disappeared into the tiny kitchen and returned with a large jug of white Gallo wine and two glasses.

"You look great, Steph." She laughed. "I love your new hairstyle."

"I grew it out and had it straightened," Stephanie announced as she poured the wine. "It's my Cleopatra look." Her gray eyes twinkled under the bangs fringed across her forehead.

"Well, it certainly suits you. But then I liked it short and curly also."

"I'm an actress now," Stephanie said in a dramatic tone of voice. "I have a good excuse for changing my hairstyle to match whatever mood I want to create. You never know, next month I may even become a redhead."

"Oh, Steph, I really have missed you."

"And this is only the beginning," her friend proclaimed as the Beatles sang "… all you need is love."

They curled up on each side of the overstuffed sofa and Jessica took a deep breath, sinking into the comfort of the pillows. She and Stephanie talked for hours until the shadows of dusk darkened the room.

"You must be hungry," Stephanie said. "I'm taking you to my favorite café in the Village."

They strolled through the colorful streets. Something about Greenwich Village reminded Jessica of Montmartre in Paris: a place to create, explore, and live fully, which was exactly what Jessica intended to do. Soon they reached a quaint little coffeehouse called The Gathering, already crowded with people. Bob Dylan's music played in the background and an air of excitement permeated the place.

"Hey, Steph, over here," a young man called from a table in the corner of the restaurant. "Who's this?"

Stephanie introduced Jessica to Jim Avery, whose shock of blond hair and sparkling blue eyes made him stand out in the crowd.

They enjoyed big bowls of clam chowder and loaves of sourdough bread. Jessica observed that women in the group were obviously infatuated with Jim. *Can anyone so handsome and charming be for real?*

"I wish you'd been here last night for the fireworks," Stephanie said. "We're in our bicentennial year here in the U.S." Lifting her glass, she made a toast. "To a new beginning for America and a new beginning for Jessica."

***

The next Monday, Jessica stood in A Clean, Well-Lighted Place, a small village gallery on Bleecker Street, awaiting her third job interview of the day. It was a perfect location, within walking distance of the apartment.

"Well, Ms. Taylor," Mr. Owens, the owner, said as he walked over to her, "what do you think of our little gallery?"

A man of about fifty, she guessed, he looked distinguished with his gray beard and mustache. She liked his casual manner.

"The paintings are evocative. I like this show, representational and yet moody with its muted use of color," she replied, not mentioning the haphazard way in which someone had hung the paintings. She fielded questions about her experience and produced a letter of recommendation from the gallery owner with whom she'd worked in London.

"Your boss thought very highly of you," Mr. Owens said in a deep, friendly voice after reading the letter. He talked with her about the hours, pay, and expectations, before telling her she was the third applicant that day.

After a few anxious days, she was surprised when Mr. Owens called to offer her the position. Jessica celebrated by taking Stephanie out to The Gathering. While they were eating, Jim Avery walked in with some friends. Stephanie invited them over and everyone toasted Jessica's new job.

"How about going to dinner with me tomorrow night?" Jim whispered in her ear. "I'll take you to my favorite restaurant in midtown."

"That sounds lovely. Thank you." *How can I resist?*

***

The next evening, Jim arrived on time. He looked fantastic, she decided, dressed in dark trousers and a soft gray jacket. His blue tie accentuated the sparkle in his eyes. She'd chosen a black dress and spiked heels, topped with a green silk blazer. She wore her hair up, allowing a few strands to fall casually around her face.

"Wow, you look stunning," he said, standing back to look her over.

They walked down the stairs to a waiting cab. The driver took them to an elegant restaurant in the middle of Manhattan.

"Good evening, Mr. Avery," the maître d' greeted them at the door.

"Good evening, Carl. I'm assuming you have a quiet table for us tonight."

"Of course, Mr. Avery," the man replied, escorting them to a cozy table, tucked away in a corner.

Jessica was impressed with Jim's impeccable manners. *He seems as much at ease here as in the casual atmosphere of The Gathering. And the staff seems to know him well. I wonder how many women he's brought here — maybe to this very table.* Nevertheless, she relaxed, enjoying the ambiance of the room, complete with crisp, white tablecloths adorned with fresh flowers, dishes and glasses gleaming in the glow of soft candlelight.

"You prefer red or white?" Jim asked her, checking the wine list.

"Actually, I like both. Why don't you choose?"

"We'll have a bottle of Pinot Noir," he told the waiter when he came to take their order. She ordered shrimp scampi to his prime rib.

Their initial conversation revolved around families and work, a typical first date. He'd been brought up an only child in New Jersey and had lived in Greenwich Village, working with a local acting group, for the past five years.

"Acting's my passion, ever since junior high."

"I'd love to see you on stage."

"And so you shall. And I'd like to visit your gallery."

"It's small, but modern, though the current artist's show is quite traditional, really."

"I hope you'll invite me in to see for myself."

"You could drop in anytime."

"Here's to many more times together, sharing our passions," he toasted, raising his glass.

"To sharing our passions," she hesitated, clinking her glass to his. *Where will this all lead? It's almost too good to be true.*

***

"I had a wonderful time," Jessica said later, as they paused in front of her apartment building.

"So did I," Jim said, kissing her gently on the cheek. "Let's do it again soon."

"I'd like that," she said as he walked away, his body language somehow out of synch with his good night. She waved hesitantly with only her fingers as he got into the cab.

He's definitely a charmer—like Dad. A shiver ran through her body. *Will he trample on my emotions if I allow myself to feel something for him?* She shook her head to rid it of such thoughts. *We had a wonderful evening. Why spoil it with what ifs?*

Joseph

Boston

Joseph sat across from the priest who'd seen him through childhood, seminary studies, and the early years of his priesthood. He had nothing but love and great respect for the man.

"Congratulations are due, I believe, now that you are Monsignor Anthony."

"Thank you, Joseph. Thank you," the monsignor responded, his dancing hazel eyes appearing much younger than his seventy-plus years. "But I'll always be a parish priest at heart. It's just that my duties have expanded to include lots of administrative details." There was a brief silence before the monsignor asked, "My dear Joseph, what brings you here today?"

"I'm consumed with anger and confusion," Joseph blurted, "and you're the only person I can think of who can help me."

"You know I'll do my best. Tell me, what has happened?"

Joseph related Natalie Shannon's story, his hands folding and refolding in his lap, as distress grew in the monsignor's face with each detail.

"And how has Father Douglas guided you?"

"Only to tell me he would take care of it, would call Ronald in, though I remain dubious of his resolve. It's been three months since Natalie first came to me. At first, she received harassing phone calls from Ronald at her parents' house. She tried to get a restraining order, but the police said she didn't have enough evidence. They *did* call Ronald, however, told him to leave her alone, or she'd press charges against him. The police told her to document each and every attempt he made to contact her.

In the meantime, Douglas called Ronald in. Of course, the man denied everything. He even said Natalie was mentally unstable—using the fact that she had suffered from depression." Joseph's voice grew louder. "But it's no wonder she's depressed. She's been living with a brute for a husband."

"Did she get the annulment?"

"Apparently it will be permitted, but not because she was abused. That bastard, Douglas, forgive me, wrote it up as if Natalie was at fault—running away from the marriage, refusing to uphold her marriage vows." He closed his eyes before continuing, "The look of disbelief on her face still haunts me. That and Father Douglas's perpetuation of the lie."

"Now I understand why you're angry."

"She looked at me like a lost lamb and there was nothing I could do to help her. She ran out of the office, saying she'd never set foot in a Catholic church again and I don't blame her in the least. I let her down, the Church let her down, and I can't forgive myself for that, nor Father Douglas." Shaking his head and continuing to wring his hands, Joseph searched the Monsignor's eyes, hoping for words his heart could accept.

"You must not blame yourself," Monsignor said gently, placing a comforting hand on Joseph's shoulder. "You did the best you could for her under the circumstances."

"I snapped when I heard the decision, and after Natalie had run from the room I lashed out at Father Douglas, accusing him of siding with Ronald only to retain Ronald's family's financial support."

"Calm down and tell me how Douglas responded."

"He told me I'd become too attached to Natalie and wasn't fit to be a priest." Joseph's hands clenched. "I could've raised my fist to him for that remark, but I remained steady, looked him in the eye, and told him if anyone wasn't fit to be a priest, it was him, not me."

"I've never known you to be so angry, Joseph."

After a long pause, Joseph announced, "I won't be staying at Saint Mary's."

"I am genuinely heartsick you have had to go through such a traumatic experience, but at least the young woman will have her annulment. She'll be able to marry again and still be a Catholic if she chooses to return to the Church."

"I don't think she'll ever return to Catholicism after this disgraceful humiliation, the blatant disrespect." Joseph stood and began pacing around the room.

"Have you requested a new assignment?"

"I need time to think and pray about this. I'm so torn, I'm wondering if the priesthood has been a mistake for me."

"I see. Well, the Church would lose a treasure, but I understand your sense of betrayal."

"It's time I told you about another issue heavy on my heart. I cannot reconcile the Church's rigidity on the birth control issue. Some of my parishioners can't afford to have more children and must manage the size of their families."

"What did they teach you in seminary about this?"

"That sexual intercourse is primarily to be used for procreation and artificial birth control makes it too easy for couples to forget this." He gave Monsignor a questioning look. "But when two people love each other, why wouldn't God want them to express that love for love's sake?"

"Joseph, you're struggling with a core Catholic issue."

"I know."

They remained in silence for some time.

Finally, Monsignor advised, "There's a retreat in Buffalo that I highly recommend. You can take as much time as you need there to contemplate and pray for guidance."

"Thank you, Monsignor. You've always been here for me, ever since I was a child. It gives me great comfort."

After returning to the rectory, Joseph sat on his bed, memories of his father flooding his mind. *Have I become a priest only to please him or to truly follow the path God wants for me? What of my love for Jessica? Should I have married her instead? Her image, her words, continue to haunt me.* He desperately needed answers to these questions; he began to plan his retreat.

***

A few days later, Joseph bought an old Volkswagen and packed up his clothes. After saying goodbye to Father Andrew and the volunteer workers in the rectory, he started on his journey. He didn't speak to Father Douglas.

Upon reaching the Buffalo Catholic Retreat Center, he cut the engine and breathed in the beauty of the place, nestled in a green valley with plenty of nature walks, streams, and places for quiet contemplation and prayer. Evergreen pines intermingled with stands of maples and aspen. Mid-October splashes of yellow and orange adorned the fading green leaves, and vibrant reds painted the tops of the maples. He marveled at God's creation.

There would be several brothers at the center along with two staff priests available to him for spiritual direction. He'd listed four reasons for coming to the center: to deal with his anger, to strengthen his relationship with God through prayer and contemplation, to come to grips with tenets of Catholicism that disturbed him, and to examine his own character and worthiness to be a priest.

After a week on retreat, he had yet to center himself sufficiently to listen to God. Sitting by a stream, he reflected upon the rushing water, so much like his own restless soul. His mind was a jumble of thoughts, like a radio station filled with static or a television set blaring out one commercial after another.

If only I still had my father's necklace. Somehow, just holding it and touching its gemstones in the past helped to quiet my mind. What happened to it? Is Jessica wearing it? Tears filled his eyes as he thought of his father's vision of him in a priest's collar. *The priesthood isn't what I'd imagined it to be. There are those, like Douglas, who abuse their authority and have little feeling for their parishioners.*

"Please stop these thoughts," he cried to God, holding his hands against his head as if to physically shut them out.

If I could only still my mind, perhaps I could ask God the questions on my heart and be quiet enough to receive His answers. Suddenly, an image of the rosary he'd left in his room came to him. It had been a gift from his mother upon entering the priesthood.

Perhaps the rosary will help me focus clearly. Rising to his feet, he gazed at the blue sky above and inhaled the fresh scent of pine, then walked humbly but with purpose to his room, thanking God without saying a word.

Settling in a chair by the window, he closed his eyes and held the rosary in his hand, the sunshine warming his face. He began to recite the Apostles' Creed. While touching each bead, he said the appropriate prayer while visualizing Christ through his life events: birth, ministry, crucifixion, resurrection, and ascension. Like Jesus, he could feel the presence of the Holy Spirit, filling and comforting him with light and love.

"Oh, God," he prayed, "I implore you to teach me your will that I may fulfill it without questioning your judgment."

"I am with you always," a tender voice said from deep within him.

He felt comforted, as if God, Jesus, and the Holy Spirit were speaking with one voice through his own heart.

"Thank you for your presence," he prayed.

Joseph poured out his heart that day and in the days ahead, continuing to use the rosary before engaging in personal prayers. He found God there, listening and guiding him from deep within.

Brother Matthew, his spiritual director, offered meditative exercises and scriptural readings that helped deepen his connection even more. He realized that his love for Jessica, though sexual and emotional in the past, now lived on a spiritual plane. She would always have a place in his heart.

As for the actions of Father Douglas, he learned that even within the priesthood, the ways of the world could distract from the love of God. Although he could not condone what Douglas had done, he was able, with the help of the Holy Spirit, to release his anger toward the other man. He became assured, too, that Natalie was in God's hands.

As for the disturbing tenets within the Church, he came to believe that Jesus took direction from God, rather than men, when going about his ministry. *Will I have the strength and courage to do the same, even if my actions go against the current policies of the Church? Will I be able to effect change in such an established institution? If my role as a Roman Catholic priest is on the line, will I be able to walk away from this path in order to follow the guidance I receive deep within my heart?*

***

After six months on retreat, Joseph felt prepared to leave. He would continue his role as a priest, but had no idea what assignment to request.

While thumbing through a Catholic newspaper, he spotted an article about a project in Brooklyn, New York. An old school building, with connections to Saint Andrew's Catholic Church, was scheduled to be transformed into a youth center. The church had bought the property and was in process of getting permits and finding appropriate staff to complete the conversion.

I've worked on projects like that before and I have some great ideas about what's needed in a youth center. Maybe I should request a change of assignment while I figure out my future.

***

Securing Brother Matthew's encouragement, later that day Joseph called and made an appointment for an interview, realizing that reinstating his architectural license could give him an advantage. Plus he'd kept in contact with a number of excellent contractors. He could say Mass at Saint Andrew's on evenings and weekends while using his secondary skills to further a worthwhile church project. It was a natural transition from the retreat center to the larger community.

***

With the assistance of Monsignor Anthony and the approval of other Church authorities, Joseph was hired as architect to create the Saint Andrew's Catholic Youth Center in Brooklyn. He moved into the rectory with three other priests.

The church bordered an area of the city where youth had few after-school choices. His goal was to provide a sanctuary that would hold the interest of Catholic teens in the neighborhood enough to steer them away from mischief and temptation. He wanted to include a family counseling center and opportunities for group counseling as well.

There would be areas for sports and after-school tutoring. He visualized it clearly and went to work drawing up a blueprint. It looked something like a mandala with rooms branching out from a center chapel in an integrated, cohesive pattern. It was perfect.

Joseph met a few days later with the contractor to finalize everything. When they agreed on a working plan, they shook hands in agreement. They would begin the following month.

Jessica

New York City

Jessica leaned her head back against the tub, allowing her eyes to close and the fresh, clean smell of jasmine bubbles to fill her nostrils. The warm water soothed her skin and her senses as she relaxed and savored the memory of last night's events. It had started when Jim offered her a puff of her first marijuana cigarette.

Hmm ... she could still hear Jim Morrison belting out, "Come on baby, light my fire ...."

Jim sure lit my fire and the grass made it all so intense. Her body responded to the memory. Grasping her breasts, she sank down in the warm water, grinning as she recalled Jim's words after their night of mad lovemaking.

"You are quite a woman, my little English bird."

She *felt* like a woman again. Not since her relationship with Joseph had she really let herself go. *It's time,* she thought, easing herself out of her bath and vigorously drying off.

***

After their initial night of lovemaking, Jessica and Jim began to spend most of their nights together at his place in the theater district. Soon, they were practically living together. *What would Mum think of this?* She rationalized that times had changed, and today's couples were much more liberal, even in England.

One morning, after Jim had left for an audition, she glanced at her reflection in the mirror. *My God I've changed since coming to America. I look like a hippie.* She laughed at the sight of herself in a long paisley skirt, peasant blouse, her hair hanging straight down with a part in the middle. *Where did the old Jessica go?*

***

After only a few months, she began to question her relationship with Jim. Sure, it was fun, but the connection between them seemed shallow. At first she'd felt relieved to just go with the flow, but now she longed for that ... *something* ... she'd had with Joseph.

That night, a compelling dream woke her with a start. The next morning the dream image was still deeply imprinted in her mind. She'd seen the beautiful tree that had been carved in the door of the convent in Paris. Before her eyes, it transformed itself into a real tree with branches reaching upward toward the sunlight and roots delving deeply into the earth. A white bird rested on its top branch. The memory of her dream was so vivid, she was inspired to write a poem.

The Tree of Life

I am the tree of life
in a garden of light and shadow.
I come through the earth
yet I am not of the earth.
My spirit soars far and wide
upward to the highest star,
for I am the white bird
who lives at the top of the tree,
coming home to rest
after long flights
into upper realms.
I am also the sturdy branches
that hold the white bird's nest.
My leaves tremble in the wind
and shimmer in the sunlight.
I am the strong trunk
with roots that travel
deeply into the earth,
channeling energy
into my being,
supporting me
as I grow,
yielding fruits of wisdom
for all to share,
for I am true to my own nature.

As she read the poem to herself, she sensed her connection to everything and everyone in the universe. It was impossible to feel lonely after such a profound experience. *If only I could share this with Joseph.*

She wrote further in her journal: *My sex life with Jim is great, especially when we smoke grass, but something is missing. On the outside, everything is fine, but on the inside, there just isn't that heartfelt connection I had with Joseph. Why do I compare every man I meet with Joseph? He's not even in my life anymore. Maybe I love Jim* in a different way, less complicated and more realistic. Besides, Jim is here and Joseph isn't. I can't change that reality.

***

"My parents asked me to bring you over for dinner tomorrow night," Jim announced the following evening. "They're beginning to hope you'll be part of the family, and, I guess you know, I'm hopelessly in love with you."

His comment threw her off guard and she stumbled over her response. "When you put it like that, how can I refuse?"

He reached down to kiss her. Pushing away all sense of doubt, she allowed herself to melt into his arms. His kisses grew more passionate as they fell onto the couch.

"Let's move in together," Jim whispered in her ear after a night of lovemaking.

"Are you serious?" Somehow the thought of it, reckless as it was, excited her.

"Yes, I'm serious."

"Do you really think we should?"

"Of course. Why not? Lots of couples we know are living together now. It's the way of the seventies."

"Okay, let's do it."

Maybe by living with him, I'll finally know if he's the right man for me.

***

"We hardly see you anymore," Jim's mother said during dinner the next evening. "Since you met Jessica, I'm afraid you've forgotten all about us." She looked at him with a little scowl on her face.

"Oh, Mother," Jim assured her, "you know you've always been my best girl." Turning to Jessica, he added with a smile, "But now I have two best girls."

Somehow the thought of sharing the limelight with Jim's mother made Jessica's stomach turn.

"Hey," Mr. Avery said, raising his glass and looking at Jessica, "we're very happy Jim has a girlfriend as lovely as you. Here's a toast to the two of you."

The tone of his voice was warm and accepting. Everyone clinked their glasses together.

"Perhaps you two will have a formal announcement to make soon?" his mother inquired coyly. "I certainly hope you're not planning to do what so many irresponsible young people do today and just live together."

Jim and Jessica blushed.

***

Jessica moved in with Jim a few weeks later. Like so many of their friends, she reveled in the idea of breaking traditions. *Surely we're mature enough to make our own decisions.*

Their friends supported them and even threw a party in their honor. With ample amounts of wine and grass, everyone was mellow, but, in the midst of the gaiety, her mind wandered to Joseph. *What would he think about my decision to move in with Jim?* Quickly she dismissed the thought. *Why should I care what he'd think?*

Joseph

Brooklyn, New York

Joseph listened intently to the female voice speaking to him in the darkness of the confessional as she admitted she'd been having sex with her boyfriend. Asking if they planned to marry, Joseph felt the pang of his own sexual indiscretions with Jessica; his inquiry sounded hollow.

"It's important that your relationship has a spiritual foundation." *Now that sounds more authentic.*

"That's why I'm wondering if he's the right man for me. He's not religious."

"Sex is a sacred union. Perhaps you two might consider couples' counseling."

"I can't imagine he'd agree to that. And, by the way, we've been using birth control."

A pang in his heart disrupted his concentration. *There's that issue again.* He gave the young woman her penance and sat for a few moments alone before addressing the next parishioner.

I've never felt guilty about my affair with Jessica. Our love was sacred, wasn't it? So how am I going to counsel these young people when I've sinned in the same way? And, as I recall, Jessica took birth control pills.

Monsignor Anthony was coming the following week to tour the center; Joseph knew it was time for another heart-to-heart discussion.

***

A few days later, Joseph led the monsignor on a tour of the newly completed youth center he'd designed for Saint Andrew's Church. The older priest nodded approvingly as they strolled about the facility.

"I've been asked to take the role of Youth Director when it's complete," Joseph reported.

"That's wonderful," Monsignor said, stopping to give him a fatherly pat on the shoulder. "I know you like working with young people, Joseph, but how do you feel about taking on such a committed role?"

The kind but serious look in Monsignor's eyes sent Joseph's thoughts back to his first Communion when a youthful Father Anthony had stood before him, offering the Holy Eucharist. He'd felt a deep connection between them that day, one that had remained strong through the years.

"I'm looking forward to it. I really am."

"I like the fact that you included a chapel in the building. Do you think the kids will use it?"

"The chapel will be part of the program I'm developing. When they come to the center after school, I will expect, if not require, them to be quiet for a while in chapel before engaging in their activities. If they want to make a confession, I'll be available to them for that. If not, they may light a candle and pray or simply sit quietly for a few moments to center themselves in God."

"It seems as if you've finally found your niche, Joseph. I am so pleased for you."

"I believe I have—for now. But something else has been bothering me."

"I sensed that. Shall we find a moment's privacy so you might share your concerns?"

Joseph's hand trembled as he opened the door to the room that would serve as his office, ushering his mentor inside. *This isn't going to be easy, but he's the only person I can trust.*

Pointing to the uncovered windows facing the hallway, Joseph said, "Eventually, we'll have blinds so I'll have privacy when I need it. I'll leave them open most of the time so I can see the kids and they can see me."

Monsignor nodded.

Two burgundy leather easy chairs sat on the left side of the small room with a round coffee table between them.

"Have a seat," Joseph said, gesturing toward one of the leather chairs. Trying to relax, he took a deep breath and walked over to the credenza to pour two cups of coffee. When he picked them up, the coffee in one splashed a bit onto the floor. Placing both cups on the coffee table, he fumbled inside the credenza for napkins and then dampened a paper towel to clean up his mess.

"Come, sit. What's on your mind? You seem nervous."

"I guess I am," Joseph admitted, taking another deep breath before continuing. "It really isn't anything new. You know I've been struggling with whether the priesthood is my true calling. I thought I'd resolved my struggle on retreat in Buffalo, but a gnawing feeling comes over me at times."

"I'm listening," Monsignor said, leaning closer.

"I'll try my best to explain it. I'm feeling hypocritical when I listen to some parishioners. You know I had a sexual relationship before I entered the clergy. So how can I advise young couples who are doing what I did?"

"I remember your telling me about the young lady in Paris, but the point is you are now a representative of the Church and you must honor your sacred contracts. I thought you had done your penance and put that experience behind you."

"I still think about her sometimes."

"Well, of course you do. She was part of your life. But now you are a priest and all that must be different."

"I know. And you're right, of course. I'm just … well, I'm still questioning whether I made the right decision."

"Joseph, you cannot be a priest half way. You must make up your mind once and for all if this is the right path for you."

"I know, I know. I realize that. To make matters worse, I remain conflicted about other Catholic principles, such as the birth control issue."

Monsignor sighed, looking again into Joseph's eyes. "Dear Joseph, you must come to some resolve. I think it would be wise to take additional time for reflection before you become more involved here."

They sat for some moments in prayer before the monsignor rose, blessed Joseph, and departed in silence. Knowing his mentor was right, Joseph asked Father Robert, the head priest at Saint Andrew's, for time off to be with his family in Boston.

***

"John and I are planning to be married," Joseph's mother announced a few days later while setting the table for dinner, "and we're going to Paris for our honeymoon."

"Mom, that's wonderful. Paris is the most beautiful city I've ever seen." While watching her mash the potatoes, he described his favorite haunts to her. *Special places I explored with Jessica,* he remembered, allowing his mind to wander.

"Sweetheart," his mother said, interrupting his reverie, "Would you like to do the wedding ceremony?"

"Mom, I'm very flattered, but I'd be entirely too emotional. Don't you think Monsignor Anthony would be a better choice?"

"If you say so," she replied, giving him a look of concern. "I know you were on a long retreat. Is everything all right?"

"Yes, why do you ask?"

"Well, you seem more distracted than usual."

"You're very perceptive. I have a lot on my mind. You know, completing the youth center and all. I'll be assigned as director after it's finished."

"That's wonderful, Joseph. You'll be working with kids, like your father. He loved being a counselor, you know. You're a lot like him."

"I'll take that as a compliment." *She's right. I am like my father; both of us drawn to helping kids — and to the priesthood.*

"Speaking of kids, I think I hear Tom and the gang at the door." His mother laughed.

A few moments later, John came in to the kitchen to make the crescent rolls, the last thing to go in the oven before they settled down to a Saturday night meal. In the midst of his family, Joseph pushed his concerns to the back of his mind.

***

Later in the week, Joseph awoke to a day free of family obligations. He rose early and walked down to the Charles River to watch the rowers glide along. It seemed effortless but he knew it took strength and forbearance. *All of us may appear to simply walk through life with ease, but within us it takes courage to stay on course, in keeping with our purpose.* Couples with their children caught his eye, arousing his imagination. *What would it be like to be married to Jessica ... and to have kids? Stop torturing yourself, Joe. She's probably married to someone else by now. Stop thinking about her. God, I need your help.*

After some moments, his inner monologue quieted and Joseph felt called to return to Brooklyn the next day, sensing that it would be the best medicine. Many of his prayers had been answered at times when he was busy giving of himself rather than focusing on his inner conflicts.

***

In a small, simple, and elegant ceremony two months later, Monsignor Anthony officiated at the marriage of Joseph's mother Dorothy to her fiancé John. The family and their guests celebrated afterward over dinner at a favorite seafood restaurant in Boston.

After their celebratory meal, Monsignor sought Joseph out as they were preparing to leave.

"How are you coping since we last spoke, Joseph?"

"Actually, I'm doing much better. The center's open now, as you know, and I love working with the kids."

"They're lucky to have you. Remember, my door will always be open if you need to talk."

Joseph thanked him with his eyes as the monsignor blessed him and gave a silent prayer.

The next afternoon, the newlyweds left for France and Joseph returned to his duties in Brooklyn. Back at the rectory, he greeted the other priests who were sharing a bottle of wine in the front room.

"Welcome back, Father Joe. Care for a glass of wine?" Father Edward asked.

"Sure," Joseph said, putting down his small suitcase and joining them. "Nice wine," he commented after taking a sip.

"It's a California Cabernet, a Napa Valley vineyard," Father Robert said.

"Lovely," Joseph said, "but nothing can top a good Parisian Bordeaux."

"I haven't been to Paris," Father Edward said. "Have you?"

"I spent a couple of years there before seminary."

"A good place to sow some wild oats before getting serious about your calling, eh?" Father Robert chided.

The way the head priest's words came across triggered something within him. Abruptly, Joseph stood and thanked them for sharing the wine, adding, "I think I'll take it to my room. I'm pretty tired."

Once inside his private space, he finished the glass of wine and opened a bottle of Merlot. Sitting on the bed, he shook his head and held up his glass, "Here's another one for you and John, Mother dear." He felt an ache in his heart. One glass became two, and, before he knew it, the bottle was empty. *What's wrong with me? I feel so damned depressed. And now I've made it worse.*

An inner voice said, "You're jealous of your mother and John. For that matter, you're jealous of your brother and his wife, too. You're not sure you should have become a priest."

Is God admonishing me? Or is this the voice of my guilty conscience? He held his head in his hands as tears began to fall. *It's been ages since I've wept like this. Something is very wrong.* "Father, help me," he prayed out loud, as if to make sure God could hear him. "Tell me what to do, please, please."

No answer came, only the beating of his heart and the throbbing of his head. Not even bothering to undress or brush his teeth, Joseph lay down and let sleep take him away from his troubles—at least until he awoke the next morning with a nasty hangover.

Jessica

Jessica nestled into the pillows of her easy chair with a warm cup of tea. Mozart's "Overture to the Marriage of Figaro" played on the stereo, lifting her up and out of herself. Jim would be late at the theater, his new play opening on the weekend. *I hope Jim's parents don't come to opening night. I can't stand being around his mother. I can just hear her now,* "Doesn't it bother you, living in sin?"

Gray clouds formed in the eastern sky, threatening rain. Interrupting her peace, Jim came bounding through the door, much earlier than expected.

"There you are. I'm so glad you're home. I want you to come to dress rehearsal with me tonight."

"Oh, it doesn't look like a good night to be out."

"Oh, come on, we'll make the sun shine, even inside," he said, pulling her up from her seat and twirling her around.

"Where did you get all this energy?" Jessica asked, giving him a quizzical look.

"It's just the joy of seeing you again, my love."

"Somehow I don't think that's the whole story," she said, her brow furrowing before she gave in to a smile at his dramatic antics.

***

The warmth of the theater with its color, music, and costumed actors filled Jessica with excitement, much like a new art exhibit at her gallery. *He really is quite a good actor!*

***

Afterwards in a small, romantic café, Jim ordered a bottle of champagne and almost shyly handed her a small velvet box. Her heart jumped to her throat. *If this is what I think it is … what should I say? Do I love him? Or do I just feel comfortable having someone of my own?* She gave him a tentative smile and slowly opened the box. Sure enough, it was a beautiful diamond ring, one of the prettiest she'd ever seen.

"It was my grandmother's. When she died, she told my mother to save it for me until I needed it. And now I do. Will you make me the happiest man in the world and say you'll marry me?"

What a sweet proposal. But I don't know what to say. An image of Joseph suddenly appeared in her mind's eye. *I should be long over him by now.* She pushed the image away. *Why shouldn't I marry Jim? We're certainly compatible in bed—and he makes me smile.*

"Yes," she whispered as Jim slipped the ring on her finger before she could have second thoughts.

"How about an August wedding in Central Park?" he asked, leaning closer to her over the table.

"That's only a few months away. Do you think we can get it together that quickly?"

"Of course. We don't want anything fancy, right?"

"I guess not."

***

Neither Jessica nor Jim felt connected to a particular church. Jim called himself a Methodist, but never went to church. Since her intimate encounters with Mother Mary and the Black Madonnas in France, Jessica had become comfortable with her own personal spiritual practices and no longer felt a need to attend regular church services.

She and Jim had attended the Unitarian Church a few times, though she found its pastor's talks more intellectual than spiritual. But they both appreciated the universal, ecumenical essence of his messages and decided to ask Pastor Sellers to perform their wedding ceremony. When he agreed and encouraged them to write their own vows, his less traditional, more liberal approach, which more suited their lifestyle, assured them they'd made the right choice.

While working with her vows Jessica found herself resisting the words "'til death do us part." *Is this a bad omen? Or am I simply being practical?* She omitted the phrase.

As the date of the wedding drew near, her mother called with regret that she was suffering from walking pneumonia and the doctor had firmly advised against her travel. Not long after, her father also called with regrets that Luann couldn't make the trip so close to delivering their second child, and, of course, he needed to be with her. Both parents wished her every happiness and assured Jessica that they would all get together soon, hopefully, they both suggested, in Britain.

"I can't believe neither of them is coming," she announced to Jim, exasperated.

"Hey, we didn't give them much notice, now, did we?"

"You're right," she said, softening her tone. "Maybe we should postpone the wedding." *Why does this whole thing feel so surreal? Maybe this is a sign to call it off.*

"But we've already made our flight reservations, and there's the honeymoon suite at Amberley Castle awaiting us. We can see your parents before our flight home."

"That's true," she said, tears in her eyes. "I'm just disappointed, that's all."

"I know, sweetheart," Jim said, taking her into his arms. "At least my parents will be here."

That certainly doesn't make me feel better.

***

A few short weeks later, Jessica stood behind a large oak tree with Stephanie, watching as their friends gathered under the bough of pink roses their florist had constructed over a collapsible trellis near Shakespeare's Herb Garden behind Central Park's Delacorte Theater. The scent of lavender wafted from the garden toward them. Jim looked movie-star handsome in his dark suit and sky blue shirt, but Jessica wished he'd refrained from the two Scotches she'd seen him down at the pre-wedding brunch. "Hair of the dog," he'd remarked when he saw her grimace, no doubt recalling his rehearsal dinner drunkenness.

Catching Pastor Seller's eye, Stephanie motioned that it was time to begin. She handed Jessica her bouquet of orchids. All eyes were on them as Jessica followed Stephanie along the pine needle aisle toward their friends. An old friend of Jim's played John Denver's "Annie's Song" on a portable keyboard. His wife accompanied him on the violin.

Jessica felt foolish in her stark white tea-length chiffon gown and wished she'd chosen the more modern yellow silk chemise with the scooped neck. She felt like a mannequin and found herself looking down at her too-silver pumps. *This is not how I'm supposed to feel on my wedding day.*

Taking her place before the trellis, she kept her veil over her eyes to hide her tears. The pastor's words sounded far away, but she could feel Jim's eyes on her. His vows sounded like words from a script. When her turn came, she cut hers short, saying only, "I vow to be honest and kind, true to myself and to you."

Pastor Sellers had to ask her if she was finished. When she nodded, Stephanie stepped forward to pull back her veil, gently wiping under her eyes where her mascara had smudged.

As Jessica heard the fated words "I now pronounce you husband and wife," she couldn't believe she'd gone through with it. When Jim leaned over to kiss the bride, for an instant, she floated away but the alcohol on his breath brought her back to the moment.

The crowd clapped and cheered as she and Jim shared their first marital kiss, but it was Jim's mother that she heard the loudest. *She is so obnoxious.* Jessica turned to look at her new mother-in-law, who was staring at her. *She doesn't like me. I know it. Well, the feeling's mutual.*

While mingling with the guests later on, Jessica spun around in the direction of a shrill, somewhat slurred, announcement her husband was making to some of their friends.

"And we're gonna celebrate our nup-tu-als in a freaking castle. Yep, a castle. In bloody Sussex, England."

Embarrassed, but trying to appear nonchalant, she'd begun to stroll in Jim's direction, hoping to quiet him down a bit, when Stephanie whispered in her ear, "Don't worry about him today. He's just celebrating."

"Thanks, Steph. Having you here means so much to me."

"I love you, my friend," Stephanie said gently. "And I wish you all the happiness in the world."

"I hope I've done the right thing," Jessica whispered, gesturing toward Jim and straightening the laurel wreath in her hair, ignoring the nagging doubt in her heart.

***

Jim fell asleep as soon as the plane took off on their overnight flight to London, but Jessica was too keyed up. In her mind, she replayed the entire wedding and reception, including Jim's boisterous behavior. *Wish he hadn't had so much to drink. Oh, well, it's not every day one gets married.*

It seemed she'd just drifted off to sleep when the lights came on in the cabin and the clanking of carts woke her up with a jolt. The smell of coffee and rolls filled her nostrils.

"We'll be landing at Heathrow in approximately forty minutes," the captain announced as Jim began to stir, yawning and stroking his tousled hair.

He looks like a little boy, she thought, her heart warming toward him.

***

Still drowsy from jet lag, Jessica and Jim decided to rest in their room before exploring Amberley Castle where they were lodging in the English countryside. When Jessica awoke in the late afternoon, her eyes were drawn to the bay window framed with purple velvet and white lace curtains. The golden rays of sunset cast a luminous glow on everything in the room.

She shook her head in astonishment as she took in the elaborate furnishings of the honeymoon suite. Rich carpet, woven with deep blues and purples, warmed the shiny wooden floor, and two wingback chairs covered in a lavender silk print sat in front of a large fireplace.

Gazing down at the sleeping man beside her in the huge four poster bed, she noted the upside down bottle of champagne in the bucket and two empty glasses on the nightstand, recalling how her new husband had swept her up in a crescendo of passionate lovemaking, leaving her nearly bruised—and unsatisfied. *I guess this makes it official. I'm a married woman now. But why does this feel more like a fantasy than a meaningful event in my life?*

***

Two days later, after dining like royalty in the elegant dining room of the castle and riding horseback through green fields covered in an array of wildflowers, it was time to leave. They drove their rented car to London, Jessica at the wheel as she was familiar with driving on the left side of the road.

When they arrived at her father's flat, Luann met them at the door, wearing a big smile and a gingham sundress, her strawberry blond curls bouncing against her bare shoulders. *How can she look so young— especially after having two babies?* Jessica grumbled inside.

"Come in, come in," Luann greeted them.

"It's so good to see you," her father said as he joined them and gave Jessica a big hug.

"You look wonderful. I like your hair longer like this." His chestnut locks, streaked with gray, hung just above his shoulders.

"Thank you, my dear. I must keep up with the times, you know, or my students will think I'm just an old fogey and not give my playing or my instruction a whit of attention."

"Dad, this is Jim," she said, turning to her husband. The two men shook hands.

"It's very good to meet you, Mr. Taylor," Jim said.

"Please, call me Jonathan."

"Jonathan it is."

Eight-year-old Tyler came bouncing into the room. With a light spread of freckles across his nose, he looked like Huckleberry Finn, Jessica thought. His hair was chestnut in color, just like her dad's, but curly like Luann's.

"Give your sister a hug," Jonathan directed his son.

"Hi," Tyler said, politely hugging her and shaking hands with Jim.

Poor thing feels awkward. So do I. I'm old enough to be his mother. "One of these days," she said, smiling and rumpling Tyler's hair, "I hope we can get to know each other better. Maybe you can come to see us in New York."

"Hey, that'd be cool," he said, grinning back at her.

"You know you're a very lucky man," Jonathan announced, turning to Jim.

"Yes, sir, I'm well aware of that."

"And congratulations to you," Jessica said. We're looking forward to seeing the new baby."

"I'll go get Annie now." Luann disappeared down the hall, soon returning with the baby wrapped snugly in a blanket, her eyes wide open.

"She's beautiful and so tiny," Jessica said, taking her little hand.

"Would you like to hold her?"

"I would, if you don't mind." Taking the baby in her arms, she gazed into the infant's sweet face, shocked when tears welled up in her eyes. "You'd better take her," she said, giving Annie back to her mother.

"Oh, sweetie," Luann said, noticing her tears. "You'll have one of these before you know it."

"I hope so," she said, wiping her eyes. *Luann is more sensitive than I'd expected her to be. Maybe I've misjudged her.*

***

After a hearty lunch of roast beef sandwiches and red potato salad, Jonathan lifted his glass of iced tea and offered a toast.

"To Jessica and Jim. May you two be as happy in your marriage as Luann and I are in ours."

"Thank you, sir," Jim said with slight hesitation. "I'm sure we shall be."

"Thanks, Dad," Jessica chimed in. *I wish just once he'd look at me with love in his eyes the way he looks at her. And here he is with two children young enough to be my kids. Damn, Tyler's nearly as old as André would be now.*

"I understand you are in the theater," her dad remarked, turning to Jim.

"Quite right, sir. I love the thrill of performing. As you must, as well. I hear you are quite the virtuoso."

"Well, now, it sounds as if Jessica has been exaggerating a bit about her old man."

"Don't be modest," Luann chimed in. "He's in demand these days for guest appearances."

"I plan to be just as spectacular in the theater someday," Jim announced with bravado.

"Hear, hear," Jonathan said, holding up his glass. Then, turning to Jessica, "I like this young man."

Maybe that's because he's just like you, she thought with dismay, *quite full of himself.*

***

Later that day, they left London and boarded an express train to the Lake District to visit with Jessica's mother and the rest of the family. Her aunt and uncle met them at the station and drove them out to their farm. Her stepfather, Donald, met them on the porch and welcomed them inside.

"Darling, I'm so glad to see you," her mother said, rising from her chair. The blanket over her legs fell to the floor as they hugged. "I'm so sorry we couldn't make the wedding."

"I know you'd have been there if you could. How are you feeling?"

"Better, now that you're here. But the doctor has commanded I stay in the house until I've finished all of the medicine he gave me."

"Poor Mum. I'm so sorry you've been so sick."

She introduced Jim to her mother and Donald. Her aunt suggested that Jim join them for a tour of the farm to give Jessica time alone with her mother.

"He's charming," Adelaide said. "Just make sure he treats you right."

"I'll be fine, Mum. He's a wonderful guy." But even as she said it, more doubts crept in. *What is wrong with me? I should be happy. After all, this is my honeymoon, for goodness sake.*

Joseph

Brooklyn

Joseph enjoyed working with the kids at Saint Andrews's youth center, but felt hypocritical trying to stay within Church guidelines while counseling his parishioners. He still couldn't accept that sex before marriage was wrong, nor reconcile the birth control restrictions.

Having heard that some of the more liberal-minded priests were forming groups to air their concerns, he'd decided to attend one of their meetings.

Joseph walked into the small YMCA conference room where the monthly meeting of Catholic Priests for Change was held.

"Welcome, everyone," the leader of the group said. "I'm Father Benjamin and I'll be leading our discussion today. As you know, attendance at our churches has been dwindling. Young people are leaving Catholicism, disillusioned with trying to uphold Church standards in the way they've been taught in the past. Vatican Two was supposed to be the beginning of renewal within the Church, but change has been sporadic and inconsistent.

"We offer a platform here for you to express your opinions, based on your individual experience as priests. Although we're not, of course, in a position to make official changes in the Church doctrine, we can support each other and perhaps join together and make recommendations as a group.

"Would anyone like to speak?"

"I would," Joseph said, raising his hand. Father Benjamin motioned for him to stand up.

"I'm having difficulty—rather, some of my parishioners want and need to keep their families small, just to pay their bills. I don't agree with Church policy that contraception devices within a marriage should never be used." *I hope I've come across clearly.* His heart was racing.

"Thank you for breaking the ice today. And your name?"

"Joseph, Father Joseph Murphy."

"Does anyone else want to add to what Father Joseph has so courageously expressed?"

The tension in his body gradually melted away as, one by one, other participants addressed the issue, some agreeing with him. *How freeing to have a place to share my feelings openly and honestly.*

"Are there other concerns to be addressed today?" Father Benjamin asked, his eyes scanning the room.

"Yes, I have a concern," a tall, thin priest said, standing up.

"Your name?"

"Father Phillip Malloy."

"Go on, Father Phillip."

"It's no secret," the man began in a quiet but steady voice, "that there are more incidents of sexual molestation by priests being reported than ever before."

Joseph heard whispers and hushed comments around the room; he strained to hear what the speaker was saying.

"I sincerely believe," the man continued, "that if priests were allowed to marry, this would not be happening so frequently." His voice grew louder. "The chastity requirements for priests, in my opinion, are archaic and should be abolished." Concluding his pronouncement, he sat down.

Joseph could feel the tension in the room as his throat tightened. *I know I could still serve God if I were married*. This was the first time he'd allowed himself to entertain such a thought without self-judgment and guilt overwhelming him.

"Well, you two have certainly woken up the group today," the leader said as the chatter floating around the room became more audible. "Anyone else care to comment on this issue?"

Joseph was about to raise his hand when another, elderly, priest, stood up.

"I'm Father William Connolly," the man said, "and I agree with Father Phillip. But we know this has come up time and time again before the Vatican and nothing has changed. What can we do?"

A lively discussion ensued, with some favoring the change and others defending the Vatican's current position.

Joseph finally had another chance to speak. "These are changes only hinted at in Vatican Two. I feel like we're on the cutting edge of something important."

"We will do what we can," Father Benjamin assured them. "My clerk is taking all of this down and we'll be putting it in a letter to the bishop very soon. Where it goes from there is anyone's guess."

"At least our voices will be heard," Joseph said as others nodded in agreement.

***

Joseph became an active participant at Catholic Priests for Change meetings. They aired their concerns and presented them to the bishop, but no Vatican attention ensued. Joseph, among others, doubted they would ever make much headway. As his disenchantment with the priesthood grew stronger, he found himself drinking more wine to take the edge off his discomfort. He knew it was time for more authentic soul searching.

"I'm feeling fatigued and burnt out," he told the head priest as summer came to a close. "The kids at the center will be returning to school soon and I won't be needed as much. Would it be possible for me to have some time off?"

"Of course, Father, if you feel you need it. I know how busy the kids have kept you lately. Take a couple of weeks and come back refreshed and ready to go again."

***

Joseph called his mother and stepfather to see if he could come to Boston for a visit.

When he arrived the next day by train, his mother and John picked him up and they drove over to Tom and Susan's for dinner.

After dinner, Joseph and his brother shared a few moments alone in Tom's den. Joseph noticed the many pictures of the boys in various stages of their lives, lining the fireplace mantle. "You have a wonderful family, Tom, and you're a great father."

"Thanks, Joe. And how is life treating our priest these days?"

"Not the best. I've been part of a group, Catholic Priests for Change, trying to make some needed changes within the Church but I think it's just a pipe dream."

"You sound fed up. Maybe it's time to leave?"

"Believe me, I've thought about it, hard. But it's easier said than done."

Tom reached over and held Joseph's arm. "You know that whatever you decide, I'll support you. If there's anything I can do to help, just say the word."

"Thanks," Joseph said, his eyes moistening. "Enough about me. How's your job going these days?"

"Great. The club keeps my schedule filled with students. Tennis seems to be as popular as ever."

"Good to hear," he said, just as Susan called them in for dessert.

***

After spending a few days with his parents, Joseph decided to rent a place on the Cape for the remainder of his vacation. In early September, most of the tourists would be gone and he could be alone with nothing but sand, sea, and sky. Surely he could connect more deeply with God in such a place and listen for direction.

Two days later, he lay on a blanket on the beach, watching the seagulls circling above him, allowing the sound of the waves to relax his mind. In this place, away from his responsibilities, life seemed to be in balance. There were no unmarried couples to counsel about their sex lives, no married couples to counsel about their birth control methods, no teens trying to make sense of the world, all of them looking to him for direction.

God, please help me understand what's happening to me now, he pleaded as the air cooled and the tide started coming in. In the roaring of the waves he heard an answer. An echo of his own mind?

"Nothing is permanent. Everything changes. Even you. Go with the flow of your heart."

Thank you, Father, he prayed in gratitude, pondering the meaning of what he'd heard and realizing it was the same message he'd received in Buffalo. *I've been afraid to put what I feel in my heart into practice.* He resolved to go back to the youth center and start anew. *I'll listen to my heart, let it be the guide. Perhaps then I won't feel like a hypocrite. I can give what I'm meant to give, be who I am.*

Jessica

Jessica immersed herself in the art displayed at the gallery where she worked. Her boss gave her full responsibility for arranging the pieces to their best advantage, and she did so with great savoir-faire.

But things were not good at home. Jim worked in starts and fits, playing in off-off Broadway shows. He often complained of not getting the parts he *really* wanted and was becoming bitter, despite her attempts to encourage him.

One day on her way to work, she caught her reflection in a shop window. *What a sad looking woman,* she thought, stopping to look closer.

For the rest of the day, while going about her work, her mind wandered. *What do I really want? A job in a prestigious museum? Would that make me happy?* She closed her eyes and allowed an inner image to form: of herself, traveling, acquiring beautiful and important paintings and sculptures to share with an eager public along with her curatorial knowledge. Her visualization pleased her, but still something was missing.

Remembering her life in France filled her with bittersweet memories, giving up André the most painful among them. A *baby. Could that fill my longing? Could it bring true love to our marriage?*

Jessica felt exhilarated for the rest of the day, imagining being pregnant again. *And this time, I can keep my baby.*

***

"You seem excited," Jim said over dinner.

"Well, I've been thinking about something. About how nice it would be … for us to have a baby. What do you think?"

"Sweetheart," he replied, wrinkling his brow, "aren't you happy with just the two of us?"

"Of course," she answered, knowing it wasn't true. "But a baby will give our lives so much more meaning, don't you think?"

"Our lives *are* meaningful. Besides, we're not financially ready to think about children. I think we should wait a year or so until I've landed a strong, reliable part and settled into it. Then we can start a family."

"I guess you're right," she said, her heart sinking and her eyes filling with tears. "But I don't want to wait too long."

"Soon I'll be working on Broadway. I just know it," he said, moving closer and touching her face gently. "Don't be sad."

***

It had been a busy Christmas season, but now, in January, things were quiet in the gallery. Jessica was alone, working on a display, when Alex Thomas, a curator from the Museum of Modern Art, burst through the door, bringing with him a rush of cold that hit her smack in the face.

"Come in and get warm," she welcomed him. "It's freezing out there."

"A snowstorm's on the way," he said, shrugging off his overcoat and sneezing. "Oh, my, I am without a handkerchief."

Jessica reached for a tissue on her desk and handed it to him, taking his overcoat and hanging it on a rack by the door.

A regular customer at the gallery, Alex was always on the lookout for new artistic talent. They'd recently discussed her background in art history and she'd shared her dream of working in a museum.

"I have an offer for you," he said cryptically.

"An offer?" she asked, surprised.

"Yes, I'd like you to come work for me. There's an opening on my teaching staff. You obviously have talent for art display," he said, sweeping his arms at the space around them, "and you have an impressive knowledge of European paintings. You could help set up various exhibits the way you do here, but on a grander scale, of course. And I trust that you'll be pleased with the increase in salary."

"Mr. Thomas, I'm very flattered," she said nervously, hardly believing what she'd heard. "It would be an honor to work for you."

"Then send me your resume, just as a formality, and next week we'll finalize our agreement." He smiled, handing her his business card.

"I will need a bit of time to give notice and at least offer to find someone to replace me."

"Take as long as you need. I trust your transition will be smooth," he said, reaching out his hand.

"You're very kind. I'll do my best not to disappoint you."

He left as suddenly as he'd come, and Jessica flinched as the cold reached her from the opened door. She stood frozen, not from cold, but amazement at her good fortune.

***

A few weeks later, Jessica began her new career at the Museum of Modern Art. She found her new boss to be an impressive curator. She admired his candor and innovative ideas about fine art's cultural influence. She also respected his willingness to live an openly gay life even in the midst of the burgeoning HIV/AIDS crisis.

Jessica loved the teaching aspect of her job as well as the opportunity to arrange art just as she'd done at A Clean, Well-Lighted Place, to show off each piece to its full advantage while conveying the breadth of a display as a whole. She was particularly proud of her Local Artists Initiative, instituted with Alex's blessing, where each season an emerging local artist would be chosen to exhibit in the West Room. Jessica's own curatorial style began to reveal itself through this effort, and Alex took notice.

After only six months at MoMA, Alex made Jessica one of his assistant curators—a position she'd always wanted—and increased her salary. That night, she wrote in her journal:

I love my work. Being appreciated and encouraged nourishes me. Plus, we're finally making ends meet and even saving some money. I want to bring up the baby issue again, but I'm afraid it will upset Jim. If only he could be happier in his career. His drinking certainly isn't helping him get the parts he wants and it seems he's drinking more and more.

But what could she do? Her thoughts turned to Paris. *Maybe we should go there on a vacation.* Joseph popped into her mind. *Bad idea.* She dismissed the fantasy as quickly as it had come.

***

When autumn arrived in New York, Central Park burst into a masterpiece of color. The cool winds blew, exciting Jessica's spirit. She called Jim spontaneously, wanting to get him out of the apartment, hoping the fresh air and a picnic would pick up his mood. Today she had the courage to ask him what she'd wanted to for months.

"Sweetheart," she said as they ate their sandwiches, "I'm so glad you came up to meet me. Isn't it glorious out?"

"It is, yes, but I see more gray than color."

"Oh, Jim, I wish you were happy with your work. I bet the right part is just around the corner. If you could only feel good about yourself."

"I'd feel better if I got the part in the Sam Shepard play. It's down to me and another guy."

"That's great news. When will you know?"

"My agent says any day, but I don't think the director's crazy about me. I think I may have been a bit out of it when I spoke to him at the

Drama Guild meeting last week."

"That could be a problem."

"Don't start."

"Oh, Jim, I just want us to be happy."

"*You* make me happy."

"It seems it's never the right time to bring it up but it's such a beautiful day and you're here and maybe there's good news on the horizon. Plus, it helps that we have money in the bank."

"*Your* money."

"What's mine is yours."

"If you say so," he mumbled. "I know what you're going to propose but I'm not ready to be a father. I can't even take care of you the way I want to."

"But, Jim, before we got married you told me you wanted a family. Now I'm wondering if you really meant it. Besides, my biological clock has been ticking for a while. I don't want to wait too long."

After a long pause and a deep sigh, Jim responded, "I do want a family. But I don't feel ready for that responsibility. Do you?"

"Yes. At least I think so. Is anyone ever really sure?"

"I don't know," he said, shaking his head.

"Jim, I think you'd make a great father. You love to play and pretend. That's the kind of person children adore."

"Do you really think so?"

"Yes, I really do," she replied, taking his hand. *He looks like a little boy needing approval from his mother.*

"Well, I guess we could give it a try."

"Do you mean it?"

"Yes, if it will make you happy," he said, pulling her into his arms.

"Oh, sweetheart, you'll make a wonderful father. I just know it."

***

Months later, Jessica still had not conceived. She told her doctor she'd delivered her first child without a problem but asked that he keep that detail confidential.

He advised her to relax and try not to worry. But Jim's drinking had become more problematic. *Maybe I'm wrong to want a child with him, but I want to be a mother, a real mother, to hold a baby on my shoulder again. My baby. Is that so wrong?*

Another two months passed and, after missing her period, she returned to see the doctor. The day after the test he called and spoke the words she'd waited so long to hear.

"Congratulations, Mrs. Avery, you are indeed pregnant."

Delighted, Jessica hung up, not remembering whether or not she'd thanked the doctor. "Oh, thank you, God."

Hearing the news, Jim said, "That's wonderful," and reached for her, but Jessica noticed a slight tremble in his voice.

"Do you really mean you're happy about it?"

"Of course, I am. I'm just a little nervous about being a father, you know that."

"I know you are, and I'm nervous, too. We'll just be the best parents we can be, and, you'll see, it'll be fine." Jessica wasn't quite as confident as she tried to sound.

***

Three months later, Jessica came home from work unusually tired.

After changing into sweats she decided to run out for Chinese food to avoid cooking after Jim got home. Once back at the apartment, she put on a Fleetwood Mac album and sat down to relax, and drifted into sleep.

She awoke doubled over with pain. In the dim light of early evening, she rushed to the bathroom. Blood stained her sweatpants and gushed onto the floor.

"Oh, my God," she shouted, wrapping a towel around herself. She managed to stumble to the phone to call 911 before she blacked out and fell to the floor.

She awoke behind a curtain in the Emergency Room, a doctor and two nurses peering down at her.

"I'm very sorry, Mrs. Avery," the doctor said softly, "you've miscarried. You've also lost quite a bit of blood. We want to keep you here overnight." His words pierced her heart.

"No, it can't be true," she cried in agony.

"Is there someone we should call?" the nurse asked.

"Yes, my husband." She sobbed in uncontrollable waves, pointing to her purse, her address book just inside.

"I'm sorry," the nurse said later after trying to reach Jim. "There was no answer. I left a message for him to come to the hospital."

Jessica glanced at the clock. It was one o'clock in the morning. *Where could he be?* She cried herself to sleep.

When she awoke hours later, Jim was sitting by the bed, his shirt only half tucked in and unshaven.

"I'm so sorry, honey."

"Where were you last night?" she asked, unable to keep back her tears. "I needed you."

"I was out with the crew and time got away from me."

"Did you even call me to let me know? I had dinner waiting. I needed you!"

Jim's looked down at his lap for long seconds. When he finally raised his head, she noticed the deep circles under his eyes. She also caught a whiff of alcohol.

"Well, you won't have to worry about being a father now," she said in a bitingly bitter voice.

"That's not fair. I'm just as sad about this as you are. Believe me."

"I don't believe you," she said flatly and turned her head away from him.

Later that morning, they took a taxi home in silence.

When a curtain of darkness finally closed the day, Jessica climbed into bed, her mind tormented. From the other room, she could hear Jim crushing ice. *Maybe this is a blessing? Do I really want Jim to be the father of my child?*

She fell into troubled sleep, broken by a very disturbing dream in which a thick fog surrounded her, blocking her view of a baby, whose crying grew fainter and fainter, then stopped altogether. "Where are you?" she shouted over and over into a great expanse of silence.

"Oh, my God, where is my baby?" she cried, waking up with a start.

She was sweating and trembling. The dream had been incredibly real. Jim stirred beside her and mumbled something before returning to sleep.

Her thoughts turned to her lost baby. *Mother Mary, please take care of my baby's spirit. And please watch over André, too. Let him know how much I love him.*

As tears moistened her cheeks, a feeling of warmth and comfort washed over her. *An angel enveloping me in its wings?*

André

Provence, France

André Casal stood with his friend Pierre, throwing pebbles into the creek. The two boys had just been confirmed in the Catholic Church.

"Do you feel any different?"

"Well, Father Baud spoke to us like we're all grown up now," Pierre smirked.

"It's a scary thought, don't you think?"

"I know. I'm the first one in my family to be confirmed. Mamà says now I must be an example for my little brother and sister."

"I'm not ready to grow up," André said. "I'm not even sure I believe all the things the nuns teach."

"What do you mean?"

"Well, what about people in other countries who've never heard of Jesus? Does that make them bad? Maybe they just have different teachers."

"André, where do you get these ideas? Not from the nuns, that's for sure."

"Do you think the nuns know everything? I don't. Remember that book, *Siddhartha*, that I told you I was reading?"

"The one your mother told you about?"

"Yes. Well, this kid, Siddhartha, from India, learns about a religion, started by a man whose name was also Siddhartha. Only *that* Siddhartha was a great teacher and became known as the *Buddha*. Kind of like Jesus was a great teacher and became known as the *Christ*. Do you see what I'm getting at? The followers of Buddha are called Buddhists and the followers of Christ are called Christians. My mother says different cultures have different teachers and that's just the way it is."

"You'd better not let the *nuns* hear you talk like that."

"Hey, maybe I'll just ask Sister Maureen next week," André said with bravado.

"I wouldn't if I were you."

"Well, you're not me," he said, laughing and pushing playfully at Pierre until both boys fell down in their laughter, wrestling as they had since they were small, keeping it up until Pierre's mother called them inside. She asked André to stay for dinner, but he told her his mother expected him before the sun set.

The day's last rays of sunlight painted the sky with bright strokes of purple and pink. André stared in awe at the heavens above him. *I know that God loves the Buddhists in India just as much as He loves us Christians.* He thought of his Papa; such a religious man. *He'd be mad if he knew what I've been thinking about, maybe even madder at Mamà for sharing her book with me. But he's a good man and I love him.* He smiled, remembering when he'd believed everything his Papa told him.

Papa wants me to be a good Catholic like he is. I think I'm more like Mamà. She's a Catholic, too, but misses Mass sometimes. She says God is in her heart, not in some building. I could tell her how I'm feeling, but I know she doesn't like to talk about religion.

André's mind wandered into the future. *It seems my parents are happy to just be at home. I want to have adventures to faraway places.* Catching sight of the old stone farmhouse where his family had lived and managed their vineyard for four generations, he smiled. *Provence is good enough for now.*

Holly

Cambria, California
Two months later

Fifteen-year-old Holly Simpson studied the painting she'd just completed, a rendering of an unforgettable image from the previous night's dream. She'd been sitting in the middle of a huge tree, its roots digging deeply into the earth, connecting her to all the elements—earth, water, air and sun—as the tree breathed them into itself. Its branches held her and emanated up toward the heavens, connecting Holly to angels and invisibles, including her mother, who had recently died of cancer.

When Holly painted her dreams and waking images she felt close to her mother. *I'll call this one, The Tree of Life. All that life is, both seen and unseen.*

Since her mother had died, she'd been painting more but was now cooking for the family. Tenth grade had lots more homework in preparation for college and she also had to help her little brother with the fourth grade work he brought home. With her extra chores, she painted less landscapes outdoors and focused more on painting from her imagination. She'd moved her bed into her mother's studio where her mother's paintings inspired her and she could feel her encouragement. Holly called her art *visionary paintings*.

Although at times she felt very sad alone in the studio, Holly could sense her mother's spirit alive in her paintings. As she gazed at one of her favorites, of Holly and her brother Randy painted only last year, tears filled her eyes. It had been just before her fourteenth birthday, a day she remembered as if it had been yesterday.

***

"Come downstairs, sweetheart," her mother called as Randy giggled from where he hid behind the dining room doors. Usually his laugh was infectious but, since her mother's diagnosis, she hadn't cracked a smile, and couldn't even enjoy her birthday.

Randy jumped out with an unsurprising "Surprise" as her mother stepped from in front of the beautiful chocolate birthday cake sitting in the middle of the table. Her mother, father, and brother beamed amidst the glow of fifteen lit candles, one for good measure, as Randy broke first into "Happy Birthday."

"Blow out the candles," her mother urged, "but don't forget to make a wish first."

Fighting to hold back her tears, Holly wished with all her heart that her mother would get well, and blew every single candle out with conviction. When her eyes met her mother's gaze, a silent understanding flowed between them. Only two months before her mother died, she knew, but did not have words for, what it meant.

***

Closing her eyes, Holly could see herself, only four years old, the first time her mother had invited her to paint with her in her studio.

"Hold your paintbrush like this," her mother showed her gently, turning her little hand in different directions to make all sorts of lines and shapes.

They painted together all morning and then went to Moonstone Beach to splash around at the water's edge, looking for shiny pebbles. They even found what looked like a moonstone. That night, her father came in to tuck her in after finishing work in the restaurant where he worked.

"How's my princess?" he asked, stroking her hair. He was big and strong, but his hands were gentle against her forehead.

"I'm great. Mommy and me made art today."

"You did? I can't wait to see it."

"I painted a picture just for you, Daddy. It's a butterfly tree."

"A butterfly tree? That sounds neat," he said, kissing her on the cheek. "Time for sleep."

"But, Daddy, I want to show you your picture, please."

"Well, okay, but put on your slippers."

Together they walked to the studio where her mother was cleaning paintbrushes.

"What are you doing out of bed, young lady?" her mother exclaimed.

"Just showing Daddy his picture," she said in her sweetest voice.

"That sounds like a good idea."

They looked at Holly's creation: a big green tree with a colorful butterfly perched on each branch.

"It's fantastic. I see now we have two artists in our family," he said sweeping her up in his arms and kissing the top of her head. "Now, let's get you off to dreamland."

That night Holly had dreamed that an angel kissed each butterfly and the tree's branches had reached all the way to heaven.

Jessica

New York City

Jessica sat in a tiny waiting room in Manhattan, aimlessly turning the pages of a magazine, when the door to Dr. Goldstein's office suddenly opened. A kind-looking woman, wearing a pale blue suit that hugged her little round body, stepped into the room. She wore her gray hair tied in a bun. A pair of half glasses completed the picture. She reminded Jessica of a professor she'd once had in England. After introductions, the psychologist ushered her into a small cozy office.

"Have a seat," Dr. Goldstein said, motioning to one of the two chairs facing each other on either side of a long coffee table. "You may call me Laura, if you'd like," she invited in an assertive but gentle voice. "Now tell me why you're here."

"I just feel numb inside," Jessica stammered. "Like I'm just going through the motions."

"You mean you have no enthusiasm for your life? Can you identify what causes you to feel so flat?"

"It's more than flat. Sometimes I don't feel fully alive."

"Now, that's a strong statement. What's troubling you?"

"Well, for one thing, my marriage is falling apart. I also had a miscarriage this time last year, and I feel heartsick all over again coming to its anniversary."

"I see," the doctor said, tapping her pen against her cheek. "Many women have miscarriages and then become pregnant later. Won't you try again?"

"No, I couldn't bear it, I mean if something went wrong."

"How does your husband feel about that?"

"Oh, he's relieved, I'm sure. I don't think he really wanted to be a father."

"And how does that make you feel?"

"Disgusted."

"Are you angry with him?"

"No, just disgusted."

"You're disgusted with your husband. Tell me more about that."

"He drinks too much. He acts like a teenager." She paused for a long moment before adding, "I think I've outgrown him."

"I see. And how do you respond when he drinks?"

"I tell him he should stop and that he needs help."

"Does he admit he has a problem?"

"No. That's the problem. I've tried to get him to go to AA but he tells me he can stop anytime he wants to. It's not true, of course. Once he got drunk and actually made a pass at my girlfriend. She finally told me a couple of weeks after it happened."

"That must have been hard."

"At first I was mad at both of them, feeling betrayed and rejected. Then I realized I didn't care how he felt about me."

"Did you ever confront him?"

"No," she said under her breath, beginning to cry. "It's just too humiliating."

Dr. Goldstein handed her a box of tissues and placed her hand on Jessica's trembling one. "Tell me why you feel humiliated."

"Because it makes me feel like … something is wrong with me. As if I'm not enough."

"If I'd told you that story, and you were my therapist, what would you say to me?"

"I'd probably say that you shouldn't blame yourself for something someone else did."

"Do you believe that's true?"

"Yes," Jessica responded, blowing her nose. Thank you. I feel better just talking about it."

"The judgmental words we say to ourselves," the doctor said slowly and deliberately, "often lead us into depression. When we take a close look at them, we find they're usually irrational. Are you willing to work with me to replace your guilty thoughts with more rational, positive ones?"

"I'll try. But I don't think anyone or anything can really help me."

"Just give it your best effort. I want you to keep a journal where you write down your feelings and thoughts."

"I do that already."

"That's wonderful. Don't you find that it helps clarify your thoughts and feelings?"

"I do, but sometimes I feel I just repeat myself and don't get anywhere."

"I understand. It sounds like we need to go a bit deeper."

***

That evening, Jessica sat up in bed with her journal, trying to go beneath the surface. It was late and Jim was already asleep, snoring peacefully beside her as if he didn't have a care in the world. She wrote:

Why do I feel so empty inside? I don't think I'm in love with Jim.

Maybe I just wanted to marry him so I could have another child. A child I could keep—or so I thought.

A few days later, Jim came home smelling of booze, as he often did lately. He stumbled through the door, weaving back and forth as he took off his coat and shoes.

"Why do you have to drink so much? Look at you. You can't even walk straight."

"Well, well, well, listen to Miss Goody Two Shoes."

"I don't deserve that," she said, turning to walk out of the room.

"Come back here," he shouted, grabbing her by the arm.

"Let go of me. You're drunk."

"Don't talk to me like that," he said, pushing her so hard she fell to the floor. Instead of helping her up, he turned toward the door and stormed back out. "That's it," she said, getting up and walking adamantly to the kitchen where she tore a piece of paper from the notepad, her hands trembling, and wrote, "I have to get away from you and do some long, hard thinking." She thought about calling Stephanie but realized she needed to listen to herself and she couldn't stay with her anyway now that Stephanie's boyfriend had moved in.

She looked inside her wallet. *Not much money.* She grabbed her checkbook, packed a small suitcase, and left the apartment. *I have no clue where to go. How could Jim do this to me? How could I do this to myself? It's certainly not the first time he's been rough with me. And the drinking has gotten worse and worse. What's wrong with me? Maybe this is what I must do. There's no turning back now.*

Through her tears, she noticed she'd walked several blocks without a destination. *Here I am wandering around Hell's Kitchen like a lost waif.* It started to sprinkle and suddenly the rain came down hard. She spied the Franklin Hotel ahead and rushed inside. Looking around, she figured it would be too expensive. *But I have to stay somewhere.*

"How much are your rooms?" she asked the clerk at the counter, hoping she didn't look too disheveled.

"They start at a hundred dollars a night," he replied, barely looking up.

"Oh, that's too much."

He glanced up, giving her a long, hard look and in a gentle voice said, "There's one small room I could give you for sixty. It faces the alley, though, and can get pretty noisy."

"No worries. That will be fine, thank you," she said, smiling through more tears.

She accepted the key gratefully and trudged to the back elevator, taking it to the sixth floor. Once inside the small, drab room, she fell onto the bed. Her surroundings matched her mood perfectly, she decided, and then proceeded to cry herself to sleep.

The next morning, after a fitful night, she woke up with a start. Loud traffic rose up from the alley below. Probably garbage trucks. She pulled the covers over her and tried to go back to sleep. It was useless. Restless thoughts tormented her. *This is a nightmare. What am I doing here? Jim will be wondering where I am. But I can't go back there!* The sun up, but barely reaching the dark room, she picked up the phone, willing herself to call him. Twisting the phone cord tighter and tighter until her knuckles turned white, she managed to dial the number.

"Look, I'm sorry I pushed you," Jim said after hearing her voice. "I was drunk and didn't know what I was doing."

"That's the problem. You were drunk. Don't you know you need help?" Suddenly, her head started to spin.

"I'm not an alcoholic," he yelled. "I can quit anytime I want to."

"Then maybe you should," she yelled back. "It's ruining our marriage."

"You're the one who's ruining our marriage," he shouted. "Ever since we lost the baby, you've pulled away from me. Why don't you go out with me anymore?"

"Because I don't want to drink the way you do," she stammered, suddenly feeling nauseated.

"Oh, is that so? You're too good for me now, is that it?"

"I'm not saying I'm too good for you," she answered, trying to steady her trembling voice. "I just think you need to make some changes in your life."

"Well, I'm happy the way I am," he said with finality in his tone.

"Happy?" She softened her voice and continued. "Look, I know you're not happy when you don't get the acting parts you want. Don't you see how you're sabotaging your career?"

Silence.

"I have the number for Alcoholics Anonymous," she offered after a long moment. "Will you please write it down and find a meeting in the neighborhood?" She was pushing him, but there was no way she could continue with him unless he got help.

"Give me the number," he grumbled.

She gave it to him only to have him hang up on her.

"God, please help me," she prayed out loud, "and help Jim realize what he's doing." Looking at the clock on top of the TV, she panicked. It was after nine, but she couldn't go to work, not like this, not until she'd calmed down and made a plan.

***

Alex's voice sounded rushed when he answered Jessica's call. "Things are frantic around here. I need you to get in here right away."

"I'm sorry, Alex, but I'm can't come in today. It's important that I take some time off."

"Nothing could be more important than getting this new exhibit ready to open," he said with exasperation.

"I've left Jim and I'm at a hotel. Please, Alex, try to understand."

"Oh, dear, I'm sorry, of course. Are you okay?"

"I'll manage somehow. Thank you, Alex. I'll make it up to you. I promise."

"Just go straighten out your life. He'd be a fool to let you go."

"Well, it's certainly a crossroad. I'll keep you posted."

She took a few deep breaths before next calling her therapist to schedule an urgent appointment. Luckily, Laura had an open session for the next day.

***

"I've left Jim," Jessica divulged, squeezing her hands together as if to hold herself intact.

"Take your time," Laura said in a gentle voice, "and tell me what happened."

She relayed the story, searching for the right words to explain.

"You did what you needed to do. You chose to leave a situation that had become unbearable for you."

"I know. It's true," she said pausing, near tears. "I gave him the number for AA. He said he was writing it down, but then he hung up on me."

"You have done all that you can," Laura said, offering her a tissue. "The rest is up to him. He must want to get sober for himself."

"I know you're right, but what if he doesn't follow through?"

"Then you face that situation if and when it comes. I encourage you to attend an Al Anon meeting for those whose family or loved ones struggle with alcoholism."

"He says I've changed and become distant toward him," she continued, as if in a trance. "Maybe I'm the reason he's drinking."

"Do you truly believe Jim's drinking is your fault?"

After a long pause, Jessica answered softly, "No, not really."

"And have you changed and become more distant?"

"Probably. I don't enjoy being around him when he's drinking. I don't even like him. I think he's disappointed, if not desperate, over the trajectory of his acting career and sees no options. He seems much younger than me somehow. I think I've outgrown him emotionally and that threatens him."

"It doesn't sound like he's the man you'd want to be the father of your child."

"You're right. I can see that now."

"So how are you going to handle this?"

"I'm going to stay away until he goes for help."

"It's not going to be easy. But you must think of yourself, take care of yourself."

"Thanks, Laura. I hear you and I'll get myself to Al Anon."

Her thoughts were racing as she left the office. *Is this really happening? How will I cope? Is it over?* Wandering aimlessly, she found herself in a small diner, ordering soup. When the waitress brought it to the table, Jessica found she had no appetite. Realizing she needed to eat, she forced down a few spoonfuls before paying the bill and heading back to the anonymity of life at the Franklin Hotel.

She took her therapist's advice and called Al Anon to find a nearby meeting, then wondered if she should call Jim. *I know Laura said I should leave Jim alone, but I just have to know if he's getting help.* When she called their apartment, a woman answered the phone.

"He's indisposed right now," she said, giggling.

"Is that my frigging wife?" Jim's voice called out in the background. "Give me the phone."

"Look," Jim said harshly, slurring his words, "I don't need you anymore. I have someone new who understands me better than you do and accepts me just the way I am."

"Clearly you have not called AA," she said sharply, shocked at what was happening, her body shaking all over.

"You got that right. Now leave me alone."

She dropped the phone, stunned by what she'd just heard.

"I hate him," she cried. "How can he be so cruel?" *I should have left him long ago. The signs were all there. I really am a fool for staying as long as I did.*

She thought about calling Stephanie but decided she wanted her mother. *She's been through it herself and will understand.* Aware that she would need to call collect from the hotel, she called the front desk to access the international operator. On the third ring, her mother answered and she said without preamble, "Mother, I've left Jim. He's drinking and cheating on me."

"Oh, no. How long has this been going on?"

"The drinking, longer than I'd like to admit. The cheating, I'm not sure."

"You're strong, dear, and have a good head on your shoulders. You'll get through it. Goodness, if *I* can recover, anyone can."

"I appreciate that you think so. But I don't feel confident of anything today."

"Would you like me to come be with you while you get through this difficult time?"

"You mean you'd come all the way across the ocean to be with me?"

"Of course, dear girl. I love you. Where are you now?"

"I'm staying in a hotel for now. Would you really consider coming?"

"Yes, dear, I will come."

"How soon could you make arrangements?"

"Give me a day or two. What's the name of the hotel and your room number?"

Jessica gave her the information.

"I'll call you soon, darling. Try to rest and look ahead, not back."

"Thanks, Mum. Talk soon," she said, wiping her tears. *I can't believe she's coming.*

***

Jessica met her mother two days later at JFK and returned to the Franklin where she'd upgraded to a quiet room with two double beds.

"I imagine I have a real sense of what you're going through, dear," Adelaide began as they sat down facing one another. "My story's different from yours, of course, but I know how betrayal feels, though your father was not a drinker."

Jessica began to cry. "It helps to know you understand, Mum, and that I'm not alone."

"I'll help you in any way I can," Adelaide assured, reaching out her arms.

"I can't tell you how much it means to me, just having you here."

Enfolded in her mother's arms, Jessica let herself cry until she had no more tears.

***

With her mother's financial help, Jessica was able to rent a small walk-up studio within walking distance of the museum. Filing for divorce was fairly straightforward, only paperwork, with New York's no-fault policy and no real property to divide. Still, it was painful, especially returning to their apartment to gather her belongings. The formerly neat home was a disaster, with clothes thrown about, dishes in the sink, and empty liquor bottles on every available surface. She had not told him she was coming; she'd watched until he left for the theater before letting herself in.

Her mother stayed until Jim had been served with the divorce papers and Jessica's lawyer assured her all would go smoothly. At the airport, they said their goodbyes with a renewed closeness, both of them in tears.

"It's strange how good things can come out of difficult situations, isn't it?" Adelaide said.

"I feel so much closer to you, Mum. I truly couldn't have managed without you. Thank you so much."

As the last call for her mother's flight came over the loudspeaker, they embraced.

Her mother blew a last kiss. Jessica waved and smiled, feeling good about their improved relationship. She'd almost told her mother about André but had decided not to.

In Al-Anon she was learning to focus on herself now instead of Jim's problem. *I have to be strong and get on with my life, even without a man, even without a baby.*

André

André paused from packing for a moment and re-opened the letter he'd received from Speos Institute several months before.

We are happy to inform you that your application for the 1986-87 school term at Speos Institute of Photography in Paris has been accepted.

By next summer, I'll have the credentials I need to begin working as a professional photographer. But I wish Papa was happier about it.

***

"I can't believe you're more interested in taking pictures than in accepting your responsibility here at the vineyard," Papa had shouted after reading the letter. "Don't you realize how you have insulted me? Insulted and disappointed me. You, my only son, ready to give up your place in the family business and just walk away."

"But, Papa, you know how I feel about photography. And Pierre will be much better than me as your apprentice. It's what he's always wanted to do. And, now that his father has died, it will help him support his mother."

"I've got nothing against Pierre," Henri continued in a loud voice. "I like him. You know that. But, as you know all too well, a vineyard is traditionally a family business, intended to be passed from generation to generation. I took over for my father and you should take over for me and your son for you. That's just how it's supposed to be."

"Papa, I can see how hurt you are. But don't you want me to be happy at what I do, like you are? I'm a good photographer and I'll make you proud of me. You'll see."

"I just don't understand you," Henri said, shaking his head.

"Henri," André's mother implored, joining them in the front room, "the boy has a different destiny than you had. That's just the way it is."

Henri stormed out, slamming the front door behind him.

"Try not to feel guilty or worry about him. He'll get used to the idea, André. He loves you."

***

Nearly packed, André spotted his personal photo album on the bottom shelf of his bookcase. Putting down his suitcase, he opened the album and sat down on the edge of his bed. There on the first page was the picture he'd taken of his parents on the happy day they'd given him his first camera, his fourteenth birthday. "Not bad for a beginner," he said to himself, as the memory of that day came into focus.

***

"I love it," he shouted after pulling a shiny black camera out of its box. "A Leica. It's amazing. Thank you so much. It's truly a professional's camera. It means so much to me! The perfect birthday present."

He stood up to give his mother a hug. She looked so pretty in her blue paisley dress, with her long brown hair tied behind her neck. "Here are the batteries." Papa pulled them out of his pocket. "Put them in and you can take some pictures."

"Thanks, Papa," he said, hugging his father. "You and Mamà sit close together and I'll take a picture of you."

Inching his chair close to his wife's, then removing his glasses and straightening his suspenders, Henri's face filled with his broad smile.

***

If only he was as happy for me now as he was then.
Looking through the other photos in his album, he came across one of himself with his girlfriend, Michelle. They were standing with Pierre and his girlfriend, all dressed up for the fall dance. Pierre's mother had taken the picture. He'd been so bashful about asking Michelle to the dance. They'd dated steadily until graduation just a few months ago.

He'd loved kissing her. And he knew he'd always remember that moon-lit evening, just before graduation, when Michelle had invited him to her house when her parents were away for the evening. She'd taken him outside where she'd already spread a blanket under the stars. *What a woman. She made a man out of me that night—and then dropped me, just like that.*

Shaking his head, he turned the page in his album to one of Pierre taken down by the creek where they always met to tell each other their secrets. *I think I'll miss him most of all.*

"Dinner's ready," his mother called, disturbing his reverie.

He closed the album and tucked it into the zipper pocket in his suitcase and went out to join his parents for dinner. Mamà had made his favorite meal: bouillabaisse with crème brulee for dessert.

125

After dinner, his mother was suddenly silent and his father's attempts at conversation seemed awkward.

"André," she finally said, "there's something we must tell you. It won't be easy for us to share or for you to hear."

"You sound so serious," he said, puzzled by her manner.

"There's something I've been saving for you, something you should take with you to Paris."

She left the room. His father remained silent. When she returned, she was holding a small wooden box tied with a black ribbon.

"What's that?"

She untied the ribbon and took out an ornate necklace and handed it to him. It was a Celtic cross, its center circle filled with mother-of-pearl on which a gold fleur-de-lis had been engraved. He marveled at the many colorful stones on the piece.

"It's beautiful. Where did you get it?"

"It's a long story. Let's go sit on the porch and your papa and I will tell you about it."

***

The next day, André sat on a train as it rumbled into the city limits of Paris, still bewildered by the story his parents had told him the night before. His heart ached as he touched the necklace they'd given him, now hanging around his neck.

I can't believe I was adopted and my mother—my real mother—abandoned me. Why did they wait seventeen years to tell me?

On what was supposed to be a joyful day, André felt nothing but confusion. *How can I be happy when I don't even know who I really am?* For the first time in his life, he felt bereft.

The train soon slowed and Gare du Nord station came into view. With a flutter in his stomach, he gathered up his things, ready to meet his future—whatever it would be.

Jessica

New York City
One year later

Jessica had a few minutes to catch her breath before guiding a group of students from Berkeley through the museum's collection of Impressionist paintings. With a yellow notepad clutched under her arm, she stood overlooking the courtyard, the latest landscaping of tall grasses around a still pond, a Japanese theme, soothing and drifting her into a relaxed state.

Turning toward the entrance, she saw and heard a group of young people entering the museum. She could make out some of their naïve, eager faces, reminding her of herself as a student back in the late sixties and seventies.

That's probably my group. She made her way toward them with a stirring of excitement. Jessica loved being with college students, many of them as curious and enthusiastic as she had been.

"Over here," she called. "I'm your guide for the morning."

"Hello, I'm Charlotte Johnson," a professionally dressed woman announced, reaching out her hand.

"Pleased to meet you. I'm Jessica Taylor," she said, shaking the woman's hand. "I'm an assistant curator here at the museum and on the teaching staff. I believe your group has requested an Impressionist tour."

"Yes, that's our main interest, though we'd like to take in as much of the museum as possible. We have the entire day."

"I'll take you through the Impressionists collection and then you can decide what you'd like to see from there. After you check your belongings, please meet me back here."

Jessica returned to her place of calm as the students checked their things. As they approached her, the group of about twenty young people spoke softly among themselves, clearly in awe of their surroundings.

Arriving on the second floor, Jessica spoke briefly about the birth of Impressionism in 1874 in Paris and its founding members Claude Monet, Edgar Degas, and Camille Pissaro, among others. As they gathered before Monet's work, she shared that it was Monet's *Sunrise* that gave the movement its name. The students lingered before Monet's *Water Lilies* before moving along to Manet, Renoir, Cézanne, Gauguin, and, Jessica's personal favorite, Van Gogh. The entire group remained attentive and involved throughout her lecture, many writing energetically in their notebooks.

One particularly inquisitive young woman, whose dark curly hair framed a round friendly face, caught her attention as she gestured passionately with her hands, revealing a small red heart tattooed on her wrist. When asking questions, her expressive brown eyes seemed to dance. After the morning tour, the young woman approached her.

"How did you get this job? I'd love to do what you do."

"Well, I majored in art history," Jessica replied, "spent some time working in galleries, and then got a position here at MoMA."

"Your presentation was awesome. By the way, I'm Holly Simpson." The girl's exuberance impressed her.

"Why, thank you very much. I appreciate your enthusiasm."

"I guess I am a bit over the top sometimes, but art really excites me."

"That's wonderful. I imagine you'll be taking in the Met, too, while you're in New York."

"That's on the agenda for tomorrow," the group's instructor said, coming over to join them. "Thanks so much for a wonderful tour and discussion. You really brought the art to life."

"My pleasure. Here's my card. Don't hesitate to contact me if I can be of further assistance."

Holly asked if she could have one, too.

"Sure. Perhaps we'll meet again one day."

Ah, to be young again. Maybe I'd even get a tattoo. Smiling, she watched as the group filed out for lunch. Holly turned and waved goodbye.

***

That evening, she sat in her Manhattan apartment, gazing out the window at the busy street below. She'd dated a few men since her divorce from Jim, but none of them seemed to click. Beneath her, people rushed about and taxi horns honked. Mesmerized, she allowed her thoughts to ramble and flow.

Not as quiet as Stephanie's place in the Village, but I love it. I love my job. I'm on a solid track toward possible curator someday. But what about a husband and children? Is it time to at least let the children fantasy go? Tears formed, but she brushed them. *I still care for Jim, but not as a husband. Stephanie says he's doing well in treatment. I wonder how Joseph is doing, where he is, what his life is like. It makes me sad to think of him. We were so close, so in love, but long, long ago.*

A tug at her heart sent her to her cedar chest in the bedroom where she kept some mementos of Paris. She opened it slowly and began to pull out old ticket stubs, postcards, a program from a boat trip she'd taken with Joseph, and, most precious of all, a street artist's drawing of the two of them in Montmartre. *We were so happy. But that was then, a long time ago. Why can't I get over him?*

"Because you're still in love with him," her heart answered, "and probably will be for the rest of your life."

Her vision blurred by tears, she carefully replaced the memories in the chest and closed the lid. *Please, God, help me let go of this ridiculous fantasy. Joseph is yours, not mine.* Her thoughts turned to their baby, who would be a young man by now. *May André be safe and happy, doing what he loves to do.*

She wandered into the kitchen, poured herself a glass of wine, and chose Chopin's *Nocturnes* to soothe her. Curling up on the sofa, she immersed herself in the progressions of laments and exaltations. Before long, she'd drifted off to sleep.

A strange dream startled her awake. Rubbing her eyes, she stood up, turned out the light and stumbled into the bedroom. *I'm glad tomorrow's Sunday. I can sleep as late as I want. Now what was that dream? It was so real.*

Turning on the nightlight, she put on her nightgown and got into bed, reaching for her dream journal and a pen.

I'm Psyche, the poor girl from the myth. I'm begging Aphrodite to give Eros back to me. She's mean and tells me I must do exactly as she says. Now I'm by a river, loathing my reflection, about to jump in and end it all. Next to my own reflection, I suddenly see an image of the Black Madonna. Out of the blackness comes a voice. "Live your life the best you can. Someday, it will all make sense to you." And then I woke up.

Her head throbbed and she went to the bathroom for aspirin. Gazing at her reflection in the mirror, she began to cry. *Who are you, anyway? Nobody's going to love you if you don't love yourself. Why is that so hard?*

***

The next day, still in her nightgown, Jessica rummaged through her books in search of her dog-eared copy of the Psyche and Eros myth *Amor and Psyche*. She wanted to reference it again in relation to her dream, but when she found it, she didn't have the focus for it. Instead, she showered and pulled on a pair of jeans and a T-shirt, deciding to clear her head with a walk.

When she got to the end of her street, she heard the sound of a kitten's meow coming from around the corner.

"You poor baby," she exclaimed, scooping up the tiny creature, cradling it in her arms and stroking its matted and dirty orange fur. "What happened to you? Where's your mother? Don't cry, sweetheart, I'll take care of you."

"I'll call you Miss Suzy," she said, wondering why, but not questioning it, as her mood shifted and she smiled. "Let's go home. You and I belong together."

The following spring

It had been a long winter in Manhattan and Jessica felt happy to be outside without a heavy coat. A riot of color filled Central Park like a Monet painting, all pink, violet, and chartreuse with early spring. Although she loved the stark beauty of winter snows and the sun-splashed beaches of summer, spring and fall remained her favorite seasons. Autumn leaves and spring flowers created nature's most spectacular paintings. Those times of year brought her alive.

She gravitated toward color and adorned herself accordingly. She'd just bought a sea-foam green suit for work that perfectly matched her eyes.

When she reached her apartment, Miss Suzy greeted her, as usual, with a loud meow. "Hi, there, baby," she said, scooping up her furry little friend, who rewarded her with a loud purr. Kissing the kitten on the head, she said, "Down you go. I want to try on my new outfit."

After putting on her new suit, she looked herself over in the mirror, startled by the professional-looking woman staring back at her. Where had the casual, artsy girl living in Greenwich Village gone? Her long blond hair had then fallen freely around her shoulders; now, as befitted her position, she swept it up in a neat French twist. She was also a bit larger in the waist than she'd been in those days. The only consolation was a decent bust size for once in her life.

"Well, I guess my skinny hippie days are over," she announced to the reflection in the mirror.

***

The next day at noon she strolled through the familiar corridor from her office to the MoMA lobby, absentmindedly playing with the pearls around her neck. She mused that, at forty-two, she felt more passion for art, its history and its making, than for any of the men she'd recently dated. Time for lunch, a pleasant break from meetings and tours. She didn't mind being on her own.

As she approached the museum entrance, a familiar figure, wearing a priest's collar, caught her eye as he made his way through the front door. The way he walked … it couldn't possibly be! She stopped short, her thoughts muddled as she moved closer to the revolving doors.

"Joseph?" she called in disbelief.

The priest turned to her in slow motion, as if refocusing from his own reverie, then stopped, his words spilling over, his whole demeanor brightening. "Jessica? I can't believe it! Is that really you?"

Her chest filled and fluttered as she gazed into the warm brown eyes she remembered so well. Still handsome, the extra weight he'd put on suited him. The gray at his temples reminded her of the years that had passed since they'd last seen each other.

"A priest now. It must be Father?" she whispered over the lump in her throat.

"Yes, I finally took my vows," he answered, noticing her name tag, "You must work here."

"Yes, I'm on the teaching staff," she replied, her voice wavering. "And an assistant curator," she continued, her confidence returning.

"That's wonderful," he said, smiling. "I thought of you just yesterday when I saw the article announcing the Monet exhibit here. I remember how much you admired his work." He paused, his hand briefly touching her arm.

At his touch, precious memories washed over her like a splash of liquid sunlight.

"I had no idea you were in New York," Joseph went on, shaking his head as if to wake himself from a dream.

"I've been here since seventy-six," she said.

"You look wonderful. And you still have your lovely English accent."

"Thanks. You look well, too." Her images of him over the years paled in comparison to the way he now appeared, in the flesh, in front of her.

"May I buy you some lunch?"

"Well, I was on my way out to grab a quick bite," she told him, her cheeks glowing warm.

"May I join you then?"

She smiled as he offered her his arm.

"There's a little café I like just a couple of blocks east," she suggested.

"Sounds great." Once outside on the sidewalk, he turned toward her and continued, "I've thought about you so often—wondering what happened to you. I'd about given up on seeing you again. And here you are in New York City."

"It's good to see you, too, Joseph," she said, looking deeply into his eyes. "Truly good."

A crowd had gathered at Café Saint Tropez, but they were soon seated in the courtyard. The lilting sounds of French music, the aroma of freshly baked bread, and the soft breeze that filled the air reminded her of their days in France so many years ago. *He still sets my heart pounding.*

The waiter brought two ice waters with lemon and took their order: an endive salad for her and lobster bisque for him.

"I can hardly believe you're actually here having lunch with me."

Before she could reply, the waiter arrived with hot tea and lemon for two, along with croissants and sweet butter. "For you, Madame, and you, Father."

She looked down, hoping to hide the flush on her cheeks. *How can I still have these feelings for a man I haven't seen in twenty years?*

They sipped their tea quietly for a few moments until he broke the silence. "So what brought you to New York?"

"I came to live with an American friend I met in London. I got a job in a gallery in Greenwich Village and made a life for myself here."

"Did you ever get married?" he asked, looking down at his tea.

As the waiter served their meals, she gathered her thoughts.

"I married an actor," she finally told him, "but it only lasted a few years." After pausing for a moment, she continued, "I had a miscarriage and the relationship went downhill afterwards, but, honestly, I was more upset about losing the baby than losing my husband."

"I'm sorry to hear you suffered, Jess," he said, a look of genuine concern in his eyes.

Suddenly flustered, she pushed away from the table, her napkin falling to the floor along with her fork. "I really must go," she said, glancing at her watch and standing up. "I have an exhibit to get ready for tomorrow." She couldn't control her tears for much longer; she had to get away.

"But, Jess, your lunch. Are you sure?"

Glancing at him, she paused, conflicted.

"Could we have dinner later? Or tomorrow?" he asked, standing up and reaching for her hand. "I must see you again."

Her mind racing, she pulled her hand away. "I don't know," was all she could manage to say.

"But it's been such a long time. Please meet me again so we can talk."

She turned to meet his gaze. *Are his eyes really moist?* "I'm not sure I should see you again," she stammered. When her tears began to flow in earnest, she turned in the direction of the door.

"Jess, please" he pleaded, grasping her shoulders. "Look at me."

She paused to catch her breath and brush her tears away. "I can't. I can't be with you, Joseph," she said. Then, looking into his eyes, she stood transfixed, absorbing the warmth that flowed from him, the familiar, comforting connection with him, still there along with the pain she'd carried since they'd separated so many years before. "I can't handle this, Joseph, not again." She pulled away and shook her head. "I have to go."

"But, Jess, we owe it to ourselves to at least talk."

"I can't think right now," she said, choking back her tears and turning to leave.

"I'll phone you at the museum tomorrow."

Nodding her agreement, she gave him a feeble smile, then walked quickly away from the restaurant—away from him.

***

Jessica stopped at the ladies' room to wipe her eyes and repair her makeup. Gripped by her reflection in the mirror, she was stunned. Her new sea-foam suit now called attention to the puffiness, rather than the brightness, of her eyes. *How can this be happening? I've spent years reaching beyond the heartache of leaving him behind and here he is again. What can we possibly be to each other now?*

She made her way to the West Room, where two of her assistants waited to help her hang the next day's exhibit of a modern New York City artist of recent fame. Relieved at the distraction, she immersed herself in the task.

She told her assistants exactly where to place the paintings, then instructed them to put a large alabaster sculpture of a couple embracing one another in the center of the room. Her eyes fell upon their nude bodies, entwined like wild ivy. Something pulled her to join their intimate space. Startled by her body's response to the alluring couple's presence, she averted her eyes like a shy young girl, focusing instead on the painting of a feminine-looking figure staring into an abyss.

I'm more like her: ungrounded. I must get a grip, mustn't let seeing Joseph throw me into a tailspin. I'm not that girl I used to be. Surely I can handle this now. She sat down to proofread the painting placards one last time but couldn't concentrate. *How can I concentrate on art when my mind is filled with Joseph, my darling Joseph?* She struggled to push her haunting feelings aside, willing herself to focus on the titles and descriptions of the featured artist's paintings.

Finally, the color, movement, and vibrancy of the art swept her out of her inner thoughts and feelings and back into the familiarity of the large airy space with well-worn but polished oak floors and natural light sweeping through western windows. In the glorious afternoon sunlight, each piece in the collection, though similar in style, came alive, revealing its own unique beauty. She admired the artist's fluidity — abstract, symbolic, and sensual — a blend of stillness and movement that felt mystical and spiritually inspired.

Painting after painting invited a fresh emotional experience — some whimsical and bright, others dark and gloomy, mirroring her conflicted feelings. The soft greens, blues, and purples rising from one painting lifted her spirits as if the fragrance of lavender emanated from its field of flowers. Then, abruptly, the bold red and blue strokes on one of the larger paintings leapt off the wall, sweeping her out of her body and into their turbulence. Golden light, radiating from the center of the painting, crept into her heart, gently returning her to the bustling preparation in the room.

"Jessica, are you in here?" a man's voice called. Alex entered the room. "Is everything ready?" he asked. She thought he seemed a bit frantic.

"Yes. I've accounted for everything and am now reviewing the details."

"Fantastic, my dear. I'm in a rush and don't have time to look at the exhibit, but I trust your judgment completely." He waved goodbye with the air of flamboyance to which she'd grown accustomed.

After her assistants left, she turned her attention back to the exhibit, a sense of comfort enveloping her. Regardless of her confusing private life, she could count on the museum to provide a safe haven. She longed to create a similar sanctuary within herself, but Joseph's appearance had shaken her to the core.

Taking one final look around the room, her eyes fell on the old wooden floor, now golden in the radiance of the afternoon sun. Like a cat seeking warmth, she moved toward the last patch of sunshine. Slipping out of her high-heeled shoes, she sank into the floor, allowing Joseph's image to fill her mind. *Now that he's a priest, what can the future possibly hold for us?*

Joseph

Brooklyn

Joseph sat on the subway, his thoughts reeling.

What an incredible day! It's like a miracle: Jessica sitting across from me. She's still so beautiful, all sea-green eyes and golden hair. Will she ever forgive me? Will she even see me again?

My God, you've brought her back to me. There must be a reason. How can we be only friends? I want to hold her in my arms again. If this is a test, a temptation, I will surely fail. No matter what, I must see her again.

The train came to a jolting stop at the rectory exit, snapping him out of his thoughts. He had agreed to say Mass at Saint Andrews later that day; a fellow priest would be taking his place at the youth center. He willed himself to put thoughts of Jessica away, at least for the time being, and retreated to his apartment to prepare for Mass.

***

That night Joseph was unable to sleep. Jessica's image flooded his mind: her beautiful face, golden hair, the way she walked, even her fragrance, but also the pain in her eyes, her tears. *I must see her, talk it through, somehow make all these years up to her.* The next day he called MoMA first thing, surprised when she answered her phone, and amazed she agreed to meet him for lunch.

At noon, he hurried into the lobby, his heart jumping to his throat when he spotted her walking toward him. She'd tied her hair back and was wearing a soft, gathered skirt and silky blouse.

My beautiful Jessica.

"Hi, I've brought lunch."

"Great. I'm starving."

When they reached Central Park, they walked quietly over to a bench and sat. He pulled out a cheese croissant, broke it in two pieces, and handed her half.

"In memory of our days in Paris." He smiled. Her eyes clouded over, which touched a deep place in his heart, and caused his own to moisten.

"This isn't going to work," she said, thrusting the sandwich back into his hand and standing. "I can't do this."

"Please, Jess." He stood, placing his hands on her shoulders. "Let's just have lunch and enjoy each other. It's been a long time."

They sat again and ate in silence.

"I don't know what to say to you, now that you're really here," Joseph admitted. "I've dreamed of this moment."

"Don't such thoughts conflict with your vows?"

"Yes, they do, but I'm troubled more by the vows than by my dreams of you."

"I've told myself over and over again to forget you, but I haven't. And now that you're here, I'm undone, feel unhinged, frightened. My good judgment tells me I should not be here with you."

"And what does your heart say?"

He saw she was trembling and reached for her hand. As his fingers closed around hers, she lifted her head and turned toward him, her eyes speaking for her heart. He put his arms around her and drew her near.

"Oh, Joseph," she said after a long pause. "How can we be friends?"

"I don't know, Jess. I don't know. But it's like a miracle to be with you again."

She gently pulled away to gather herself, moving down the bench.

"Are you living in New York?" she asked cautiously.

"I am, in Brooklyn. I designed a youth center on the edge of Park Slope as head architect and then the Church placed me there as the center's director."

"A way of combining your architectural skills with your pastoral interests, like you did in Paris."

"Yes, a bit like Paris, but without you." He sighed. "Where did you go after you left me there?"

"After *I* left *you*?" she replied, the tone in her voice hardening. "I'd say it was the other way around." Jumping to her feet and starting to walk away, she said, "This is too much. I can't do it again."

"Jess, please, try to understand." He stood and reached for her arm, stopping her. "Maybe God has brought you back into my life to help me work through something."

"What do you mean?"

He led her back to the bench before answering. "I'm changing. I've been seriously questioning some of the basic tenets of Catholicism and have been for some years."

"I knew, of course, that you were ambivalent about your decision to take your vows, but I thought you had absolute faith that, for you, Catholicism was the only true path to God."

"After much silence and even six months of secluded retreat, I'm slowly coming to the conclusion, through prayer and reflection, that the Catholic path may not be right for me."

"What do you mean?"

"Working with the kids has given me a chance to redirect my energy until I know what I'm called to do next. I'm also involved with a support group for priests who are committed to making changes in fundamental Church principles, though it's a tough road."

"You sound different, not like the Joseph I used to know."

"I *am* different. I'm learning to listen to my heart in deciding how to advise my parishioners, even if it's not exactly what I was taught in seminary."

"You really *have* changed."

"I must, however, resolve the conflict between listening to my heart and honoring my vows."

"I hear how you're struggling."

"You've— *we've* suffered enough over this. I am so sorry to have hurt you, Jess, and myself. I want us to be free, free of conflict, free to at least be friends, for now. I will never hurt you again, Jess. Never."

She looked at him in disbelief, the wind swirling about them, as if holding them in an imaginary world.

Jessica

Spring turned into summer and Jessica relished her time with Joseph. Their natural friendship flourished again, just as it had in Paris. She enjoyed a genuine connection with him that couldn't be explained in words. It was as if they'd always known each other and always would. At first, they shared picnic lunches in Central Park at least every other week. Soon their time together expanded to include excursions on their days off to various museums or long walks around the city. Joseph patiently listened to her talk about the art that moved her while she enjoyed his passion for urban architectural styles. She shared the deeply moving experience she'd had walking the labyrinth at Chartres Cathedral. He spoke of the highs and lows of his life as a priest.

His questioning of his vows encouraged her and she believed he would not hurt her again. But she wondered if she was hurting herself.

***

Jessica was looking forward to a long overdue lunch with Stephanie, her old friend from Village days. They'd not seen each other in a long time, a fact that was mainly Jessica's fault. After she and Jim divorced, she'd separated herself psychologically from all of her friends in the Village, from anyone who reminded her of her painful marriage and divorce. Stephanie had eloped with her boyfriend and was now busy with her own life.

Looking up from her seat at a table in The Gathering, she smiled as her friend practically danced through the door.

"It's great to see you." Stephanie laughed as Jessica stood to hug her. "I'm so glad you could make it."

"It's been much too long," Jessica replied, studying in Stephanie's new hairstyle of brown bouncing curls framing her vibrant face and clear gray eyes. "I love your hair. Married life certainly becomes you."

"Thanks. I guess you can see how happy I am," Stephanie said, sitting and pulling her chair closer to the table. "And I have news for you." A radiant smile accompanied her announcement. "I'm pregnant."

"Oh, Steph, that's wonderful. But, at your age, are you sure it's safe?"

"I'm only thirty-nine. I know *lots* of women who've had perfectly healthy children *at my age*."

Her friend's smile gone, Jessica regretted what she'd said. "I'm sorry. I just want everything to work out better for you than it did for me."

"Oh, Jess, I'm the one who's sorry," Stephanie said, reaching out to touch her friend's hand. "I didn't mean to make you feel uncomfortable."

"It's okay. I'm so happy for you, truly I am. I just want you to take good care of yourself."

Enjoying their lunch, Jessica reflected on how easy it was to be with Stephanie, how she'd missed her. Still, she didn't feel ready to tell her about Joseph.

Over tea—and splurging on cheesecake—Stephanie asked if she was seeing anyone special.

"I'm really not interested in dating right now," she replied, trying to sound natural.

"Why not?"

"I'm too busy with my job," she said, averting her eyes.

"Well, it doesn't sound natural to give up dating for your job."

"I haven't exactly given up dating. I'm just concentrating on other areas of my life right now."

"You sound serious. Is everything all right?"

"Sure. How about you? What have you been up to lately, besides making a baby?"

"I've been attending some lectures at the library near our old apartment. There's one tomorrow evening I think we might both enjoy. It's based on the book, *A Course in Miracles*. Have you heard of it?"

"I don't think so."

"It's was supposedly channeled by Jesus through a Jewish psychologist in New York."

"Come on, you don't really believe in channeling, do you?"

"Why not? God channeled information to the Jews through their prophets." Stephanie tossed her head and rolled her eyes, a gesture Jessica remembered well. "As you know, I'm not a Christian, but it intrigues me to think that Jesus would channel information through a Jewish woman."

"You amaze me. I think of myself as a seeker of truth but I don't always live what I learn. I do feel connected to a kind of sacred feminine energy since my time at Chartres Cathedral years ago. I saw that experience as connecting to a feminine face of God. But I don't practice it, call on it, as I could. I wish I trusted myself more, what I'm called toward, the way you do."

"You can. Go with me to the lecture."

"Okay. Let's do it."

***

"A Course in Miracles," the lecturer concluded, "teaches that guilt and judgment are blocks to our happiness. We need to embrace love and forgiveness in all that we do."

When he finished speaking, Stephanie and Jessica went up to look at a copy of the large text from which he'd been reading.

"I like the emphasis on forgiveness," Jessica said. "I need to work on forgiving myself for leaving Jim when he was in so much trouble."

"Hey, he finally got the help he needed, didn't he? Maybe losing you was what he needed to finally bring him around. By the way, have you been able to forgive the guy in Paris for leaving you, the one who became a Catholic priest?"

"That's another story altogether," Jessica replied, her cheeks growing warm.

"If you're still holding on to that pain, maybe the *Course* could help you."

Even after they'd parted, her friend's last words stuck with her. *Am I fooling myself? I do fear that Joseph will hurt me again. And as things are, we have no future together.*

***

"You'd better sit down," Alex said as Jessica walked into his office the following Monday. "I have some good news for you."

After she'd done as instructed, he continued, a big smile on his face. "How'd you like a huge promotion?"

"Who wouldn't? What's up?"

"There's an opening for a curator at a lovely museum on the West Coast and I think you should apply for it."

"The West Coast? Why would I want to leave New York?"

"Because, my dear, it's a great opportunity for you."

"Where?"

"Laguna Beach, a beautiful little town in southern California. Joshua Martin, the curator, is retiring in a couple of months. I found out about it from his assistant, Clay Sebring, at the conference in San Francisco last month."

"Hey, are you trying to get rid of me?"

"Of course not. I'd miss you terribly."

"Why wouldn't Clay Sebring be taking over that position?"

"Because he wants to move to New York." Lowering his voice to almost a whisper, he said, "Look, Clay and I are old friends. Well, maybe more than friends. Anyway, I could offer him your job if you get the position out there."

"Oh, so that's what this is all about."

"It's a win-win situation if you decide to go for it, but if you don't, I think Clay will be moving here anyway, so don't feel pressured one way or the other."

"I don't know, Alex. California's a long way from New York."

"Just give it some thought." He wrote down Joshua Martin's phone number and handed it to her. "If you decide to apply, I'll write a recommendation he can't refuse. Besides, I think you'll make a great curator."

***

After work, in the quiet of her apartment, Jessica imagined herself as a curator, in charge of her own museum.

It's what I've always wanted, but moving to California would be a huge transition—and even farther away from Britain. It would create distance again from Joseph, maybe not a bad thing, until he decides how to resolve his quandary. I don't want to be away from him, but it may be the best thing for me.

The next day she called the Sea View Museum of Art in Laguna Beach and scheduled an interview. Joshua Martin sounded pleasant—and interested. Jessica pulled together her resume and sent it off, promising a solid recommendation from MoMA if and when he was ready for it.

Joseph

Brooklyn

Joseph sat in his small bedroom at the rectory, relaxing on his day off. He decided to give Jessica a call before she left for work.

"What've you been up to?" he asked when she answered the phone.

"Well, I attended an interesting lecture the other night. Have you ever heard of *A Course in Miracles?*"

"No, what is it?"

"It's a new spiritual path based on a book Jesus supposedly channeled through a Jewish psychologist here in New York."

"Surely you're not serious."

"Yes, I am. It's an attempt to get back to the essential teachings of Jesus, without all the rules and regulations added to Christianity over the years."

"That's interesting," he said, seeing a resemblance between what she was saying and his experience with his support group. "I'm trying to do the same things, but I'm definitely skeptical about the notion that someone can *channel* divine knowledge in such a way as you describe."

"I guess I am, too, but something about it speaks to me."

"Jess, I'd love to see you, talk more. Why don't you come out to Brooklyn after work? It'll give us a chance to visit and I can finally show you around the youth center. We can have supper afterwards, if you'd like."

"That'll work. Besides, there's something else I need to talk with you about."

The seriousness in her voice took him aback. "Okay, so I'll see you about six? Take the F train to Fifteenth Street at Prospect Park West. We're just after the circle; you can't miss it."

"Sounds good, but it may be closer to six thirty. You never know with rush hour trains."

I wonder what's bothering her. I hope she's not upset with me.

***

At just after six, Jessica arrived at the youth center. "I'm amazed at how beautiful this is," she proclaimed, her eyes scanning the place, "but you were always a great architect."

"I'm so glad you came," he said, excited, as always, to see her, and for the chance to share a closer look at his world. "The kids are gone for the day, I'm afraid, so you'll have to come back sometime and meet them."

"I'd like that," she said, following him out a door to the courtyard.

In the middle of the open space stood the chapel. Opening the door with loving care, he ushered her inside.

"It's beautiful and so serene," Jessica whispered as she looked at the stained glass windows, each representing a Station of the Cross. Their colors shone brightly as the last light streamed through, adding a soft glow to the room, accentuated by lit candles on the altar.

"I'm glad you feel the sanctity of the space," Joseph said, smiling. "It gives the kids a place to sit and unwind after the busyness of the school day before getting involved in their after-school activities."

She gazed at him with what looked like tears in her eyes, which touched him deeply. They stood still, connecting heart to heart, until her eyes darkened and she suddenly turned and walked out the chapel door.

Joseph followed and reached for her arm. Jessica turned to him as he asked if she was okay.

"Fine," she said, smiling half-heartedly and glancing at her watch.

"You must be pressed for time, so we'll take a modified tour today and then grab some supper. Okay?"

She nodded.

Something was wrong. Of that he felt sure.

He kept the tour to a minimum, showing her the library, the gym, the counseling corners, and finally the arts and crafts room.

"Oh, how wonderful! I would have *loved* to explore art in a place like this. I'm sure the kids treasure having such a special place. I can tell you love working with them. It suits you," she said, touching his arm gently.

"I like to think I can make a difference in their lives," he said, pausing to take her hand. "I'm glad you like the place, Jess. It feels good to share it with you."

She smiled into his eyes for a brief moment and then glanced again at her watch.

"There's a little café just around the corner. They have great soup and sandwiches. We could split one if you're in a hurry."

Again she nodded, but dropped his hand.

***

"Sit anywhere you'd like, Father Joe," a motherly woman called from behind the counter.

They each ordered a bowl of soup and decided on a sandwich. Joseph brought their food to the table on a tray.

"Tell me more about *A Course in Miracles*," Joseph said as they ate.

"Yes, well, it teaches that people who hurt us usually do so because they've been hurt themselves. When we forgive them, it helps them to realize that they aren't really so bad. They just need to be loved."

"And by being loved, they can learn to love themselves."

"You've got it." She smiled.

"You sound more like a priest than most of the ones I know."

"I'll take that as a compliment. I'm finding that it's much easier to forgive others than it is to forgive myself."

"I know that one," he agreed, grimacing. "God reaches us in a myriad of ways. For you, right now, through this *Course in Miracles,* and, for me, through the Catholic Priests for Change support group. Maybe, just maybe, we can raise awareness about those Church practices that truly hinder parishioners' lives every day."

"What was that you said?"

"Are you okay? You seem distracted somehow."

"I'm okay, just a lot on my mind, I guess. Tell me more—or again. You sound excited."

"I am. Some members of our group actually speak of changing the chastity requirement for priests. Just think of the possibilities if that happened."

"Joseph, you're living in a dream world," she told him, her voice growing louder. "You know the Vatican won't agree to that."

"But—"

Before he could say more, she interrupted. "You made your choice to be a priest, knowing full well what would be required of you." Her voice had grown high pitched and nervous.

"I didn't mean to upset you, Jess. You know how I feel about you."

"No, I don't. How *do* you feel about me?"

"I love you," he said, holding his breath.

They sat staring at one another without speaking.

"Jess," he finally spoke again, "I love you with all my heart. I know I have critical decisions to make about my future, and I think God led me to this group for that very reason."

"I can't get my mind around what you're saying," she whispered, her eyes filling with tears. "I came out here to see the center but also to tell you something."

"What is it, Jess? It sounds serious."

"I'm considering," she finally said, averting her eyes before finishing her sentence, "moving to California."

"California?"

"Yes. My boss told me about an opening in a small museum in Laguna Beach. He has an intimate connection out there. I'd be the principal art curator," she said. "You know it's something I've always wanted to do."

"But California's so far away," he protested.

"Maybe that's a good thing," she said after a noticeable pause. "You need to figure out your life and I need to get on with mine."

"Don't do this, Jess," he pleaded.

"I can't wait any longer for you. As long as I stay near you, I'm putting my life on hold."

"Just give me a little more time, please."

"I've already set up an interview for next week," she explained, her voice trembling. "Please, don't make this harder for me than it already is."

"Jess, please, give this very careful thought. We just found each other again and—"

"And what?" she asked with raised eyebrows, staring through him. "I know you said you love me, and I love you, too, but that usually leads to a couple creating a life together. In this case, you're still essentially unavailable to me. I can't live like this anymore. I need someone who can really be with me."

She broke down and cried. The woman behind the counter looked at them and other customers began whispering.

"I hear you, Jess," he said, taking her hand. "I hate that my indecision is causing you pain, more pain. But the message I'm waiting for isn't clear yet. It's a life-changing decision. Right now, I'd have to break my vows and leave the Church. I'm praying, praying constantly, but I'm still not sure how to proceed," he said quietly, his own eyes moist.

"So that's the way it is," she said, pulling her hand away and standing.

He stood also, but she turned and started to leave.

"Wait. Let me walk you to the train."

"No, Joseph, I need to be alone. Look, I'll call you when I get back from California."

I can't believe I'm losing her again. God, please help me, please answer my prayers.

Jessica

A few weeks later, perched on the edge of a box in the living room of her Manhattan apartment, Jessica sighed at the sight of all her things packed and ready to go, walls bare, suitcases near the door. In the dim light of the fading sun, the room had a cold, eerie feel, causing her to shiver. Everything had happened so fast.

Her interview with Joshua Martin had landed her the job in Laguna Beach. Closing her eyes, she recalled an image of the museum where she would soon be curator. Perched atop a hill, it offered a stunning view of the cove below, where turquoise water kissed a honey-colored beach in ever-changing patterns of tidal ebb and flow. Nearby paths carved into the bluffs ran along the shoreline.

Life will be peaceful there compared to the hustle and bustle of Manhattan and Paris. It's a beautiful place and I'll be in charge of my very own museum.

Although her job wasn't slated to start until January, she'd decided to move to California early enough to familiarize herself with the area. She loved Joseph but had to remove herself from his indecision as soon as she could. She'd rented a small cottage near the center of Laguna Beach village. *Tomorrow's moving day. Time to say goodbye. For now? Forever?*

Miss Suzy rubbed her orange furry self against Jessica's leg.

"Let's get us both some dinner," she said, scooping the cat up in her arms.

Jessica fed Miss Suzy and heated up the last piece of food in the fridge—a slice of pepperoni pizza—for herself.

Returning to the living room with her meager meal, she stared out the window as though trying to memorize the scene she'd soon be leaving. Brushing her tears away and taking a deep breath, she said out loud, "I've got to stand my ground. This is what I need to do to find myself again, and that is that."

***

The next day, after the movers loaded up her belongings, Jessica took one last look at the empty apartment that had been her home. *It's not easy, leaving it behind.* With a deep sigh, she picked up her purse, one large suitcase, and Miss Suzy, who meowed loudly inside her pink carrier.

***

That evening, at the Airport Hilton, she sat in the lobby in her comfortable soft gray slacks and a white angora sweater, waiting for Joseph to arrive. Soon she saw him, making his way toward her, conspicuously without his priest's collar.

"Hi, there," he said, leaning in to kiss her on the cheek. "You look beautiful tonight."

"Hi, yourself," she responded, standing to greet him.

When he reached out to embrace her, she didn't resist.

"I'm going to miss you so much," he said, holding her close.

"I'm going to miss you, too," she whispered, lingering in his arms before pulling gently away and motioning toward the restaurant on the other side of the lobby. "We have a reservation at seven."

They were soon seated at a table by the window. She noticed how the candlelight accentuated the gray at his temples. He looked at her intently, as if attempting to burn her image into his mind. In memory of Paris, they ordered chateaubriand for two and a bottle of French Bordeaux.

"Jess," he began, "it's meant so much to me, being with you these past few months. I can't imagine not having you here."

"It's better this way," she said, trying to sound confident about her decision. "We can't go on trying to be friends when we both know our feelings go so much deeper." She shuddered at her own words, even though they were true.

Lingering over tea, they sat holding each other's hands.

"I'd like to walk you to your room," he said. "I don't want our goodbye to be in a hotel lobby."

"Of course," she said, taking his arm. *I don't want to say goodbye at all, but we must. For now.*

They rode up in the elevator in silence.

Standing outside the door of her room, Joseph held her close and she molded into his arms with no resistance as he reached down to kiss her. When their lips met, she could feel the intensity of his yearning. Her heartbeat fell into a rhythm with his. The more intense it became, the more frightened she felt.

"No," she said, disentangling herself from his embrace. "I can't bear to have you tonight and lose you tomorrow." Unable to stop her tears, she pulled away. "Take care of yourself, Joseph. I'll always love you." She opened the door and walked into the room without looking back, closing the door behind her.

***

The next day, flying cross-country, farther and farther from New York City and Joseph, she saw the endless desert below. *It mirrors the emptiness I feel inside.* Closing her eyes, she remembered the pain in Joseph's eyes just before she'd left him alone outside her door. *Why didn't I make love with him? It could have changed the course of our lives.*

She knew in her heart that it would have only made things more complicated. *Why do other people close to me seem to find partners so easily? Mum and Donald, my father and Luann, even Stephanie and Bob? How could I have fallen in love with a man destined to be a priest?*

She glanced at the title of the big blue book in her lap. *A Course in Miracles.*

If only I could open to receiving the guidance that comes to me. How can I commit to any spiritual practice without that openness, without that trust?

Joseph

Brooklyn

Over the next few weeks, Joseph worked diligently and enthusiastically with the children at the youth center, especially the teens. In quiet moments, he thought of his father, who'd also spent his life counseling kids.

Jessica had become a permanent resident in his mind, heart, and body—even when he knelt to pray. In quiet moments, he allowed his thoughts to flow toward her. *She's the only woman I've ever truly loved. I must be a fool. If she hadn't pulled away from me that night, I'd have broken every vow I've ever made to God.*

In not so quiet moments, after drowning himself in wine and wallowing in self-pity, he cried in the night, "Oh, God, why did you bring her back only to take her away again? I can't stand this anymore. I'm not fit to be a priest, not the Catholic way, with feelings like these."

Yet with each dawning day, he rose, dressed himself, and set about the daily routines. The children, their laughter and tears, their endless questions, temporarily filled the lonely place within his heart as he opened to their worlds and put aside his own concerns. It became increasingly clear that he must get away again to more deliberately consider his options.

"I feel I need a change of assignment," he finally told the bishop. "I don't know what kind of change, but perhaps Monsignor Anthony's good counsel can help me figure it out. We've known each other a long time."

"I certainly won't keep you if you feel you need a change, but, honestly, I believe it will be hard on the kids. They've come to depend upon you. I think we all thought you were very happy at the youth center."

"I have been happy, but, well, my heart is conflicted and the children deserve more, much more than I can give them now. I need time, real time, for reflection."

"It won't be easy to replace you, but I imagine that God will send us the right person. If you believe that the monsignor can offer you the spiritual guidance you need, by all means consult with him."

"Thank you, thank you so much," Joseph said, relieved that he'd finally taken action.

"You'll be missed, Joseph," the bishop said, taking Joseph's hand in both of his own.

***

Mesmerized by the sound of the train's wheels rumbling through the countryside, Joseph closed his eyes and let his thoughts wander. *Am I really doing the right thing? I'm already missing the kids and the Center. I hope the bishop finds the right person to replace me. But I can't wait any longer. I must focus wholeheartedly on coming to a decision about my future.*

When the train pulled into Boston late that afternoon, his mother and stepfather stood at the station waiting for him. He'd be staying with them for a few days before taking a sojourn to Paris. He needed to be where he had been happy with Jessica and where he had left her behind.

***

The next day the entire family gathered in the backyard of Tom and Susan's house. Joseph relished times like these, especially seeing how well his two nephews had turned out, so different and yet so wholesome, Sean soon to be a psychologist and Charlie a high school coach. He realized again how it saddened him to not have a family of his own.

After dinner, Joseph and Tom stole away to the den for another of their brotherly talks.

"You seem uptight, Joe. What's wrong?"

"You're right. I'm tense."

"Talk to me, man."

"Well," Joseph began, "remember the woman I told you about, the one in Paris?"

"The one you had the affair with?"

"That would be the one and only," Joseph said with a wan smile. "I ran into her last spring in New York and we rekindled our friendship. Turns out our feelings are as deep as when we parted years ago, but you know my situation."

"Wow, that's something. How've you handled it?"

"Not so well. Truth is I'm in love with her. She couldn't stand any more of my indecision and took an art curator position in California. I can't blame her, of course, but my feelings have me on edge. I must do something and I'm more confused than ever about the priesthood."

"That's huge. What's your next move?"

"I'll talk with Monsignor Anthony and then … I don't know. It's not just about Jessica, either. I've been going through the motions of being a priest for some time, but I'm in constant conflict. I can't accept and uphold many of the Catholic tenets, especially around necessary abortion and birth control. Personally, I'm struggling with the chastity issue, not to mention marriage and family. I may simply be out of my element. I can see myself as a counselor, a guide, perhaps, but I'm questioning my call to the priesthood. It just isn't working."

"Whew. I feel for you, Joe. It's a tough situation."

"I'm wondering if I became a priest to please Dad, not because I genuinely heard the call."

"Dad did pressure you a lot. Maybe it was his call and not yours."

"You have no idea how much it means to me to hear you say that. Thanks, Tom. Thank you so much," Joseph said, embracing his brother.

Jessica

Laguna Beach

On a chilly Saturday morning in late October, Jessica warmed her hands with a cup of tea while sitting at the small wooden table in the kitchen of her new home. Her eyes scanned her new surroundings: dishes now unpacked and put away, pale yellow walls displaying some of her prints, Miss Suzy snoozing on a cushion in the chair next to her. The peach chintz cushion matched her cat's orange furry body. *What a picture.* She smiled, sneaking off to the bedroom to fetch her camera.

With the morning sunshine pouring through the southeast-facing windows in her living room, the cottage felt warm and cozy. Her eyes fell on the mantle over the small fireplace where she'd placed photos from childhood. She especially liked the one of herself standing between her mother and father. "I hope you two make it here to visit me someday and see my sweet little home," she said out loud, feeling the pang of separation from those early days when they'd lived together as a family.

Her eyes paused on a poster of one of Monet's *Lily Pond* paintings set off by the soft green walls. *It brings Paris to California.* The thought made her smile. She'd also placed some personal sculptures on a low table under the picture window; abstract pieces mostly, but also the very sensual Embracing Couple. She'd admired the original at MoMA and bought a replica of it, just after, she suddenly remembered, her first encounter with Joseph in New York. Tears filled her eyes as that bittersweet memory played out again in her mind.

But that was then and this is now, a firm voice in her head reminded her. Brushing her tears away, she looked around and admired her eclectic decorative style, pleased with the comfortable home she'd made for herself. *I needed this time to settle in before starting work.*

Later that morning, wrapped in a light wool shawl, she strolled through the quaint streets of little Laguna Beach village, marveling at how she needed the rarely employed outer garment to stay warm. An image of Stephanie, bundled up to stave off the cold autumn wind, flashed through her mind.

Passing by several art galleries along the streets, Jessica followed her nose into the French bakery, feasting her eyes on rows of fancy, luscious looking pastries, but ordering her usual, a chocolate éclair and a cup of black tea.

Remembering the *patisseries* in Paris brought her thoughts again to

Joseph.

Stop thinking about him, she scolded herself. She'd made him promise not to call. And he hadn't, not once in the nearly full month since she'd left New York.

Leaving the bakery, she continued her walk, passing the library and post office, appreciating the row of shops and sense of authentic neighborhood. *Everything I need is here. I'm determined to make this work.* Though she'd passed the small, lovely steepled building in front of her a number of times, this time its decorative sign, Unity Church of Laguna Beach, called to her. She couldn't believe it when she read the announcement at the bottom: *A Course in Miracles* group meets on Thursday nights at six o'clock. All welcome.

This feels like synchronicity. I've wanted to learn more about the Course. From what she'd heard the ecumenical Unity Church emphasized a metaphysical view of Christ's teachings.

***

The next day, with the intention of hiring an assistant, Jessica settled into Joshua Martin's office, soon to be her own, at The Sea View Museum of Art to begin conducting her interviews. The first applicant was a young woman named Holly Simpson. According to her application, Holly would be graduating from UC Berkeley in January, with a Bachelor's degree in Business and a Master's in Fine Art—not the art history degree Jessica had specified, but, she sensed a head for business could be a supportive plus, if the young woman's knowledge of art impressed her.

"Have we met before?" Holly asked after introductions.

"I don't know. I just moved here from New York. I worked at MoMA before coming to California."

"That's where it was. We met when my Art History class from Berkeley was visiting. You were our guide, remember? I was really impressed with your knowledge of art and how you carried yourself. It was you who inspired me to apply for a museum job."

"Now I remember you. Of course. You approached me after the tour to inquire about my work."

"That was me," Holly said, suddenly shy. "Forgive me for saying so, but I don't believe in accidents."

"You mean like it's our destiny to work together? Now that's an ingenious interview technique." Jessica laughed openly with delight.

"Maybe, but in any case, I'm glad our paths have crossed again."

"Me, too. Let's see, basically I need someone who has a passion for art and can discuss it with the people who visit here. I also need someone who's capable of managing things when I'm out in the community promoting the museum and raising funds. Do you have any professional experience?"

Holly looked up at the ceiling as if thinking about the question and finally said, "I worked as an assistant to Dr. Evans in the Art Department this past year. I took care of the class whenever he was away giving lectures in the community. Sounds like this job will be something like that, right?"

"Well, yes, there's a similarity."

"You can request my placement file at Berkeley. The letters of recommendation should be there. I brought copies of my transcripts with me. I won't complete my Master's thesis until January, but I trust I'll get my degree. My supervisor has been supportive of my work, even if he doesn't understand it." She pulled out some papers from a folder and gave them to Jessica.

"Well, you certainly are prepared, aren't you? 'Fine Art as Symbolic Healing' sounds fascinating. I look forward to hearing more about it."

"Does that mean I'm hired?" Holly asked, her joy at the thought evident.

"I think it does, as long as your references check out, and I'm sure they will. Welcome to Sea View."

***

On Thursday evening, Jessica slipped into the community room adjacent to the Unity Church, carrying her *Course in Miracles* text. A couple approached her, warmly introduced themselves as Tim and Marcia Banning, leaders of the group, and invited her to join the circle. Six of the twelve seats had been occupied. Jessica sat next to an elderly woman who held the *Course* text in her lap. They exchanged smiles as more participants entered the room and filled the remaining seats.

Tim and Marcia brought two more chairs into the circle for themselves. Tim asked that each person introduce themselves for the benefit of new members of the group. Jessica smiled at each one, but was particularly drawn to a rather large-framed man whose chiseled features, olive skin, and flashing dark eyes made him stand out. *He looks Italian.* When his eyes met hers, she quickly turned away, feeling her face warm.

"For our newcomers," Marcia said, "let me point out the formatting of most *Course* books. The first section is referred to as the Text. That's the section we cover in class. We call the second section the Workbook. It includes daily lessons for reading and practicing on your own. The last section is the Teachers' Manual. It provides answers to many student questions."

"Before we begin," Tim said, "are there any questions from your reading this past week?" Since no one brought up a question, he directed them to turn to the section in the Text entitled "The Gift of Freedom."

Jessica listened carefully as each participant read one of the passages aloud then paused for questions or comments. When it was her turn, she read: "Light does not attack darkness, but it does shine it away. If my light goes with you everywhere, you shine it away with me."

She paused to consider the words.

"What does that passage mean to you, Jessica?" Tim asked.

"Well, the words comfort me. Maybe we're never really alone."

The woman beside her said, "I lost my husband three years ago and I still cry myself to sleep at night."

"Perhaps it would help you to read this passage before going to bed," Marcia suggested.

The next person's reading suggested that by freeing others we actually free ourselves.

"That makes sense to me," Jessica said, "but it can be painfully difficult to let go of the ones we truly love."

She and the woman who had spoken about her husband shared a smile.

Now that I've freed Joseph to do what he needs to do, I'm free, too. Why does that make me so sad?

***

As Jessica turned to leave, she was stopped by a touch on her elbow. The man she'd noticed earlier extended his hand. "Ken Abbrazizzi," he said in a husky voice. "Welcome to our group."

"Jessica Taylor. It's good to be here," she said, feeling her cheeks warming again and hoping he wouldn't notice.

"Would you like a cup of tea?" he suggested with a smile.

"I'd love one," she said, following him into the kitchen.

"How long have you been reading the *Course*?" he asked while pouring.

"Oh, just a short while. I heard about it in a lecture last year in New York and bought the book, but I've only scanned through it casually until now."

"I'm still a novice, too."

"Every sentence seems packed with layers of meaning."

"I know. I've found myself rereading sentences two and three times. No wonder I haven't gotten too far."

"I know. That's so true."

"I love your accent."

"Why, thank you. I was raised in London."

"I would have guessed that. My parents are first-generation Italian. I was born and raised in Chicago. How long have you been living in the U.S.?"

"Since 1976, about thirteen years, but the accent seems here to stay."

"That's fine with me." He smiled.

"You're too kind."

After an awkward few moments, Ken asked, "Do you live in the neighborhood?"

"I do and I love being able to walk wherever I need to go. You?"

"I drive up from San Clemente each week just for the meetings. I met Marcia and Tim when they gave a talk at the Unity Church down there and I've been attending ever since."

"Well, it was lovely to meet you, Ken," she said, putting down her cup and turning to leave. I'll probably see you next week."

"You, too, Jessica. I'll walk you out."

Out in the front courtyard, Ken said, "Maybe we could grab a bite before or after the meeting sometime, talk about the reading, you know?"

"Sounds good," she said lightly, offering her hand as goodbye.

He held it a bit too long, placing his other hand also on hers. Jessica pulled away gently, with a simple, "Good night, Ken."

She felt his eyes following her as she left. Something about him made her uneasy. He was very intense. His hands on hers had sent a shiver through her. *Is this attraction or foreboding?*

Walking home, she continued to wonder about Ken. He was kind of exciting. She'd been on hold, hoping that Joseph would make a decision about his future, even reconsider his call to the priesthood.

Isn't it better for me to move on, before I get hurt again?

André

Provence

Since graduation, André had been working as a freelance photographer. He'd just completed a shoot in Arles for a Paris publication. He'd come down to Provence from Paris to see his parents and Pierre for a few days. He also wanted to pay off his motorcycle so he could travel the way he was born to—in the open air. Touching the stones in his necklace, he sighed deeply. *It's been three years since I got this necklace. It's high time I found out where it came from and who I really am.*

After making his last payment on the bike, he tucked his photography equipment into the saddlebags as best he could and spent the afternoon riding through the beloved scenery near his boyhood home. He could hardly wait to show his bike to Pierre.

Before driving up the hill to his family's vineyard, he cut the motor for an instant and sat still. *What a stunning place to live, even in winter.* Smoke rose from the chimney, giving his home a storybook look. *If I had to be adopted, I'm glad I ended up with these parents in this beautiful place. I do hope Mamà and Papa will accept that I'm ready to find out about my natural parents.* Still touching the necklace, he took a few deep breaths for courage.

As he turned into the old dirt driveway, his parents ran out to meet him. Mamà had her arms out, ready to enfold him, and Papa wore a grin that lit up his face. "We heard you coming," his father said.

After hugs all around, André pulled his camera out of its case. "Stay right there. I want to get you just as you are." His parents stood arm in arm in front of the house and he snapped a few shots before turning to capture the last golden rays of early evening sun.

"Come, sit by the fire and get warm," his father said. "I'll get the wine." He soon returned with a bottle of Beaujolais. "I think you'll like this."

"I'm sure. It's so good to be home."

"We've missed you, sweetheart," his mother said. "And we're so proud of you. A professional photographer. It seems only yesterday that we were sending you off to school in Paris."

"It's hard to believe, isn't it?" he replied.

"You look happy," she said. "But I do wish you weren't living so far away."

"Don't worry, I'll always make time to come back home to see you."

"We're going to Mass tomorrow morning. Are you coming with us?" his father asked.

"I don't think so," André told him. "I'm really tired from my trip. Besides, I'm not feeling very Catholic these days."

"What do you mean?" his father asked with a look of surprise on his face.

"Let's just say I'm exploring some other religious philosophies."

"What kind of religious philosophies? You're still a Christian, aren't you?" The concern in the older man's voice was clear.

"Could we not talk about religion just now? I'd like to take a shower if that's okay with you two."

"He's just gotten here," his mother exclaimed. "Give him time to settle in." She turned to André with a gentle smile and a knowing look. "Take your shower, dear, and I'll get dinner ready."

He could feel his father's eyes on him as he left the room.

His mother had encouraged André to think for himself. Likewise, she'd never tried to change her husband. "Let him be himself," she would always say. *I'm really a lot like her, even though I'm adopted.*

***

Later that evening, after dinner, his father raised the topic again. "So, I'm curious to know more about the religious philosophies you spoke of earlier."

"Only if you want to talk about it," his mother chimed in.

"It's just that I don't believe that one religion can be right for everyone. For example, what about the Protestants? They can't all be wrong because they aren't Catholics, can they?"

"Yes, they can be wrong," his father said matter-of-factly.

"Well, I'm exploring other belief systems to find what's right for me."

"So what have you found out?" his mother asked.

"I attended a weekend retreat with a Vietnamese monk named Thict Nhat Han. He has a monastery here in France."

"What can a Vietnamese monk teach you that could possibly be relevant to your life?" his father questioned.

"He says it's in the stillness that one can come to know the truth of one's being. So, I'm learning how to meditate."

"André," his mother said, "I think that's great. You know how I spend time alone in prayer. I find that much more useful than going to the priest."

"Seems like you two are teaming up against me," his father said, raising his voice a bit. "I was just going to suggest that you, my son, do talk to the priest."

"I don't want to talk to the priest," André said, rising from his chair.

"Henri, André's just gotten here," she admonished her husband. "Sit down, son. Let's change the subject, shall we? When do you think you'll be displaying some of your photographs?"

"I've been looking into that," he said, relieved that his mother had intervened before the conversation got further heated, "and I've made a connection with a small gallery in Montmartre. The owner likes my work and thinks I'm almost ready to have a show of my own. He suggested I come up with a theme and create an exhibit around it for him to consider."

"That's sounds very promising. Papa and I would love to come see your work in a gallery."

"Are you sure you'd want to travel all the way to Paris?"

"We may be old," Henri joked, "but we're not dead yet."

"I didn't mean to be impolite." André smiled. "It's just that you two are such homebodies. I'm surprised, that's all."

"When your show is ready," Henri said in a delighted voice, "we'll be there."

"Thanks, both of you," he said sincerely, standing and leaning to kiss each of them. "And now, forgive me, but I've got to get some rest."

"We'll see you in the morning, son," his mother said. "Let me know if you need anything." She gave him a look that told him she understood his questioning heart.

André retired to his room upstairs. The familiar bed he'd slept in since childhood sat next to the window, covered with one of his mother's handmade quilts, an always welcoming sight. On the wall by the window hung an old poster of a red Yamaha motorcycle. *Dreams can come true.* He smiled, climbing into bed and turning out the light.

Just as he'd done almost every night since he was a child, he leaned on the windowsill and gazed out at the vast night sky, filled now with millions of stars. He fingered the mysterious necklace around his neck, wondering about its significance. Tomorrow, in a private moment, he'd broach the subject of his adoption with his mother. No need to upset his father again. *Maybe by locating my natural parents, I'll better understand myself.*

***

The next day, while his father showered, André helped his mother clean up the breakfast dishes.

"Mamà, I don't want to upset you, but I think I'd like to find out more about my birth parents."

"André, you know how much your father and I love you, just as if you'd been born to us."

"Yes, Mamà, I know that in my heart. And I love you in the same way. I'm curious, that's all. It's the seeker in me, you understand."

"I do. It's okay, son. It's only natural for you to wonder about your roots."

Lifting the necklace away from his chest, he continued, "Did the adoption agency tell you anything about this that might help me locate the woman who left it with me?"

"Only that your mother was English and wanted you to have it when you were old enough to appreciate it." She turned to look directly into his eyes. "The fleur-de-lis, it's so very French. I wondered why an English woman would have it."

"I believe it's used in other countries, too, for special insignias, coats of arms, and so forth."

"Yes, and," she said, reaching out to touch the center of his necklace, "I remember my grandmother always wore a brooch with a fleur-de-lis in its center. I think it might have had these same colors embedded in the petals—blue, gold, and pink. I wonder what happened to it. She even wore it at her funeral. It was the first time I'd seen a dead person. I tried not to look but when I saw the brooch pinned to her blouse, I felt better somehow. It made her look just like she'd always looked. I was grateful I could remember her that way."

"When I'm upset about something," he said, "I touch my necklace and, like you said, it makes me feel better somehow."

"I love you so much, André," his mother said, reaching out her arms.

"I love you, too, Mamà."

"It's time to go," his father's booming voice called from the front room, startling both of them. "Are you ready, Jacqueline?"

"I'll be there in just a minute, Henri," she answered, brushing a tear from her eye and giving André another quick hug. "I'll speak to your father about this after Mass. Then, if you still want to go, we'll give you the directions to the adoption agency in the morning."

"We're going to be late," Henri called out again, his voice becoming irritated.

"Coming," his mother shouted back, smiling and rolling her eyes at André. "You know your father loves you in his own stubborn way."

André smiled, too, knowing she was right.

***

The next morning at the adoption agency, Sister Maria held André's file and gazed up at him over her horn-rimmed glasses. "Your mother's name is listed as Jessica Taylor. She told us your name was André. Now that you're over eighteen, you're entitled to know."

Jessica's a pretty name.

"Do your records say anything about my father?"

"I'm sorry. There's no mention of him."

"Do you have any other information that would help me find my mother?"

"It says here that she was from London. It also says she left a necklace of some kind with you."

"That would be this one," he said, pulling the necklace out from beneath his shirt.

"That's an interesting piece of jewelry. It's really beautiful," she said. "I've never seen anything like it."

"Neither have I," he said, leaning in toward the desk. "May I see my mother's handwriting?"

"Certainly," she said, showing him her signature.

"Do you mind if I have a copy of that page?"

"Well, I guess it couldn't hurt. We're obligated to help our children find their parents, if that's what they want to do when they grow up."

After leaving the agency, André folded the paper and tucked it in his pocket before straddling his motorcycle. He stopped by Pierre's house on the way home. Pierre had lived on his own for a while but had recently moved back with his mother and siblings after his dad died.

"Come out for a ride," André called to his friend, the roaring sound of his motorcycle bringing Pierre running out the front door.

"Man, this is hot. When did you get here?"

"Yesterday," he said and off they went, racing with the wind.

When they returned to Pierre's house, they walked down to the creek where they'd spent so many days as children.

"I went to the Catholic adoption agency today," André said, bringing the necklace out from under his shirt. The afternoon sun made the gems sparkle. "The nun in charge told me my mother's name. She's from London." He pulled out the folded paper and handed it to Pierre.

"Jessica Taylor. That sounds English, all right. Are you going to look for her?"

"Not right away. But when a shoot comes up in London, I'll seriously consider it, though I wouldn't know where to start."

"London's a big city. There are probably a lot of women with that name."

"Maybe I'll photograph this necklace and put an ad in the paper," he said, only half joking.

"I don't think that's a good idea. There's no telling how many kooks would answer an ad like that."

"I guess you're right. I'll figure something out."

"Be sure to keep me posted," Pierre said.

André rode home, nervous but excited about his upcoming quest. A thousand questions skittered through his mind. *Even if I find my mother, what will she be like? Will she be glad or sorry to see me?* When he thought about the way she'd abandoned him, he shuddered. *Why am I even looking for someone who'd abandon her child?*

Jessica

Laguna Beach

Jessica busied herself making what she hoped would be a superb pumpkin cheesecake. It was her contribution to Thanksgiving dinner with her new friend Ken, at his son's home in San Diego. She'd gone out with him a few times after the *Course in Miracles* class, discussing the *Course* and sharing a bit about their lives.

While lining the pan, Jessica recalled their conversation about his divorce and how cold he'd sounded toward his ex-wife—and his daughter.

"I can't do anything about it," he'd said in a huffy tone. "Marlene sided with her mother when we got divorced and hasn't forgiven me for what she sees as my breaking up the family."

Married with two children, Marlene lived in Chicago, where Ken's ex-wife also lived. Ken had not even seen his grandchildren since leaving the marriage and moving to California. *I can't imagine having grandchildren and not seeing them.* Then it dawned on her that her own son was grown now. Someday, she, too, could have grandchildren and not even know they existed. *That's so sad I can hardly stand it.* Her heart ached.

She finished the cheesecake, then put on her favorite cream-colored silk blouse, throwing a turquoise print shawl around her shoulders. She would meet Ken in San Clemente and then he would drive them to his son Fred's place in San Diego. *At least he's remained on good terms with his son.*

***

"So, did you hire your assistant yet?" Ken asked as they drove down the coast in his shiny black Mercedes.

"Yes, I did. It's funny, we'd actually met in New York when she came to MoMA with her class from Berkeley. What an enthusiastic young woman! I think she'll be great."

"It's January, isn't it? When you begin?"

"Yes, and I can hardly wait. Of course I've enjoyed having time to get settled but I'm ready to get back to work. And the museum is absolutely beautiful. Not only does it house fantastic pieces of art but the location is stunning. It even has a view of the ocean. I feel very fortunate."

"I can see that you're quite passionate about this opportunity."

"It's true, I am." She paused. "Tell me about *your* work, Ken. You said real estate, I believe. Are you a broker?"

"Not exactly. I'm more of an investor. I've been into buying houses, upgrading them, and then flipping them for some years. Now that I've made pretty good money with houses, I'm moving into commercial real estate. That's where the real cash is."

"Do you enjoy your work?"

"There's nothing more satisfying than making a successful pitch, you know, convincing people to see things my way. I get such a high from that."

"Sounds like you can be very persuasive when you want to be."

"I guess you could say I'm a born salesman," he said, giving her a suggestive look.

I'd better watch out for this guy. Turning her head to gaze out the window, she changed the subject. "How are you coming with the daily lessons in *A Course in Miracles*?"

"Funny you asked. I'm having trouble with the idea of giving up my ego. I certainly don't want other people to walk all over me, especially in business."

"I don't think we're being encouraged to *give up* our egos, rather realize that we're *more than* our egos. It's about not identifying with our egos, as if that's all we are. I find it freeing to think of myself as part of a bigger picture, not only this person called Jessica Taylor."

"Hey, don't downplay Jessica Taylor. I happen to like her very much."

"So, tell me about your son," she said, changing the subject.

"Fred's a great guy. He's doing well in advertising, works for a very reputable agency. He's a good salesman—like his dad."

"How old is he?"

"He's twenty-eight now, and pretty serious about his girlfriend, Elena. She teaches school in San Diego. Nice lady."

"I'm looking forward to meeting them."

"Well, we'll be there soon. Just a few more beach towns to go through. They live in a condo. Nice area, not far from the ocean."

***

Fred met them at the door. "Come in, you two," he said, slapping his dad on the back and turning to greet Jessica. "Elena's in the kitchen. We bought all the food at one of our favorite local restaurants and we're just heating it up."

"Great idea," Jessica said. "I brought dessert." *He looks a lot like his father*. They met Elena in the kitchen. She was a petite brunette with a very sweet disposition. Everyone pitched in and helped, and before long Thanksgiving dinner was on the table.

"Hear, hear," Fred said, raising his wine glass. "A welcome toast to you, Jessica. Dad has told us so much about you. All good, by the way."

"It was so kind of you to include me in your family gathering."

"How's business going?" Ken interrupted.

"Great," Fred answered his father, then turned back to Jessica, "Basically, I go out and obtain contracts, new clients, for the advertising firm I work for."

"A goddam regional sales rep for one of the finest ad agencies on this coast," Ken said, beaming at his son.

"That's because I learned from *you*, Dad."

"I guess you could say I've done pretty well," Ken said.

After an awkward pause in the conversation, Elena spoke. "Since today is Thanksgiving, why don't we share something that we're grateful for? It's a tradition in *my* family."

"That's easy for me," Fred said, reaching over to hug her. "I'm grateful to have you in my life."

"Oh, Fred, that's so sweet," Elena said, giving him a little kiss on the cheek. "And I'm grateful for you."

"Looks like moving in together was a good thing for you two lovebirds," Ken said, raising his glass.

"The best," Fred said with a big smile, giving Elena's shoulders a squeeze before turning to Jessica. "Dad tells me you're an art curator. That sounds like a great profession."

"It is and I love it. But I haven't actually started yet. In New York, I was an assistant to the curator at the Museum of Modern Art. In January, I'll begin my first job as an actual curator, and, speaking of gratitude, I couldn't be more excited and grateful about this opportunity."

"I love my job, too," Elena said, smiling. "I'm teaching a class of first grade students who are the most amazing kids I've ever met. There's nothing more rewarding than hearing the excitement in their voices when they discover they're actually reading. Now if they'd just be quiet when I ask them to."

"I admire people who go into teaching," Jessica said. "I bet we've all had teachers who have influenced us in a positive way."

"I hope I can make a difference," Elena said quietly.

"My sister Marlene is a teacher, too," Fred added. "But she's staying at home right now while the kids are little."

"How old are they?" Jessica asked.

"They're twins, a boy and a girl. They're about four now, aren't they, Dad?"

"Something like that," Ken mumbled, abruptly pushing back his chair and standing. "How about some more wine?"

"I guess any talk of Marlene is off limits," Fred said, his voice growing noticeably louder as Ken started for the kitchen.

"Fred, don't start," Elena admonished, getting up to help Ken with the wine.

"If only he'd bite the bullet and go see her," Fred said to Jessica, "they might be able to work things out."

Jessica remained quiet.

"I heard that remark," Ken said, returning to the table, Elena close behind with an open bottle of Pinot Gris. "Marlene doesn't want to see me and I don't want to see her. Can't you get that through your thick skull?"

"Stop it, you two," Elena exclaimed. "It's Thanksgiving, after all. Why don't we finish our dinner, enjoy it, and then get back to what we're thankful for?"

After a long silence while they ate, Jessica surprised herself by saying to Ken, "It's your turn, I think. What are you thankful for?"

He looked startled as if from sleep, stammered, and finally said, "I'm grateful to be sitting at this table today with all of you. The food is good, but ... I remain disappointed that my son cannot face facts."

Elena reached to take Fred's hand. Jessica stood suddenly and asked, "How about some pumpkin cheesecake?" The tense atmosphere lifted as Jessica picked up her beautiful pie from the sideboard and set it in the center of the table.

***

"Your pie was quite a hit," Ken said on the drive back towards San Clemente.

She could only muster a basic "Thanks," her breath short. Ken's attitude at dinner had unnerved her. After a few minutes, she added, "Too bad dessert didn't really help. Everyone still seemed uncomfortable."

"The problem is," Ken said, "Fred just won't give it up. His sister and I don't see eye to eye, and never will. That's all there is to it."

"But she's your *daughter*. Wouldn't you like to mend things with her?"

"I really don't want to talk about it," he said, his voice hardening.

"Well, I guess that ends that," she said in a clipped tone.

"Look, Jessica," Ken said, his tone softening. "I like you. You know that. I don't want to argue with you." He reached for her hand.

She removed it from his grasp as gently as possible and gathered her shawl around her. "It seems cool in here."

He shook his head and turned on the heater. They rode the rest of the way in silence.

"Here we are," Ken finally said. "This is our exit."

"That was a quick trip," she said, inwardly relieved.

"Would you like to come in for a while?" he asked, pulling into his driveway.

"No, but thanks for including me today," she said, extending her hand.

He pulled her close instead and looked deeply into her eyes. She tried to resist, but his desire stirred her body. When he kissed her, hard, she let him. He drew her even closer, kissing her all over her face, one hand on her thigh. She became uncomfortable and pulled away.

"Ken, I can't. Please, I'd better go," she said, catching her breath.

"Oh, Christ, really? I wish you'd stay."

"I'm not ready for this."

"Okay, then I'll see you Thursday," he managed with an awkward half-laugh.

"I … I might not be there. I don't know. I need to start my Christmas shopping. Posting to Britain takes much longer. And, Ken, honestly, I need some space."

"I hope you don't mean that," Ken said with a worried look on his face.

"I really must go now. Good night, Ken."

She opened her door and got out of the car.

***

Why did I let him kiss me that way? He's not my kind of guy at all. But I enjoyed it. What's wrong with me, anyway?

That night, she wrote in her journal: *I like Ken's son. He doesn't seem to be angry like his dad. Ken's anger scares me! Still, there's definitely chemistry between us.*

If only Joseph were here —for that I would be thankful. I wonder how he is. It's as if we never came together again, like it wasn't real and never will be. Ken is here … in the flesh.

Didn't I learn anything from my mistakes with Jim? Chemistry isn't everything! I'll just read the text and skip classes for a while.

***

A few days later, Jessica's mother and stepfather invited her to spend Christmas with them. She'd already sent off their packages and things for her dad, Luann, and the kids. She was happy to be able to travel light.

Jessica decided to visit her father's family first for a few days, enjoying the children and watching him interact with them.

After Christmas but before New Year's she sat with her mother and Donald, enjoying teatime the afternoon before her planned departure. She wanted to be in her own home to start the new year. The shrill ring of the phone startled them as they sat relaxed by the fire. Since it sat on the table next to her, Jessica answered.

"Your dad had a stroke," Luann said in a breathless voice. "He's in the hospital."

"What? When? What hospital? How is he?"

Luann's jumbled words relayed the necessary information, suggesting that the stroke had been mild.

"Are you all right, Luann?"

"I think I must be in shock. I was terrified when he collapsed."

"I can only imagine." Covering the mouthpiece, "Dad's had a stroke—a mild one, Luann says."

"A stroke!" her mum exclaimed.

"He's in the hospital," she told them, turning her attention back to Luann. "I'll be there as soon as I can."

***

Later that evening, Jessica sat with her dad in the hospital. The stroke had affected his left side. Being left-handed, he was having difficulty eating, so she was helping him.

"Thanks for coming, Jess."

"I'm so sorry this happened to you."

"At least I get to see you again before you go," he said with a chuckle.

"Not the best of circumstances, but I'm glad I'm here."

"Me, too," he said, grasping her hand. "I'm lucky this happened at home and not during a performance."

"Dad, I'm sorry to ask, but when are you going to retire?"

"Not until they kick me out. I'm only sixty-eight."

"Only sixty-eight? You say that as if you're twenty-four." She smiled and poured him some milk.

"I'll be back on my feet in no time. By the way, how's that new job of yours?"

"It hasn't exactly started yet. Not until I get back. But I'm really happy about it; it's such a good fit for me—an impressive collection in a beautiful setting with lots of possibilities. Why don't you come for a visit?"

"My sweet Jess, I wish you weren't so far away. We haven't had much time together, have we?"

"No, we haven't, Dad. You've had a busy life of your own and so have I." She lowered her eyes, recalling the many times in the past she'd wished he'd been available to her.

"I know I haven't been the best father to you," he said, as if reading her mind, "but I've always loved you."

"Sometimes it doesn't feel like you do," she admitted, fighting back her tears. "If you'd just call me every now and then ...." Choked up, it was hard for her to speak, but she needed to ask, "Why do I have to be the one to call every time?"

"Dear Jess, I'm so sorry."

***

Jessica called Clay and asked him to stay on at the museum until she could return. She needed more time with her father. For three days she held his arm as they walked together up and down the hospital hallway.

"Didn't you worry about me, Dad, when you left us for Luann?" she suddenly asked one afternoon.

"Oh, honey," he whispered, hanging his head.

"I'm sorry, Dad, I don't mean to make you feel bad. I guess it's a little girl's question."

They sat down on a bench by the window.

"I didn't worry because I knew your mother would take good care of you. I was selfish. We've been through it, Jess. Please let it go. People change."

"I hear you. I want to. It's just that it still hurts. It's only now, since you've been sick, that you've even shared how you feel."

"That's true. I've struggled to express my feelings, most men struggle with that. Don't they?"

"Not all men."

"Oh, really? Sounds like you know that firsthand. Well, that's how I felt with Luann, like we could talk, connect, in words ... and in silence. I didn't have that with your mother. With her, everything was my fault. You can't imagine how difficult that was for me."

"I'm sorry, Dad," she said, her heart softening. "I know Mum can be difficult. Sometimes, growing up, I felt more like the mother in our relationship than the daughter."

"Really?"

She nodded her head. "Of course, she's much better now. She helped me out tremendously when Jim and I divorced. But that wasn't always the case."

"I want you to know that my leaving had nothing to do with you," he said, looking at her intently.

"Thanks for telling me that," she said. "I just wish you'd told me when I was young."

"I'm telling you now," he whispered.

That evening, Jessica wrote in her journal: *It felt good to finally have some time with Dad. How sad it has taken a stroke to bring it about! He didn't exactly say it but I sensed he didn't feel truly close to Mum, as if they didn't fit together.*

Joseph and I fit together, not just sexually, like with Jim, or possibly Ken. Joseph and I are good friends. In Paris, when we made love, we were one being and, at the same time, part of something bigger, something more. I've never felt that kind of union with any other man. But he isn't here. Must I learn to be happy alone? Or wait? Or not? I have so much to learn!

André

Paris
January, 1989

André hung the last piece of his first photo exhibit, "The Children of Paris," on the wall of the *Galerie d' le Beau*, a Montmartre gallery owned by his new friend Anton Deschamps. He'd captured the many moods—joyful, sad, angry, lonely—of children he'd seen throughout Paris and its outskirts. Doors would open in two hours. He hoped his parents would make it on time.

He stood before one of his favorites, young boy crouched on the steps of an upscale flat while a fashionable woman, who appeared to be his mother, argued with a man off to the side. The faraway look on the child's face still moved him. The adults in the scene, obviously caught up in their own problems, remained oblivious to the boy.

"Is everything ready?" Anton asked, bringing him back to the present moment.

"I think so," he answered nervously. When he saw the staff usher in his parents, along with Pierre, he ran over to embrace them.

People drifted into the gallery, filling it comfortably. A young, pixie-ish woman circulated among the group, carrying a tray of small sandwiches, her bright smile lighting up the room. Another offered plastic cups of champagne. André milled about, eavesdropping on the comments.

"What an adorable child!"

"How utterly sad this one looks. Makes me want to cry."

"This one looks a lot like my granddaughter. Isn't she beautiful?"

After the show, Anton approached him, clearly pleased with the turnout and sales. "You've charmed them! Please, brother, stand over here by the first row of photos. The local newspaper wants to take your picture."

André smiled obligingly at the camera, his heart full. This was the first time he'd been photographed with his work—and for the newspaper, no less.

"You are not only a photographer, you are an artist," André's mother gushed, hugging him and then giving him a warm pat on his cheek after the photograph had been taken. "I'm so proud of you."

"Well done, son," his father echoed, embracing him as well.

"Looks like you're on your way," Pierre agreed.

"I'm so happy you could all be here," André said with a relieved sigh. "It means more to me than you know."

Since his studio apartment was too small to accommodate everyone, André had booked reasonable hotel rooms nearby, one for his parents and another for himself and Pierre. After a celebratory dinner, they all headed back to retire. It had truly been a beautiful evening.

"I believe congratulations are in order," Pierre stated in a formal tone after they'd entered their room.

"Thank you, thank you," André said animatedly, as if addressing a crowded room before bowing deeply.

Like a magician, Pierre produced a bottle of Burgundy from his suitcase.

"All right!" André exclaimed with a huge grin, unwrapping two plastic cups he found on the bathroom counter, his shoulders releasing tension he'd been unaware of until that moment. He realized how very much he'd missed his friend.

With the pop of the cork, the evening began anew.

Loosening shirts and kicking off shoes, they each claimed a bed, plopping down to catch up. The two laughed and shared until the conversation shifted to quieter tones. André's mind again returned to the haunting image that had been troubling him beneath the surface all evening, stealing the smile from his face.

Pierre gave him a curious look.

"It's weird," he admitted, sitting up cross-legged on the bed. "One of my photos haunts me, makes me wonder about my natural parents, who they are, why they left me for adoption."

Pierre stood and gave him a reassuring pat on the shoulder, pulling another bottle out of his suitcase before sitting on the other bed, facing him. "I'm sure they'd be proud of you tonight if they knew what you've accomplished. *Any* parents would be."

Holding up his cup with one hand, André toyed with the gems on his necklace with the other. "Even though I have no clue what I'll find, on assignment in London next month I want to look for Jessica Taylor."

They pretended to clink cups and took a sip. With a long, knowing look, Pierre said, "I wish you luck with that, my friend."

"Let's change the subject, okay?" André said, tucking the necklace under his shirt. "I want to hear about life in the vineyard."

"I'm having the time of my life cultivating grapes and making good wine. Who could ask for more?" Pierre replied with gusto. "Your dad is a great teacher."

Something about Pierre's excitement gnawed at his heart. "That's ... fantastic," he managed to say, averting his eyes.

"You don't look very happy," Pierre noted, pouring them both more wine.

"It's just that ... well ... you know, it feels awkward not to be the one working with Papa."

"Look, buddy, if you've changed your mind, just let me know. I can get a job in another vineyard, no problem."

"No, no. You know I love being a photographer. It's right that you're the one working with Papa and not me, but I still am aware that I've hurt Papa."

They sat, lost in their own thoughts for a while, then looked at each other in a moment of brotherhood.

Pierre's eyes grew moist. "I guess we're both fulfilling our dreams," he said gently, raising his cup and downing its entire contents this time.

"*Vive la différence*," André echoed, smiling at his friend and doing the same.

Joseph

Joseph wandered through the majestic Notre Dame Cathedral, absorbing the history and grandeur of its creation and relishing the sacredness of its magnificent interior paintings and sculptures. He'd decided to return to Paris in hopes of making his decision, once and for all, about the priesthood.

He knelt to pray before a statue of the Virgin Mary, her invisible, loving Presence enveloping him. He poured out his feelings of profound love for God and his deep need for guidance, remaining until he'd released the concerns of his heart, then straightening, drained and yet somehow filled with peace. At last, God was with him. He wasn't alone in his quest to understand the meaning of his life. He would be shown—in God's time—what path to take into the future. Of this he was certain.

Back at the Hotel Louvre, he picked up a newspaper in the lobby and carried it with him into the tiny lift barely large enough for two people. *This hotel must be for couples only.* He smiled inwardly.

When he exited the lift, a hall light flickered on above his head. *The French are so thrifty, compared to Americans.* Unlocking the door to his room, he chuckled at its small size. The double bed, covered in a red, flowered chintz bedspread, took up most of the space, with a small desk and chair somehow crowded into the corner near the window.

He squeezed his tall body into the chair by the desk and spread out the newspaper, scanning the headlines. *My French still isn't very good. I'm not going to get much of the news this way.* Flipping to the Arts section, he scanned for exhibits that might be of interest. *Maybe I'll go to Montmartre.* He remembered when he and Jess had their portrait drawn there by one of the street artists. *I feel her presence all around me today. This was our city.*

His eyes fell upon a haunting image of a child, a young boy, his longing palpable. "The Children of Paris, André Casal's first photography exhibit, now on display at the *Galerie d' le Beau*." *This looks worthwhile.* He scribbled down the address.

***

The next day, Joseph strolled around the *Galerie d' le Beau*, impressed with Casal's exhibit, the photos of children mesmerizing, touching him deeply. *He's truly captured their emotions and inner life. Reminds me of some of my kids at the youth center in Brooklyn.*

At the end of the exhibit, a large poster of the photographer sat on an easel. *Sure looks young to be such a serious photographer.* He noted the artist's unruly chestnut hair and innocent-looking hazel eyes. Suddenly, his stomach clenched. The young photographer wore a very familiar looking necklace over his dark turtleneck sweater.

I was sure my necklace was one of a kind ... but this looks exactly like it.

***

I'm sorry, but Monsieur Casal isn't in Paris just now," Anton Dechamps, the owner of the gallery, explained. "He left for London a few days ago on assignment. He's a talented photographer, don't you think?"

"Yes, very talented," Joseph replied.

"I met him and some of his friends at Speos a few years ago."

"Speos?"

"Speos Photographic Institute. I was very impressed with André and his work. His show did quite well."

"When do you expect him back?"

"The exhibition hangs for another two weeks. He'll be collecting his photographs soon after."

"I won't be in France that long, but I would very much like to meet Mr. Casal, perhaps buy one of his pieces. How might I reach him?"

"I can inform him of your interest. Would you like to leave your name and number?"

"Yes, thank you. Here is the number of my hotel. I'll be there through the week. Does Mr. Casal have a card?"

"Take one of the exhibit brochures. I'll be sure to share your enthusiasm with André and give him your contact information in Paris."

The necklace. Why would this André Casal have it? There must be an explanation. I trust he'll call the hotel if he wants to sell his work.

Strolling around Artists' Square, a feeling of déjà vu suddenly enveloped him. *This is where the street artist painted us, Jess and me. I see her everywhere.*

An hour later, he caught the Metro from Montmartre back to the hotel. Before returning to his room, he wandered down to the Seine where riverboats gave excited, curious tourists glimpses of famous Paris landmarks from the river. Like the floating boats, his thoughts drifted gently over his past—viewing, analyzing, questioning. *Do I regret my decision to become a priest? No.* He knew he'd followed the strong yearning in his heart to serve God and the priesthood had given him that opportunity, at his father's urging. *But is the Catholic way my true calling?*

What am I to do about Jessica? I thought I could remain a priest while carrying a spiritual love for her in my heart. But now seeing her again, in the flesh, everything's changed. I want to be with her every day—spiritually, emotionally, and physically. She brings meaning into my life like nothing else. Nothing seems right without her. Leave the priesthood? How could I consider it? Yet how can I not? I can't continue to be a representative of a faith I've come to doubt. But, my decision cannot depend upon my feelings for Jessica ....

***

Joseph had heard nothing back from André Casal. Hoping to connect with him before leaving Paris, he called the *Galerie d' le Beau.*

"I'm sorry, but Monsieur Casal is still in London," Monsieur Dechamps informed him.

"I'm leaving for Boston tomorrow, but, please, take this number where I can be reached in the U.S." He gave the man his mother's number, knowing she would forward any messages to him. For now, André Casal's connection to the necklace would remain a mystery.

On his last night in Paris, at Mother Marian's invitation, Joseph attended a performance of the convent choir. He couldn't believe she was still in charge after so many years. The exquisite beauty of the chanting touched his soul, excited his senses, and lifted his spirits. He closed his eyes to receive it all. *If only Jessica were here, if only my Jessica were here.*

Suddenly, his heart opened as he pondered his destiny, hearing the message: *Tell me what you long for and I will tell you who you are.*

In that instant, for that moment, he knew that God wanted him to follow his heart, just as he'd done when he'd entered the priesthood. Only this time his heart wanted to lead him in a new direction, still unclear, but away from the path he currently walked. *Do what you love. Be with your love. Love is what truly matters.*

He bowed his head in gratitude for the clarity he'd been given, finding what he believed was the answer he'd been searching for. He longed to tell Jessica what had come to him, but he knew he must continue to listen deeply. *In good time. In God's time.*

Jessica

Laguna Beach

Jessica returned home from England satisfied with how her Christmas trip had gone, but more than ready to return to her casual California lifestyle and to finally take over as official art curator of the Sea View Museum of Art.

Looking out her front window at the sky striated with hues of pink and violet, she decided to take a sunset walk along a trail she'd discovered but not taken that followed the jagged Pacific coastline.

She began with a power walk, then slowed her pace as other people arrived at the trailhead to view the sunset. She was lucky to find an empty bench. As the sun began its daily ritual of sinking into the vast Pacific Ocean, Jessica allowed her whole body to relax into itself, letting go.

I am the Way and the Light. The words came to her as she sat quietly contemplating the incredible sight before her: golden rays fanning out beneath passing clouds, illuminating a path on the water, and running all the way to the beach in front of her. She'd been working on a lesson from *A Course in Miracles* that dealt with looking at life from different perspectives. An image of Joseph flashed through her mind. But this time, instead of feeling saddened, she turned her attention to the beauty of his character.

He's such a good man, always trying to do God's will and ministering to others. No matter if we can't be together, I will always love him. I wonder if I should at least let him know I'm doing well and not resenting how things stand between us.

"No," a voice inside spoke. "He'll call you when—and if—things change. Your work is to focus on moving ahead with your own life."

She did not fight her tears and resolved to do her best to let go of her attachment to Joseph.

***

Jessica awoke earlier than usual the next morning, her eyes opening to the beauty of sunlight peeking through the partially closed blinds in her bedroom, reminding her of the sunset the night before. Miss Suzy, who'd been sleeping at the foot of her bed, stood and stretched, then strutted up and nestled into her arms.

"I love you, sweet kitty," she said, running her hands through the cat's soft fur as her thoughts wandered back to England. It had been sweet to spend a little time with her half siblings, Tyler and Annie. They loved their kitties, too.

Dad really dotes on Annie. I wish that didn't trigger me. She's just a little girl like I once was. It's silly to wonder if Dad loves Annie more than me ... but I do. That's the wounded little girl who's still inside of me, no matter how mature I think I am. I hope Annie grows up more secure in her father's love than I did.

And Tyler already wants to be a musician like his dad. "But not in an orchestra," he'd announced. "Playing keyboard in a rock band is more my style."

André would be Tyler's age. I wonder what he is dreaming of doing with his life. The shrill sound of the telephone pushed away that bittersweet thought.

"Welcome home," Holly greeted her. "Clay told me your dad was ill. I hope he's better now."

"Yes, he's much better. Thanks for asking."

"When will you be coming in?"

"In just a bit. This will actually be my first official day."

"I can handle things if you need more time."

"No, it will be good for me to get to work."

"Great. I'm looking forward to seeing you."

Well, Holly sounds eager. Her attitude will no doubt help my spirits.

After her usual California breakfast of yogurt and fresh fruit, she hopped into her new Honda and drove toward the museum. What freedom she felt driving along the coast in her own little car. After parking, she gazed another moment at the Pacific: blue water, blue skies. *How this expansive view soothes me. It's so good to be home. I'm feeling more at home here than I did in New York or England.*

Holly greeted her with an unexpected hug.

"Thanks for the warm welcome."

"I'm so excited to tell you about my new project," Holly said.

"Oh?" Jessica was struck by the young woman's exuberance. "Clay didn't mention anything about a new project."

"Well, he didn't know about it," Holly explained. "I had the idea the day after his last day, when I was here on my own. I was closing up late on Friday afternoon and there was such energy on the street. Lots of kids hanging out. I imagined what it would be like to open the museum on Friday nights for special community events, particularly for young people interested in the arts."

"That sounds like a great idea! I think you're on to something. We can brainstorm about it, but it will take some planning," Jessica advised.

"Well, honestly, I probably jumped the gun, but last Friday night I brought in a local band and people loved it."

"You what?" Jessica asked, stunned. "Did any of the Board members attend?"

"Well, they didn't exactly know about it."

"What?" Jessica exclaimed, stunned by Holly's announcement. "You mean you didn't get their approval first?"

"I didn't even know there was a Board. Clay didn't mention it and, honestly, neither did you. Anyway, I found out about the Board when one of the members called me the next day. He told me a few of the neighbors had complained about the traffic and volume of the music."

"Oh, dear, it's clear to me that we need to clarify museum procedures. I'd been working on that with Clay in preparation for my transition."

"But you haven't heard the whole story. I've invited the entire Board to the next event so they can see for themselves how well this idea will work."

"The next event? You've already scheduled something?"

"An exhibit of local school children's art. I coordinated an impromptu contest for the elementary school last week with the help of one of my friends who teaches there and the winning pictures will be announced and on display in just two weeks."

"Though it sounds lovely, Holly, you need to slow down."

"What do you mean?"

"I mean I think you have great ideas brewing here, but we need to talk about how to implement them without overstepping the Board. Let me get settled myself and we'll meet first thing in the morning to go over procedures and your ideas."

She'd asked for an assistant with initiative, but was hardly prepared for someone like Holly.

***

Two weeks later, after a very successful Friday night event, Jessica told Holly that not only was the Board impressed with the children's art contest and exhibit, so was she.

"My intuition *told me* it would be successful," Holly stated in a matter-of-fact way. "That's why I went ahead and implemented it — even though you weren't here."

"You must have a strong intuition," she replied, impressed by the young woman's confidence.

"Yes, quite strong. I've been wanting to tell you about that. I had a premonition about getting the job here at Sea View."

"A premonition?"

"Yes, well, actually it was a *vision*," Holly explained. "I was meditating during an intuitive development class with a Spiritualist minister. In the vision, I saw myself arranging beautiful pieces of art in a room. Outside the window was a view of the sea. When I came to Sea View, I recognized the room I'd seen in my vision."

"Really? That's fascinating. What led you to study with a Spiritualist minister? I don't even know what such a person does or is."

"A spiritualist is essentially a highly intuitive individual who, as minister, can counsel less developed intuitives on their paths. I've had sporadic psychic experiences since I was a child. I usually get a hunch about what to do, you know, like a strong sense of 'yes' or 'no' when I have to make a decision. Sometimes I also get a kind of vision—like the one I told you about."

"That's an amazing gift."

"I'm glad you didn't say it's weird. It used to freak out some of my college friends. They thought I just had a vivid imagination."

"On the contrary, I believe some people can pick up information most of us can't even perceive. I once went to a psychic myself. She told me I'd live in a foreign country, and here I am, living in America. I've been curious about psychic phenomena ever since."

"I'd love to visit Paris. I feel sure that I had a past life in France."

"What makes you think you had a past life there?"

"Dreams, visions, you know, just a very strong connection to all things French. Also, my mother spent some time in Paris when she was young, painting and studying art. Her stories made France come alive for me."

"So your mother is a painter."

"*Was* a painter. She died when I was fourteen."

"Oh, Holly, I'm so sorry. That must've been terrible for you."

"Yes, it was. Still is. I really miss her."

After a long pause, Jessica asked shyly, "Holly, I don't want to put you on the spot, truly, but with so many transitions in my life, I wonder if you sense a clear direction for me, something perhaps I can't see for myself?"

"You're not putting me on the spot," Holly said, looking her in the eye. "I sense that you are a very deep person who has suffered a lot. Maybe one day you'll be willing to share some of that with me."

"Maybe I will."

"I hope so. My mother always told me that we all have intuitive capacities, but we must practice our own inner knowing."

"I've heard that. I guess I've not yet had the patience," Jessica said, glancing at her watch. "I could talk with you for hours about this, but it's getting late. We should call it a night, don't you think?"

"Yes, it's been a long, but exciting, week. I'm so glad you were pleased with the event. On another note, speaking of patience and its antidote, relaxation, I thought you'd like to know about a wonderful yoga class early on Thursday mornings, down in the village."

"I've wanted to try yoga."

"Why don't we go next week?"

"Sounds like a plan."

***

On Thursday morning, Jessica arrived at the Yoga in the Village studio just after Holly. They hugged spontaneously. This time, Jessica wasn't taken aback. It felt right.

"I'm so glad you came," Holly said, smiling and handing Jessica one of her yoga mats and a fragrant eye pillow. Jessica had also brought a light blanket per Holly's instructions.

When they entered the room, most students had already unfolded their colorful mats and lay on the floor in restful poses. Holly and Jessica joined them, stretching out like the others, relaxing to the sound of soft, soothing music.

Jessica stretched and twisted her body, loosening muscles she'd neglected for much too long.

After a number of standing poses as well as poses on their backs and stomachs, the music stopped and the instructor asked the students to lie down on their mats to prepare for savasana. Jessica gave Holly a quizzical look.

"Savasana is the corpse pose," the teacher shared, as she darkened the room, "the time for final relaxation. Keep your palms up as your arms rest beside you. Close your eyes and melt into the floor. Let all your thoughts simply drift away."

Breathing in the scents of the lavender and flaxseed sewn up in her eye pillow, Jessica relaxed more deeply, as her body released all tension. To her surprise, tears filled her eyes. When the instructor's quiet voice told them to begin to move their hands and toes, Jessica continued to lay still. Soon, someone gently nudged her. She took off the eye pillow and looked around. Holly smiled at her and motioned for her to sit up.

Everyone else was sitting cross-legged with their hands in a kind of prayer position. When Jessica joined them, they spoke in unison: "The light in me greets the light in you. Namaste." With that, they all bowed to one another and class was over.

"I'm sorry I stayed in savasana longer than I was supposed to," she apologized to the teacher after class.

"Not to worry. You probably relaxed deeply enough for your emotions to rise to the surface."

Jessica nodded.

Holly approached Jessica, "I know a café that opens early just down the street. We could get some coffee or tea after we've changed."

"Great idea. A good cup of tea is just what I need."

They walked together to the Sunrise Café and sat near the window, where the morning sun brightened up the table. The aroma of fresh baked bread and coffee brewing permeated the air.

After they'd ordered, Holly asked, "What did you think of your first yoga experience?"

"It was good for me, I think, but I'm puzzled by something. During savasana, I felt like I dropped into a trance and it was difficult to come out of it."

"That can happen. It has to me, especially when there's something I need to process on a deep level or something I'm avoiding."

"I felt very sad."

"You were probably quiet and still enough to pay attention to something painful in your life."

Holly's comment struck a nerve, but Jessica reflected rather than reacted while enjoying her tea, after which they walked arm in arm to their respective cars and drove to the museum

***

Later, eating their lunch on the museum patio, Jessica asked Holly if she'd heard of *A Course in Miracles.*

"I have the book," Holly said.

"What do you think of it?"

"I like the content, but I don't like how the masculine pronoun is used throughout the book."

"That bothered me, too, at first. But so much of it speaks to me. I figure it's written in the language of the Bible. I started going to *A Course* class at the Unity Church on Thursday nights but I haven't been in a while. Would you like to come with me tonight?"

"Why not? You came with me to yoga. Now I'll try something new with you."

Jessica smiled. It would be easier to see Ken again if she came with Holly.

***

When they walked into the *A Course in Miracles* meeting room,

Jessica introduced Holly to the members of the group.

"We've missed you," Ken said, motioning for them to sit next to him.

I guess I can't very well ignore him. It's funny how repulsion and attraction can walk the same edge.

The discussion centered on the importance of forgiveness. *I want to forgive Joseph for not choosing me over the priesthood. As for Ken, there's nothing to forgive. If I judge him as intolerant, perhaps the antidote is to tolerate him.*

"Would you two like to join me for dinner?" Ken asked them after the meeting.

"I don't know, what do you think, Holly?"

"Sounds okay to me."

Turning to Ken, Jessica said, "Tell us where, and we'll meet you there."

Ken gave them directions to a French bistro he'd discovered not far away. Jessica decided not to tell Holly about her altercation with Ken the last time they'd been together. *I'll just let her get a sense of him on her own.*

The restaurant was small and popular, so they had to wait for a table. While Ken and Holly chatted, Jessica scanned the room, its French décor transporting her to another time and place where she and Joseph stood waiting in their favorite café in Montmartre.

"Where are you, Jessica?" Ken asked. "You seem far away."

"Oh, sorry," she said, blushing. "The ambiance reminds me of the time I spent in Paris as a young woman."

Both Ken and Holly gave her inquisitive looks, but before anyone could respond, the beautiful young hostess approached, ready to seat them.

"It's about time," Ken snapped, his tone unnerving Jessica.

The young woman apologized dryly and placed the menus on the table. "Enjoy your meal."

"An experienced maître d' would have engaged us much earlier, taken better care of us at the bar with the long wait," Ken said.

"Ken, we just left *A Course in Miracles* class," Jessica said, her words clipped. "Why so harsh and judgmental?"

"I'm not being judgmental. I simply won't tolerate incompetence."

Jessica and Holly ate their dinner in relative silence amidst Ken's attempts to charm them.

***

"There's a mean streak in Ken," Holly said while they were driving home. "I get very bad vibes from him."

"I know what you mean. I've seen that intolerance in him before."

"Well, I wouldn't get too close to him if I were you," Holly advised.

***

Jessica thought about Ken on and off as she readied for bed, wondering who he really was and why she cared. Holly was right. She should be careful of him.

Turning out the light, she remembered her yoga class and the deep sadness that welled up in her. It just wouldn't go away. *If I could only speak with Joseph one more time, maybe then I could let him go or ….*

***

The next day, during her lunch break, Jessica willed herself, with only minimal success, to be calm while dialing the number of Saint Andrew's Catholic Church rectory in Brooklyn.

When the volunteer who answered told Jessica that Father Murphy no longer lived at Saint Andrew's and had left the center, Jessica was so shocked she forgot to ask if he had left a forwarding address or number.

Where could he be? Her hope rose, but then her thoughts turned realistic. *He's probably just gotten a new assignment. If something had changed, he would have called.*

André

André arrived at the hostel in London, determined to begin his search for Jessica Taylor. The next day, he planned to photograph Princess Diana at a local benefit in hopes of landing a magazine gig. He also intended to contact London galleries that featured photography.

After washing up and settling down with a glass of wine, he decided to make a few calls. Sitting on the bed, he scanned the telephone book. Dozens of J. Taylors. *Well, what have I got to lose?*

After ten or more unsuccessful tries, his voice had stopped trembling, "Hello, my name is André Casal. I'm trying to reach Jessica Taylor, and I saw your number listed under J. Taylor. Does Jessica Taylor live here by chance?"

"The J. in this Taylor house is my husband, Jonathan."

"I'm sorry to have bothered you," he responded, his heart again sinking.

"Wait, before you go, I do *know* a Jessica Taylor, my husband's daughter. Why are you trying to reach her?"

"I have a necklace that might belong to her. A nun in France passed it on to me at Miss Taylor's request."

"A nun? That's intriguing. I do remember Jessica working in a convent in France many years ago."

"That sounds promising. Do you know where I might find her?"

"I'll have her father call you."

André spelled his name and gave her the name and number of the hostel where he was staying, emphasizing to the woman how grateful he would be for a call back. She assured him that she would give her husband the message.

The next day, André awoke to pouring rain, not a day to photograph a princess at her best. He dressed, grabbed his camera and hurried to the Carlyle Hotel where Princess Diana would be attending a breakfast benefit.

At first glimpse, Diana's radiant smile shone more brightly than he'd been told—even in the midst of the inclement weather and some distance away. "She's like a beacon of light in a storm," he said to himself, juggling to protect the camera from the rain. *Even if my pictures don't capture it, I've seen her for myself.*

***

When he stopped at the hostel's front desk to ask for his key, the clerk handed him a phone message.

"Is this Adelaide Townsend?" he asked the woman who answered his call.

"Yes. Who is this?"

"André Casal. You left a message for me this afternoon."

"Oh, yes, Mr. Casal. I received a call this morning from my ex-husband. His wife told him you were looking for Jessica Taylor, my daughter. You have a necklace that might belong to her?"

"Yes. It was given to me in Provence. I believe it may have at one time belonged to her."

"Provence? What kind of necklace?"

He described the necklace in detail.

"I vaguely remember my daughter wearing a necklace that fits that description when she returned from Paris years ago. Come to think of it, I never saw her wear it again after that. It was quite unusual, even stunning as I recall. But I'm confused. You say it was given to you, but you believe it belonged to Jessica Taylor? Why?"

"I'm afraid it's a long story," André replied, trying hard to remain calm. "Could you tell me how to reach your daughter?"

"She doesn't live in the U.K. anymore. Besides, I'd better contact her first before giving you any more information."

"That's understandable, certainly. I would really appreciate it, though, if you could get back to me soon as I will only be in London for a few more days."

"Does she know you?"

"No, we don't know each other."

"Well, all right then, I'll get back to you as soon as I reach her."

What have I started? Thanking her profusely, André put the receiver in its cradle as if in slow motion, drinking down the rest of his glass of wine in a single gulp, jumbled thoughts racing through his mind. *What if her daughter really is my mother? How will she react? Excited? Upset? I wonder if she even told her mother.*

***

André awoke to a sunny day and did his best to put thoughts of Jessica Taylor aside while visiting several galleries in London and showing his portfolio. Delighted about the gallery owners' enthusiasm for his work, he returned, content, to the hostel ready to go out for a good meal.

The desk clerk once again gave him a message that Adelaide Townsend had called. He hurried to his room to call her back.

"Madame Townsend, this is André Casal. I received a message you'd called."

"Hello, Mr. Casal. I've been thinking," she said. "Before I call my daughter, I'd like to meet with you, if possible. Maybe if I actually see the necklace, I'll know if it's the one I saw her wearing way back when."

"Of course," he managed.

"I can take the train to London tomorrow. Could we meet for tea?"

"Certainly. Do you have a favorite spot?"

"I adore the Carlyle."

"I know it," he said, smiling to himself at the coincidence, as he'd just been there to photograph the princess the day before. "Will three o'clock be suitable for you?"

There's no turning back now. A surge of both fear and excitement coursed through him.

***

After an interminably long morning and lunch-time, three o'clock finally came and he hurried into the lobby at the Carlyle. *I forgot to ask what she looks like and didn't describe myself.*

He pulled the necklace out from under his shirt. *Maybe this will draw her attention.*

Before long, an older woman with short, salt and pepper hair and a warm smile walked through the door and directly up to him.

"You must be Mr. Casal," she said, looking him over, necklace and all.

"It's great to meet you, Madame," he said, reaching out his hand. "I've reserved a table for us by the fountain." He gestured toward the other side of the lobby.

"Your necklace is exquisite," the woman commented after they'd placed their orders. "Very unusual. Not really gender-specific, more of a keepsake, it seems. It could well be like the one my daughter wore. As I recall, she told me a friend had given it to her. I remember that even now, over twenty years later, because I thought to myself it must be a very special friend."

Unclasping the necklace and handing it to her, he asked, "Do you think it's the same piece?"

The waiter appeared, interrupting their conversation with the tea service, an array of English teas, and a tiered display of crustless sandwiches, scones, and chocolate-covered biscuits. Adelaide continued to study the necklace while they nibbled.

Running her fingers over the colored gems, she affirmed, "Now that I look closely, the colorful gems and the fleur-de-lis in the middle, it's unmistakable. Though, mind you, I only saw it once when Jessica came to help me recuperate from hospital years ago. I never saw her wear it again."

André sipped his tea while gathering his thoughts—and his nerve. "Do you remember what year she returned to Paris?" he asked quietly, holding his breath.

"I believe it was in the late sixties. Yes, she came home in 1968, the year her father asked me for a divorce. Then she left and I didn't see her for almost a year."

Suddenly, his eyes filled with tears.

"Young man, what's the matter?"

"That necklace was left with me when I was a baby," he said, choking on his words, "in Provence—in 1969. My mother left me there to be adopted." He pulled out the page with his mother's signature on it and handed it to Adelaide.

"Oh, my," Adelaide exclaimed, looking at the paper. She covered her mouth with her hand and searched his eyes. "This is my daughter's handwriting."

Jessica

Laguna Beach

Jessica awoke with a start. She'd dreamed again of the tree design on the convent door that she'd so resonated with long ago in Paris. This time it appeared in her dream as a real tree, growing atop a hill, solitary, its branches silhouetted against the sky. She sensed the tree's loneliness as her own, tears coming to her eyes. She picked up her pen and journal.

A Solitary Tree

A solitary tree stands against the sky,
lovely and lonely on her hill.
She needs the touch
of branch to branch, root to root,
with others of her kind.
She whispers to the wind:
"Please, caress my leaves and take my seeds
and plant them nearby
so I may never be alone."

While practicing her *Course in Miracles* lessons, Jessica often asked the Holy Spirit for guidance. Closing her eyes, from deep within her heart, she asked, "Why am I so sad?"

"You are carrying the weight of all your hidden secrets," she heard within. "Open your heart, allow what is hidden to emerge into the light where you may be healed."

Her tears flowing freely and gratitude filling her heart, she made a conscious decision to share her secrets with someone she could trust. *Holly. With her intuitive awareness, I know she'll understand.*

***

While sharing lunch with Holly on the museum patio, a cool breeze off the ocean, all right with the world, she took a chance.

"Holly, since practicing the *Course in Miracles* lessons, I've learned to ask the Holy Spirit for guidance and I did that this morning after a disturbing dream." She took a deep breath and continued, Holly looking at her with compassion. "The message that came told me that

I'd been carrying a painful burden for many years and that it was time to share my secrets with someone I could trust." Taking another deep breath, she went on, "I believe that person is you." Relieved, her tears began again.

"Oh, Jessica, it's good that you're listening so deeply to your inner guidance. I would be honored. How about tonight after work?"

"Well ... okay. Thank you so much, Holly."

"You'd do it for me, I know."

"I would. You know, if I had a daughter, I'd want her to be just like you."

"That's so sweet. I don't know what to say."

"Now that's a first."

They laughed.

***

Holly poured two glasses of Merlot and handed one to Jessica as they settled in the living room, the wine and a box of tissues on the coffee table between them.

"I'm ready to listen if you're ready to talk."

"You're getting right to it, aren't you?"

"Only if you're ready. I sense a bit of hesitation in your voice."

"I'm ready." Jessica took a sip of her wine before carefully taking out the sketch she'd brought with her, the one of her and Joseph in Montmartre.

"That must be you in the peasant blouse. And who is the good-looking man?"

"That's Joseph when we were together in Montmartre."

"Montmartre? That's where my mother painted when she was young. I wonder if she was there at the same time."

"Wouldn't that be amazing?"

"It feels like my mother's here with us in spirit," Holly said.

Taking Holly's hand, Jessica willed herself to go on. "When I was only nineteen, I fell in love with Joseph, the man in the sketch. He was an architect from Boston working on a project in Paris. I became his interpreter."

"You still have feelings for him, don't you?"

"Our relationship ended when he followed his father's wish for him to become a Catholic priest."

"That must've been very painful for you."

"I shouldn't have let myself become involved with him. I know that now. He told me early on that he was interested in the priesthood, but the attraction was genuinely mutual and I let myself fall in love with him."

"You followed your heart. Sometimes that's all we can do."

Taking a deep breath, Jessica stood. "Excuse me a minute."

She looked at herself for a long moment in the bathroom mirror. *This is harder than I'd expected. Should I be sharing such vulnerabilities with my assistant?* The answer was clear. *I can trust Holly. Besides, she knows things.*

"As you might have guessed," she said when she returned to the couch, "he left me to enter seminary. But, even worse, I was pregnant. I didn't tell him."

Holly asked softly, "What happened to the baby?"

"I'm ashamed to tell you," Jessica replied, wiping the tears from her eyes. "The only other person who knows is my therapist in New York."

"I can see this is extremely hard for you," Holly said, reaching out to touch her friend's arm, "but, please, go on."

"I gave up my baby boy, my son, for adoption," Jessica said. Her voice broke, and she looked down at her lap, unable to say more.

"You were so young. Wasn't it the best thing, maybe the *only* thing, you could do?"

"I suppose. I don't know. The nuns in the convent where I was staying convinced me he should be brought up by both a father and a mother—preferably Catholic."

"I'm sure your intentions were good."

"I can't begin to tell you how relieved I am to get this out—and to feel your understanding." Jessica sighed deeply. "I've had so many different feelings about it. Sadness, anger, grief, guilt, regret. You name it, I've felt it. Therapy helped me forgive myself to some extent, but not completely. If only I knew my son is okay, that he's happy and the people who adopted him love him the way I do." She stopped to wipe her eyes and blow her nose. "If only he knew how much I love him."

"I'm so honored that you trusted me with this. And I'm glad you're getting it off your chest, Jessica. You must forgive yourself *wholeheartedly*."

"There's more," Jessica continued, grateful for Holly's willingness to listen, pouring each of them more wine. "I ran into Joseph in New York before I moved out here."

"That must have been a shock."

"It was—for both of us. We haven't seen each other since we broke up. It's been over twenty years. I still love him, Holly, but, we can't be together, not as long as he's a priest." Saying those words out loud affirmed again that she must let go of any fantasy that Joseph would come back to her.

"Is he in love with you?"

"He says he is, and I believe him, but he's tortured with the decision to leave the priesthood. When the opportunity arose at Sea View, it felt like a blessing. I just couldn't abide the pain of it all, waiting for him — for so long — to make up his mind."

"I'm so sorry you've been carrying this."

"I broke down and called the rectory the other day. They said he'd left and they didn't know where he'd gone."

"Maybe he's making his decision."

"You think so? Oh, Holly, I can't live like this. That's why I started spending time with Ken, just to see what it would be like with someone else."

"Well, I don't think he's the right man for you," Holly said in a stern voice. "Please think carefully before going out with him again. I don't want to tell you what to do, but my feelings are very strong where he's concerned."

Jessica picked up her glass. "To our friendship, and especially to your good listening and sound advice."

"To our friendship, and to your honesty and trust," Holly added, clinking her glass with Jessica's.

André

André felt as though he was living in a dream. Adelaide, the woman likely to be his natural grandmother, had decided to stay in London a while longer so they could get to know each other. She'd encouraged him to move from the hostel to a better hotel and had even rented a room there for herself. She'd also insisted on picking up his tab.

Adelaide had asked about his photographs, eager to see them, and the day that he moved to the hotel they sat together on a sofa in the lobby with an assortment from his portfolio spread before them.

"You have a *wonderful* talent," Adelaide stated with conviction.

"Thanks. I've met with a few gallery owners here in London and one plans to visit my exhibit in Paris."

"You must be thrilled." After a pause, she said, "I still can't believe you might be … my grandson."

Her words sounded surreal to him. "I can hardly believe it, either."

"But I can't just call Jessica out of the blue and ask her about all of this over the phone. We have to figure out another way." She tapped her hand on her chin and gazed at the ceiling. "How long will your photography be on display in Paris?"

"Just for another two weeks," he replied, puzzled by her question. "Why?"

"Jessica is an art curator in a museum in California. What if I tell her I've discovered a young French photographer whose work she really should see? When she comes, we can talk with her in person."

"But I doubt she'd drop everything to come see my work."

"You have a point there. But I know she respects my ability to recognize artistic photography. I once considered being a professional photographer myself and I'm certainly a collector."

"Perhaps one day you'll show me your collection."

"I suspect that will happen. In the meantime, I know a jeweler who might be able to shed a bit more light on the origin of your necklace."

Wanting to hug her, André realized a new chapter in his life was unfolding.

***

"Hmm, the fleur-de-lis is very French," the jeweler said. "I suspect it came from southern France and has a Cathar origin."

André's eyes widened. "My great grandmother, my mother's mother, wore a brooch with a symbol very similar to this. She was from southern France."

"But there's something more." He studied the necklace closely under his eyepiece. "Most Celtic crosses have open circles in the middle. In this one, the center's been covered with mother-of-pearl. It looks like a locket, but, strangely, its two sides have been soldered together."

"Can you open it without damaging it?" André asked, eager to know what was inside.

The jeweler told them he could and took the necklace to his workroom to do so. He returned to show them what he had discovered: an engraved tree, with a meditative figure in its center, branches and roots swirling around it.

"It looks like some kind of symbol," Adelaide said, her eyes widening. "Do you know what it is?"

"I'm not sure," the jeweler said, "but the local branch of the London Library is only a short taxi ride away. I'd explore ancient symbols, perhaps Celtic, perhaps with a focus on the Cathars."

"I know it well," Adelaide said. "I used to work there."

***

At the library, they located a number of references to ancient symbols in the card catalogue. They pored over various illustrations and informative descriptions in the texts until André discovered an image that looked very much like the design in his locket.

"It's an important symbol of an ancient Jewish sect known as the Essenes. They called it the Tree of Life. It says Jesus and his family, including his cousin, John the Baptist, were thought, by some, to have been members of an Essene community."

"Some of the Dead Sea Scrolls, discovered earlier this century, are thought to be Essene documents," Adelaide added.

André continued reading in a whisper, "Not as well known as the Pharisees and Sadducees mentioned in the Bible, the Essenes were quite secretive and kept to themselves. They strongly believed that a Messiah would come to free the Jews from Roman oppression."

Adelaide interjected, "And they believed that Jesus was that person."

Skimming the text, André said, "It says here that the Essenes broke away from the mainstream when Paul became accepted as one of Jesus's rightful apostles. It seems they thought Paul interjected some of his own ideas into Jesus's teachings, such as making money through the church and requiring ministers to intercede when communicating with God. The Essenes apparently believed individuals had the right to ask for guidance from God directly, without the need for intermediary authority from the Church. I believe that, too."

"So do I." Adelaide smiled. "It looks like they were forced to go underground to preserve what they thought to be Jesus's pure teachings. I guess they were in danger of being persecuted as heretics by mainstream Christians."

"Just like the Cathars," André exclaimed. "I wonder if there's a connection between the two sects. The Essene symbol was soldered shut inside the locket. I wonder if that was to protect its owner from being persecuted."

"And I wonder," Adelaide echoed, "how my daughter came to own this necklace. I want to sleep on all of this and then give her a call tomorrow evening. It'll be earlier there and she'll be at work."

His heart jumped to his throat. "I can't help being nervous," he stammered.

"You're not the only one, André. But if anyone can convince Jessica to travel to Paris to meet you, it would be her mother." Adelaide laughed, then put her hand to her mouth as the man next to them gave them a stern look.

"Adelaide, do you have a picture of Jessica? Maybe in your wallet?"

"I do," she said, rummaging in her bag. "Here's my Jessica," Adelaide said proudly a few moments later, handing André a somewhat worn picture.

He stared at the smiling woman in the picture: blond hair, standing on a balcony, with skyscrapers in the background, and a fluffy, orange kitten nestled against her shoulder.

"She's lovely," André whispered. *And if she's anything like her mother, I know I will like her. But will she like me?*

***

The next day, André and Adelaide met in the hotel café for dinner.

"I think it's time to call Jessica," Adelaide said cautiously over dessert.

He nodded, taking a deep breath and willing his heart to stop racing.

"We'll use the phone in my room." she said.

Sitting at the desk in her room a few minutes later, she placed a call to the Sea View Museum of Art in Laguna Beach. "This is Adelaide Townsend, Jessica Taylor's mother. May I please speak with her? … Oh … When will she be back? … No, I don't want to bother her at the conference. Here's the number where I'm staying in London. Please tell her I've met a young French photographer whose work I really think she should see."

Hanging up the phone, Adelaide shook her head at André. "She's at a conference in San Diego, but she'll be home on the weekend. We'll just have to wait."

He was disappointed, but also oddly relieved. *Is this really happening?*

Jessica

Jessica sat in the back seat as Tim Banning drove her and his wife, Marcia, to San Diego to attend a six-day *Course in Miracles* conference. *I'm glad Holly agreed to take over for me at the museum. This is just what I need—the perfect arena in which to explore more about the Course.* Then she thought of Ken.

"How well do you know Ken?" she asked, eager to hear what they had to say.

"He's been coming to the group for quite some time," Marcia replied. "He seems interested enough in the material, but I'm not sure he has a good understanding of how to apply it. Why do you ask?"

"Well, Holly and I had dinner with him the other night and he became quite brusque with the hostess."

"Ken's always been polite in the group," Tim said, "but I've sensed that he carries some pent-up anger. I think it's because he went through a nasty divorce before moving to California."

"Did you know he'll be at the conference?" Marcia asked.

"No," Jessica replied, feeling suddenly queasy.

***

On Sunday morning, Jessica, Marcia, and Tim walked the short distance from their accommodations to the Unity Church of San Diego where Reverend Arlene proceeded to the stage to welcome everyone and introduce the keynote speaker. Just as he began his talk, Jessica felt a tap on her shoulder and turned to see Ken, who had taken a seat behind her.

"Hi, it's good to see you," he whispered.

"You too," she whispered back. *Why did I say that? It isn't true.*

"Let's have lunch together today, okay?"

"I'm having lunch at Reverend Arlene's house," she said. "Maybe another time." *Why can't I just tell him the truth? I don't want to be alone with him again.*

"I'll hold you to that. I'm staying with Fred. I know he'd like to see you while you're here."

Not knowing how to respond, she turned back toward the speaker who was discussing the basis of *A Course in Miracles*.

"Whereas mainstream Christianity tells us we're all sinners, Jesus, in his new teachings through the *Course*, tells us we're magnificent creatures, still living in the heart of God. The problem is we've forgotten who we really are and need to awaken to the truth of our being. The *Course* also teaches that people, who strike out in anger toward others, do so because they are *crying out for love*.

"We're all here to heal ourselves by waking up to our true potentials. By loving and forgiving ourselves and others, we allow our inner magnificence to shine. We need to practice love, not judgment, for this healing to take place."

Her heart felt the truth of his words. The audience agreed as they broke out in loud applause.

After lunch, the participants divided into small experiential groups in various locations throughout the building. Wanting some personal space, Jessica was relieved when none of those she knew were assigned to hers. She followed the young woman facilitating her group to a small conference room with mostly beanbag chairs on the floor and a few traditional comfortable chairs. A box of tissues had been placed near each seat. The woman introduced herself as Sally, and instructed them to find a place where they could work comfortably on their own. Jessica chose a soft blue chair near the back of the room and settled into it as best she could, making sure that she could reach the tissues.

"Now, close your eyes," Sally said softly, "and visualize someone who you *feel* has wronged you in some way. Be with that person for a while and pay close attention to your feelings. Then begin to imagine forgiving them. Feel how *that* feels. When you have finished with one person, move on to visualizing someone else. Continue until I ask you to stop, which will be in about forty-five minutes, after which I'll invite you to write about your experiences in your journal. If you finish your forgiveness ritual before I stop you, go ahead and begin writing."

Jessica closed her eyes and immediately saw Ken's image in her mind.

I've been judging you since Thanksgiving, when I heard about the grudge you held against your daughter. Then you lashed out at that hostess. Though it's hard for me to believe, I hear that you were really crying out for love ... and ... I forgive you, Ken.

Jim came next to mind.

I know it wasn't your fault that we lost the baby and yet I've blamed you. Tears started, and her heart ached at this new insight. *I realize now that our marriage was in trouble even before I got pregnant. We were just like two kids in a way, playing at marriage. I forgive you, Jim — and myself — for making such immature choices.*

Next up was her father.

I forgive you, Dad, for leaving me and Mum. She paused to reach for the tissues. *I forgive you for not giving me the kind of love I needed from you in* the past. *I now know it's not because there's something wrong with me. It's just that you weren't capable of giving me what I needed when I was young.*

Last of all, she visualized Joseph.

I forgive you for choosing the priesthood over me. I'll always love you and I respect you for loving God the way you do. Now it's my turn to love God and, in so doing, to learn to love myself.

After everyone was finished, the facilitator suggested, "You can do this on your own whenever you find yourself feeling negative toward others. We'll work more on forgiving ourselves as the week unfolds. For most of us, that's no easy task."

During the afternoon break, emotionally drained from the forgiveness exercise, Jessica strolled outside for some needed fresh air, then returned to the refreshment table to pour herself a cup of tea. Suddenly, Ken's familiar voice startled her from behind.

"Are you enjoying the conference?"

"Not exactly enjoying it, but appreciating its value. You?" she answered, glancing over her shoulder.

"I like the lectures," he said, pouring himself a cup of coffee, "but the exercises are pretty intense."

"Intense, but helpful, I think," she said as they turned to face each other.

"Shall we have dinner tonight and discuss what we've learned?" he asked, giving her a pensive look.

Maybe I should give him another chance. "You know, that sounds like a good idea."

"Great," he said, grinning.

In jeans and a soft blue denim shirt, he looked more relaxed than she'd ever seen him. *He really is quite handsome. There's also something appealing about him, as if he's lost and can't find his way.*

"Do you like sushi?"

"To tell you the truth, I've never tried it." She laughed.

"Great. I'll pick you up at six thirty."

***

Jessica sat across from Ken at an outdoor table at Mikko, a Japanese restaurant in Old Town, San Diego. The lanterns around the patio cast a warm glow over the table as they sipped hot saki from small blue and white ceramic cups while waiting for the sushi rolls Ken had ordered.

"It's nice to be out with you again," Ken began. "It's been a long time."

"Yes, it has," she agreed, "but, you know, your treatment of the hostess the last time we went out really put me off."

"I know it did, but she was incompetent. I think I was helping her, actually, to be better at her job."

"Well, I do believe there are more discreet ways of making such a point."

"Oh, Jessica, you're soft as a grape."

"Maybe I am, but I believe you can speak your mind without intimidating people. I was about to tell you about my experience in the forgiveness group, but now I don't feel you'd understand at all."

"Hey, I'm sorry I gave you that impression. Sometimes, I don't know why it is, but I put my big foot in my mouth. I'd really like to hear about your experience."

Before she could respond, the waiter arrived, placing three dishes of colorful sushi rolls on the table, along with two steaming bowls of miso soup. Giving their full attention to the meal, Ken acquainted Jessica with sushi, putting their conversation on hold.

"How did you like it?" Ken asked after they'd finished eating.

"I'm not sure. The textures aren't appealing to me and I don't find raw fish particularly appetizing, even dressed in seaweed wrappers. But I enjoy new experiences," she pronounced.

"Speaking of which, I'd really like to get back to what you wanted to share about your forgiveness exercise—if you still want to talk about it."

"Among others, I placed you in my mind's eye and forgave you for the way you treated that hostess and I forgave myself for judging you for holding a grudge against your daughter."

"I'm flattered that you cared enough to do that. Thank you."

Jessica nodded and smiled. "How about you? Were you able to forgive someone?"

"Well, I tried to forgive my father but that wasn't very successful," Ken reported.

"I have a feeling there's a long story there."

"There is, but not a very hopeful one. My father was a cruel man and he took out his anger on me."

"I'm so sorry you had to endure that."

***

Ken drove Jessica back to Reverend Arlene's house. Before she could open the door, he pulled her close. "Thanks for going out with me tonight," he whispered in her ear. "And for listening."

"You're welcome," she whispered back. When he reached down to kiss her, she did not resist, in spite of her earlier reservations. It had been a long time since she'd been kissed.

Joseph

A light rain fell as Joseph rode in a taxi to Monsignor's office in Boston. He'd been secluded on the Cape since returning from Paris, processing his thoughts and feelings, praying for guidance. *Without help I can't follow through with what I must do. I feel like part of me is dying. How can I go through with this? I've been a priest for so long. I don't know how to be anything else. But I must be true to myself. That's all there is to it.*

Despite the cold rain outside, Monsignor's office was cozy and warm. *This is a safe haven for me, a place where I know I can bare my soul.*

"You look drained, Joseph," his mentor said, motioning for him to sit down in a comfortable leather chair in front of his desk. "I'll get some coffee." He returned with two cups of steaming brew. "Now, tell me what's bothering you."

"All this time," Joseph began, "I've been trying to live up to my own idea, and, I must admit, my father's idea, of how best to serve God. But I haven't been happy with one foot in the priesthood and the other foot wanting to walk away from it."

Monsignor nodded empathically. "I've been concerned about you, and I'm glad you're finally able to see the situation more clearly." After a short pause, he asked, "And what about the woman you told me you're in love with?"

"You seem to be reading my mind," Joseph replied, leaning forward in the chair. "I returned to Paris, where we met, and it became clear to me that my heart is with her and that God wants me to tell her so. Of course, I don't know if she'll trust me after all these years." He stood and paced for a moment, then sat again. "But I must tell her how I feel."

"And the priesthood?"

Joseph closed his eyes and held his head in his hands for a few moments, trying to gather courage. Finally, dropping his hands to his lap, he opened his eyes and looked directly at the older man. "I'm beginning to realize that it is not my true calling," he said, choking on the words. "It's not easy to give up what I thought was my destiny. But if the priesthood was my true calling, wouldn't I have peace in my heart like you seem to have?"

"That wasn't always the case," Monsignor told him, "but, over the long haul, I've come to love my work. And with that love comes the peace you're referring to."

"I became disillusioned with many of the Church tenets long ago, as you know," Joseph said. "I even joined a group of liberal priests, hoping to change things, but I was kidding myself. I can't, in good conscience, continue being a representative of Catholicism when I have so many misgivings about it."

"Joseph, it takes courage to face the truth within ourselves. The Church will be losing a good priest, but I'm sure God will find other ways of using your talents."

***

Joseph began the arduous task of disengaging himself from the priesthood. Each step he took felt like giving up a part of himself—or at least the self he'd thought he was. Now he faced an unknown future, trusting that God would lead him in the right direction.

He'd taken a hotel room in Boston, knowing he wasn't ready to tell his family about his decision. After spending a few days gathering his courage, he finally placed a call to the only number he had for Jessica: the museum where she worked.

"Sea View Museum of Art. This is Holly Simpson," a cheery voice answered.

"May I please speak with Jessica Taylor?"

"She's away at a conference, but due back in Laguna on Saturday or Sunday. May I take a message?"

"Just tell her that Joseph Murphy called. I'll try again later."

Realizing who he was, Holly said, "I *could* give you the number where she's staying if you want to call her there."

"Sure, I'll take that number. Thank you."

She gave it to him and he wrote it down, thanking Holly again.

What kind of conference is she attending? He tried to decide whether or not to call her there. *What will I say to her? I can't just tell her over the phone that I'm leaving the priesthood. That should be done in person. But, what if she doesn't want to see me? What if she's found someone else?* He'd wait until the next day to call, he decided.

Jessica

San Diego, California

The last day of the conference was for tying up loose ends, purchasing materials, and having a final luncheon with the group.

In the first break-out session, Jessica and the others in her group found their special spots, flashed nervous smiles at each other, and prepared for the morning's experience. Jessica sat down on her blue chair and awaited the facilitator's instructions.

"Today," Sally began, "we are going to work on self-forgiveness." After leading them in a short meditation, she continued with her instructions. "Now, allow an image of yourself to appear before you. Greet yourself gently and begin to recall how you have blamed yourself in the past and how you hold onto that self-blame. With each remembered instance, allow yourself to forgive yourself. You will have forty-five minutes for this experience. When you are complete, write about your experience in your journals."

Jessica's image was of herself at twenty, unmarried and pregnant. Feelings of love and elation mixed with confusion and despair washed over her.

"I know you're young, Jessica, and you don't know what to do," she said to the image of herself. "I know it feels like you're all alone, but the Holy Spirit is with you and that great love lives through you and your baby, no matter what."

As she spoke those words to her young self, the image faded and another arose, still young, talking with the nun in the adoption agency about leaving André in Provence. She could hardly bear it.

"Jessica," she said to her young frightened self, cringing and ridden with guilt, "you're doing what you think is right for your child—giving him a home with two good people who will love him as their own."

A wiser voice spoke. "You feel you've abandoned your son, but André may very well be living the life he was meant to live. It's time now for you to live the life you are meant to live. God forgives you. Now it's time to forgive yourself."

She paused to wipe away her tears. "I forgive you," she finally whispered, as every muscle in her body went limp.

***

Jessica had lunch with Ken in a nearby deli where the only available table was outside. Even though the sun shone brightly, the February weather had grown cooler. She pulled her sweater close around her as they sat down.

"That was a powerful exercise," she remarked.

"Yes, it was. I saw myself as a little boy, standing up to my father, telling him just what I thought about him, regardless of the consequences. I felt very proud of that little boy. His father was a brute."

"You still haven't forgiven *him*, have you?"

"No, I haven't."

"It takes time to get there, Ken, but it's well worth it. Have you ever been in therapy?"

"I tried once, for almost a year, but the therapist gave up on me—or maybe I gave up on her."

"Perhaps you could try again with a different person, maybe a male therapist."

"Hey, let's leave early. I get more out of talking with you than I do in being here with the group."

"I don't know, Ken," she said, unsure of her feelings.

"I'd love to drive you home. It'll give us time to talk some more. Besides, there's not much going on this afternoon."

"Well, you've got a point. It would be nice to get home a bit earlier," she said, attracted to the look in his eyes. "Okay, you've talked me into it."

While packing up, Jessica reviewed what she'd learned at the conference. She felt lighter and at peace. *Forgiving others was powerful but finally beginning to forgive myself, for giving up my baby, my André, this is long overdue.*

Joseph

Boston

Joseph finally gathered the courage to call Jessica. Gripping the phone cord as he dialed the number, he held his breath until someone answered.

"Hello, this is Reverend Arlene."

"Hello, Reverend. This is Joseph Murphy," he said, trying to stay calm. "I'm calling to speak with Jessica Taylor. I understand she's staying with you while attending a conference."

"I'm sorry, but she and Ken already left."

His heart sank. "Oh, thank you, anyway. I'll try to reach her in Laguna."

Numb inside, he hung up the phone. *Who is Ken?* He closed his eyes and sat on the bed, stunned. *Have I waited too long?*

***

Early the next morning, Joseph rented a car and headed west, then off the Mass Pike north toward Vermont and the Green Mountains. He needed to get out of the city and think things through. He pulled over into a park by a frozen lake and buried his head in his hands, releasing tears he'd been holding back since his call to San Diego. *What if I've really lost her, even before telling her that my priesthood days are over?*

He bought a bottle of French wine and checked into a bed and breakfast nearby. The room had comfortable country furnishings complete with an antique four poster bed and a small wood stove. He loosened his shirt and kicked off his shoes, then lit a fire. *Maybe Ken's just a friend. And maybe he's not.* The idea that the woman he loved could possibly be with another man at that very moment was impossible for him to accept. He shut his eyes, hoping to erase the thought from his mind, but it didn't work.

Taking a sip of wine, he remembered all the romantic moments with Jessica: the night long ago in Paris, after the university riot, when she'd shown up on his doorstep, looking like a waif, all bruised up and in need of his comfort. *If only we could go back in time.* The day in New York when they bumped into each other again at MoMA. *It was wonderful being with her for those precious months. If only I'd been able to make this decision then when she was with me. But, no, I just couldn't make up my mind.*

Wallowing in self-pity, Joseph poured another glass of wine and then another, until the bottle was empty. Tossing it in the trash can, he shook his head, ashamed of himself. *What am I doing? This isn't going to solve a thing. It only makes me feel worse.*

While showering, he affirmed: *I've got to get myself together. I feel paralyzed.*

Nothing eased his mind. Taking out his mother's rosary, he closed his eyes and began to recite the familiar phrases that centered him.

"I've got to be strong," he asserted, after emerging from his prayers. *Even if Jessica is lost to me, I must stay true to myself and get on with my life.*

Jessica

Jessica and Ken stopped to see his son Fred before making the trip to Laguna Beach, arriving in time for dinner at The Cottage, once a charming old house. The sun had set before they'd finished eating and Jessica felt a chill caused as much by her anxiety as from the drop in temperature.

Did I make a mistake leaving the conference with Ken? When they arrived at her house, she unlocked the door and invited him inside. Miss Suzy greeted them, meowing insistently.

"Hello, my sweet kitty," she said, picking up her cat. "Did Holly visit with you while I was gone?" The cat stopped meowing and began purring in her arms.

Over dinner Ken had told her how resentful his ex-wife had been when he'd asked for a divorce. According to his story, she'd hired a tough lawyer and *took* him for most of their money, as well as their house. Ken was more than a little angry about it. Jessica, in turn, had told Ken about her miscarriage, Jim's heavy drinking, and her divorce, though afterwards she had some misgivings about having been so open with him.

"Would you like a cup of tea?"

"I'd rather have a beer or a glass of wine if you have any."

"I do have some red wine."

She left him in the living room while fetching the wine. When he'd first asked to drive her home, she'd considered the possibility that they might spend the night together. *Having him in the house feels ... well ... unnatural. What have I gotten myself into?* She opened the wine and poured two glasses, nervously taking them back to the living room. They sat on the couch together.

"To us," he said, clinking his glass to hers.

"To our friendship," she said, taking a small sip of her wine.

"Well, I'd hoped for more than that," he said, looking deep into her eyes.

"I need to be honest with you, Ken. I realize, now that you're here, I can't give you anything more than friendship."

A look of disbelief shown in his eyes.

"That's ridiculous. You're just nervous." He pulled her nearer to him. "I know you want more than that."

He reached down to kiss her, but she was unresponsive.

"What's the matter with you?"

"I'm sorry," she said, pulling back and sitting up straight. "I don't want to hurt you, but I can't do this." She searched his face for a glimmer of understanding, but a dark shadow had fallen across it.

"You're a phony, Jessica," he shouted, standing, his voice harsh and his eyes accusing. "You led me on."

"I didn't mean to. I've felt ambivalent ever since we met."

He gave her a look of disgust, his large frame towering over her.

"What a bitch," he shouted louder, his eyes narrowing. "You act like you really care and then you go cold." He grabbed her arm and pulled her up. "Maybe I should give you something to remember me by."

"Let go of me, Ken. You're hurting me."

The phone's ring startled them both. She pulled free and ran to answer it, saying a desperate "Hello."

"You're out of breath. Are you okay?" It was Holly.

"Yes, I'm ... I'm fine. I was just saying goodbye to Ken." She shot an angry look at him.

Ken picked up his jacket. The indignant look on his face reminded her of a child who couldn't take no for an answer.

"Fuck you," he bellowed, slamming the door behind him.

"What's happening?" Holly asked frantically.

"I'll be right back," Jessica promised, dropping the phone.

She ran to lock the door and heard Ken's engine start up and speed away.

"Holly," she cried, retrieving the phone from the floor, "you saved me from a bad situation."

"What happened?"

"Ken offered to drive me home and I agreed, somehow seduced by his vulnerability after the conference." She was stumbling over her words. "I invited him in, but I knew right away I'd made a mistake. I tried to tell him we couldn't be more than friends. He got angry and verbally abusive. Just when you called, I thought he was going to force himself on me. I was starting to get scared. Thank God, you called when you did. He left in a hurry."

"I was afraid something like this might happen," Holly said quietly. "He's got serious anger issues."

"I sensed that but didn't trust myself—or you, for that matter. We shared some quality time at the conference and I thought I could give him another chance."

"Well, now you know for sure he's not right for you. Oh, I almost forgot. I didn't expect you home until tomorrow but I wanted to leave you an important message so you'd get it as soon as you got in."

"What is it?"

"Joseph Murphy called the museum this afternoon."

"Joseph called?"

"He seemed disappointed you weren't here so I gave him Reverend Arlene's number. I guess you left before he tried to reach you."

"Did he leave a number?"

"No, he didn't. I should have asked but I thought he'd reach you in San Diego. I'm so sorry, Jessica."

After hanging up, Jessica sat down with Miss Suzy.

I was honest with Ken, and he showed his true colors. And Joseph was trying to reach me all the while. Hearing his voice would have been so comforting after that scene with Ken. "I'll have to leave the comforting to you, kitty," she cooed, stroking soft fur as tears of longing and relief ran down her cheeks.

Joseph

Pleased to find another cottage on the Cape as secluded as the first he'd enjoyed, Joseph continued the difficult process of cutting the strings that had bound him to the priesthood for years and to Catholicism for as long as he could remember. He had no idea what the future would bring, only a deep conviction that he must sever himself from his past identity. With each priestly garment he packed away, a sense of loss, combined with a new sense of freedom, swept over him. *It is high time for the exterior man and the interior one to live in harmony.*

"What is it you truly long for?" a voice inside whispered.

To tell Jess how much I love her. But is it too late? He couldn't bear to hear her say she loved another man.

"Look deeper," the inner voice insisted.

I long to live authentically—not just the way other people think I should live. I long to be at peace with you, Father—and with myself—whether or not Jessica becomes part of my life.

He *knew*, as he never had before, he was not alone and that he never would be. With that realization, a deep sense of peace swept over him. He was ready now to tell his family about his decision, but not quite ready to call Jessica again.

***

"Joseph," his mother smiled, hugging him and kissing him on the cheek as she greeted him at her home a few days later. "It's so good to see you. And no collar today. I guess you're feeling pretty casual."

"Yes." He smiled. "Are Tom and Susan here yet?"

"They sure are. Charlie drove them over. And, Sean's here, too, with his girlfriend, Tanya. Do you remember her?"

"Of course."

He followed her to the kitchen where his stepfather stood opening the refrigerator.

"How about a beer?" John asked, smiling at him.

"Love one."

"We have a new puppy and everyone's gathered out there in the yard to meet him," John explained.

"Fantastic," Joseph said as they walked outside.

The air was crisp, and the gray clouds overhead threatened rain.

"Uncle Joe," Sean shouted cheerily, "good to see you, man." He and

Tanya came over to greet him warmly.

Charlie brought over the latest member of the family, a little blonde cocker spaniel puppy.

"Her name's Trouble." Charlie laughed. "She's into all kinds of mischief, chewing on every shoe she finds and even the chair legs."

"Hi, Trouble," Joseph said, patting the puppy's head. "You are a wiggly one, aren't you?"

Charlie put her down and gave Joseph a bear hug.

"So good to see you, Uncle Joe."

"Great to see you, too, Charlie. How's your internship going?"

"It's keeping me pretty busy," Charlie answered, "but I love it."

Tom and Susan wandered over and greeted Joseph. "Hey, what took you so long to come back for a visit?" Tom chided, slapping him on the back.

"Well," Joseph explained, "a lot's been happening over the past few months." Tom gave him a curious look.

"Dinner's ready," Dorothy called from the kitchen. They filed inside as she placed a large pot roast on the dining room table.

Soon everyone was seated and, as usual, his mother asked Joseph to say grace before they started to eat. He thanked God for the food as well as for the love of family and friends. In unison, everyone said "Amen."

With a huge grin on his face, Sean announced, "Tanya and I are engaged." Tanya blushed as Sean reached over to give her a kiss on the forehead.

"That's wonderful news," Dorothy exclaimed.

"Hear, hear," Charlie said, raising his glass. "To Sean and Tanya."

"We haven't picked out the ring yet," Sean said, "but that's happening next weekend."

"I'm so happy for you two," Joseph said, beaming at his nephew.

"We'd like to get married next spring," Sean said, "and we'd like you to perform the wedding, Uncle Joe."

Joseph looked around the table at each of them and said slowly, "I'm afraid that won't be possible. I also have an announcement to make. I'm not exactly a priest anymore."

No one spoke.

"Hey, it's a good thing," Joseph explained, "not a bad one. After much prayer and good counsel, I realize I must follow my heart and, right now, it's leading me toward something new. I'm not sure what exactly, but I know it is *not* the Catholic priesthood."

"So you've finally made your decision," Tom said.

"It's taken me a long time but I know this is the right thing to do."

"I had a feeling you were struggling with a major decision when you went to Paris," his mother said, a look of loving concern in her eyes.

"You're right, Mom. That's exactly why I took that trip—to make my decision. Monsignor Anthony has been a great help to me as well. We've had numerous talks about this and he agrees I'm doing the right thing. In fact," he said, turning to Sean and Tanya, "I think *he'd* be honored to officiate at your wedding if you ask him."

"To letting go of the old and welcoming the new," John stated, holding up his glass.

Again in unison, the family raised their glasses.

***

"Tom, can we talk alone for a few minutes?" Joseph asked after the meal was over.

"Sure. Let's go outside."

Joseph followed his brother out the back door onto the patio.

"So what's on your mind?"

"You know about Jessica and my feelings for her, but there are other reasons for my decision to leave the priesthood. I don't believe Catholicism has all the answers to life's questions anymore and …."

"What's the matter?"

"I have reason to believe that Jessica may be involved with another man."

"What makes you think that?"

"Well, when I tried to call her a few weeks ago where she was staying for a conference, I was told 'she and Ken' had already left. It sounded like they were a couple."

"Maybe they're colleagues or just friends."

"I know that's a possibility. But I don't think I could handle it if she's fallen in love with someone else."

"You need to find out for sure, buddy. If you don't connect with her, tell her what's going on, she won't even know you're available."

"I know, I know. You're right, but I feel like I need more clarity about my next step, career-wise. I don't want to confuse or worry her."

"Sounds like you're stalling. I wouldn't wait too long," Tom said, patting him on the back.

***

"Mom, could we talk for a bit before I go?" Joseph asked after everyone else had left.

"I'm going on up to bed now," John said. "I think you two need some time together."

"Thanks, dear," Dorothy said, kissing her husband goodnight and motioning to Joseph to join her on the living room couch. All was quiet except the ticking of the grandfather clock in the hallway.

"Talk to me," she said, looking intently into Joseph's eyes.

"Well, you know I've always wanted to follow God's will for my life," he began, "but, after much soul-searching and prayer, I've realized that it was Dad I was trying to please."

"I'd often wondered about that. Your dad was quite adamant that the priesthood was your destiny. I never felt that way. I always thought you'd miss having a wife and children."

"I *do* miss those things. And I've become disenchanted with the Catholic Church. I'm not even sure if my spiritual path includes finding another church. I may decide to go back into architecture or maybe even social work."

"Oh, my darling son, I trust you will find your way."

"Who knows, maybe one day I'll even marry."

Dorothy's eyebrows raised and then a smile spread across her lips. Joseph could tell she liked *that* idea.

Jessica

Laguna Beach

Jessica woke up late on her day off. Throwing on her robe and stepping into her slippers, she stumbled to the kitchen, fed the cat her favorite tuna meal, and stared vacantly out the window, trying to recall her dream. Something about being in the woods, searching for Joseph, but he was nowhere to be found.

She suddenly caught sight of an elusive rainbow created by the sun shining through the colored glass bottles in her kitchen window. *The rainbow after the storm?* She recalled her ordeal with Ken and that Joseph had been trying to reach her almost simultaneously. But nearly a full week had passed and he hadn't called back. *He should've left a number. Doesn't he know this is driving me crazy?*

After indulging in a bagel and cream cheese along with her usual tea, she slipped into sweats and headed for the beach trails. The soothing sound of waves breaking over jagged rocks helped to calm her busy mind as she continued to think about Joseph's call and what it might have meant. She walked south, enjoying the sun's warmth as a soft breeze played with her hair. Her attention turned to her mother's call to the museum earlier that week when she'd spoken to Holly and told her she'd discovered a young French photographer whose work she felt Jessica and the Sea View would do well to consider.

The timing was actually spot on as the museum had been focusing more directly on international photography. Jessica trusted her mother's judgment when it came to photography. Adelaide had acquired an impressive collection over the years and could perhaps, in Jessica's estimation, have been a professional photographer herself, if she'd had the confidence to follow through with her art.

The Sea View had already exhibited some photographic landscapes from England and the Tuscany region of Italy, but needed more urban, people-oriented photographs to balance them out. *I hope he fits the bill.* She decided to return her mother's call while she was free, wondering why she'd called from a London hotel, the Carlyle. It would be near dinner time there. Of course, there a good possibility that she'd already returned to the Lake District.

Her mother answered on the first ring.

"Hi, Mum. Holly told me you'd called."

"Hello, darling, I'm so glad to hear from you."

"I've been away … and also had a very hard week."

"Oh, dear, anything you'd like to share?"

"Not really."

"Well, I've been in London now for nearly ten days and enjoying myself immensely but I must soon get home. I'm so glad you caught me. I was just about to leave for dinner."

"Tell me about the young photographer you're so excited about."

"The short of it is, you must see his work. He has a remarkable eye, both sensitive and provocative. His name is André Casal. He's recently been on display at a gallery in Montmartre, an exhibit entitled Children of Paris. It's garnering such excitement, he's been here in London showing his portfolio."

"How did you meet him?"

"Oh, I was on my way to high tea and I saw him in the lobby of the hotel with some of his work spread out on a table, people gathered around. I went over to take a look."

"What were you doing in London?"

"Oh, you know, shopping, visiting some of my friends, that sort of thing. But the important thing is this: Mr. Casal's exhibit will only be featured in Montmartre for a week or so. Is there any chance you could fly to Paris and see his show?"

"Oh, I don't think so. I just got back from a conference and there's so much to do around here. But it just so happens I *am* looking for international photography right now and I'm quite intrigued to hear that he's working with portraits of children. I'll have an opening for another exhibit within the season."

"Oh, Jess, you don't want to miss this opportunity. I know talent when I see it. Plus, he's such a lovely young man, and very talented."

"You sound quite taken with him. And it is Paris. Perhaps I could clear my desk enough to come for a short trip. Even if I miss his show, maybe I can meet him and get a good look at his portfolio."

"Try to make it happen, darling. You won't be sorry."

***

Holly had never been to Paris, so Jessica decided to surprise her and take her along to meet André Casal. Having a strong administrative team in place made it easier to decide. Jessica knew the volunteer docents would look after information and tours at the museum in their absence.

André

Entering the quaint Jeanne d' Arc Hotel where Jessica was staying in Marais, André noted its charming ambiance. *Jessica has good taste.*

Riding the lift to the third floor, he took a few deep breaths to calm his nerves. *What will she be like?*

When a winsome blonde woman in a business suit opened the door, his breath caught in his throat. He recognized her immediately from the photograph Adelaide had shown him, but she was even more attractive in person.

"*Bonjour*, I'm André Casal."

"Jessica Taylor. Come in, please."

He stepped into the French provincial-appointed room complete with marble top buffet, a soft green damask sofa with facing arm chairs, and a welcoming open balcony that allowed the afternoon sun to warm the space with light. Jessica invited him to sit on the sofa in front of a coffee and tea service that included an array of small pastries.

The door next to the buffet opened and a young woman with dark hair and expressive brown eyes walked into the room.

"Come join us," Jessica invited. "André Casal, meet Holly Simpson, my assistant."

"*Enchanté*," he said, standing and taking Holly's outstretched hand and kissing it lightly. He smiled as her face took on a charming pink glow.

"I'm very pleased to meet you both," he said.

"Your English is very good," Holly remarked, her large brown eyes smiling into his.

"Thank you, Mademoiselle. *Parlez-vous français*?"

"Uh, I think you're asking me if I speak French and the answer is no, but I'd love to learn someday."

"Then I'm sure you will if that is your intention."

"Oh, it is. I'm so excited to be here. My first trip to Paris."

"It would be my pleasure to be your guide, Miss Simpson, if you would like." André smiled.

"Thanks so much," she said. "And please call me Holly."

"Holly it is."

"We'll only be here for a few days," Jessica said, motioning for Holly to sit. "Not much time, but we'll make the most of it."

"Tea or coffee, Mr. Casal?" Jessica asked.

"Coffee, and please call me André."

"André, yes, thank you. And feel free to call me Jessica."

He nodded his head in agreement, thankful things seemed to be going well so far.

"Is this also your first visit to Paris, Jessica?" he asked, knowing what her answer would be.

"No, I was a student here back in the sixties," she told him, her soft green eyes appearing wistful, even nostalgic. Touched by her expression, André didn't know what to say next.

"I'm looking forward to seeing your work," Holly said, breaking the silence.

"And I'm eager to show you. Are you ready now?"

"Of course," Jessica and Holly said in near unison as they stood to clear the coffee table.

"Oh, please, let me." André said, reaching to help them.

"No, no, you get out your portfolio. We'll put these things on the buffet, but do continue to help yourself."

"*Merci*," he said, pulling forward the portfolio, realizing he was a bit nervous. "The collection is entitled Children of Paris," he explained, turning to the first image: a little girl, sitting at the top of a sliding board, excitement in her eyes, her hands in the air, ready to take the plunge, while an elderly woman waited with arms outstretched at the foot of the slide.

"Just look at her face," Jessica commented with enthusiasm. "I feel her sense of freedom but also how she needs her determination to take the risk."

"And the older woman, with her arms outstretched," Holly added, "appears to be her grandmother, encouraging the child's latest adventure. It's very moving."

"I found many children in the city whose grandparents seemed to take care of them while their parents worked, but there were many more, like this next child, who may have had no one." He turned to the next photo, a little boy in ragged clothes sitting against a building in the city, alone, a faraway gaze in his eyes as if he was imagining another time, a better life. "I bought him an ice cream from a vendor on the street. Just look how his face lit up." He turned to another photo of the same boy, fully enthralled by his treat, eyes shining with delight.

"Your technique is very effective, André," Jessica said. "I appreciate your choice to fade out the background, allowing the child's expression to come forward, to be the focal point of the photo. Well done."

"Usually, I prefer color," Holly added, "but your use of sepia makes your subjects appear timeless."

"You're both very perceptive. Those were my intentions on both counts."

One by one, he shared his photos with them, and Jessica and Holly spent several moments with each one. When he reached the back of his portfolio, Jessica nodded approvingly and said, "They are truly exquisite, Mr. Casal—André. You have captured such an array of emotions in the children's expressions. Like Holly, I'm quite moved by your sensitivity."

Her words touched his heart. *Why do I care so much what she thinks?*

"*Merci beaucoup.* Children are so honest and unpretentious—unlike most adults—with such fluid and unmasked expressions. The photographer's primary job is to be present and quick, to be truly there with his subject."

"I must admit," Jessica said, "I was skeptical that someone your age could capture such depth of emotion. But I was wrong. Our museum, the Sea View in Laguna Beach, California, will have an opening for a photography exhibit very soon and we'd be honored to exhibit your work."

André's could barely speak. "Thank you, Madame. But it is I who would be honored."

"And, with our new endowment for emerging artists, I believe we can cover your transportation as well."

"I am very grateful. *Merci, merci.*"

"You are quite deserving of the opportunity," Jessica assured him.

"Have you ever been to America, André?" Holly asked.

"No, but I've dreamed of it. Now, do let me show you Paris through this photographer's eyes!"

"We've certainly seen some of your Paris through your photos," Jessica said, "but I imagine Holly would very much like to see more. As for me, well, I need my solitude here. There are such memories."

André noted again the wistful look in her eyes and smiled gently, turning to Holly. "How about it, may I show you Paris?"

***

The next day, André met Holly in the lobby of the hotel. Her eyes shone with excitement.

"Where would you like to go first?"

"Could we start with Montmartre? My mother painted there when she was beginning to take her art seriously."

"Of course. The Metro is at the end of the block. It's just a short ride to Montmartre."

"Even with jet lag, I'm so excited to be here," Holly exclaimed.

André bought their tickets and guided her to the appropriate train.

"What a beautiful church," Holly said as they exited the Metro to see a massive building at the top of the hill in front of them.

"It's the *Sacre Coeur*, Church of the Sacred Heart," he told her as they began the long trek up steep steps, his hand lightly touching her back. At the top, André motioned for her to turn around. "Just take a moment to enjoy this amazing view."

Paris lay before them; the Eiffel Tower looked miniature in the distance.

"It's beautiful," she said, bringing her hand to her heart. "A dream come true."

"Stand over here for a moment," André said, taking out his camera. "I want to capture the excitement in your eyes."

"If you insist." She laughed, then smiled brightly at him.

"Beautiful."

After strolling through the church with its windows of sparkling blues and gold, André took Holly's arm and guided her down the narrow, curving street that opened into a large square filled with artists painting and sketching at their easels.

"I love it here. I can imagine my mother there behind one of those easels. She told me stories about her time here before she married my dad."

"Is your mother still painting?"

"She ... died when I was fourteen."

"I'm so sorry," André said, reaching for her hand. They stood for a few moments while Holly gathered herself.

"My mom taught me everything I know about art."

Just then a young woman rushed up to them, holding up black cut-out images that she had created of the two of them.

"Look," the woman insisted, placing the images against white paper, framed with pre-cut mats, presenting them as silhouettes.

"André, look, she's even cut out my heart-shaped earrings and my beret. And you, your long hair just so. These are wonderful!"

"How much?" André asked, and proceeded to negotiate the price.

"Thanks so much, André, I love them."

"You're welcome. Now you can't forget me or Montmartre."

Holly looked down shyly.

"You were telling me," he said, "that your mother taught you all about art. Are you an artist, too?"

"I like to think so, though these days I work with other people's art."

"What's your favorite medium?"

"Watercolor. I enjoy capturing *plein air* landscapes, but I most love painting visionary images from my imagination," Holly shared, the joy in her face unmistakable.

"*Vous êtes adorable,*" André pronounced, taking her hands, his heart throbbing.

"*Merci,* I think," she whispered, blushing.

After exploring the square and visiting with the artists, they walked toward the *Galerie d' le Beau,* where André's photos had been on display. The gallery owner was out to lunch, but his assistant invited them to enjoy the latest exhibit.

As they were leaving, André said, "I look forward to seeing some of *your* paintings when I am in America."

"Maybe we'll have a chance to go to Cambria where I grew up. All my mother's and my paintings are there. My father and brother seem to enjoy having them, but if I settle permanently in Laguna Beach, I'll likely want to have some of our work with me. It keeps me close to her."

"I understand."

They walked a while in silence.

"How about an authentic French lunch?"

"Lovely."

"You'll like the ambiance of *La Cremaillere 1900.* Cabaret singers entertain large groups of tourists in the back room, but we'll enjoy them from an intimate table upfront."

André ushered her into the café, which was decorated with colorful posters and murals.

"May I order for both of us?"

Holly nodded her agreement, captivated by the French conversations and local color. When the carafe of red wine arrived before their soup, salad, and baguette, he poured some for each of them and then raised his glass.

"To you, Mademoiselle."

"And to you, Monsieur."

Somehow this feels oddly familiar, he thought.

PART THREE

Jessica

Jessica spent the day wandering around the city, first along the Seine, visiting her old haunt, Shakespeare and Company, and then walking toward the Sorbonne, where she had taken classes in the sixties. Crossing Saint Germain, she found herself standing in front of Joseph's old flat. She stood looking up at the wide window, reliving the past, her heart filling with bittersweet memories.

As the sun dipped low in the sky, she stopped in a little café but didn't have much appetite. Daydreaming for a while, she decided to make her way back towards the Pont Neuf Bridge, breathing in the evening air as she gazed out at the Seine before crossing from the Left to the Right Bank. *How many times did Joseph and I walk this route together?* In the setting sun, the bridge took on a luminous quality.

I feel pulled, but to what I'm not sure. It's as if the threads of my life are weaving me, making sense of it all: my days as an art student, falling in love, living on the edge between heartache and promise, transitioning from girlhood to womanhood, even motherhood, the journey to New York, work in the art world, and now California. Still I'm alone.

Tears filled her eyes but she didn't bother to wipe them away. *Let them fall. I can't hold them back anymore. Paris, the City of Light. It brings old and new together in a way that transcends the ordinary, merging the past and present, circling, spiraling, flowing like a river through two sides of me, connecting me to Source.*

She walked to the center of the bridge and gazed down at the water, its ripples reflecting the dancing city lights. *If only Joseph were here to share this with me. In a strange way, he is here. He is here because I am here. He's my soulmate. It's clear if not simple.*

The night air grew cooler as she stood, shivering and alone.

***

Holly had not arrived when Jessica got back to the hotel. Although it was still early, she'd begun to feel the effects of jet lag. *I'll just slip under the covers for a quick nap. Mother Mary, I need your support, your guidance, your strength.*

Jessica awoke to the sound of the shower. Sunlight poured in through the window. Rubbing the sleep out of her eyes, she pulled herself up and wandered into the sitting room. *I've slept through the night!* From the bathroom, she heard Holly singing, "Blue skies, nothing but blue skies …."

"Jessica, you're up," Holly exclaimed moments later as she danced into the room, her hair wrapped in a towel.

"Yes … at least I think I am."

"It's a beautiful day. André wants to meet us downstairs after breakfast and then take us to the Louvre. Are you up for that?"

"I really don't think so. I'm still feeling quiet."

"Are you okay, Jessica?"

"Lots of memories here for me, you can imagine."

"Yes, I can." Holly gave her a sympathetic look, then grinned. "I really like André."

"I gathered that."

"Paris is such a magical place."

"I know you'll enjoy the Louvre. I spent many hours there when I was a student here."

"Will you be okay by yourself?"

"Absolutely. I just want to go where the day takes me, maybe return to some of my old stomping grounds."

"Thank you, Jessica, for everything: bringing me here with you, being such a wonderful mentor, a wonderful friend."

"You are most welcome, my dear."

***

After breakfast in the hotel, Jessica and Holly found André at the lobby entrance, waiting for them.

"*Bonjour*," Holly called.

André turned, his face brightening as he came toward them.

"Are you ladies ready?"

"You two enjoy the Louvre. I've already told Holly I want a bit more time on my own," Jessica said.

As Holly and André walked side by side toward the lobby door, Jessica smiled and watched them for a moment. *They're really cute together. His walk, it's so familiar. Funny.*

Jessica followed soon after them, turning toward the square. *Perhaps to the Bastille. Hugo's house.* Tears surfaced. *I'll just keep walking, see where my body wants to go.*

Soon she stood at a bakery counter, admiring the many treats behind the glass.

"A double cappuccino… and a chocolate éclair." *Delicious, the perfect way to begin my day.*

Next, she crossed the bridge and made her way back toward Saint-Germain-des-Pres. She admired the elegant designer clothes that filled the shop windows. She passed a café historically known to literary types, and an old stone church. *Where is the convent? Can I possibly be lost?*

She walked to the end of the block, the smell of pine turning her head, and there it was, the wrought iron fence to the convent and, through its gate, beyond the once miniature pine, the Tree of Life door, repaired and re-painted. Like the bridge, it beckoned to her. But she could not bring herself to enter the sacred space and instead stood outside the entrance, gazing at the branches reaching upward, the roots reaching down, carved in the golden wood. It moved her but she could not explain why. *Nostalgia? Longing?* No, more than that, a symbol meant for her. But meaning what? She turned and walked back down the block, the image, long imprinted in her mind, brought alive again.

She wandered aimlessly until pausing at the top of the stairs of a Metro station. *Luxembourg Gardens is more than a healthy walk. I could take a bus.* But the day had turned gray and the underground route better matched her melancholy mood.

***

Stepping out of the Metro station and onto the sidewalk, Jessica buttoned her jacket and retied her scarf to buffer the chilly air as she entered the great garden. Although the skies remained gray, a strange light pierced the dark sky. *It's no wonder Paris is called the City of Light.*

She heard the splashing water from the center fountain and walked toward it. The surrounding sculptures transported her to timeless time, music from the gazebo reminding her of a painful conversation with Joseph while standing beside it. They'd been discussing the turmoil in Paris—and the Vietnam War—when he had stopped, looking hard at her.

She could hear his voice saying, "On one hand, I'm so grateful for our connection. On the other, I wonder if it's a test of my faith."

"A test of your faith?" she'd said, incredulous. "If that's all I am to you, I've been a complete fool."

Have I been a complete fool? "No," she heard herself say out loud. *All of my choices, the good and bad, contributed to the person I've become. In a way, my dreams have come true: I love my work, now have my own museum.* "But," a voice within reminded her, "You don't have Joseph."

Tears came again to her eyes and she sat on the edge of the fountain, its energy enveloping her. *I'm glad Holly and I are going home tomorrow. It's high time I listened to my inner wisdom, trusted the Holy Spirit, Mother Mary, the Goddess, the Source, God, whatever the greater good may be called, to help me let go of the past, forget about the future, and learn to live fully in the present—whatever it brings.* Jessica gathered up her things and returned to the hotel, determined to move on with her life.

In the hotel room, she found a note from Holly.

André is taking me on a dinner cruise on the Seine. I'm so excited! Thank you again for this, for everything. I could stay in Paris forever. Holly.

Holly

Holly smiled at him as André helped her board the riverboat for their moonlit journey down the Seine. *This feels like a dream. André looks so handsome. How amazing of him to suggest this. I hope Jessica is okay.*

André ordered champagne.

"You look very beautiful tonight."

"Thank you, and for taking me to the Louvre today. I'm still in awe at how immense it is."

"All the more reason for you to come back, *mon cherie.*"

"The Mona Lisa was much smaller than I'd expected, and yet such a thrill to see in person."

"It brought tears to your eyes."

"They're welling up again just thinking about it, about *everything.* My trip to Paris has been a dream come true."

"Shall we dance?" The three-piece band was playing a soft, slow song.

"I'd love to."

When André held her close, every cell in Holly's body seemed to awaken. When he kissed her tenderly on the cheek, she melted into his soft embrace.

After the music ended, their lips naturally met, transporting her into a dimension where only the two of them existed.

"I think I'm falling in love with you, Holly Simpson."

"You can't be. We just met."

"Maybe so, but I've never felt like this before." He pulled her closer.

They danced through several songs before returning to their table where their champagne had been poured. The boat ride lasted just long enough to enjoy a lovely French buffet and their bottle before coming to dock, the landing jolting them back to reality.

Back at the hotel, Holly wistfully thanked André again for everything.

"You are most welcome," he whispered, standing back to study her. "I want to photograph you someday, really photograph you. You are a natural beauty, Holly: unpretentious, real, not unlike the children that have captivated me."

After a short pause, he whispered, "May I kiss you good night?"

When their lips met again, her body trembled as she drew even closer to him, not wanting the moment to end. *I've never been kissed like this before yet it feels so natural, so perfect.*

"I wish you weren't leaving tomorrow. We're just getting to know each other."

"I know, but soon you'll be in California. Then I can show you around."

"I can hardly wait. *Au revoir, mon cherie. Au revoir.*"

They kissed again, holding each other's hands, parting ever so slowly.

***

The next morning, Holly awoke to Jessica's, "Time to get up. Our cab will be here in less than an hour."

"Oh, my goodness!"

"Well, it was pretty late when you came in last night. How was it?"

"Only the most romantic evening I've ever had."

"You really like him, don't you?"

"I'll be leaving a bit of my heart in Paris."

"I know what you mean."

André

Reflecting on his time with Holly and meeting Jessica, André sat quietly in his studio, realizing his life had changed. *It's time to tell Mamà and Papa what's going on.*

"I have good news," he announced when his mother answered the phone in Provence. "I'm going to the United States in a few weeks."

"You are?"

"Yes, I've been invited to exhibit my photographs in a small museum in California."

"André, sweetheart, that's great news. Tell me how this happened."

"Maybe you should sit down, Mamà. It's quite a story."

André relayed what had transpired, beginning with meeting Adelaide, but not sharing details about the necklace's hidden contents. Sensing that she would be intrigued by the Essene/Cathar connection, he wanted to show her the Tree of Life symbol in person.

"So now you know." He held his breath, anxious about how she would react.

"You must do what's right for you," his mother said in a faint voice.

"Mamà, you and Papa will always be my real parents. I'm just curious about my origins, you know?"

"We've always loved you, André," she said in a choked voice.

"I know that, Mamà, and I love you, too. None of this will change how I feel about you and Papa."

"I just don't want you to forget about us."

"Mamà, how could I ever forget about you?"

"Your papa will be so proud when he hears you'll be exhibiting your photographs in America."

André smiled, moved by the sound of her voice.

"Mamà," he said timidly, "do you believe in love at first sight?"

"For some, love comes instantly—at least the chemistry happens right away. But real love, deep intimacy and trust, takes years to blossom. Why do you ask?"

He told her about Holly, his voice full of joy.

"Oh, André, she sounds lovely. You are clearly enamored of her, but, a word of caution: go slow, be present, enjoy each moment without expectation."

"You're a wise woman, Mamà."

"And you're a very special young man."

"Will you explain everything to Papa? I know you can do it better than I could."

"Of course. And, André, I couldn't possibly be prouder of you than I am at this moment. You are a talented photographer and a wonderful son. I love you so much."

***

One month later, an excited and nervous André Casal landed at Los Angeles International Airport. He was ready to begin a new chapter in his life, but plagued by anxious questions. *What will Jessica think when I tell her who I am? Should I really be doing this?*

Holly had offered to meet him at LAX but he preferred to have his own transportation when he reached Laguna Beach and so had reserved a rental car. She had reserved a room for him and would be meeting him at the hotel. He found himself very excited at the prospect of seeing her again.

André rolled down the car window and breathed in the fresh ocean air as he drove down the coast, looking forward to seeing the Pacific in the daylight. *Southern California. Am I really here?*

When he walked into the lobby of the hotel, he spotted Holly curled up in a comfortable chair with her eyes closed, looking gorgeous in black jeans, boots, and a purple knit top, a colorful shawl draped around her shoulders.

"Holly," he said softly, tapping her on the arm.

She opened her eyes and looked up at him with the pretty smile that dazzled him.

Pulling her up, he wrapped his arms around her and held her close, kissing her forehead.

"The bar's still open in case you want a nightcap," she said, smiling at him.

"A glass of wine would be nice. I'm eager to compare California wine with the French wine I grew up on."

Carrying his bag in one hand, he held her arm in the other as they walked toward the bar.

"In the daytime, you can see the ocean through these windows," Holly told him as they sat down at a table in the corner of the room.

"We'd like a bottle of California Cabernet, something special from the Napa Valley," André said to the waiter.

She took off her shawl, revealing a small tattooed heart on her wrist.

"That's cool. I hadn't noticed it before."

"I've had it since I turned sixteen." She laughed. "My best friend and I were such good girls we decided we had to do something wild to celebrate our coming of age. She has a butterfly on her ankle."

"Good and wild, that sounds promising," he said, looking at her seductively.

"Oh, stop," Holly said teasingly, kicking him gently under the table as the wine arrived.

He continued to gaze at her as the waiter poured.

"I can't believe you're really here," she said, nervously pushing an unruly curl from her eyes. "I reserved the same room for you that I stayed in when I first came to Laguna for my interview at the museum. You can see the ocean from the balcony." The reflection of candlelight danced in her eyes.

"Fantastic." He smiled, reaching out to touch her hand.

"Tomorrow is Monday, so the museum is closed. You'll have a day to settle in. We can still begin setting up your exhibit later in the day. Jessica likes to use Mondays to get a jump on the week."

Anxious, he idly pulled the necklace from under his shirt. As usual, touching it helped to calm his nerves.

"That's beautiful, André. I don't recall seeing it in Paris. May I take a closer look?"

"Not now. Tell me how you've been," he said awkwardly, trying to change the subject.

"What's up? Is something bothering you? You seem testy that I asked about your necklace."

André stayed quiet, taking a sip of wine and looking down.

"I have a feeling it has a deep meaning for you."

"You're very perceptive. My parents gave it to me when I left home for photography school in Paris."

"I sense there's some kind of mystery associated with it."

"What makes you think so?" He stared at her with curiosity.

"Sometimes I get intuitive messages about things, and this is one of those times."

"Tell me more."

"I don't know how to express it in words. The intuition came as an image."

"Of what?" he urged.

"I see a woman wearing your necklace. She has a baby in her arms, reaching for it."

His eyes brimmed with tears. *I have no other choice but to tell her.*

"Holly, I can't believe you just said that. My mother, I mean my birth mother, left this with me in a convent in Provence when I was a baby. I only learned I'd been adopted when my parents gave it to me four years ago."

"Wow, that gives me angel bumps," she said, shivering.

"And I'm here not only to exhibit my photographs ... but to meet the woman I believe to be my real mother."

She looked at him wide-eyed. "Who?"

"Jessica Taylor," he said quietly.

Holly gasped. Before she could respond, the waiter came over to tell them the bar was closing.

"Could I still get a cappuccino?" André asked.

"Sure," the man said. "I'll make it to go."

"Make that two," Holly said, still stunned.

As they waited for their coffees, André suggested they take a walk on the beach, unless she was too tired.

"Are you kidding? I'm wide awake."

Carrying their steaming cups, they crossed the main street and sat down on a wooden boardwalk, dangling their feet over the side, facing the surf, now glowing in silvery moonlight.

"Please, André, tell me your story. I can't believe what you just said. Jessica? Jessica may be your birth mother?"

He explained how he'd gotten Jessica's name from the adoption agency and had gone to London to look for her, called several J. Taylors in the phonebook until by chance he'd reached her father's house, his ex-wife, Adelaide, Jessica's mother, returning his call.

"She recognized this necklace." He paused, touching it again. "You can imagine how shocked she was when I told her my birth mother had left it with me at the convent. We compared notes and, well, Jessica had been in France during the same year I was born."

"I can hardly *believe* this," Holly, her brow tensing as she recalled the night Jessica had told her about her long-ago pregnancy, Joseph, all of it.

"What is it?" André asked.

"I don't know what to say. It's too much," she said.

"I know it's a lot to absorb."

After a long pause, André reached for Holly's hand, asking anxiously, "How do you think Jessica will react?"

"Initially, she'll be in shock. But once she calms down, I imagine she'll be overjoyed."

They sat together in silence for some time, allowing the soothing sound of waves crashing on the shore to envelop them.

No matter how Jessica reacts, I know I was meant to meet Holly. With that knowing came instant peace.

Holly

The next day Holly awoke with the same sense of astonishment that she'd taken to sleep. *Jessica is André's mother? It's surreal. And I'm falling in love with him!*

Later, she and André shared an egg salad sandwich on the boardwalk, both of them short on appetite, before heading to the museum to hang his exhibit. His photographs had arrived a few days earlier. Holly and Jessica had planned a prospective display sequence, but André had the final say.

After some placing, deliberating, and re-ordering, André stood back to look at the exhibit as a whole, then walked it front to back, finally smiling with satisfaction.

Waiting for Jessica to arrive and give her approval, André and Holly sat together on the outside patio, sipping a cup of tea, gazing out at the teal-blue Pacific. André put his cup down and reached for his necklace.

"You're nervous about telling Jessica, aren't you?"

"You've got it."

"May I hold your necklace for a moment?"

André unclasped it and handed it to her.

She held it to her heart and closed her eyes. Opening them after a long pause, she looked deeply into André's eyes, tears coming into her own.

"Are you okay?" André asked.

"Yes, but the tumultuous images that came are disturbing: people crying and running about. The one who wore this necklace had been hurt badly, but the vision did not show me a face. I have no idea what it meant." She studied the fleur-de-lis at the center of the necklace, its pink, gold, and blue petals. "This probably represents some kind of trinity."

"You mean Father, Son, and the Holy Ghost?"

"Well, that's one version, or perhaps body, mind, spirit … or even mother, father, child." She took a breath and continued, "Pink commonly relates to the feminine, blue to the masculine. The gold could be what they create together: a child perhaps. But, honestly, I may be pushing my imagination a bit hard."

"Keep going," André urged, touching her arm.

"These stones surrounding the center, they map to the chakra system in our bodies."

"What's a chakra?"

"Chakras are energy centers emanating along the length of the spine. I visualize them when I meditate."

"I meditate, too, but I just count my breaths until my mind goes quiet. But touching the stones also helps."

"It's no wonder. You're probably picking up their energy. I always use the chakras as a focal point in my meditation, but I don't have these stones to touch. Instead, I visualize the colors associated with each chakra's place in my body."

"Tell me more."

"Well," Holly said, touching the ruby. "I visualize the color red at the base of my spine, the root chakra. This helps me feel grounded."

Touching the coral stone, André asked, "What does this one represent?"

"Orange is the color of the sacral chakra, the seat of creative potential and … sexuality."

"Fascinating." He smiled, putting his arm around her shoulders.

"The solar plexus chakra, at the center of the body, is a golden yellow, representing strength and personal power or authority. I visualize it as a small sun in the center of my being. Green's the color of compassion and love," she went on, placing her hands over her heart.

"I think there's a lot of green energy surrounding us, don't you?" He squeezed her shoulder affectionately.

Blushing, Holly touched her throat. "Light blue represents our self expression, speaking our truth, and trusting Creator's will for our lives. From this place, we make our creative potential real." Then, touching her forehead, she continued, "Indigo is the color of the brow chakra, the seat of wisdom and intuition, the connector to inner vision." Finally, she touched the top of her head and said, "The crown chakra, represented by the necklace's amethyst, connects us to Source and the heavenly realms."

"No wonder the necklace helps me focus more clearly. And look at this." André opened the locket to reveal the meditative image inside. "It was too dark last night to show it to you."

A chill ran up Holly's spine as she gazed at the intricate design in André's necklace. "Incredible," she exclaimed. *It's just like the tree from my dream.* "André," she said, after finding her voice, "I painted this design years ago after dreaming about it."

"What?"

"I painted this same image years ago—the swirling branches and tree roots with a meditative figure at its center. Do you know what it means?"

"I didn't even know it was a locket until Jessica's mother and I took it to a jeweler. He's the one who told us it had been soldered shut."

Her heart raced. *I wonder if it had been kept a secret and, if so, why?*

"We researched it in the library and found an illustration almost identical to it called the Essene Tree of Life."

Her mouth dropped open. "André, I named my painting The Tree of Life. In my dream I was sitting in the middle of the tree, just like this image. I felt connected to everything in life—especially my mother, who had already passed away."

"Do you know anything about the Essenes?" André asked.

"I do recall reading about them in a book by Edgar Cayce."

"Who is Edgar Cayce?"

"He was a famous psychic healer, born here in the United States in the early part of the century. He would enter a sleep-like trance and answer all kinds of medical and philosophical questions that people asked in sessions with him. And he was quite accurate. People were healed by following his directions. His messages have been recorded and are available for present day researchers. As I remember it, he said that Jesus was born into an Essene family and that Mary had been groomed to become his mother so that he would be brought up amidst the Essenes. Apparently, as a group, they were well versed in the mystery schools and mystical teachings of the time, including those in India, Egypt, England, and Ireland."

"Wow. Our research revealed that the Essenes were a Jewish sect in existence at the time of Jesus's birth, so what you've said makes perfect sense."

"Whoever originally owned this necklace must've been an Essene," Holly said. "And that person must have been hurt or killed. I think that's what my vision referred to."

"I don't think I should wear the necklace when we meet with Jessica," André said.

Holly nodded in agreement, feeling even closer to him now. She handed him back the necklace and he put it in his pocket, finding a piece of paper there. He pulled it out, looked at it for a moment, and said, "I almost forgot. Anton, the gallery owner in Montmartre where I exhibited, gave me this number. An American who saw my work in Paris wants to talk with me about it, maybe buy something. I want to call him while I'm in the States."

"Wait a minute, let me see."

André showed her the note with the name and phone number.

"What? Joseph? André, I think I know who this man might be."

At that moment, Jessica walked out onto the patio, startling both of them out of their chairs. André pushed the piece of paper into his pocket.

"Oh, hi, Jessica. You're here," Holly announced the obvious.

"Yes, and the exhibit is beautifully displayed. Come on inside. Let's review it again together."

Together, Holly thought. *In more ways than you know, my dear friend.*

André

André and Holly strolled barefoot on the sand as the waves of the Pacific lapped around their ankles. Holly had changed into a pair of cut-off jeans, with a soft white gauzy blouse tied at her waist. Her dark hair, with its reddish tint, looked beautiful to him in the sunlight. He splashed water on her and she splashed back, giggling and chasing him playfully. He drew a heart in the sand with his big toe and wrote her name in the middle of it. When she paused to look at it, he put his arm around her and held her close, feeling her heartbeat against his own.

"It's as if we've known each other forever," he whispered, then kissed her gently.

Everything in his body warmed as a charming blush painted her face.

"Look, the sun is about to set," she said, pointing to the western sky.

"I should have brought my camera," he said as he observed the sky's canvas, filled with bright blue, purple, yellow, and magenta.

"I'm sure you'll get another chance."

"This is a magical place, especially with you here with me."

"André, I have something to tell you. Let's get some cappuccino and talk privately in your room."

"You sound serious. Do I really want to hear what you have to say?"

"I've been struggling with whether to tell you. It won't be easy to hear, but you should know."

They walked in silence back to the hotel.

"You know the number you showed me yesterday, the one Joseph Murphy left for you? I think it's important that you call him."

"I plan to, but why is it so urgent?"

"André, Jessica confided in me one night that she had never truly gotten over a man she'd fallen for many years ago. His name is Joseph Murphy, and he's from Boston. The number you have is a Boston area code."

"That *could* just be a coincidence."

"He actually called the museum a couple of weeks ago, wanting to speak with her. It rattled me and I told him how to reach her at a conference she was attending but forgot to get his number. He didn't catch her there, and he hasn't called back."

André looked at her quizzically. "I don't get it."

"There's more. Jessica fell in love with Joseph Murphy twenty-something years ago when she was working in Paris."

All the color drained from André's face. "Go on."

"He left her to join the priesthood. He never knew—"

"She was pregnant," André said, finishing her sentence. Tears filled his eyes.

"Yes," she said gently, her own eyes moistening. She reached for his hand. "If this man is a priest—"

"He's probably my father," André said, reaching for his necklace.

After a long pause, Holly said cautiously, "Maybe you should call him."

"I can't. I can't handle anymore right now," he said, standing and pacing around the room, his head spinning. "It's just too much, Holly. I'm on overload."

"I'm sorry. Of course," she said, standing and gathering her things. "I should go."

"I know you only want to help me, but …."

"I understand. I'll see you tomorrow, okay?"

"Okay," he said, touching her face lightly before opening the door for her.

***

André woke to the soothing sound of waves. Glancing at the desk, he saw the paper with Joseph Murphy's phone number on it, and shuddered at the thought of actually talking with the man who could be his father. *If he doesn't know about me, how would he find my exhibit in Montmartre?*

He dressed and went downstairs for breakfast. Though the buffet looked delicious, he had no appetite. Grabbing some coffee and a sweet roll, he went back upstairs to his room. *There's only one way to find out what I need to know.*

Holding his breath, he dialed the number.

"Hello," a woman answered.

"This is André Casal. May I please speak with Joseph Murphy?"

"Joseph doesn't actually live here," the woman said. "But I'm his mother. I'll be glad to give him a message for you."

"Do you have another number where he can be reached?"

"How important is it that you reach him? My son is on retreat for a few days."

"Is Joseph, by chance, a priest?"

"Yes … and no. How do you know him?"

"I don't really know him, but he saw my photography exhibit in Paris and left this number with the gallery owner. I think he's interested in my work."

"I'll be happy to pass this information on to him if you'd like to leave your number."

"I'm exhibiting at a museum in Laguna Beach, California," he said, giving her the Sea View number.

***

"I called him," André said without preamble when Holly answered the phone.

"Really? How did it go?"

"It was his mother's number. She said he was on retreat. I asked if he was a priest. That seemed to surprise her. She said yes and no. What does that mean?"

"Are you glad you called?"

"Yes. I mean, I guess so. Actually, I can't believe this is happening. I came here to find my mother and now I might even find my father. It's mind boggling."

"My mother told me once that when destiny is at work, unexpected connections align and things just fall into place. It's called synchronicity."

Joseph

Boston

The shrill sound of the telephone in his hotel room jolted Joseph out of a dream where he was late for Mass. *What time is it? Who could that be?*

"Father Joseph," he answered, forgetting he was no longer using that title.

"You sound groggy," his mother said. "Did I wake you?"

"It's all right," he replied, rubbing his eyes and glancing at the clock on the night stand. It was already mid-morning.

"I know you need your solitude, but I had a call from a young man who seemed eager to reach you, a Frenchman, I believe, André Casal. He said you'd seen his photography exhibit in Paris and requested he contact you."

"André Casal, yes, I remember."

"He's now exhibiting at a museum in California and left his number."

"Thanks, Mom," he said, reaching to grab a pen and paper. "Okay, what is it?"

***

Stumbling to the bathroom, Joseph splashed water on his face and stared into the mirror. *You look awful.* He'd been up most of the night, struggling with what next steps to take, with no peace, no sense of deep faith.

Joseph retrieved his address book from the desk and located Jessica's number at the museum. He compared it to the number his mother had given him for André Casal.

"Identical."

***

To get to Laguna Beach, he'd have to fly to Los Angeles, rent a car, and drive down the coast. Everything inside him shook with excitement, coupled with anxiety, but he believed he'd made the right decision.

Joseph began to pack his bags and then stopped short. *I'd better let someone know where I'm going.*

"Mom, I wanted to let you know I'm going on a short trip to California," he said when she answered the phone.

"But I thought you were on retreat."

"I have been, but, well, I must take care of something, something important."

"Is everything all right?"

"I pray it will be. I'll call you."

***

Gazing out the plane window at the night sky, thoughts raced through his mind. *I know this is going to be a shock to Jessica, but it's time to tell her I'm leaving the priesthood, even if I don't know how she'll respond. She may have moved on. And is there a deeper connection between Jessica and André Casal? Could it be my necklace that he wears?*

He closed his eyes and recalled his last encounter with Jessica. She had pulled away from him that night. *I may have already lost her for good.*

He soon drifted off into a light sleep, carried away in a beautiful dream: dancing with Jessica in a garden of flowers, the blue-green sea just beyond, her hair golden in the afternoon light, a gardenia over her ear.

"The captain has turned on the seatbelt sign," a loud, clear voice declared, jolting him out of the dream. "Please place your seat backs and tray tables upright. We'll be on the ground momentarily."

Joseph Murphy walked off the plane and out of his past into the future moving ever so surely toward him.

André

Laguna Beach

The Museum Board reviewed André's exhibit with resounding approval. They assured him that his talent would catapult him into a successful career as a photographer in the U.S. and that they would do what they could to help him. Relieved, he prepared himself for the next, even greater, hurdle: dinner with Holly and Jessica at Holly's apartment. He had agreed with Holly that it was time to tell Jessica the truth.

André felt wet under his arms, anxious from chest to groin. He realized he was scared to death. *What if she can't handle it, doesn't want to know? Maybe it will bring up sore memories and she'll resent me for it. I don't know, maybe it's too soon, just on the other side of the Board's accolades. It feels manipulative.*

Arriving at Holly's complex, he hurried in, hoping to arrive before Jessica, realizing he needed a glass of wine, maybe even a shot of vodka, to soothe his nerves. Holly saw how nervous he was and moved close to hug him. He hugged her, but half-heartedly. Catching himself, he patted her on the back. With excruciating ambivalence, he felt torn in half.

She poured him a glass of Chardonnay but he opened the freezer looking for vodka, surprised to find it.

"Oh, I see you want a *real* drink."

He nodded, poured one and threw it back, reaching around Holly's waist from behind and saying, "I'm sorry I'm so jumpy. I feel like a child."

"You *are* someone's child, a few people's child. That's why you're so anxious."

He laughed and said, "You're too wise."

"I love you," she said, handing him the Chinese food that needed to be a bit warmer.

He looked at her, loving her back but not saying so.

Jessica arrived, giddy with excitement over André's exhibit, chattering on about how grateful she was for her mother's good eye for art. "Maybe I've been too hard on her," she said at one point. "I'm like her in more ways than I've realized."

"Our parents certainly live in us, and so do our grandparents," Holly said.

"Unless we're adopted," André blurted.

Jessica looked stunned and Holly gave him an "I can't believe you said that" look before enlisting their help with getting the food on the table.

Though everything was quite tasty, André found himself toying with his food, plagued with anxiety. *How can I tell Jessica I'm the son she left behind in France? I don't think I can go through with this.* Holly had agreed to bring up the topic and he nervously awaited her cue.

After they finished their meal, Holly brought out three fortune cookies. Jessica shared hers first.

"The stars smile upon you today," she said, her voice trailing off, looking at the two of them across from her. "It's lovely to see the two of you looking so happy together."

Holly looked warmly at André and he held her gaze for a moment before turning back to Jessica. He couldn't look too long into her eyes.

Holly was next. "You are lovable and affectionate." She blushed, smiling at André, who said, "I'll second that."

"You have many gifts to give to the world," André read. He looked down shyly, then admitted, "I do have lots of photos."

They all laughed.

"And wonderful ones at that," Holly added. "Why don't we go sit in the living room? I'll put on water for tea. Speaking of gifts, André has something to share with you, Jessica."

His heart skipped a beat and he nervously began clearing the table, following Holly into the kitchen as Jessica took her wine glass and moved to the sofa.

Holly gave him an encouraging smile as he set the dishes on the counter, shaking her head when he started to scrape them. He ambled into the living room and sat in the least comfortable chair.

"So, what's up, Mr. Casal?" Jessica asked playfully.

"Let's wait for Holly." André forced a weak smile.

Holly soon came in with a tray of English tea, complete with milk, sugar, and a few chocolate-covered biscuits.

As Jessica poured her own tea, she said, "I've gotten out of the habit of my daily teatime. May I pour yours?"

"Thank you, sure," Holly said.

André nodded.

Taking a deep breath, André reached inside his shirt and carefully pulled out his necklace, unclasped it, and laid it flat on the tray in front of them.

Jessica's eyes widened. She turned to Holly and then back to André. "Where did you get that?" she asked, a look of shock on her face.

"My ... parents told me it was left with me when I was— that is, when they adopted me."

Jessica jumped from her chair, her face ashen. She shook her head in disbelief and strode around the room, hugging her shoulders with her hands, stopping, shaking her head again, turning to look at André, walking, and stopping again.

"This can't be happening," she stammered. "That can't be the same necklace … you must be mistaken." Gathering herself slowly, she finally walked over to face him. "Are you telling me that you're … you're my son?"

"I'm sorry to surprise you like this."

"André? Are you sure?" Jessica asked in a trembling voice.

He nodded, reaching for her hand.

Holly said, "It's true, Jessica."

Jessica reached for his other hand and their eyes met.

"I can't believe it's you."

"I was so nervous about this. I'm still nervous, but now you know."

"I've thought about you most every day," she said. "I can't believe it."

"Neither can I."

Holly's eyes were moist as she said, "Why don't you two sit down? I'll get some wine."

"Great idea," Jessica said, slumping onto the sofa. André sat beside her.

"How long have you known?" Jessica asked Holly when she returned from the kitchen.

"Since the night he arrived," Holly said, placing a small tray with three wine glasses next to the larger tea tray that she whisked away, returning with corkscrew and bottle, and handing both to André.

André opened the bottle and poured them each a glass.

"I still can't believe this is happening," Jessica said, staring at André in amazement. "How did you find me?"

"I went to London," he said, "and found your mother."

"You found my mother?" Jessica asked, her eyes widening.

"Yes. I searched the London metropolitan directory for J. Taylor and reached your father's house. I told his wife that I had a necklace that I thought belonged to you. It was probably a strange enough inquiry that he called your mother and then she called me. At first Adelaide thought she'd call you about the necklace but, thankfully, she decided instead to meet me in London. She recognized the necklace. She remembered seeing you wear it after you came home from Paris. When I showed her your signature on the form I got from the adoption agency, she recognized your handwriting. Then we knew."

André took a deep breath and exhaled a heavy sigh.

Jessica was quiet for a long moment.

"No wonder she wanted me to see your photographs," she finally said.

"I think she also *liked* them," André said with a smile.

"No kidding. Remember the response today from the Board? Wait until the public sees them."

"It feels like a dream," André said shaking his head and topping off their wine.

"*This* feels like a dream," Jessica said. "I agonized over whether the nuns were right, that it was best for you to be with two parents in a loving Catholic home. Were they good to you?"

"The most loving parents anyone could possibly have."

"I always had a sense you were okay, but now I can see that with my own eyes."

"Jessica," André said quietly, "I want to know about my father."

Jessica froze, uncertain how to answer.

"Of course you deserve to know," she said finally. "I never told him I was pregnant. You see, he believed he'd been called to the priesthood. It was his father's dream. When his father was dying in Boston, he promised that he would seriously consider it. When he returned to Paris and told me he'd made his decision, I was devastated—angry, hurt, disappointed. I was so young, only nineteen. I didn't know what to do. I revealed my situation to a nun I'd come to know at the convent where I was working as a translator for your father. He was the architect for the convent's renovation."

"So my father is a priest now?"

"Yes," Jessica answered quietly, "as far as I know."

"Is his name Joseph? Joseph Murphy?"

"How did you know that?"

"He somehow happened to see my exhibit in Montmartre and left his name and number with the gallery owner, asking me to contact him. Holly made the connection when I mentioned it to her. She recognized his name from what you had told her about him."

"Amazing, but why, how? It just doesn't make sense. How would he know you?"

Holly interjected, "I'm sorry if it seems I betrayed a confidence. It all happened spontaneously … synchronistically."

"I understand that," Jessica said, less disturbed than confused by the revelations.

"I called him this morning."

"You what?" Jessica asked, standing.

"The number in Boston must be his mother's. She answered and said he was on retreat and would tell him I called."

"André gave her the number of the museum," Holly added. "I hope you don't mind."

"Why not his hotel?" Jessica shook her head in disbelief. "This is more than I can take all at once. I haven't seen him since I left New York."

"You saw him in New York?" André asked, confused.

"Yes. I ran into him a year ago. We hadn't seen each other since Paris. We tried to be friends, but it was impossible. He's a priest! I finally lost my patience and took the job out here," she finished, a bit breathless, and slumped back down on the sofa. "I think about him, us, almost every day."

"You're still in love with him?"

"We've never stopped loving each other, but Joseph believed God wanted him to be a priest. That's why we couldn't be together."

"Jessica," André said, "I truly appreciate your sharing about you and Joseph, but I still don't understand how you could abandon your child, no matter what the circumstances."

Clearly startled, Jessica sputtered, "Oh, André, I didn't mean to abandon you."

But her words sounded empty to his ears.

As her tears came, Jessica reached for a tissue. "I was so young, remember, only nineteen, so in love, but rejected and heartbroken. I couldn't tell my depressed mother. I couldn't tell my father. He was all wrapped up in his new wife and unavailable to me. And how could I tell Joseph, who was following God's will?" She began to sob in earnest. "I felt so alone. The Mother Superior delivered you at the convent and convinced me you should be brought up in a Catholic family. But," she continued intently, "I've always regretted it." She gave him a helpless look.

"It's okay. I get it." He reached out to touch her trembling hand, his heart softening.

***

André and Jessica decided to take a short hike together on a nearby beach trail early the next day, before the museum opened.

"It's beautiful here," André said, stopping to look at the expanse of sea and sky. "I feel a lot better today, much less awkward."

"I'm glad," Jessica said.

André felt he'd found his way home inside, relieved, full. Even though Henri and Jacqueline would always be his parents, now Jessica could also be part of his life. He walked quietly beside her along the beach until they came to a jetty and sat down.

"Would you tell me more about my birth?"

"Well, I was only twenty when you were born, just a year younger that you are now," she began. "It seems like such a long time ago. You were born in Provence, at the convent near Arles. I went into labor very fast and there wasn't time to go to the hospital. The doctor came, but Mother Superior, I think I mentioned, delivered you into this world before he arrived."

"Born in a convent," André, mused, smiling.

"Yep." She laughed. "With nuns all around to adore you—just as I did. I didn't want to put you down, even to sleep.

"I was so confused, André. My faith was shaky and I was angry with all the men in my life, especially your father. I began to realize that the nuns were right. I didn't want to raise you in an unstable, troubled atmosphere. While praying over the necklace you're now wearing—did I tell you it belonged to your father? To Joseph? He gave it to me when he left me in Paris. I always carried it with me after that. Anyway, one day when I was holding you, imagining how it would be without you, I had a vision of a little boy running through the sunflower fields."

"And that's just what happened. I grew up in such a place. Do you realize that if you hadn't left the necklace with me, we probably wouldn't be together now? By the way, I want to show you something." He took off the necklace and opened the locket to reveal the symbol inside. "Your mother and I discovered this when we took it to a jeweler in London."

"It reminds me of a design on the door of the convent in Paris where your father and I met," she exclaimed. "I once had a vivid dream about that door and actually wrote a poem the next day. I called it The Tree of Life."

"Jessica," he said incredulously, "Holly had a dream that she was sitting inside a tree just like this. It was so vivid that she painted it the very next day."

Jessica shivered, pulling her shawl around her shoulders, as she looked up at him.

"Adelaide and I looked up the design in a London library. It's called the Essene Tree of Life."

"What does Essene mean?"

"It's the name of an ancient communal Jewish sect during Jesus's day but which also spread throughout India, as well as France, England, and Ireland. They are most notable in the current day for their connection to the Dead Sea Scrolls."

"Fascinating," Jessica said after he'd finished. "And the connections; the necklace, the convent door, Holly's dream. Synchronicity again?"

"I guess. Where did the necklace originally come from?"

"Joseph's father gave it to him. It had belonged to an ancestor who was a priest."

"Probably an Essene priest."

The incoming tide lapped around their feet. They laughed and ran to higher ground.

When they reached the boardwalk, Holly was walking toward them. "Hey, you two," she called. "It's time to open the museum. We've got an exhibit to show to the world."

Joseph

Joseph awoke to the sound of waves. He'd rented a room at the Laguna Beach Hotel, leaving the inside door open so he could hear the water. *It rocked me like a baby.* Ambling out to the balcony, he closed his eyes and inhaled the salt air, exhaling an equally deep sigh of gratitude. *Here I am, in the place where Jessica lives. She could be walking the beach right now. Please, God, help me stay true to your will and the love you have given us.*

After dressing in a pair of jeans, a light sweatshirt, and sandals, he searched through the hotel guidebook for museums. *That's it, The Sea View Museum of Art. I'll head over there after breakfast and just follow my heart.*

After a nourishing breakfast, he drove to the museum. He stepped out of his car and turned again toward the water, giving himself over to its immensity. His nerves surprisingly calmed, Joseph walked through the front door of the museum where a pleasant, middle-aged woman greeted him warmly at the front desk, took his fee, and told him about the current exhibits, including one of photography by André Casal.

"Did you say André Casal?"

"Yes, it's right down the hall, on the right," she said, pointing toward the entrance to that gallery.

I don't think I'm quite ready for this.

Stalling, he entered a room filled with the museum's impressive Native American collection. Admiring the many authentic historical paintings, drawings, and sculptures depicting Native American life and culture, some familiar, Joseph found the modern work, primarily artists from the Southwest, rich with vibrant color and images. A soundtrack of drums and flutes subtly echoed through the room evoking the Native American experience. *Such mood, a transporting sense of presentation. Jessica seems to have found a wonderful place to share her love of all things art.*

I guess it's time.

Peering into the room that housed the photography exhibit, he saw a young man he recognized as André Casal pointing to one of the photos and discussing it with patrons. "Children of Paris," Joseph noted. *Just as in Montmartre.* He strained to see if the young man was wearing the necklace.

"May I help you?" an attractive young woman asked, startling him.

"Oh, hello. Why, yes, I was actually looking for Jessica Taylor. Do you know where I might find her?"

"I'm Holly Simpson, her assistant. Do you have an appointment?"

"No, but I'm here from Boston and would very much like to see her."

"If you'll give me your name, I'll let her know you're here."

"Joseph, Joseph Murphy."

He watched her walk down the hall, looking back at him briefly before turning the corner at the end. *She looked at me oddly. I wonder if Jessica has mentioned my name.*

"Ms. Taylor said she'd be right out."

Within a moment, Jessica appeared at the end of the hall walking towards him. The young woman passed him, a slight smile playing about her lips.

A familiar warmth came over him as she approached with a look of pure astonishment on her face.

"Jess, it's you," he said. "You look … wonderful."

She held out both hands, and he took them in his as she said, "Joseph? What on earth are you doing here?"

"I had to see you."

"But … why?"

"I know I shouldn't have barged in on you at work. Forgive me. Can you steal away for a coffee? Or could we meet for lunch? What I came to tell you must be said in person."

"The timing is a bit awkward, but come on back to my office. We have some coffee made," she said, taking his arm.

Once in Jessica's office, a bright room with an array of blooming plants in the window, she stepped toward the coffee machine, poured them both a mug, and handed his to him. "Black, right?"

"Yes, thank you," he said taking it, his hand a bit shaky. "Could we sit down?"

She offered him the couch in front of the window and sat next to him, perched up on its edge.

"What in the world have you come to tell me?"

"I've finally left the priesthood."

Jessica stood again, stunned, pushed her hair back off her face, and turned to look at him. "My first internal response is a bitter something like why now? Or it's about time. But I know you've been ambivalent for years, so it must be a huge relief." She sat at her desk.

"It's true, I've been seeking clarity for many years, almost since I took my vows, maybe even before," he said, his head dropping toward his chest.

"Oh, Joseph, I don't know what to say. Your dilemma has cost me a lot. But I *am* happy for you."

"Thank you. I know, Jess, and I hate that I've hurt you so."

She suddenly stood, straightening her skirt. "I really can't give this any more time right now. I'm sorry," she said, looking at her watch. "I have a meeting straightaway … and other things, too, on my mind. Let's meet later, after work."

"I'm staying at the Laguna Beach Hotel. Why don't you call me when you're free?"

"I will," she said with what Joseph saw as a near perfunctory smile. "Joseph, it's good to see you." She hurried out the door.

"Great to see you, Jess. I'll find my way out."

Not exactly a warm reception. He walked out into the fresh air, forgetting all about André Casal. *At least she agreed to see me later.*

***

As the hours passed, Joseph became more and more anxious. He walked into the hotel bar with the intention of having a couple of glasses of wine to calm his nerves. A fire had been set in the fireplace, giving off a warm glow. He changed his mind. *I want to be sober and fully present when I talk to her.*

She sounded more relaxed but still a bit distant when she finally called, but agreed to meet him for dinner on the hotel terrace.

***

They shared a bottle of Chardonnay before dinner, under a sky heavy with billowy clouds that promised a brilliant sunset. Already hints of pink showed high above the horizon.

"I can't believe I'm really sitting here with you." He reached for her hand. "I've missed you so much, Jess."

"I've missed you, too," she said nervously, pulling her shawl more snugly around her shoulders.

"Thank you for seeing me tonight."

"There's no need to thank me," she said, looking at him and then away toward the horizon, a pensive look on her face.

"I'm sorry I was so unavailable today at the museum," she said. "I was shocked to see you and already flustered by something else that's happened. And then your news, and you standing there telling me. I didn't know what to say, how to respond."

"I understand. But I'm concerned to hear that something else is bothering you."

Joseph's brows furrowed but he tried to relax, afraid that her news would somehow exclude him from her life. They sat silently, leaning towards each other, as the sun melted into the sea, streams of light illuminating the clouds from beneath them, the earlier pink now a full, gleaming coral.

"Joseph, I need to tell you something."

His breath quickened. "I think I know what you're going to say. It's another man, you've found someone else."

"Another man? No, Joseph, that's not it."

"But you were with Ken in San Diego."

"Ken? How in the world do you know about him?" she said, almost irritated.

"Your assistant gave me your number at the conference you were attending and I called you there. The minister told me that you and Ken had already left. I just assumed ...."

"No. I mean, that's all over now. In fact, it never really began. We were never—we're not even friends anymore."

"I shouldn't have jumped to conclusions—or sprung my visit on you."

"It's just as well you're here. I mean, yes, it is a shock, and, honestly, I don't know quite how I feel about it all, but I can't help being glad you're here."

"That's generous of you, Jess. I should have called ahead. It's just that it's been such an ordeal, waiting for guidance, not knowing the right thing to do. And, now that I'm sure, I had to tell you in person."

"I understand." She paused. "Joseph, I do want you to know that I'm not the same woman you reunited with in New York last year. I'm much stronger now. I can certainly live on my own. Quite well, in fact. It's been a monumental move for me, in many ways. I wonder if you, too, have grown, are truly ready now to leave the priesthood behind you. It's been your chosen path for many years."

"Jess, I understand your concerns. I really do. You of all people know I've struggled with this decision for years. I've been in seclusion on long silent retreats. I've sought my mentor Monsignor Anthony's counsel. I've prayed and prayed about it. I've even realized that I've been numbing myself a bit with wine," he paused, noticing his glass was still full. "I know now that I must follow my heart's deepest desires and not only try to please others—especially my father. I wanted to please him as much as I wanted to please God, maybe more."

"I always thought that."

"I guess such life decisions take the time they take, though I deeply regret how much hurt and upset I've caused you through it all. I hope you can one day forgive me."

"I do forgive you. But you're right, it has been very hard on me."

"I know. I know."

"What are your plans?"

"I still do truly want to do God's will, to serve in some way, but today I don't know what form that will take. The only thing I *do* know, deep in my heart, is that ... I want to be with you."

She looked at him with love in her eyes and squeezed his hand affectionately. "I don't know what to say, Joseph. I hear your words but ... I'll need some time."

They sat in silence, the soothing sound of the waves and the fragrance of the night air enveloping them.

Holly

Holly could feel André's eyes on her as she cooked her specialty for him: salmon, sweet potatoes, and asparagus. She lit candles on the table, creating a soft glow in the room.

"I still need to decorate this place. Soon, I'll bring some paintings down from Cambria to make it more my own."

"I think it looks charming, especially with you in it," André said, opening a bottle of wine and pouring two glasses.

She smiled and walked toward him as he held up his glass and handed her one.

"To our new love," he said, smiling back at her.

Feeling her cheeks heating up, Holly clinked her glass to his.

"To us," she said, uncomfortable with the formality, remembering her casual "I love you," while they'd waited for Jessica to join them the other night. *Maybe he didn't even hear me. He was a mess that night.*

"I could never have told Jessica without you," Andre said. "And kudos to Adelaide, Jessica's mother, too. If I hadn't listened to her, I might not know you. And that, even more than meeting Jessica, has changed my life."

"Oh, André, meeting you has meant the world to Jessica, I'm sure. And, me, well that goes without saying," she said, leaning up to kiss him lightly on the lips.

"I was so nervous about meeting her, and now it feels so natural."

"And soon, forgive me for reminding you," she added, "you may also be meeting your father." She'd told him earlier about Joseph's surprise visit to the museum.

"When do you think she'll tell him about me? The exhibit here, him here, me here. It spooks me when I think about it, how we've all come together."

"It's a miracle," Holly agreed. "Really, if there are such things, and I believe there are, this is one. I think it's just a matter of time before she tells him," she said gently. "By the way, she called to tell me she's not coming into work tomorrow."

"Oh, God, it's surreal for me—and nerve-wracking—knowing that Joseph is with her." He reached for his necklace.

"André, I'm so glad we're together."

"As far as *I'm* concerned," he said, putting both arms around her, "we'll *always* be together."

She smiled. "By the way, I told my dad about you. He wants to meet you. And so does my brother Randy."

"So, when things calm down around here, maybe we can make that trip to Cambria."

"Did I tell you Randy's a senior in high school this year and wants to be a chef? He's had lots of experience in our family restaurant."

"You did. Sounds like your parents have been very supportive. That's so important. Mamà has always believed in me, but Papa doesn't understand about being an artist. He still wants me on the vineyard."

"I'm sure my dad would prefer me to be closer to home, too. With Mom gone, it's been incredibly hard for him." Tears filled her eyes. "I wish you could have known her."

***

After they'd cleaned up the dinner dishes, they took their wine out to the balcony and sat together on a comfortable wicker sofa. It came as no surprise when he took the glass from her hand and placed it, along with his own, on the small table in front of them, drawing her into his arms. She melted into his embrace, her desire for him growing as he kissed her lips, her face, her neck.

"*Mon cherie, l'un, je vous aime,*" he whispered. "I love you."

Joseph

Walking the side street to Jessica's cottage, Joseph felt on edge. Summoning his best source of courage, he prayed silently for God's will, stepped back one step, and rang Jessica's doorbell.

When she opened the door, Joseph gasped. She wore the same slacks and angora sweater she'd worn when he'd said goodbye to her in September. "You … look beautiful." *Just as I've pictured you since our last time in New York.*

Before Jessica could respond, Miss Suzy, her little orange cat, greeted them noisily. He reached down to scratch the cat's back.

"She must be glad to see you."

He stood, closed the door behind him, and pulled Jessica into his arms. "I'm glad to see *you.*"

He held her close for several moments, savoring the feeling of her body next to his until a warm wave of passion washed over him. As his lips met hers, his desire grew more intense. "I've missed you so much," he whispered in her ear.

She pulled him closer and kissed him deeply, running her fingers through his hair and pulling his shirt out of his pants. In response, he gently reached inside her sweater. Their hearts beat together in harmony, her breathing intensifying with his own.

When Jessica unclasped her bra and placed his hand on her bare breast, every nerve in his body quivered. She broke away, gazing into his eyes for what seemed like an eternal moment. When she removed her sweater and bra, it took his breath away.

"You are so beautiful," he whispered, pulling off his shirt and drawing her closer, his bare chest pressing against her breasts. *I've been celibate for so long, I hope everything works right!*

As he caressed and kissed her lips, abdomen, thighs, and between her legs, his passion grew and he realized he could satisfy her again, when, in a rush of excitement, she cried out. Her body shook as she pulled him inside her, matching her movements with his until every bit of his passion exploded. *Nothing will ever separate me from her again.* At home in her arms, he felt peace at last.

***

In the middle of the night, Joseph awoke to find Jessica nestled in his arms, fast asleep. In the moonlight, he could see Miss Suzy lying at the foot of the bed. When the cat noticed his stirring, she walked up to him and rubbed her head against his arm. Jessica opened her eyes and looked sleepily into his.

"Is it morning?" she asked, smiling up at him with a look of contentment.

"No, and I'm not ready to let you go."

"There's no need to let me go," she said, reaching her arm around him. "I can't believe you're really here. I've dreamed about us, like this, but never thought ...."

"It has been a long journey, but we're together now. I know this is where I belong, where God wants me to be."

Jessica kissed his lips, his neck, his chest.

They made love until dawn.

***

Joseph sat with Jessica on a swing in her backyard, drinking a cup of coffee while she sipped her tea. The sound of the birds singing in the trees echoed the happiness in his heart as his eyes fell on the ruby-red bougainvillea blossoms, creeping up the corner of her house.

"The weather's amazing here. In Boston, it could be snowing. Do flowers bloom here year-round?"

"They do. Of course, I do miss the beautiful snowfalls in New York."

"I'd say this is paradise. Of course, that has everything to do with you, my love. Are you sure we're not dreaming?"

"No, it's real this time." Her eyes widened and her voice changed to a deeper, more sultry tone. "Especially after last night."

"Somehow this feels like a honeymoon—one I hope never ends." It seemed as if they'd never been apart. He placed his cup on the table in front of them and she did the same. They moved towards each other like partners in a dance and kissed tenderly. *This is how I want to feel in my new life.*

"Joseph," Jessica said, "there's something I must tell you."

"Uh-oh, what is it, love?" The serious tone in her voice grabbed his full attention.

"After you left Paris and decided to become a priest," she began, turning away from his gaze, "I knew I couldn't tell you what I need to tell you now." When she looked back at him, a shadow had fallen over her face.

"What's wrong, Jess?"

"I wanted to tell you before you left Paris, but when you got back from your father's funeral, you had clearly made a decision. I was so young, heartbroken, angry, and alone. I didn't have the courage to tell you that I was—"

"Pregnant?"

"Yes," she said quietly, holding his gaze. "We have a child, Joseph. We have a son."

"What?"

He stood abruptly and stared down at her in disbelief. She rose, too, and reached for his hands.

"Why didn't you tell me before? You know I would have come to you."

"That's *why* I didn't tell you. You were so set on becoming a priest— and your father had just died."

"Oh, my God," he cried, dropping her hands to walk around the yard. *All the while, I had a son.*

"I'm so sorry, Joseph. Please understand. I didn't want you to give up your dream for me, for us, and then resent me for it later."

He looked directly into her eyes, now clouded over with pain. She's been all alone with this, he realized, pulling her to him. They clung together for several moments. "Where is he? Does he know about me?"

"I've only just found out myself, only met him a month ago in Paris. And, yes, he knows about you, about us." Tears filled her eyes. "I was so young, Joseph, and all alone. I didn't know what to do. Mother Marian suggested I go to Provence and stay in a convent there, and I did. Our baby was born there. He was beautiful. I was with him for some months, and then ... the nuns convinced me I should give him up for adoption, so he could be raised by Catholic parents."

Her look of anguish matched his own. *How could she have given up our child? Why didn't she tell me?*

"But who raised him? Do you know them?"

Something in him snapped. *I can't hear anymore now. I have to get out of here.*

"Never mind. Don't tell me. I'm overwhelmed. The rest will have to wait."

How could you have had our child and not even told me until now

"I need some space, forgive me, Jessica. I can't hear anymore. Not yet, not now."

***

He walked around the side yard to the street, pausing for a brief moment before turning toward the beach. His walking pace became a jog. The soft morning air cleared his mind, little by little, as he let go of the holding in his throat, and let himself cry. The sound of the surf soothed him as his stride slowed. At last, Joseph felt himself walking more deeply into a new life that he could ever have imagined.

Jessica

After Joseph's sudden departure, Jessica stood unable to move. *What have I done? I've never seen that look on his face before, detached, as if he didn't even know me.*

After a long while, she went inside and sat in the comfortable chair by the front windows, looked out to the turquoise sea beyond, and prayed for guidance.

He's in shock. He needs time to process everything. Surely he wouldn't leave. No, he wouldn't leave, not now, not this way. Suddenly, it dawned on her. *He doesn't even know it's André who is our son. Surely he wouldn't leave before knowing.*

Though her intuition gently urged her to slow down, Jessica ignored it, her mind racing as she grabbed her denim jacket and rushed out the door.

***

When she reached Joseph's hotel she hurried inside and made her way to his room, knocking hard on the door.

"Joseph, it's me. I need to talk to you. Please let me in."

No response. *Maybe he's out on the beach.*

On the beach, she saw only a young mother building a sandcastle with her daughter, seagulls screeching as they searched for breakfast, and the silhouette of a couple walking together in the distance. She sat on the sand, pulling her knees up to her chest. *I'll just wait here for him.*

Whatever happens, I will be all right. And so will Joseph. She took off her jacket and spread it out on the sand, lying down in the warmth of the sun.

***

A familiar voice spoke her name. Opening her eyes, she saw Joseph standing over her.

"I didn't mean to startle you," he said, kneeling beside her.

"I must've fallen asleep," she mumbled, rubbing her eyes.

"You looked so peaceful, I didn't want to disturb you."

"Well, I'm glad you did. Are you okay?"

"Yes. At least I think I am. I had a long walk on the beach and hiked the marsh trail. It really is beautiful here."

"I know, it's a special place." Something inside told her to just wait and let him take the lead.

"I'm ready now to hear about ... our child." He sat and looked expectantly into her eyes. "Do you know if he was adopted and who his parents are?"

"I know that he was adopted, and André tells me they are good people."

"André? His name is André?"

"Yes."

Joseph paused, searching for a recollection. "And how did he find you?"

"The adoption agency told him I was from London and actually gave him my name—with a copy of something I'd signed, so he had my signature."

"I didn't know adoption agencies gave out that kind of information."

"Apparently, when such children become adults and want to trace their birth parents, some agencies help them."

"So he went to London. What then?"

"He said he called a number of J. Taylors and eventually reached my father's house, Jonathan Taylor. Apparently Dad passed his message on to my mother and she called André."

"I see. So he met your mother and she told him where you were?"

"Not exactly. You see, she didn't know about my pregnancy or about my giving André up. No one knew except Mother Marian and the nuns in Provence. I couldn't tell my parents. They had their own problems and wouldn't have understood. You probably don't remember, but my mother was very depressed at that time. My father had just asked for a divorce. She was much too fragile to hear such news."

"Yes, I remember now."

"I wanted to tell her—and you—but you'd already made up your mind. What was I to do?"

"I just wish you'd told me. All those years not knowing we had a child, all those years lost. We could have been a family, raising our son," he said, the helpless expression on his face underscoring his sadness.

"There were so many times when I regretted not telling you. But you belonged to God. Who was I to take away your dream? I felt so alone." She broke into tears.

"I'm so sorry, Jess. So sorry you suffered over my ambivalence. I thought surely after my father's death that I was following the path meant for me. But I can't undo what's done. I can only be with you now, for as long as you'll have me."

His sincerity snapped her out of her despair. "It's going to be all right," she said, reaching for his hands and speaking with conviction. "The past is behind us. Neither of us was ready to be a parent. Neither of us knew for sure what path to take. Now we know. Now we can be together."

"I love you so much, Jess."

"And I love you. I always have."

He held her tight for a few moments and then stood, pulling her up beside him. "Let's walk. I want to know more about how ... our son found you and where he is now."

Together they walked to the water's edge.

"So after your mother contacted André, what happened?"

"They met and, though he had that paper with my signature on it and showed it to her, it was the necklace she recognized, your necklace. I'd left it for him with the nuns. I'd been wearing it the day I went to see her when she was recuperating. And André wore it intentionally when he met with her in London."

Bringing the heel of his hand to his forehead, he stared at her, wide-eyed. "André. Why didn't I put it together before? He's the photographer, André Casal, isn't he? André Casal is our son."

"But how did you know?" she asked, puzzled.

"I saw his photo on a poster advertising his exhibit at a gallery in Montmartre. I'd been traveling and I ended up in Paris, searching for answers. I immediately noticed his necklace. It wasn't totally visible, but it looked identical to the one I'd given you."

"So *that's* why you left your number at that gallery. André told me he'd tried to call you back."

"He tried," Joseph explained, "but he reached my mother instead and left the number of your museum with her. I wondered about it, but I still didn't make the full connection at first. Now it all makes sense."

"When I left the necklace for him when he was a baby, I hoped it would help him make his way in the world. But the necklace has reunited us, brought us together, all of us."

He held her in his arms and kissed the top of her head.

"It's more than amazing. For me, it's one of God's miracles."

A wave rushing in over their feet surprised them and they laughed.

Relieved that the mood had lightened, Jessica suggested they order some sandwiches, pick up beach towels back at the hotel, and have a picnic on the beach.

"I think we can both take a bit more sun. What do you say?" She splashed Joseph again as she flung her jacket over her shoulders, carrying her sandals in her hand.

***

Lying on their backs on beach towels after lunch, Joseph asked Jessica to tell him about André's exhibit at the Sea View and how it had come about.

"Oh, that's how Mum lured me to Paris to meet him in the first place. When she called to tell me about André's photography, she never mentioned anything about the necklace or that he was looking for me, only that she'd met an extremely talented young man and that I must come to Paris to see his work for my museum."

"And you just took off like that?"

"The timing was right, and I'm a sucker for Paris." She laughed. "Anyway, I took Holly with me. The exhibit had ended but André met us at our hotel with his portfolio of very sensitive and provocative photographs. I was very moved by them, as was Holly, and I invited him to show at the Sea View. It was also clear that Holly and André had a strong chemistry, so it's possible that colored my decision as well."

"So when you invited him here you had no idea he was our son?"

"None. I've known for less than a week myself. We were all relaxing after dinner at Holly's one night when André took the necklace out and laid it before me on the table. I nearly fainted."

"Wow."

"Did you know there's a locket in the center that had been soldered shut?"

"A locket?"

"When you meet André, he can show you and tell you all about it. He's fascinated by the research he and Mother did in London."

"Do you think it's time for us to meet?" he asked, sitting up and searching her eyes.

"When you're ready. I guess, when you're both ready."

He sighed and lay back on the sand.

Jessica dozed lightly, opening her eyes to find Joseph looking at her.

"I haven't felt so good in years," he whispered, propping himself on one elbow.

"I can see it in your eyes, even though you're processing a lot, quickly."

"I've been questioning my faith, my commitment to God, most all of my adult life, but now I'm sure of I'm where I'm supposed to be, even if I don't know yet how my work will unfold."

"I imagine you'll miss aspects of the priesthood."

"It's true. I'll miss counseling, being there for parishioners, also the children. It's bittersweet."

"I'm sure you'll find another way of serving others, Joseph. That's just the kind of man you are."

"Being here with you, knowing we have a son, those things come first now. In learning to trust my heart, I can better trust God to guide me."

Jessica put her arms around him, a feeling of peace sweeping over her with the soft breeze. Deep in her heart, she knew whatever happened in the future, they would face it together.

"I'm ready to meet him." Joseph said.

Joseph

Joseph's mind raced as he helped Jessica prepare dinner for Holly and André. *What will I say to him? What can I say? Will we get along?* The weather had shifted and a chill hung in the air.

"Do you want me to light a fire?"

"Great idea. Use one of those tall matches on the mantle and turn on the gas switch. It's not like a real, wood fireplace," Jessica said with a laugh, "but it'll do."

Soon a feeling of warmth pervaded the cottage. Jessica had stuffed and baked a chicken and delightful smells wafted from the kitchen. Joseph was on edge, couldn't sit still and, when he did, his mind raced again.

He opened a bottle of Cabernet to let it breathe. She put some wine glasses on the counter and began to slice cheese for appetizers.

"Has Holly told you how she feels about André? Are they serious?"

"I know she's crazy about him and he's obviously smitten, but she hasn't told me how deep it goes."

"I'm a bit edgy, no longer the serene priest that my parishioners saw, but a middle-aged man soon to meet his grown son for the first time, *our* son. I may never have been this anxious."

"I'm nervous, too."

The doorbell rang and they went together to answer it.

Joseph found himself looking at a younger version of himself, with lighter hair and eyes.

"Joseph, this is André. You've already met Holly, I think."

"Good to see you again, Holly," Joseph said, turning to André and extending his hand, their grip holding steady for a second.

"Good to meet you," André said tentatively.

"And you," Joseph responded, looking directly into his eyes.

"Come in, come in," Jessica said, ushering everyone into the living room. "Joseph, will you pour us some wine?"

"Sure," he answered, ducking into the kitchen and breathing a deep sigh.

Jessica joined him and gave him a quick hug.

"He's a fine looking young man," Joseph whispered.

He poured the wine and placed the glasses on a tray, taking another deep breath as he noticed his hands slightly shaking. Jessica picked up the plate of cheese and crackers and they returned to the living room. Holly and André stood as they approached.

"I feel as if I've just come home from a long journey," Joseph said, giving them each a glass of wine and clearing his throat. "I want to thank each of you for making this moment possible." He raised his glass and continued, "To the love of family and friends."

Joseph turned to André and spoke from his heart, his voice cracking. "I've been walking around in a daze this week, with so many mixed emotions. This is a huge crossroad for me: leaving the priesthood, reuniting with the true love of my life," he motioned toward Jessica, "and knowing I have ... *a son*." Tears filled his eyes. "I'm overwhelmed with gratitude."

André's eyes brimmed with tears as well though he only nodded.

"I don't know what to say," André said after a long pause.

"You don't have to say *anything*," Jessica assured him. "When I left that necklace for you at the convent I never dreamed it would bring us together this way."

"And I recognized it in your exhibit poster in Montmartre," Joseph added.

"Oh, so that's why you left your name and number at the gallery."

"Yes, but I was also impressed with your photography, though admittedly I didn't take a close enough look. I'm eager to remedy that here in Laguna."

"Amazing," Holly interjected, "how the necklace brought your family together."

"André," Joseph said, "Jessica tells me that you discovered a locket at the center. What did you find inside?"

André took off the necklace and opened the locket, handing it to Joseph for a better look.

"What marvelous workmanship. It's beautiful. Since the Celts were all about symbols, I wonder what it means," Joseph said, looking at it closely. "It feels potent, somehow, and the tree so familiar."

"The tree looks remarkably like the design on the door of the convent in Paris," Jessica said, as if reading his mind.

"You're right," Joseph said. "A miniature rendition of the same symbol."

"I had a dream about that design," Jessica told him, "and even wrote a poem about it."

"I dreamed about that tree once too and painted a picture of it. I called it The Tree of Life," Holly added. "It seems we've all been touched by the same image."

"It's the Essene Tree of Life," André said with confidence.

"Essene?" Joseph exclaimed. "That's one of the early Jewish sects. Some scholars even theorize *Jesus* was an Essene. I wonder why my great grandmother would've owned such a necklace. I always assumed she was Catholic."

"The Essene sect influenced the Celts, I'm told, and even a good Catholic can still be a Celt, I imagine," André said.

"Probably true," Joseph acknowledged, looking proudly at his son.

"So the necklace originally came to you from your great grandmother?" André asked. "Did you ever meet her?"

"I never met her, but we did travel to Ireland for her wake and funeral. Her daughter—my grandmother—gave the necklace to my father. I think it's time to trace its history more directly. My mother saves everything, so I'm quite sure she'll have my father's ancestral photographs and documents."

"It'll be cool to match the ancient history to your own family," André said.

"*Our* family. And, speaking of my mother, she'll be over the moon when she finds out she has another grandson."

Joseph smiled at André, but the young man's face had grown ashen. "What's wrong, André?"

"I'm ... a bit overwhelmed," he said, rising. "You all seem so ... warm and accepting, but I don't really know you." He turned to look at Jessica. "I still can't understand how you could just *leave* me the way you did. And how could you not tell him that he had a son? I just don't get it." He shook his head and folded his arms.

Although his heart went out to André, Joseph felt a need to come to Jessica's defense. "It's not her fault," he said, standing up to meet André's gaze. "She was just a kid, even younger than you. This is all new for all of us."

"Sorry," André said, looking at Holly for support, "but I've really got to go. I just can't deal with it all. It's just too much."

"It's okay. We can go. Maybe tomorrow." Holly gave Jessica a worried look.

Jessica said, "I'm sorry, André. I'm so sorry."

He gave her a bewildered look, then turned to leave, Holly close behind.

"What can we do?" Jessica cried when they heard the car leave. "This was supposed to be a joyful evening."

"It's okay, love," Joseph said, holding her. "I recognized a bit of myself in André's behavior. I think he just needs some time alone to let it all soak in. These are life changing days for all of us."

André

André didn't speak while Holly drove back to the hotel. The thoughts in his head were relentless. *I just couldn't take it anymore. Who do they think they are, anyway? They don't know me. And I don't know them. What would my real parents say?*

They reached the hotel and Holly turned off the ignition. "André," she began.

"I don't want to talk about it. I just need to be alone."

"Okay."

"Look, I'm sorry. I know you all wanted everything to turn out well, but I just can't let it all go: the secrecy, the deception. How could she abandon her child, a child with someone she loved? I don't understand and I don't need it."

"I can understand how you feel, but Jessica was so young—"

"How can you understand?" he interrupted, opening the car door.

"Because," she said, her voice trembling, "because ... *my* mother left me, too."

He felt slapped.

"Oh, Holly, I know. I'm sorry," he said, his voice tender as he turned toward her. "But your mother couldn't help dying. It's not the same."

"Don't we both feel abandoned and don't we both resent their leaving us? You've got *two* mothers and I don't have *any*. Maybe you should think of *that* instead of running away from people who want to love you."

He reached out to hold her hand. "I'm sorry. Truly I am. I don't want to argue with you."

She looked up at him, tears filling her eyes.

"Please, just let me hold you. He moved closer and put his arms around her. "Maybe I'll give Joseph a call in the morning."

Holly pulled back to look at him.

"I think that would be a good idea, a gracious gesture."

After waving goodbye until her car turned out of sight, he walked slowly toward the hotel. *My life is spinning around me. I don't know who I am anymore. I really don't know.*

He didn't get much sleep, unable to turn off his thoughts. *Mamà and Papa are my real parents. Maybe I shouldn't have even come here. Now I've gone and told Holly I'd call Joseph. And I will do that. After all, he hasn't done anything wrong. He didn't even know I existed.*

***

The next morning, he called Joseph at his hotel but got no answer. *I'll bet he's at Jessica's and I don't want to call there*. He left a message for Joseph at the hotel.

Only a few hours later, Joseph returned his call, and they agreed to meet for coffee.

They sat at a corner table in a brightly decorated bakery/café, enjoying cappuccino and warm croissants.

"Sorry about freaking out last night. It's all so *unreal*. I have parents at home who love me and here I am with you."

"It's okay, really. I was struck numb at first myself and not happy with Jessica about her withholding," Joseph assured him. "I couldn't take it all in, either. When you reacted as you did, I saw a bit of myself in you."

"Cool. Was Jessica all right after I left?"

"Not really," Joseph said, "but we stayed up a while and talked it through. You know, her father walked out on the family when she was quite young. When you walked out last night…and when I walked out the day before, not to mention twenty-odd years ago—I think it triggered her *own* abandonment issues. She broke open when she realized her decisions, whether young and ill-advised or not, had caused us to suffer just as she had suffered."

"I didn't know about her father," André said.

"It was really hard on her. He left her mother for a younger woman and they had two more children. Jessica felt, and to a degree still feels, that he basically forgot about her."

"That sucks. But her mother, Adelaide, obviously cares. That must count for something."

"I'm sure her father cares, too, in his own way. The older I get the more I realize how complicated we humans are. We have many aspects to ourselves and play many different roles in our lives. Some we live better than others. I'm learning to have more compassion for others, to forgive. But the hardest one to forgive, it seems, is myself."

André listened intently, then said, "My Papa has a hard time understanding me. We seem to be nothing alike. It makes me sad, but I do love him. I just can't be who he wants me to be. I blame myself for letting him down and maybe I'm feeling guilty about being here with you."

"I get it. My father didn't really understand me, either. You're lucky. I'm twice your age and have just realized that I can't complete my father's vision. I must be true to my own."

"Exactly," André said, realizing he was fingering the necklace. "It's all so strange. I grew up with my parents on our vineyard in Provence and knew nothing about *any* of this. Then they gave me this necklace and everything changed— at once, it seems."

"Maybe it couldn't have happened any other way."

"I guess so, but it still hurts," he said, looking directly into Joseph's eyes. "This necklace rightly belongs to you." He unclasped it and offered it to Joseph.

"I wouldn't hear of it," Joseph said emphatically, refusing. "You're my … son, and I want you to have it. My father would have wanted that, too."

"I love this necklace. Thank you. Thank you so much. Maybe the energy it carries knows best," André said, returning it to its place around his neck.

"Just watching you put on that necklace warms my heart."

This kind, gentle man, this wise man, not unlike me, is actually my father. "Why did you give the necklace to Jessica when you left her in Paris?"

"It was a part of me, part of my history, a kind of talisman. I used to hold and touch it as you do. I didn't plan it, but when we parted—I think on some level I knew the priesthood would become my destiny— I spontaneously took it from around my neck and gave it to her, a token of my love that I hoped she'd keep forever. I had no idea Jessica was pregnant." He paused, looking down at his lap. "If I'd known, I would *never* have abandoned *her* or *you*."

"I have no doubt about that."

They sat quietly for several moments, both needing time.

Joseph broke the silence and said, smiling, "I hope you'll give me a personal tour of your exhibit. I was so distracted in Montmartre. Jessica says you are an exquisitely sensitive photographer. She's certainly your champion in that regard."

An image of Mamà flashed through André's mind. "I do like Jessica, and understand her choices better, but my real mother is in Provence. She's the one who loved me and raised me."

"I understand, André, and respect your feelings. These are tough dynamics to accept. But Jessica is a good woman, a gentle soul, and would never have intentionally hurt you. She'd much more likely forsake herself. I hope you'll give her a chance."

André nodded, and then asked, "What do you know about your— I mean our—ancestors?"

"My great grandparents, who would be your great great grandparents, were from Ireland. I never knew either of them, but I know they had three children, all girls. My grandmother was one of them. She and her husband were both born in Ireland but immigrated to America after they married."

"What were they like?"

"My grandfather died before I was born, but my grandmother was full of stories about 'the old country.' I loved being around her. She was the one who shared the necklace's legend with my father, her son. She said whoever owned it would receive messages from God."

"I don't know about receiving messages from God, but when I hold the necklace I concentrate more clearly, feel somehow connected, and can better trust myself."

"I used to hold it when I prayed. It helped me focus, too."

"Maybe Jessica has mentioned it to you, I don't know, but if she hasn't I don't think Holly would mind me telling you that she's kind of psychic. When she held the necklace the other day, she had the distinct feeling that someone in the past wore it when he or she was hurt, or maybe even killed. It made her very sad."

"That's fascinating. No, Jessica didn't mention Holly's gift. I wonder what her vision points to."

***

Late that afternoon, the two men retreated to André's hotel room where André brought out the illustration he'd copied from Edmond Bordeaux Szekely's book *From Enoch to the Dead Sea Scrolls*. It exactly matched the design inside the locket.

"Jessica's mother and I found this in a London library. From what the caption says, this root represents our Earthly Mother and this branch our Heavenly Father. The others—six earthly roots and six heavenly branches—represent angelic forces which connect heaven and earth," André said. He paused before saying quietly, "The necklace helps me focus but I mostly use it when I meditate."

"I think I told you that I used to use it when I prayed," Joseph said. "I've also used my mother's rosary to obtain a similar effect. When did you start meditating?"

"I studied briefly with a Buddhist monk in a monastery in France, but it's all about the practice for me. When I meditate, I experience the vast space around and through me, as if I'm connected to everything in the universe. That kind of experience means more to me than what I learned as a child in church."

"I know what you mean. When I was actively practicing as a priest, I often felt restrained by the Catholic Church's rules and requirements. Over time, I developed a much more personal relationship with God," Joseph said. "When I am quiet, in prayer, a knowing comes, sometimes, speaking through my heart. I've come to believe that's the way God communicates with me."

"Maybe this symbol of the Tree of Life, no matter what its tradition, is a reminder that all of us remain linked to the Source of our being, whether we call that God or Mystery or another sacred name."

"I think you're right."

"It's really great to be able to talk with you about this. My Papa can be pretty rigid in his Catholic beliefs. I don't believe he could even entertain a conversation like this."

An image of Papa came to him and André suddenly felt disloyal.

"But Papa is a wonderful man, in other ways. He taught me the value of hard work, and, I think, finally has accepted my path, though he's terribly disappointed that I won't follow in his footsteps and manage the vineyard."

"I'm sure he's a fine man, for I see he has raised a fine son."

"Thank you, that means a lot to me."

"I also understand all too well about the danger of pleasing a parent instead of following your own heart. Your choice—and mine—have broken chains."

Jessica

Jessica stood admiring Holly as she finished up her session with a group of schoolchildren who were studying Southwestern culture. They had come to explore the museum's collection of Native American art and artifacts.

After the children left, Jessica stuck her head into Holly's cubicle and told her how impressed she was with her way with them. "They were spellbound while you were talking."

"I love kids," Holly said, brushing off the compliment. "I hope someday to have a houseful."

"Good for you." Jessica smiled, lowered her gaze, and turned to leave.

"Jessica, do you have time for tea? We haven't really checked in about everything."

"Give me a bit to tie up some loose ends. Come down in fifteen minutes. I'll put the kettle on."

***

Sitting across from Jessica in her office, tea in hand, Holly wasted no time in small talk. "Jessica, how are you handling all of this? I mean, André showing up and then Joseph, and André's behavior last night. That must have been so hard."

"No kidding. I'm really out of balance. I spent so many years longing for Joseph, wondering about André. Finally, I learned to find peace and happiness deep within, even though I was alone. Now everything has changed. I guess I naively thought things would go more smoothly than they have with André. I thought surely he would understand why I let him go. But I, of all people, should have been more attuned to his feeling of abandonment. It's very disorienting. I'm having to work hard to stay centered and grounded. Know what I mean?"

"I do. Ever since I met André, I've been in a kind of daze myself. Our feelings for each other run deep and yet we've known each other such a short time. I'm vulnerable but also comforted. Maybe we were together in a past life."

"I love your perspective, Holly."

"And what about all of us? You, me, André, and Joseph somehow connected to that image, the Tree of Life. My painting, your poem, André and Joseph's ancestral connection to the necklace."

"It's certainly got my curiosity up."

"I'm telling you, it's a miracle. That necklace holds a potent energy. And the Tree seems to represents its source."

The two women sat together sipping their tea, being together with all that they carried.

***

After work, Joseph called to tell Jessica that he and André had spent a good bit of the afternoon together. Her spirits lifted at first, but all Joseph would tell her was that André was sorry for running out but needed time alone.

***

As Jessica and Joseph finished dinner, her mother called to confirm their travel plans. She and Donald would be arriving in a couple of days to see André's exhibit and visit with Jessica.

"What did you think of André?" her mother asked tentatively.

"Mum, he told me *everything*."

After a short silence Adelaide said softly, "I just wish you'd told me. Maybe I could have helped."

"Mum, you were depressed at the time, had been hospitalized, and I was very young. Can we let it go, please?"

"Of course. Not another word."

"When do you think André will be ready to see me again?" Jessica asked Joseph after the call ended. "I know my mother will want to see him."

"Why don't you try to get together with him alone before your mother gets here?"

She nodded, but couldn't quite speak. He pulled her close and comforted her.

***

Early the next day before she drove into work, Jessica called André's hotel room. When he didn't answer, she left a message for him to call her, either at the museum or at home. For the remainder of the day, she could think of nothing else.

It wasn't until she'd gotten home from work that André returned her call.

"I'm happy to get together, Jessica. We're professionals, as well. I apologize for my behavior at your house. It was inappropriate."

"I appreciate your willingness to see me outside the museum. I can make us a light dinner with leftovers, if you don't mind. Are you okay with coming here?"

At his unexpectedly easy, "No problem," they agreed to meet in an hour.

***

After an only slightly uncomfortable meal, André and Jessica sat together in the living room.

"I hope you'll try to understand why I did what I did," Jessica began. "I wasn't very emotionally strong in those days. I'd put Joseph on a pedestal. Since he believed God wanted him to be a priest, I didn't think I had a right to stand in his way, even though it meant I would lose him. If I'd told him I was pregnant, I thought he'd feel obligated to marry me, and I didn't want his devotion out of obligation."

"Don't you think he had a right to know you were carrying his child?" André asked.

"You're right, he did. But it's too late to change what happened."

"I see what you mean."

"I don't want to push you, André, not in any way. For now, perhaps we can start by being friends."

"You seem like a good person, Jessica. I know you mean well. It's just a lot to absorb. Give me some time."

"Of course, I understand."

After an awkward silence, Jessica told him that her mother and stepfather would be visiting in a couple of days. "I know that she's excited about seeing your exhibit."

"That's great news. It will be wonderful to see Adelaide again. We got on famously in London." *My grandmother.*

"That's what she said too. How wonderful that is."

"And I'm very grateful to you for introducing me to Holly." He touched his necklace. "I've fallen in love with her, you know."

"I can see that. And I know how fantastic that feels. Trust your heart. Trying to figure things out can create unnecessary obstacles, can change the path of destiny."

"Maybe this necklace has helped rectify that," André said. "It seems we're all intended to be together, to work something through, and I'm willing to play my part in it. I appreciate your honesty, your willingness to be real. Thank you, Jessica."

"Being real is being free. I'm a late learner. Maybe knowing our story, mine and Joseph's, will help you avoid some of the mistakes we made."

André nodded in agreement. *Jessica is wise and kind, still innocent somehow. I do feel something for her.*

***

Two days later, Jessica left work to meet her mother and stepfather at a popular deli in town. They brought home some sandwiches for lunch and after they got settled, Donald took his sandwich down to the beach so that Jessica and Adelaide could have some alone time together.

"That was thoughtful of Donald," Jessica said.

"Donald is a love, it's true. I'm very lucky to have him. Now, dear, tell me everything. Where is André now?"

"Actually, he's with Joseph."

"Joseph?" her mother said with a questioning look.

"It's a long story, Mum. Joseph is the man I fell in love with in Paris many years ago. When he decided to become a priest, I kept André a secret from him."

"Oh, so Joseph, a *priest*, is André's father?"

"Yes, Mum. But now, after many years of soul searching, he has finally left the priesthood and wants us to make a life together."

"Too bad he couldn't have done that in the beginning, before André was born."

"I know, Mum, but this is how it is."

"I wish I had known you were pregnant, sweetheart. Maybe I could have helped."

"Mum, I thought we agreed to let that go. And, besides, you *have* been there for me in so many other ways. Without you, André might never have come into our lives. And for that, I will be eternally grateful."

They took each other's hands. Adelaide's eyes filled with tears. "I just wish we'd known André when he was a little boy."

"Me, too, Mum. Me, too. It breaks my heart."

They sat in silence for a while until suddenly Adelaide asked, "What time are André and Joseph coming over? Shouldn't we be thinking about what we'll have for dinner?"

"They made an appointment at an Essene Center in San Juan Capistrano. They said they'd be home for dinner—spaghetti, by the way, your recipe."

"I could tell André's curiosity was piqued in London when we were researching the symbol inside his necklace."

"And Joseph's hooked, too. It's such a blessing that they're excited about something in common."

"It bodes well for them for creating a solid relationship."

"Joseph is a gentle man, and I think he mirrors a sensitivity in André that encourages each to trust himself and the other."

"That's very perceptive, dear. I suspect I will come to care for Joseph as I already do about my grandson."

"You're going to love Joseph, Mum. He's such a good man. I've waited so long for him. It seems as if letting go somehow brought him back to me, both of them."

"I can see that. When I realized that your Dad was not coming back to me, I began to open my heart again, and then …."

"Sounds like we both learned a lesson," Jessica said, hugging her mother.

By the time Donald returned from the beach, they had dried their eyes and were laughing together like school girls.

Joseph

Joseph and André drove down the coast to the Essene Center in San Juan Capistrano, just south of Laguna Beach. They'd heard about it at the library in Laguna and had called to make an appointment.

A fish pond had been built in a shaded area off to the side of the entrance and benches had been placed in various locations around the grounds. A woman sat in a meditative position on one of them.

"Look over there," André said, pointing to a small group of people doing Tai chi. "I see more and more people practicing in the parks in Paris and I've noticed them in London, too. It's very balancing for body and spirit."

Peace pervaded the entire place. A man and woman approached them.

"Welcome," the man said, extending his hand. "I'm Michael Southerland, and this is my wife, Heather. We're both priests here."

Michael wore round, wire-rimmed glasses and sported a beard and mustache. Heather wore her auburn hair pulled back in a ponytail. Joseph guessed they were in their late thirties or early forties. His curiosity was aroused. *Obviously, these modern-day Essenes allow their priests to be married and also welcome women to be ordained.*

Michael ushered them into a warm, cheery room where they sat down to talk.

"We've been in this location for about ten years," Michael said. "It was a small inn before Heather and I purchased it."

"We added a chapel a year later," Heather said, "and then classrooms and a library three years ago."

"It's very peaceful," André remarked.

"It's our aim," Michael said, "to create a place where people can connect with the essence of nature and, at the same time, the essence of themselves."

"We were hoping you could help us understand the symbolism in this necklace," André said, taking off the necklace and opening the locket. "It used to belong to my great great grandmother."

Michael and Heather both inspected it. "It's the Tree of Life," Michael said, "a sacred symbol of the Essenes."

"It's beautifully designed," Heather exclaimed. "Are you Essenes?"

"Not yet or not that we're sure of," Joseph responded, "but it appears our ancestors might have been."

"Even if you aren't practicing our religion," Michael said, "it's possible you're carrying a spiritual blueprint of the Essenes, inherited from your ancestors. This necklace may be an aid in helping you recognize your heritage—and your destiny."

"That's an interesting concept," Joseph said. "My father gave me the necklace many years ago. As far as I knew then, his grandmother was a practicing Catholic in Ireland. I always thought the necklace was Celtic until André discovered it was actually a locket that had been soldered shut, concealing this symbol."

"Fascinating," Heather said. "The fleur-de-lis and seven stones on top probably symbolize our threefold nature—body, mind, and spirit— and the sevenfold peace that we teach."

"And the Tree of Life inside," Michael added, "reveals the mystery of our true purpose in life: to fully incarnate in life, to embody divine consciousness in the physical world."

"I'd love to learn more." Joseph said.

"You're welcome to look through some of the books in our library," Michael suggested. "I think you will find those by Edmond Bordeaux Szekely particularly useful. We base many of our teachings on his work. Szekely translated about a third of the complete manuscripts of *The Gospel of Peace* from Aramaic to English. He found it in the Secret Archives of the Vatican."

"I saw a book by Szekely in London," André said. "In fact, I copied an illustration of the Tree of Life from it that looks remarkably like the design in our necklace."

"Then you've already been introduced to the *Gospel of Peace*," Michael said, smiling at André. "A copy of the manuscript, written in old Slavonic, is held in the Royal Archives of the Hapsburgs, now the property of the Austrian government."

"This is all quite intriguing. I have so much to learn," Joseph said, feeling his pulse quicken with excitement.

"You know, the Essenes were persecuted for many years," Michael explained. "Perhaps your ancestors soldered the locket shut to keep their spiritual beliefs secret at that time."

"André and I had wondered about that," Joseph said.

Heather left to pick up their son from school, and Michael took André and Joseph to their small chapel. Behind the altar, a large, clear window had been installed. Outside, trees and flowers created a natural backdrop. A smaller stained glass window depicting a dove with an olive branch in its beak had been installed above the clear window. A brass cross stood on the altar, with a fresh vase of roses before it. All elegantly simple.

"I wonder if you might tell us more about the actual Essene practices and its origins, at least the basics," Joseph asked Michael quietly.

"Well, the Essenes were originally a Jewish sect," Michael explained, "though today we're from both Jewish and Christian backgrounds, with a metaphysical view of Jesus' teachings. Not all of our churches are alike, for there are different interpretations of Essene teachings. The most basic teaching, however, posits that the Holy Spirit lives within each of us. Jesus referred to this in the Bible as the Kingdom of God. By meditating and allowing our minds to become still, we can awaken to this Spirit and allow It to guide us in everything we do or say so that we may purify our outer lives and live in love and truth, just as Jesus did."

"That's helpful. Thank you."

After they left the chapel, Michael escorted them back toward the larger of the two buildings beyond the main house. They entered through a side door and came into a spacious room with books lining the walls. Two small rooms adjoined the large one.

"This is where we conduct classes," Michael said, "for those who want to study for the priesthood or explore our spiritual beliefs for themselves."

"You hold theological training here?" Joseph asked, his curiosity growing. He glanced over at André and smiled.

"Yes," Michael replied. "As ordained ministers, Heather and I share the teaching. We're working now with three students who've completed their preparatory studies and are in the final phase of their training."

"I was a Catholic priest for several years," Joseph divulged, "but have decided, after many indecisive years, to leave that path. I'd be interested in learning more about the Essene philosophy."

Just saying the words excited him even more.

"You're welcome to study with us anytime," Michael said, smiling at both of them. "We also invite guest lecturers from other spiritual paths to offer workshops and to share their meditative practices to enhance what we teach. As an Essene, Jesus traveled to Egypt, India, and even France and England, studying with the spiritual masters from many different traditions prior to his ministry."

"I've heard that theory," Joseph said, "but the Catholic Church, of course, does not accept those notions. Having been on the edge of Church doctrine for some time, I am becoming more and more open to such possibilities."

"You must excuse me, the afternoon is getting away from me with such attentive company. Do take a look at our library before you leave and please come back again anytime."

Joseph and André hunkered down in the library for a good part of the afternoon.

"I'm surprised to feel so much at home here and with the Essene teaching," André said as they drove back toward Laguna Beach. "It feels more inclusive of both Eastern and Western spiritual perspectives than organized religions."

"It's certainly not Catholic." Joseph laughed. "Maybe that's why I'm so drawn to it."

It was near sunset when they arrived at Jessica's house to find her sitting on the front steps with Holly and an older man and woman.

"That's Jessica's mother," André said, recognizing Adelaide. "The man must be her husband. I think his name is Donald."

"It's weird," Joseph joked, affectionately punching André's upper arm as they got out of the car, "you've met Jessica's mother before I have."

André reached out his arms spontaneously to Adelaide, all smiles.

"This is my grandson," Adelaide said proudly, turning to her husband.

"And this is Joseph," Jessica said, taking his hand and drawing him close to her.

"Lovely to meet you both," Joseph said, a bit shyly extending his hand to greet them, relieved when Jessica called them in for dinner but realizing he and André were late.

"Where were you two? I was beginning to worry," Jessica asked Andre as he helped her bring the wine and glasses to the table

"An amazing place. We're both knocked out by it. We'll tell you all about it."

Joseph warmed when he saw the two of them talking animatedly with one another.

When Holly and Adelaide brought in the spaghetti and salad, he noticed how Holly's cheeks turned pink when her eyes met André's. *There's some sweet chemistry there.* Jessica, beautiful in aqua, her lips a glossy rose, smiled at him and leaned over the table, as if in slow motion, to place sourdough rolls on the table. *I love her hair up away from her face.*

"Since André showed me the necklace in London," Adelaide said, "I've done a bit of research on the Essenes. Apparently, since 1947, when the Dead Sea Scrolls were found, there's been a resurgence of modern Essene groups, especially since it's believed the Essenes wrote the text. I'm curious to hear about your trip to the Essene Center."

"Well," Joseph replied, "the center is managed by a husband and wife team, both Essene priests. They have created a beautiful environment for retreat and study. And, I have to admit," he said, taking Jessica's hand, "I was quite intrigued by their sanction of marriage within the priesthood."

"I bet you were," Donald said, with a funny grin.

"Donald!" Adelaide scolded him. "How much wine have you had?" Her question brought good-natured laughter from around the table.

"And Adelaide," André jumped in with excitement, "remember the illustration we found that matched the symbol inside the necklace? They had a number of books by that author, Edmond Szekely. I noted some of the titles."

"Good boy," Adelaide said, as only a grandmother could get away with. "Please remember to share them with me. It's a fascinating topic."

"I'm so glad you two enjoyed yourselves. I hope you'll take me down there soon so I can see it for myself," Jessica added, her skin glowing in the candlelight.

"We definitely will," André promised, his face relaxed and open.

Joseph saw both Jessica and Holly noticing his ease. *Thank you, God, for this moment, this day, this new life.*

Later, while helping Jessica with the dishes, Joseph told her that he intended to go over old photos and documents with this mother. "That may give us some idea of the link we have to the Essenes."

Jessica leaned over and kissed him on the cheek. "We had a good day, all of us together."

Joseph smiled inside and out, thinking of how relieved his mother would be, how delighted, at how his life was unfolding. *I can't wait for her to meet Jessica ... and her new grandson.*

André

André held a map in his lap while Holly drove through a mountain pass north of Los Angeles on their way to her hometown, a full day's drive from Laguna Beach.

"Look, we're out of the mountains now, headed toward the coast," Holly pointed out excitedly.

He loved the way the flush in her cheeks lit up her face.

André gazed at the expanse of land opening in front of them, then checked his map. "Oxnard and Ventura are just ahead."

"Santa Barbara, where the Wagner Gallery is located, is just beyond Ventura. It's a prestigious gallery. It's quite impressive that Dolores Wagner wants to show some of your work. It should sell well."

They'd agreed that André would both hang and sell the photographs Dolores had selected from his Children of Paris exhibit. He planned to rotate his images, leaving most at the Sea View.

"I'm really surprised. It wouldn't have happened without your support—you and Jessica."

"It's easy to be supportive of you. Your work is very alive. And Jessica recognizes talent."

"I'm looking forward to seeing *your* paintings in Cambria."

"Well, I'm certainly not a professional, like *you*, so don't expect any masterpieces," she said, turning to him and wrinkling her nose.

"I won't judge your work; it's an expression of who you are."

"Well, *who* I am is very personal and so are my paintings. It's not easy to share them. My work is far from mainstream, especially my visionary paintings, like the Tree of Life."

"If art doesn't come from the heart, from the artist's essence, it really isn't art in my mind, regardless of the professional standards it meets."

"That makes me feel more comfortable about showing you my work."

"Would you tell me a little more about your visionary paintings, about your process?"

"They can start as dream symbols or images that come during meditation, or when I'm receiving inner guidance. I sometimes bring the symbol or image into my body through movement or active imagination, where I actually dialogue with it. That helps me fully embody it. If I don't want to embody an image, I visualize it outside of me, sometimes far away, and use that perspective to express it, releasing it from my psyche."

"That's fascinating. Tell me more about the inner guidance that you receive. Is that what happened when you saw what you did when you held my necklace?"

"The inner visions usually comment on my own life, but sometimes they show me something concerning someone else, like that one I shared with you. I felt the vision was really meant for you."

"Have you ever considered using your gift professionally?"

"There's that word, professional, again, as if somehow that substantiates its value. No, I'll help people if they come to me, but I've never considered marketing my gift, if you know what I mean."

"I get it."

He smiled and squeezed her hand affectionately. Her touch, warm and loving, excited his senses. *Not only is she beautiful, she's an inspired artist.*

A few hours later, they arrived in Cambria. "What a quaint little town," André said, noticing the antique quality of the buildings on the main street.

"Isn't it picturesque? I'm so glad to be home." She soon turned into the driveway of a two-story Victorian house, where a teenage boy stood in the front yard, working on his bicycle.

"Hey, Randy," Holly called as they got out of the car. "How's it going?" She ran over to give him a big bear hug. "I've missed you so much."

"I've missed you, too. Why'd you have to move so far away?"

"Because that's where the work is." She stood back to admire him. "You've grown at least two inches since I saw you last. André, meet my brother Randy."

Randy looked a little embarrassed, but extended his hand to André.

"I've heard a lot about you," André said, smiling and shaking the boy's hand. Like his sister, Randy had dark, full hair and big expressive eyes.

"Uh-oh. I'm in trouble now." Randy laughed. "So you're the Frenchman Holly's been raving about."

"Sounds like I'm in trouble, too," André joked, turning toward Holly, whose cheeks had turned crimson.

Just then, a man opened the front door and walked out to greet them. He looked a little tired but wore a big, warm smile.

"How's my girl?" he said, wrapping his arms around Holly.

"Never better, Dad. It's so good to see you."

After they broke away from each other, she introduced him to André.

"Just call me Sam," her dad said, shaking André's hand. "Come on in. How was the trip?"

"Great," André said. "I'm so impressed with California. It has just about everything—mountains, deserts, valleys, and the ocean."

"My favorite area is Big Sur," Holly said. "It's a little further north, mountainous with redwood forests and steep cliffs overlooking the Pacific—just breathtaking."

"Sounds like a photographer's dream," André said as they entered the living room furnished with country antiques and wall after wall of artwork. His eyes rested on the large painting, hanging over the couch: a watercolor depicting a grove of windswept trees clinging to a hillside, overlooking the ocean.

"Holly painted that," Sam said, smiling at his daughter. "It's Moonstone Beach."

"It's fantastic," André said, putting his arm around Holly. "I knew you were underestimating yourself."

"Well, the landscape around here begs to be painted ... and photographed," Holly said, blushing. "You'll see what I mean."

"I've got my camera ready."

"This one over here," Sam pointed out, "was painted by Holly's mother Karen."

"Is that Holly and Randy?"

"Yep, that's them when they were little tykes."

"Your wife was a wonderful painter," André said.

"She sure was, and she passed her talent on to her daughter."

Holly hugged her dad. They held each other until Randy entered the room and blurted out, "Hey, is anybody hungry?"

"Do we get to sample any of your special concoctions?" Holly laughed.

"My Chicken Vegetable Supreme is on the menu at the restaurant," Randy said. "I dare you to try it."

Sam explained to André that his family owned the Green Garden Café and that the head chef was tutoring Randy.

At the restaurant, André tried Randy's special dish and thought it delicious, then asked if he'd tried any French recipes.

"No, but Holly sent me a cool cookbook from her trip to Paris."

"Maybe you'll consider one of the French culinary schools when you're ready to study to become a professional chef."

"We have some pretty good schools in California, too," Randy said. "Plus I want to stay a bit closer to home."

"I like that idea," Sam said, looking lovingly at both his children.

***

The next day, Holly took André on the scenic coastal highway up to the Big Sur area.

"It was good to meet your dad and Randy. They clearly love each other, and you, very much. It's rare to see a teenage boy and his father so close."

"It is special. I'm grateful for that."

"And were you right about the beauty of this place," he exclaimed, taking many shots at Ragged Point. They continued further north, stopping frequently so André could take more pictures. He had never seen such tall trees and photographed the redwoods from base to bough.

***

They spent the next morning with Sam and Randy at the house in Cambria. Then, while Sam was helping Randy with a particularly thorny homework assignment, André asked Holly if she would show him some of her visionary paintings, in particular her Tree of Life.

She held his hand and led him into her bedroom, where several ethereal paintings adorned the walls. He immediately spotted the Tree of Life.

"It's nearly identical," he said, looking from the painting to the design in his necklace and back again.

"I want to take it back with me to Laguna. I think both Jessica and Joseph might like to see it."

She showed him a few more examples of her visionary work, some vividly colorful, others filled with light, some shadow figures, all of it inspired.

"I can tell that you've reflected, and embodied, as you said, some of these images before painting them. They're very vital, totally alive. Your work is very strong, Holly, and tender."

"I like to describe the images experientially in my journal, enter them not only physically but also through poetry."

Looking around the room, André said, "If you wanted to show your work, I'm sure you could. It's wondrously beautiful, really, and provocative."

"I'm not ready for that."

Randy suddenly burst into the room. "Do you two want lunch?"

"Are you always hungry?" Holly laughed.

"Yes," he shouted, leaving as fast as he'd come in.

André leaned over and kissed Holly lightly on her lips. "I love you."

***

On the way back to Laguna Beach, they decided to stop for a bite to eat. Holly pulled into the driveway of a small café, next to an old inn.

"This looks like a cozy place for a dinner," she said.

The sun was low in the west, creating a spectacular palette of color.

"You look beautiful in this light," André said, pulling her to him and kissing her long and tenderly. "I love you, Holly," he whispered.

She looked directly into his eyes. "I want to let go, give you my heart, but I'm afraid I'll lose you."

"You're never going to lose me."

"But we're so young, and your career just beginning. The travel, the time apart." She paused and took a deep breath. "Maybe I feel vulnerable because I loved my mother so much and then lost her. No matter how much I prayed she'd get well, she didn't."

"I'm not going anywhere," he said, kissing away the tears that filled her eyes.

"Oh, André, I *do* love you," she whispered in his ear.

Her words set his heart racing and he pulled her closer.

Finally, she broke away. "We should eat."

After feasting on steaming bowls of clam chowder and fresh bread, André suggested they spend the night.

"We could, if it's not too expensive. Jessica isn't expecting me to come in tomorrow."

They got a mid-week rate on a room with a fireplace.

"I'll light a fire," André said in a cheerful voice.

"You already have," Holly teased.

***

André awoke somewhat disoriented a few days later in his tiny flat in Paris after dreaming of his time with Holly in California. No soothing sound of waves greeted him and very little sunlight shone through the window. His eyes fell on Holly's picture by the bed, the one he'd taken in Montmartre with the Eiffel Tower behind her.

"Ah, there you are, my darling."

He stood up, rubbed the sleep out of his eyes, and looked around. All of his photography equipment stood in the corner by the window. The tiny stove, sink, table, and refrigerator, and his bookcases filled the remaining space. His unpacked suitcase sat next to the closet door.

He'd arrived early in morning after a night flight from California and gone directly to bed, sleeping for several hours. Still in a daze, he rubbed his eyes again, images of Holly, Jessica, and Joseph flashing through his mind. *Everything's new, everything's changed. I've changed.*

The shrill ring of the telephone brought him back to the present moment. *"Bonjour,"* he answered in a groggy voice, picking up the receiver.

"André, this is Joseph. I'm calling from Boston."

"Oh, hello, Joseph," he said, shifting to English. "I thought you were flying out just behind me."

"I did. I'm already in Boston. I need to wrap up some things here before I make a permanent move to California."

"You must be happy about that."

"I am, indeed. André, I wanted you to know I told my family about you."

"How did they take it?"

"They were all amazed. And as I was telling them the story, I realized that I'm still amazed myself."

"I know what you mean."

"I really called to tell you that my mother and I found some very interesting photos buried, maybe hidden, under the false bottom of an old box among my father's things. I dropped the box by accident and the bottom fell out, along with the pictures. One was of a wedding couple. On the back we could barely make out the date, 22-2-75, and the names Gaston and Anne-Catherine Benet. We guessed the wedding date to be February 22, 1875."

"The name sounds French. Do you know who they were?"

"After seeing a second photo of Gaston, the man from the wedding picture, standing next to a young girl, we came up with a good guess. They appeared to be greeting people as they came out of a quaint church. The faded names, Gaston and Anne-Elizabeth, were written on the back, dated 14-7-91, July 14, 1891, sixteen years after the wedding picture. We assume that Anne-Elizabeth was Gaston's young daughter. My mother recognized the name Anne-Elizabeth. That was my father's grandmother's name. He knew her as Anne-Elizabeth O'Brian."

"Sounds like you've identified some of our ancestors."

"There's more. Guess what's clearly visible around Gaston's neck in the second picture?"

"The necklace? Really?"

"And Gaston is dressed like a priest."

"An *Essene* priest?"

"Well, with a wife and daughter, he sure wasn't a Catholic priest."

"I guess not." André laughed.

Joseph told him he'd gather all the old photos and documents and bring them to California.

"We'll unravel the puzzle together," André said. "I'll be in Provence with my parents for a week or so, then back to Paris to figure what's next. I have things to take care of myself."

"I know you'll be glad to be with your parents."

"I will. I've missed them. I want to share everything, all that I've learned and experienced, but I want them to feel included. It won't be easy."

"Good luck, André. I'll be thinking of you."

"You're the best," André said, noticing how surprisingly close he felt to Joseph, touching the necklace that lay close to his heart.

Joseph

Joseph and his mother continued poring through his father's documents and photos, hoping to unearth more information about his ancestors. They found some papers suggesting that Anne-Elizabeth had, indeed, migrated to Ireland from France and had married Joseph O'Brian, Joseph's namesake.

"She could be the one who soldered the necklace shut," Joseph commented. "Living amongst Irish Catholics, she may have had to keep her Essene background a secret."

"Makes sense," his mother said. "Oh, look, here's your grandmother's birth certificate. Carlotta O'Brian, born to Anne-Elizabeth Benet and Joseph O'Brian. We knew her as Carlotta Murphy. She married your grandfather Raymond. Your father was born shortly after they moved here from Ireland."

Joseph and Dorothy spent the afternoon together discussing Joseph's grandparents, both maternal and paternal.

"This has been great fun, but let's talk about the future." Her face lit up. "When may I meet Jessica … and my grandson? I can hardly believe I'm saying that."

"I don't know, but we'll figure a way to get us all together soon."

Dorothy began putting things away.

"Mom, there's something else I'd like to share with you."

"What is it, dear?"

"It's about the priesthood."

"I thought you'd decided to leave that path. You're not having second thoughts, are you?"

"No, certainly not about Catholicism. But I am intrigued by the Essene Way, its inclusive philosophy, and simplicity, especially now that I know it's in my blood. I'm considering theological training at an Essene Center in southern California."

"Are they established? I mean, would you be officially ordained and qualified for the ministry?"

"Yes and no, but, that said, my intuition tells me I must follow my heart on this and, for now, I'm exploring the possibilities."

"What about architecture or social work? I thought you were considering one of those fields?"

"Mom, I've been a servant of God for many years. It comes natural to me. Plus, the Essene Way sanctions marriage for its priests."

"Whatever you decide, Joseph, I agree with following your heart. And I welcome your getting married, having a family."

***

Two weeks later, Joseph approached Michael and Heather Southerland in San Juan Capistrano with the intention of continuing his theological studies at their Essene Center.

"I want to learn everything you know about the Essene Way of Life," Joseph told them. "Now that I've discovered that my ancestors were likely Essenes and my great great grandfather a priest, I'm inspired to study with you and, if it's God's will, to become a priest again. Will you help me?"

"I'm so glad you came to us, Joseph. Your heart is clearly open and your intentions, pure and noble." He glanced at Heather, who nodded her agreement. "We could start right away, whenever you're ready."

***

Now living with Jessica in her small cottage, Joseph surprised her one evening with pizza and salad and then told her of his decision to study with the Essenes.

"Coming home to you and Miss Suzy, with dinner all prepared. I think I like this new routine," she said, collapsing in her most comfortable chair. "I'm also excited about your decision."

After dinner, Joseph surprised her again with a bottle of champagne and two chilled glasses. "Before we pour the champagne," he said, getting down on his knees in front of her, "I want to ask you something."

Taking his outstretched hands, she bit her lip as he continued shyly, "It will make me the happiest man in the world if you will marry me, Jess. I love you with all of my heart."

Tears glistening in her eyes, she was lost for words, but soon said, "Of course, I'll marry you. You're my one true love and you always have been."

He stood, pulling her up into his arms, bursting with joy. He kissed her deeply. "I don't have a ring yet," he said. "I want you to pick it out, since you'll be wearing it for the rest of your life, I hope."

He poured their champagne, held up his glass, and handed the other to her. "To our love, ever present, ever expanding."

André

André spent a week with his parents in Provence before returning to Paris to decide his next move. Back in his flat, he sat alone at the small table, enjoying a glass of the Bordeaux his father had sent back with him, reviewing the highlights of his visit.

Sitting together on the porch, he'd done his best to fill them in on all that had happened to him in California: meeting Jessica and Joseph, and, of course, being with Holly. They'd shared their feelings, shed tears, and explored misunderstandings. He'd also shown them the locket and the mysterious Essene design. His mother offered a possible connection between the Essenes and the Cathars; her people hailed from the Cathar region.

Papa, at first angry and hurt that this new man, Joseph, had become a part of André's life, had thrown himself into his work, refusing to talk about it. But when André had helped him and Pierre in the vineyard, their camaraderie had returned.

"You've always shown me the value of good work," he'd said to his father on the last day of his visit, "and to do my best, always, even when things go wrong. You'll always be my father. How could it ever be otherwise?"

"I love you, son," his father had said, placing his arms around him. They returned home with a new bottle of wine to share with Mamà, a father/son ritual.

He cherished, too, his time in the garden with his mother. While picking early flowers with her, he'd shared his deepest feelings and listened as she'd shared hers. She'd wanted to know all about Jessica, of course.

"She sounds so beautiful, and successful," she'd said. "I'm so much older and not educated the way she is. I hope you will still need me."

"Oh, Mamà, it's *you* who made this home for me and Papa. You're always been here for us, for *me*. Sure, it's impressive to be educated and to have a smart career, but to create a loving home takes a special gift. I love you more than words can say."

André could still hear his mother's response: "Thank you, my dear son, my André. God sent you to us and made life worth living. Now you must follow your dreams, your heart."

"I've come to believe that it was no accident that I grew up here in France with you and Papa. I am part of this family and this land is my home."

He took another sip of wine. *And it's true. Provence is my home. I love Holly, want to marry her. Could she come to know Provence as home?*

He opened the locket, gazing at the Tree of Life design inside. *All Trees of Life include the roots and the branches. My tree includes Mamà and Papa and Pierre, and now Holly, Jessica, and Joseph.*

***

The next day, Holly called.

"André, I've got big news!"

He loved how excited she got when she had something special to tell him

"Jessica and Joseph are getting married. He *proposed*. Isn't it exciting?"

"That's great news. When is the wedding, and where?"

"I think they're going to have it here, on the museum terrace. You remember the gorgeous view. Jessica wants a Summer Solstice wedding. That date has a special meaning for her, related to her visit to Chartres Cathedral in France. It will be such a blessed new beginning for both of them."

"I've been missing you. And it's only been two weeks."

"Me, too, but I've been keeping busy. I'm *painting* again, trying portraiture, like my mother. I'll have a surprise for you when you get back."

"That's wonderful news. I can't wait to see what your visions have inspired."

"How about you, how was the time in Provence?"

"Much better than I expected, after all the news from my California days. We all enjoyed being together at home, but I look forward to the day when you'll be with us."

"Not too far from now, I hope."

"In the meantime, while I'm in Paris I must focus on selling my photographs and saving money for our future. I love you so much."

Jessica

Laguna Beach
June 21, 1989

At The Sea View Museum of Art in Laguna Beach, excitement filled the air. From her office window, Jessica peered out onto the terrace where friends and family had begun to gather. Her eyes grew moist when she spotted her father's tall frame and thinning gray hair. Next to him stood his son Tyler, who would be playing the keyboard for the ceremony. Luann was there, as well. *I can't believe they actually came. And Mum and Donald, across the aisle from Dorothy and John. Joseph is so happy his brother Tom and family could also be here.*

André and Tom ushered friends and other relatives down the spring flower-adorned center aisle to take their seats. Clouds passed, allowing the sun to shine through and clear the view to the turquoise sea. It was the happiest day of Jessica's life.

Holly came to join her, wearing the soft, flowing lavender dress she and Jessica had picked out together, along with a lilac garland in her hair. "I think they may be waiting for us." She smiled.

Jessica's heart beat faster. Outside, Tyler began to play Pachelbel's Canon. Suddenly Annie, her half-sister, also dressed in lavender, appeared in the room carrying a basketful of flowers. "It's time. Dad's outside the door."

Jessica stood tall, her antique lace dress falling gracefully around her as Holly placed a bouquet of tiny white roses, jasmine, and baby's breath in her hands. Annie stepped forward first, tossing her flowers to the right and left as she slowly walked down the aisle toward the altar. Holly followed behind her.

Jessica's heart raced as she glimpsed the man she'd loved for all of her adult life. Now, so many years later, God had brought him back to her—and also their precious son. *My cup runneth over.*

Tears came to her eyes as she watched Holly take her place at the altar next to Annie. On the other side, Tom and André stood with Joseph.

Finally, her father reached out his arm to her, beaming with pride. They waited for Tyler to begin the Bridal Chorus before beginning their slow walk down the dark red carpet. As everyone stood up and turned toward them, Jessica's heart overflowed at the sight of their familiar, smiling faces.

She leaned on her father's arm for support but focused all of her attention on her beloved Joseph, waiting for her in front of the altar. *This is love, real love.* When they reached the altar, she handed Holly her bouquet, smiled at her father, and took Joseph's hand.

"Dearly beloved," Michael Southerland, the Essene priest, began, modifying slightly the otherwise traditional ceremony.

"And now, with these rings, please offer your vows to one another in the witness of those who cherish you."

"I pledge my love to you in trust, in doubt, in light, in darkness, for all of my days," Jessica said.

Joseph followed with, "And I pledge my heart to you, body, soul, and spirit, always."

Michael's resonant voice rang out but he sounded far away as Joseph lifted her veil and kissed her lips.

They were together at last.

André

For the next eight months, André continued taking photos of the people of Paris, earning a fine reputation for his street scenes, while supporting his art projects doing commercial photography. He made regular trips to California to see Holly, while also nurturing his contacts with galleries in Laguna Beach and Santa Barbara.

Joseph was well into his Essene priesthood studies, and Jessica and Holly continued working together at the museum.

As André sat alone in his small studio apartment, changing lenses in his camera, his thoughts naturally turned to Holly.

When he was in California for the wedding, Holly had surprised him with a portrait she'd painted of him from a snapshot. He loved it, but it was her visionary paintings that he felt were her most inspired and creative works.

Putting his camera away, he picked up the picture by his bedside. He'd taken it on their first day together in Paris. He missed her terribly, and decided to call.

"How's my girl?"

"Glad to hear your voice! How are you?"

"I'd be better if you were here with me. Please take some time off and come to Paris."

"Now there's a dream."

"Let's make that dream come true. I want to take you to Provence to meet my parents."

"You're serious. Maybe when we get this exhibit up. I'll talk to Jessica."

"That sounds promising. Make it work, will you? It's too long and too far. I want to be together."

"It'll be at least ten days. Maybe more. But I agree, we need some time. Love you."

***

To André's delight, Holly called a few days later able to make plans. She could come within a week; Jessica had suggested she take one of her two weeks of vacation.

"We'll see a bit of Paris and then take the train to Provence. I want you to see the beautiful countryside on the way south."

"I can hardly wait."

***

André counted his stashed cash that evening; he'd saved enough for the engagement ring he wanted to buy for Holly, an emerald surrounded by seed pearls in an antique setting. He'd put down a small deposit and would pick it up that day. *It's time. We've waited long enough.*

That afternoon, he called his parents. His mother answered and explained that his father was busy in the winery. He told her of his plans to propose to Holly.

"But, André, we haven't even met her yet. And you're still so young. Are you sure you're ready for this?"

"Mamà, I'm almost twenty-two. You married Papa when you were nineteen."

"But that's the way we did things in those days."

"Mamà, we're both working and supporting ourselves and, most importantly, we're in love."

"But, André, where would you live?"

"I don't know. But I know she loves France. Maybe she would consider moving here."

"What about her father and brother there in California? Do you think she'd want to leave them?"

"I don't know."

"André, we would miss you terribly if you moved to California."

"I know, Mamà, and I would miss you, too. But I haven't even proposed yet. Hopefully, she'll say yes, and then we'll figure out those details."

"But maybe you should figure out those details first, before you talk about marriage."

She sounded worried, unlike what he'd expected.

"But, Mamà, after you meet her, you'll know why I don't want to wait any longer."

"When will that be?"

"She'll be here in about a week. We'll come down by train and stay for a few days, if that's okay."

"It will be wonderful. Thank you, André."

André heard Papa in the background, just in from the winery.

"It's André, he wants to bring Holly here to meet us."

"Let me speak with him."

His mother put Henri on the phone.

"So, we finally get to meet this young woman you're crazy for."

"I'm going to ask her to marry me."

"What?" his father hollered. "You want to get married?"

"Yes, Papa. I plan to ask her when she gets here."

"So you aren't going to wait until we meet her?"

"Don't worry about it. I know what I'm doing. Trust me."

"Son, if that's what you want, then that's what I want for you, too."

Much to André's relief, his father's voice had softened. *Maybe I need to stand up to him more often.*

"Thank you, Papa. Your respect means everything to me."

"Call us when you're ready to come. We'll be here, waiting."

***

When Holly finally got to Paris, they spent three days exploring the city, even taking a moonlight cruise on the Seine like they had when they first met. On the fourth day, they boarded a train for Provence.

"I can't wait for you to meet my parents," André said nervously as they found their seats. Touching the ring box in his pocket, he sighed. "But there's something I want to show you in Lyon. It's about half way, with a rest stop. I thought we'd have lunch there and spend a little time down by the river." *It's the perfect place to propose.*

"Whatever you think," she said quietly, gazing out the window as the train started.

They rode in silence, resting, for some time.

When André noticed Holly's eyes open, he said, "This is the train I took back and forth to photography school in Paris. That was right after my parents gave me this necklace and told me I was adopted."

"This ride must bring back those memories," Holly said, taking his hand.

"It does. I left the countryside for the city, left my youth behind, you know, to make my way in the world." He sighed. "Provence will always be my home."

"I know what you mean. I really enjoyed taking you to Cambria to meet my dad and Randy. And now you're sharing your family with me."

When the train pulled into Lyon, he reached into his pocket again, palms damp, to make sure the box was safe.

André took Holly down to a special place he remembered where two rivers came together. They sat together on a bench.

"This is the point," he said, "where Lyon straddles two rivers, the gentle Saone and the restless Rhone. It's here the two converge as one, more expansive river, meeting their destiny, the Mediterranean Sea."

"That's beautifully spoken, André."

"I brought you to this place for a reason," he said, taking the box out of his pocket and showing the ring to her. "Will you marry me, Holly?"

When she threw her arms around him, he thought his heart would burst with joy. "I've loved you since the day we met."

"I remember that day," she said.

"Let's try on the ring."

She held out her hand and he placed it on her ring finger. It looked big on her small hand, but she claimed to love it, holding it out now and then so she could look at her new adornment.

He pulled her into his arms and kissed her deeply, their coming together echoing in this place where the two rivers made one.

***

As they approached Provence, entering wine country, Holly commented more than once about the beauty of the landscape.

"In summer, those fields will be filled with lavender."

"I'd love to see that," Holly said as the train pulled into the station.

Mamà and Papa stood nearby, waiting for them.

"This is Holly," André announced. "Holly, these are my parents, Henri and Jacqueline."

"André told us you were beautiful," Henri said, flashing a smile at André as he kissed Holly on both cheeks, "but that was an understatement."

"Just like a Frenchman," Jacqueline apologized.

"I'm very happy to meet you both."

André smiled as he noted Holly's cheeks turning the rosy pink color he loved so much. "Show them the ring," he urged.

Holly held out her hand, "I'm a little embarrassed by the fuss, but very happy."

"Oh, my, congratulations," Jacqueline said. "You're really engaged."

"Yes, Mamà," he said after they embraced. "We really are."

"Welcome to our family," Henri said, kissing Holly yet again on both cheeks and giving André a hug. "Congratulations, son."

Back at the house, they enjoyed the authentic Provencal meal of stuffed cabbage, chickpea flour fries, and fish stew that Jacqueline had cooked for the occasion. "For dessert," she announced, "we have *biscolins* and *crème brulee*."

"*Biscolins* are pastry wrapped hazelnuts," André explained to Holly, "and you know what *crème brulee* is."

"I made my *crème brulee* especially for André," his mother said, her eyes moist. "I can't believe you're about to get married. It was just yesterday you were a little boy. I can see you coming to that door in your knickers, dirty up to your elbows. My little man all grown up." She shook her head and wiped her eyes.

Henri poured each of them a glass of his best Pinot Noir and raised his glass high. "To André and Holly," he toasted. "What joy it would give us both if you would marry here in the vineyard."

Holly and André looked at each other and smiled their agreement.

***

Later that evening, sitting on the front porch after his parents had gone to bed, André asked Holly how she would feel about living in France after the wedding.

"I don't know," she said. "I know Dad and Randy wouldn't like that idea. Laguna is bad enough, but France? I'll have to give it some serious thought."

"I understand."

"I love France, but, I also love my job. Maybe you could move to California."

"I've considered that, too, but my audience is here, in France. And Provence is my true home. You can understand why I might want to lure you here."

"You've done a pretty good job already." She laughed.

"Let's not worry. We have time to figure out these big decisions."

He stood up, taking her hands, trying to reassure her that everything was okay.

"You're right, I'm just a little overwhelmed. You remember that feeling, right?"

"That's an understatement. Let's get some sleep. Tomorrow, I want you to meet my best friend, Pierre." He walked her to the guest room and kissed her goodnight at the door, whispering in her ear, "I wish we could sleep together."

"Me, too."

Holly

Laguna Beach

Holly breezed into the museum, looking forward to showing Jessica her engagement ring.

She held her left hand out the moment Jessica greeted her outside her office.

"An emerald! And the white of the pearls set it off beautifully. It's so you!"

"André has an eye, it seems, for more than street scenes and flowers."

"I'll say. He wants to marry *you*, doesn't he?" Jessica laughed, giving her a big hug.

"You're so wonderful to me," Holly smiled, twirling around. "I'm very happy ... as you can see."

"How romantic to get engaged in France. Tell me all about it."

Holly told her all about the surprise stop in Lyon and their visit with André's parents.

"The big question left to answer is where are we going to live?"

"Oh, that is an important question. Where are you leaning towards?"

"California, of course. Or France. I know André would prefer France, especially Provence, but I worry about being so far from Dad and Randy, not to mention my job and you."

Later on, Jessica took Holly to a deli in town where they bought sandwiches and drinks. Holly suggested they sit at a picnic table in a park across the street, overlooking the ocean.

"I have something to share with you, too." Jessica smiled.

"What is it? You sound excited."

"Well, Joseph will be finishing his theological studies next year and we're talking about setting up an Essene Center in southern France."

"Really? You mean you'd leave the Sea View to live in France? What about your career?"

"We're talking about including an art studio and gallery in the center. Perhaps I could curate local artists and even consult at local museums, even in Paris, from time to time."

"I'm in shock. This really adds weight to André's desire to stay in France."

"I thought it might," Jessica continued, her eyes sparkling. "We envision a retreat center for spiritual seekers as well as artists, those seeking direction and those who connect their artistic life to their spiritual paths. Joseph would offer classes in the Essene Way as well as spiritual guidance. I'd manage the administrative and artistic arm. I also want to explore and perhaps teach about the influence of the Sacred Feminine in southern France as well as the *Course in Miracles.* We'd also provide meditation activities, including yoga and Tai chi."

"This is huge, life-changing, and very exciting."

"I know. It won't happen overnight, of course. It will take time. And we'll need others to help us realize our vision, other creative thinkers, other artists. "What I'm getting at is maybe you and André would be willing to help us?"

Holly paused, images of Provence flitting through her mind's eye.

"Oh, Jessica, this is sounding more and more right," Holly said, stunned.

"We're hoping to purchase a parcel of land in southern France, preferably Provence."

Holly's mind began to spin. *We could live in France … and Jessica and Joseph would be there*. She took a deep breath. "This is so sudden. I have to sit with all this, consider my dad, and then I'll talk to André."

"Of course. Right now, it's a dream, a dream we hope to share with both of you."

"Oh, Jessica, it's a beautiful dream."

***

After work that day, Holly retreated to her apartment. Her whole world had changed since meeting André, expanding in directions she could never have predicted. *Why not move to France? I love Paris and Provence would give us a simple life, good for our art.*

That night she dreamed she and André were saying their vows amidst vineyards and lavender fields, with familiar smiling faces all around. When she woke, a phrase she'd learned when researching the Summer Solstice echoed in her mind: *love blooms in summer's warmth.*

The Summer Solstice, just like Jessica and Joseph. Why not? The lavender will be in bloom. That will be our wedding date, and it will take place in Provence.

Provence
The following June

Holly had been staying in the guest room at André's parents' home in Provence for a full week, preparing for the wedding in the vineyard at Solstice. Jessica had shared all that she had learned about the Summer Solstice celebration from her experience years before at Chartres Cathedral and Holly looked forward to visiting Chartres herself with André.

Maybe for our first anniversary. But right now, Solstice is only two days away. Our wedding day. Her heart beat faster just imagining it all. She would be moving nearby into the Sunflower Inn for the next evening so that André wouldn't see her on their wedding day until she walked down the aisle. She shivered with excitement.

The out-of-town guests would all be staying at the Sunflower Inn, too, including Jessica and Joseph. They would all be arriving the next day. Her father and brother had been at the Sunflower for a couple of days, mostly helping out and getting to know the area. Dinners with Henri and Jacqueline had been delightful, even with the language barrier.

Jessica's mother and stepfather, along with her father, would be arriving the following day, too. Jessica's father would be coming alone as Tyler and Annie were both very busy with summer activities and Luann had to stay behind. *Probably just as well. Luann seemed to make Adelaide very uncomfortable at Jessica's wedding. How wonderful, though, that André will have grandparents on hand.*

She thought of her mother. *Mom, I know you'll be here in spirit but, oh, how I wish you could be here next to me.* Suddenly a calm feeling came over her and she knew that her mother truly *was* with her in spirit.

With the lavender in full bloom, Holly and Jacqueline had placed many pots of fresh lavender around the arbor where the ceremony would be and also hung abundant bouquets of dried lavender around the eaves of the front porch and around the arches to the reception area. She smiled, remembering her dream. *Love blooms in summer's warmth.*

Her father had been quite skeptical about her engagement at first, but assured her he wanted more than anything for his children to be happy. When Holly told him they would be making their home in France, he again relented, as long as they promised to have a visit in Cambria or Provence, maybe even Paris, once each year.

Holly loved that Randy was enjoying learning about the Provencal cuisine from Jacqueline, and Henri clearly enjoyed sharing his knowledge of wine with him. Randy had recently completed a chef apprenticeship in San Francisco and had become the weekend cook at the family restaurant.

Joseph, of course, would perform the ceremony—now that he was a full-fledged Essene priest. Because of his prior training, it had taken him only one year to complete his studies. Pierre would be André's best man, and his papa would stand up next to them.

Jessica would be Holly's matron of honor. Jacqueline had felt left out until Holly delighted her by asking her to stand in her mother's role.

***

The day of the wedding finally arrived.

Standing in front of the mirror while Jessica finished the last buttons on her dress, Holly noticed the beauty in the room where they were dressing. *Such grace. I love them all so much.* Jessica wore a long lavender lace skirt and a white, gauzy, off-shoulder top on which tiny purple and green flowers had been embroidered. She wore a garland of white baby's breath in her hair.

Holly hardly recognized the radiant woman in her own reflection. She straightened her pearls—the ones her mother had given her before she died—and the off-shoulder sleeves of her white organza dress on which tiny lavender flowers had been sewn.

Jessica whispered, "You're gorgeous," as she leaned in to arrange her veil.

"I'm ready," Holly said, beaming as she picked up her bouquet of white lilies with sprays of lavender.

When they arrived at the vineyard, a man with a kind face ushered Holly and Jessica into the wine tasting room through a back door, so no one would see them in the Casal Winery courtyard, where the wedding would take place. While they waited for the guests to be seated, Holly peeked out the window. *Everything looks perfect! The arbor is just how I imagined it.*

"Are you ready?" she suddenly heard behind her. Her father's eyes glistened as he offered her his hand. "My little girl is all grown up. And so beautiful, reminding me of her mother," he said gently, kissing her on the cheek.

Holly took a deep breath and said, "Okay, let's go, Daddy."

Joseph and André had already taken their places in the arbor. Joseph wore a short white robe that just covered his suit jacket, with a purple scarf hanging around his shoulders. Candles and flowers had been carefully placed on a table in front of him.

André stood next to Joseph, wearing a charcoal dress shirt and lavender print tie under a soft gray sports jacket. *André will soon be my husband.* Her eyes locked onto his. All the faces smiled at them just as in her dream. As they reached the arbor she could feel her father letting go of her hand as she stepped beneath the lavender adorned arch to stand beside André.

Holly knew now what Jessica meant about feeling five feet off the ground at the altar. She heard Joseph's voice and trusted the flow of his words, coming back from her reverie each time she heard her name or André's. Soon she must speak.

"Holly, as André's partner in this life, what vows do you pledge to him?"

"I pledge to stand by you always, even when we disagree. I pledge to give you freedom for your creative work as I trust you will give me the same for mine. I pledge to tell you the truth even if it hurts and to laugh more than you may want to. I pledge to love you for all eternity."

André kept his vows traditionally simple: "I will care for you in sickness and health all the days of my life. So help me God. I pledge this and all my love."

Soon the magic words came: "André, you may now kiss the bride,"

Everyone cheered and clapped as they kissed passionately, turning to their family and friends, radiant and joyful.

Hugs and kisses abounded throughout the afternoon along with Henri's wine, the overflowing champagne, and the cornucopia of Provencal delights. Holly and André danced before their guests but in their own world, hardly taking their eyes off each other. He twirled her and she fell more than once back into his arms.

While Holly danced with her father, André danced with Jacqueline. Jessica confided in Holly later that she and André had come to a loving understanding. "Even though he didn't dance with me while you were dancing with your dad," she'd explained, "I understood completely."

The dancing continued well into the night and soon the tiny string of lights surrounding the arbor and reception arches twinkled like the night sky.

Love blooming in summer's warmth.

Epilogue

Summer Solstice
2002

Twelve years had passed since Joseph, Jessica, André, and Holly had purchased the land that now housed the expansion of the Essene Center in Provence that they had all helped to create.

Joseph had placed the chapel in the center of the complex as a reminder that God was at the center of their lives. Covered walkways branched out in seven directions to buildings where classrooms had been constructed.

The two family houses stood off to the side, along with a few guesthouses for those on retreat. Vibrant lavender fields formed a beautiful backdrop for the entire complex.

On this auspicious day, the Summer Solstice, they gathered in the chapel to connect—heart to heart—to each other before opening the doors to visitors, who would tour the newly completed center while also being part of a video that Andre would create. This would be the official christening of The Essene Center for the Arts and Spirituality. It now had ample space for artists and all people dedicated to expanding their creative and spiritual practices.

As they sat in a circle in the beautiful chapel, sunlight streamed through the stained-glass Tree of Life high above them.

Joseph spoke first.

"Everything I've ever worked for has been in preparation for creating this place. We have come full circle since my great grandmother migrated to Ireland when it was life-threatening to reveal that she was an Essene. Yet, the Essene teachings live on through us. We can thank our ancestors for passing down the symbol of that faith in the necklace that André now wears."

André spoke next, taking a deep breath before he began. "I believe that the necklace has revealed its mystery. Last year, after the tragic events of September 11, it became clear that we four were meant to create a place of light in a dark world. Like our ancestors, mine and Joseph's, we will strive to create beauty and harmony here, rather than alienation, separation, and discord."

Holly, pregnant for the second time, spoke. "I choose to believe that the child I'm carrying represents the light-bearing generations to come, who, like the Essenes, will realize human beings are much more than their physical bodies. We are sparks of Mother/Father God, who have forgotten—but are now remembering—that our true purpose on earth is to transform darkness into light and hatred into love. Our little Anne-Elizabeth Casal carries the same light of truth within her heart that her great great great grandmother, Anne-Elizabeth Benet, carried in hers from France to Ireland. The necklace she passed down to Joseph's father, to Joseph, and to André, symbolizes this truth: that we are not alone. Our angels are with us, assisting us in all that we do."

Jessica smiled at her loved ones and then began to speak. "We are very grateful to our master architect, Joseph, who designed and created the foundation for our beloved center. And each of us has added to it, using our creative talents to fill it with our own versions of beauty and love. As our students come, they will add even more beauty and love to this place and will go out into the world to share what they have learned and created, ever expanding what we have begun—or, rather, carried on from what our ancestors began. For me, in a way, this is like opening an art exhibit, but, in this case, our Center is the work of art. We humbly open it to all those of like mind who will come after us."

When the doors opened and visitors filed in, they all introduced themselves and Holly offered to take the small children "to a special room where Joseph will be reading a special story."

After the children followed Holly and Joseph to the children's center, André raised his camcorder to capture what Jessica pointed to as she described the stained glass window over the altar inside the vine-covered chapel. It had been her idea to create the window design to represent the Tree of Life, as depicted in André's necklace. Smiling brightly, she explained how the Tree's seven earthly roots and heavenly branches were held together by the meditative figure at its center.

Around the window, seven colors shimmered in the afternoon sunlight. "Because of its sacred nature, the number seven," Jessica explained, "occurs over and over again in Essene teachings. For example, we teach a seven-fold peace here: peace within the body, the mind, the family, our humanity, each culture, Nature itself, and, of course, peace with our Creator."

"It seems you focus on the arts as much as you do on spirituality," an elderly woman commented after Jessica had finished speaking. "Could you please explain why?"

"I'd be glad to. You see, we believe that the creative process is spiritual in nature. That's why our Center focuses on both the arts and spiritual studies. When we're receptive, God's creative light flows through us. Some of us express this through our art, others by co-creating beautiful, harmonious lives."

The guests nodded their heads in approval.

After they toured the rest of the facility, they stopped by the children's center to pick up their children, who were still listening to Joseph's story.

Giving Joseph a knowing look, Jessica motioned for the visitors to sit. Then she sank down on the soft rug to listen while Joseph finished reading *The Velveteen Rabbit*, a story about a child whose love turned a toy rabbit into a real live being.

A feeling of deep peace, love, and gratitude washed over Jessica as she glanced at Holly, who met her gaze, then broke into a smile, placing her hands over her heart. She caught André's eye after a moment. He pointed toward Anne-Elizabeth. The little girl sat at her grandfather Joseph's feet, her eyes wide with wonder and transparent innocence.

Like the meditative figure at the center of the Tree of Life, Jessica felt her connection to everything and everyone around her.

About the Author

Pamela Smith Allen earned her Bachelor's and Master's degrees in General and Special Education from the University of Florida in Gainesville, and her Doctorate in Psychology from the United States International University (now Alliant International University) in San Diego, California. She has worked as an educator and psychologist in public schools as well as in colleges and private settings

In an effort to piece together a worldview that unites, rather than divides, people from one another, she explored eight spiritual traditions in her non-fiction book, *Awakening to the Spirit Within: Eight Paths*, before completing *The Necklace*, her debut novel.

Dr. Allen has traveled extensively and now lives with her two cats in the mountain community of Julian, California in San Diego County. She enjoys spending time with family and friends, writing, gardening, and teaching Tai Chi Chuan classes.

ALL THINGS THAT MATTER PRESS

FOR MORE INFORMATION ON TITLES AVAILABLE FROM
ALL THINGS THAT MATTER PRESS, GO TO
http://allthingsthatmatterpress.com
or contact us at
allthingsthatmatterpress@gmail.com